Goodnight Sunshine

Mark Cameron

Catch Our Drift Productions Inc.

Catch Our Drift Productions Inc.
15-292 Gower Point Road
Gibsons, BC, Canada
V0N 1V0

www.catchourdrift.ca

ISBN 978-0-9940953-0-5

Dedicated to Tom Aylesworth
for teaching me the meaning of selflessness and grace.

"We both set out to do something ... and we did it."

Prologue

"Are you sure he's dead?"

"As sure as we can be."

She looks up from the memo on her desk. "What about the recovery effort?"

"It's like raising the Titanic," he replies. "I'm not hopeful."

"And his work?"

"There's no sign of it. Not the part that matters, anyway."

"Any indication of foul play?"

"No."

"So that's it then?" she asks.

"Well," he says, "we could monitor his wife and colleagues for a while. Something might turn up."

She takes off her glasses and wipes them with a small cloth.

"I know how you feel about—"

"It's okay," she says, holding up her palm to hush him. "If his work is still out there, we need to find it."

Part 1 - Impacto

One

First the horn, then the crash—a gunshot explosion of glass and steel. Floating sideways ... aimless, senseless, inert. Another impact. Expansion ... contraction ... I am pushed and pulled, torn apart and put together all at once.

Then everything comes to a halt.

I turn my head and stare into the grill of a transit bus.

A burning smell. An eerie silence. Then a muffled sound—my own heartbeat, pulsing through my head, pounding in my eardrums.

I turn further. The hood of a large truck fills the space behind me.

My door cranks open and I hear a man's voice, frantic. "Are you okay? Is there anyone else?"

I reach out and touch the deflated airbag that hangs from my steering wheel like a used condom—limp, spent, its sole purpose fulfilled.

"Is there anyone else in there?" he repeats, almost yelling, looking into my vehicle.

"No, just me." I feel calmer than I should.

"Are you okay?" he asks again. "You turned in front of the bus, then the dump truck nailed you on the driver's side. I thought—shit! Nobody could survive that! I was just waiting to cross the road and I saw you go and I couldn't stop it. I was like—holy crap, man—"

"Is ... everyone ..." It doesn't feel like me speaking.

"They're okay. You got the worst of it. It's like—wow! shit, man—you're one lucky dude." He continues to ramble, but I tune him out and look around me.

Another man surveys the damage on the front of the dump truck. He looks at me through a window frame that holds a few nuggets of shattered glass and pulls a cell phone from his pocket. I swing one leg out onto the ground and begin to get out of the vehicle. The first man steps back, still babbling, barely allowing me room to stand up and take in the mess that I've created.

"Thank God you're okay." Another voice—gruff but cheerful—belongs to a large mustached man in a King County Transit uniform.

"The passengers," I say. "Are they—"

"They're fine. I only had two people on board."

Two sirens, each carrying a different tune, become louder as the scene around me falls into focus. My SUV is a tangled heap of metal and fiberglass wedged between two much larger vehicles and surrounded by pools of glass and liquid.

An ambulance pulls up, lights flashing. The bustle of background noise returns.

A flurry of questions leads to a series of tests to ensure that I am unscathed, at least physically. The busy road that serves the mall—a major street perpendicular to the island's main highway—is blocked off from a growing crowd of onlookers while two policemen attempt to reconstruct the accident. Babbling man talks to everyone—cops, firefighters, reporters, onlookers. The size of the crowd does not surprise me. A crash of this magnitude is front-page material for this island of ten thousand people.

"Oliver?" A regular customer from the café that I own two blocks down the road comes toward me with a look of concern. "Are you okay?"

I glance at this man whose name I do not remember, then look at my SUV. A voice screams from within, trapped inside, refusing to surface. A voice that says I am not okay. A voice that rages with emotion—anger at buying a business that leaves me little time for life beyond the daily grind; frustration at the disconnection I feel from my wife and kids; sadness that penetrates me for reasons too complex to fully understand. A voice that says I have lost faith in the world, and I fear it has lost faith in me. I want to say all of this and more. Instead, I gaze blankly at the remnants of a vehicle that I pay six hundred dollars a month to pretend I own. Then I look at the man and find the smile that I have honed through years of customer service. "Yes, thanks. I'm just glad nobody was hurt."

~ ~ ~

Molly is unloading dishes when I walk into the kitchen of the Sunshine Café.

"What are you doing here on a Sunday?" She looks up briefly, then reaches deep into the dishwasher to retrieve stray silverware. A slim twenty-five, Molly is beautiful in the way that twenty-five-year-olds are, with a porcelain complexion, long auburn hair and a thin, curvy build. Although she does little, if anything, to maintain her appearance, the honesty of age has not caught up with her yet. I hope it doesn't find her any time soon.

"I just wrote off my SUV, over by the mall."

She turns and looks me up and down. "No shit? That was you? Are you okay?"

"Yeah, I'm fine."

"Wow," Molly says. "I had no idea that was you. Sounds like you were lucky, huh?"

"Guess so. It was my fault."

"How so?"

"I don't know. Distracted, I guess." I realize I am mumbling. Molly turns back to the dishes, giving me space. I turn inward, to the scene of the accident. I had been thinking about the journal page I'd thrown into the recycling bin— my manifesto. Coming to grips with my own insignificance … my compromises … setting my sights on more achievable goals. I had thrown it out, but the words were still riding along with me. Then—bang.

"Have you told Emily yet?" It takes me a moment to process her question.

"No. I just went out to run some errands. My cell phone was in the glove box, which no longer exists. Guess I'd better call Em to see if she's noticed me missing."

Molly flashes a sad smile. She is my right arm around here, and she knows me well enough to read the thoughts behind my words. "Hey," she says, "I can give you a ride home after lunch. I'd go now, but the church crowd could roll in any minute."

"Thanks. I might take you up on that. You need a hand?"

"Nah." She shakes her head. "We got it covered. Frank's here somewhere, and Sal should be in soon. Why don't you grab a bite and settle your nerves?"

I nod my head, but my nerves are not at all unsettled. The sense of calm that I continue to feel—a dead, numb calm— feels unnatural given the circumstances. It's like I have died and haven't realized it yet. Or perhaps numb is my new normal.

I pick up the phone on the wall and dial my house. After three rings I am directed to an adorable, rambling message that my daughter, Isabella, recorded years ago. A distant memory of happiness casts a shadow of nostalgia over my mind, suppressing the fact that even in the brightest moments parenthood has never come easily to me.

The voice mail beep brings me back to the act that is my public persona.

"Hey Em. I got in a bit of an accident near the mall. Everyone's okay, but the SUV's a write-off. Molly offered me a lift home after lunch, so I'll hang out until then. Love you."

"*That* was a slight understatement," Molly says as I hang up the phone. "A *bit* of an accident? You were sandwiched between a bus and a dump truck!"

"Thanks for reminding me."

"So do you want anything to eat?" Molly asks.

"No," I say. "I think I'll go for a walk while you handle lunch. See you around one thirty?"

"Sounds good."

I walk out to the street and look toward the mall. It gives the appearance of business as usual. I stretch out my arms and wiggle my fingers. All ten of them. I look down at my feet and lift my toes, watching my slip-on loafers bulge toward me. *My* feet, at the end of *my* legs. My body is alive, but my mind struggles to catch up—the way feeling returns after anesthesia, one part at a time. I open my mouth in a forced yawn and my ear pops, clearing slightly. My right calf is tender—or my Achilles tendon. I know it felt fine before the accident.

I look again toward the mall—and the recycling bins. The discarded page from my journal floats around in my head. *Why did I throw it away?* I move in the direction of the accident.

My pace quickens as I reach the intersection kitty-corner to the recycling bins. I cross both streets as soon as traffic allows. A warmth spreads through me. I feel like a child's glow stick—freshly snapped—my insides breaking in a million tiny ways, my whole body springing to life. Half walking, half running, I arrive at the paper bin. I notice a hinge on the top and a latch on the bottom. Seeing no lock on the latch, I pull it up and slide it sideways to dislodge the door. I lift the door above my head and give it a shove, allowing it to land on top of the container with a loud crash while half of the bin's contents spill out at my feet, leaving me knee-deep in paper.

I glance around the parking lot. A number of people are staring at me. An elderly man carrying bags that seem too heavy for his frame. A mother putting groceries in her trunk while her toddler wails. Two teenage girls passing through the parking lot, clad in shorts—and goose bumps, I'm sure, given the overcast sky.

My eyes well up with tears carrying a mishmash of emotions. Then, suddenly, I break into laughter.

Two

"Care to let me in on the joke?"

I stop laughing and glance up at a large man speaking through dry lips that hold an unlit cigarette butt. One of the dozen or so islanders who search these recycling bins for discarded treasures. I avoid looking him in the eye. I do not know how to answer his question.

He leans over and peers closely at me. Stubbled face, scruffy clothes and unkempt graying hair—oily curls squeezing out from under a dirty Seattle Mariners cap like that of an aging clown. A tragedy of inner city America, out of place on this affluent island.

"Hey, aren't you the guy from that accident this mornin'?"

I nod.

"Close shave," he mumbles. "I'm Arlo." He removes his cigarette with one hand and holds the other out to shake mine. I reluctantly accept his offer.

"Oliver."

Arlo sticks his head into the adjacent bin of tin cans while I sort through the paper. After a short search I see the envelope that I deposited in the bin this morning. Reaching down to reclaim it, something else catches my eye. Part of a handwritten note. I start to look away, but it pulls me back, its words calling to me from the page. I pick up my own envelope, then grasp the fragment of paper and read it as I stand to full height.

—ng with the PV schematics. The results are astonishing so far. The absorptive potential and conversion efficiency are beyond expectation. We must weigh the benefit and disadvantage of filing a patent: protection vs. disclosure. My friend, the future is in our hands. I'll call you when I'm in Quito next w—

I re-read the message. "What d'ya got there?" Arlo's voice startles me.

"Just … I'm not sure. Some kind of letter."

"What's it say?"

"Not much." I shrug off his question and look toward my feet. I reach down and pick up half of an envelope with handwriting that appears to match the message. It contains a return address in Seattle, under the name *Porter*; and part of the destination under the name *Dr. Robert Mc.* It is addressed to a post office box on Vashon Island, but the box number has been cut off. Kneeling down, I sift through the paper at my feet to look for more matching text.

"Ever think about where all this shit comes from?" Arlo asks as he reaches deep into the slot that reads *plastics*, pressing his face against the side of the bin. "Or where it goes from here?"

"Sometimes," I reply, immediately regretting my answer as he launches into what has all the earmarks of a rant.

"Recyclin's a double-edged sword." He pulls a pop bottle out of the bin and puts it in a cloth bag. "We sort our trash into these bins like they'll magically transform it into somethin' useful. But it's at least half bullshit." He glances at me to see if I am listening. Unfortunately, I am—a signal for him to forge ahead. "What we're really doin' is turnin' oil into garbage. We hoard stuff like the apocalypse is comin'. Then our shit piles get so big we can't find anythin', so we throw it all in here and go home with a clear conscience. Right?" His hard stare demands an answer. But before I have a chance to reply, he tops off his diatribe. "This, my friend, is our modern day version o' confession. Yep, we sin all week long, then we seek redemption in a row of shiny green bins."

He is making me nervous but I find him somehow compelling, though I am not about to commit myself to siding one way or the other with his observations. Instead, I dig a bit deeper into the pile of paper. Seeing no more matches for the letter and envelope, I place them into my own envelope containing my manifesto, and fold it into my back pocket. Then I close the paper bin lid and begin to stuff handfuls of paper back into the opening.

"Wanna hand with that?" Arlo asks. "Got everythin' I need." He sets down two bags that appear to be filled with refundable beverage containers—I would guess a dollar's worth at most.

"Sure," I say, though I don't really want his help.

We make short work of the cleanup, Arlo collecting a small stack of magazines to add to the rest of his treasure. When we are done, he sits down and leans against the paper bin, picking up a magazine containing the headline *Who Do You Fear Most?* above pictures of the two main nominees for the upcoming presidential election.

"Nice choice we have." Arlo's speech is calmer now. Quieter and understated, though the passion is still there. He is staring at the magazine headline. "Madame Baldwin, the great orator; or Edwin Mann, the evangelical preacher."

"Yeah," I grunt. I gave up on politics a long time ago. Once a passionate member of the Young Democrats Society at the University of Minnesota, a long string of disappointments with leaders of both stripes left me disillusioned with our political system. With society in general. That and the numbness of corporate life drove me to this quiet island, turning me from an aspiring writer into a restaurateur. I thought that moving to Vashon would reinvigorate my soul and recharge the optimism that had briefly fueled me during college. Instead, it lulled me further into a state of indifference.

"Fear?" Arlo asks, interrupting my thoughts. His tone is quiet, but his words are coated in anger. "They *want* us to fear. That's how they keep us in line. Maintain the status quo. Convince us *they* need more control so *they* can protect *us.*" His voice quavers as he continues. "You want fear? Try seein' your friend's leg blown off by a mine. These fuckers recruit us from shoppin' malls, high schools … the nation's great soldier factories. Catch us when we're most screwed up. Yeah, our leaders send their kids to Harvard while we send ours to war. Now that's scary."

I am surprised by Arlo's social commentary, but I contain my judgment to the confines of my brain. His penetrating stare mesmerizes me as he speaks with a slow, measured tone. "Do you really think we're free?"

He continues before I have a chance to answer. "We're about as free as caged birds. Only the dream of flight keeps us goin'. They keep the cage just big enough to create the illusion o' freedom, and they put enough shit in the way that we don't notice the bars."

Arlo looks beyond me, pointing skyward without breaking the intense connection he has created. "Look closely and you'll see 'em. The bars. They're all around us."

I turn to look at the gray sky. "All I see is clouds."

"All part of the mask," he says. Then he begins to laugh.

Three

"Hey Izzy-bee. How are you?" The words are barely out of my mouth when I notice Isabella's muddy soccer cleats by the door. "Oh … I missed your game, didn't I?"

"Yeah." She looks up from the couch where she is reading a teen mystery.

"How'd it go?"

"We lost. But I scored."

"Awesome." My daughter's first goal in an organized game. "Sorry I missed it."

"It's okay." She offers me a weak smile and goes back to her book.

Isaac runs into the room and says, "Dad, how much pi do you know?"

"Let's see"—I answer this question for at least the tenth time this month—"apple, blueberry, rhubarb …"

"Not that kind of pie," he groans, continuing to talk as he fades into the hallway toward his bedroom, "3.141592653589 …"

"Where's your mom?" I say. Silence. "Izzy?"

"What? Oh—mom? In your room, I think."

I walk down the hall and into our bedroom. Emily looks up from the laundry pile she is folding. "Where the hell have you been?"

"Hi to you too." I match her cold tone. "Didn't you get my voicemail?"

"No. We just got home from Izzy's soccer game." She pauses, then adds for effect, "I had to skip my meeting at the Arts Co-op to take her."

I stare blankly at the laundry.

"I noticed the SUV was gone. We waited for you, but ..."

"I went to run some errands. If you'd gotten my message—"

"What did it say?"

"I was in a car accident."

Emily turns toward me. "Are you okay?"

"Yeah."

"Was anyone else—"

I shake my head. "Nobody was hurt."

"What happened?"

"I was pulling out of the mall. Daydreaming, I guess. I drove in front of a bus. And a dump truck."

"Oh my God." Emily looks at me more closely, her anger fading to concern. "Why were you at the mall?"

"I took the recycling."

"Why?" she asks. "I usually take it on Tuesdays."

"Felt like getting out of the house. You were in the shower." I say nothing of the discussion we had this morning, bordering on a fight. About my frustration with our fruitless search for a new home. About selling our house before we found another one. About the dismal prospect of moving into our motor home in less than three weeks.

Emily looks down at the shirt she is holding. "How bad is the SUV?"

"It's … totaled."

She continues to stare at the shirt in her hands, my shirt—empty, lifeless. "Sorry for my reaction. I'm glad you're okay."

"It's alright. Sorry about our vehicle."

I walk over to the bed and pick up a pair of pants. Folding laundry is one of the few things that Em and I almost enjoy doing together. After a few minutes of folding in silence I ask, "Where's Quito?"

"Ecuador," she replies with a puzzled look. "Why?"

Four

Molly is already scurrying around the kitchen when I arrive at the café, and Frank is nowhere to be found. It is usually the other way around.

"Where's Frank this morning?" I ask.

"He called from his dad's place," she says. "He was trying to talk him down from the roof."

Frank's father, who goes by Henry since most people on the island cannot pronounce his real name, is the one person who can cause Frank to be late for work. If his ninety-two years have slowed Henry down, I would love to have seen him in his youth.

"Hey," Molly says. "Jake called. Said he tried to reach you on your cell. I told him you lost it in the accident."

"Oh yeah. Guess I'd better update my message…. Hello, you've reached Oliver Bruce. My phone is now embedded in the front of a transit bus. If I can convince my wife that I really do need a new phone, then I will be happy to call you back when my new one arrives. And while I'm at it, I will be lobbying for a new SUV and a nice Dutch Colonial home with a two-car garage and a painting studio. Thanks, and have a nice day."

Molly laughs, then adds, "He wants you to drop by the Jakery if you have time this morning. I told him you would."

"Thanks. Didn't realize I had a personal secretary."

As Molly and I rush around the kitchen getting ready for breakfast, I hear Frank pull up in the clattering rust-bucket that used to be a blue Honda Civic. He is grumbling when he walks through the back door into the kitchen, wearing his trademark fur hat and trench coat that have been part of the Fung family since they first arrived in the United States over fifty years ago.

"Morning, Frank," I say. "How's Henry?"

"Morning, Chief. Dad crazy. Decide to clean gutters at five o-clock. Wanted to see sunrise from roof. Took me hour and half to talk him down. Stubborn old fart."

"At least there was no snow to clear this morning."

"Yeah, crazy old fart gonna have heart attack one day."

Frank laughs his unique chortle, accompanied by the wide grin that exposes two missing teeth. I am convinced that his strong accent and skipped words are part of an act to keep people from getting too close or expecting too much. Just once I saw him speak with authority, in perfect English, his eyes boring a hole in the bully who belittled Molly over a cold plate of French fries. I remember the exact words Frank used that day, which sent the unwanted customer out the door without a word. *If you don't leave this restaurant in the next ten seconds, you will find out how far a skinny black belt can kick an overweight asshole.* He may have been bluffing, but in that moment—while I stood idle, paralyzed by the discomfort of the situation—I envied Frank's strength and resolve.

For all the times I have thought of letting him go for insulting a customer or ignoring a best-before date, Frank is an integral part of the Sunshine Café. I expect to employ him forever, or until he dies, whichever comes first.

~ ~ ~

The Jakery is a rich mug of hot cocoa on a cold day—literally and metaphorically. Whereas the Sunshine Café provides a kind of ageless comfort, Jake's place is current. Hip. I openly admit—to Jake, at least—that I would rather discuss life at one of the maple tables beside his woodstove than the vinyl chairs and retro booths that adorn my café.

"Sounds like a helluva scare." His warm smile tells me he is thankful that I am still alive.

"Yeah. Woke me up, that's for damn sure."

"What happened? You're usually with it behind the wheel."

"I don't know. Had a lot on my mind yesterday."

"Things okay with you and Em?"

I sip my liquid dessert and consider taking Jake's bait. I know he is giving me an opening to vent, but I have nothing to add to my usual lament about the frost that coats my relationship with Emily. So I slouch in my seat and say, "Same old."

"Is she still pushing for that holiday?"

"Yeah," I say. "Maybe I'll entertain the thought once we agree on a house."

"Why don't you hold off for a while? Live in that home on wheels for the summer, take off for a few weeks when you can, buy again when the market cools down in the fall."

"That's what Em says. Like we'll have some sort of epiphany after a few months in a motor home. I'm thinking a homicide's more likely."

"I'd bet on the epiphany," Jake says. "You're like a Venus Flytrap. You sit there looking comatose, then snap—you're moving to an island … buying a restaurant … selling your house. You remind me of this book I read called *Spontaneous Evolution*. It's like, change isn't linear the way we think it is. We go for long periods with little change, and then—suddenly—we evolve."

"You're losing me."

"It's like that restaurant of yours. You've hardly changed a thing in all the years you've owned it. But it wouldn't surprise me to walk in there one day and find that you've turned it into some cool tapas bar that serves tiny pickled things for ten dollars a piece."

"Hah!" The volume of my laugh causes the customers around me to go silent. I wait for them to return to their own conversations before continuing. "You're hallucinating, my friend. If I ever knew what cool was, I've forgotten. I've become a slave to the domain that I'm the master of."

"A slave to the domain …" Jake repeats, trailing off as he analyzes what I said. "Hey, that's kinda deep. Did you just come up with that?"

"I guess. Just popped into my head and out of my mouth."

"See?" he says. "I'll bet that thought's been forming all morning. That stuff doesn't just pop into a person's head."

"Sure, whatever you say." I look at a clock above the service counter and realize lunch time is approaching. "I guess we'd better get back to work."

As Jake reaches to gather our mugs, I remember the message that I found yesterday, which I stuffed into my back pocket again this morning. I hand it to Jake. "Hey, before I go ... I found this at the recycling bin yesterday. What do you make of it?"

Jake reads the letter fragment and looks at me. "I don't know. Sounds like some kind of invention."

"Yeah," I nod. "I looked up some of the terms yesterday. I think it might have to do with solar energy."

A bewildered look crosses Jake's face as he hands the message back to me. "And you just found this sitting at the recycling bin?"

"More or less. I found an envelope too. The return address is someone in Belltown. It's addressed to a Dr. Robert Mc-something. Know anyone by that name on the island?"

"No," Jake says. "There's Dr. McKenzie, but his first name is Chris."

"Yeah. I checked him out. Christopher Robin McKenzie."

"Christopher Robin?" Jake echoes. "Classic."

"Yup."

"Is this like your glass slipper?" Jake says. "You're gonna try it on every Robert Mc-something in the kingdom?"

"Yeah, something like that," I reply. "But seriously, I've had a nagging desire to seek out the person who sent it."

"Because ... ?"

"Because it spoke to me."

"Okay ..." Jake is waiting for me to continue.

"I've been questioning a lot of things lately. Existential stuff, y'know? That accident, it ... I don't know—jarred me, I guess. I'm feeling really ..." He keeps staring at me, prompting me to complete my thought. "Raw, I guess. That message seemed ..."

"Seemed what?"

"Like it was intended for me."

"Hmm."

"You think?"

"I think that if I was in your shoes, I'd be thinking that as well."

I am a little surprised by his answer, but comforted. "Okay, that's what you think *I'd* think. But what do *you* think?"

Jake shrugs. "I don't know. Stranger things have happened. But I'd suggest you sit on it for a while, see if you still feel that way once the dust has settled from your accident. I think we sometimes look for meaning where it doesn't exist, especially when we—"

"Narrowly escape death?"

"Yeah."

"You're probably right," I agree.

Five

Almost every seat on the one hundred and fifty passenger catamaran is full as it pulls away from the dock. The MV Melissa Ann, which runs between downtown Seattle and Vashon Heights ferry terminal during peak hours, bears little resemblance to the Mosquito Fleet of steam vessels that first served this route in the late 1800's, followed by the various auto ferries that have run almost continuously since the end of World War I. Cool spring air magnifies the Olympic Mountains to the left and Mount Rainier to the right. There is no sign of the high-rise buildings that will greet the boat when it passes the point that contains the Admiral District of West Seattle.

Numerous threads fill my head in the twenty minutes it takes to cross Puget Sound. I think of the island that I have chosen as my home for the past decade, with its giant cedars, rocky beaches and infinite shades of green. Even the undergrowth has undergrowth here, in stark contrast to Minneapolis, where I spent my first twenty-four years. I love the ocean and the greenery, but the clouds here get me down. I still miss the clear blue skies that brighten even the coldest days inland.

If it were not for the paradise that Mother Nature delivers for a few months each year—long, warm days with modest humidity and a surprising absence of airborne pests—I might have left the coast before it took hold of me. While my reason for moving west—a girlfriend who dumped me shortly after my arrival in Seattle—has long since become a footnote in my life, this community has wrapped its arms around me. It is, quite simply, home.

It sometimes feels like a dream to live on Vashon full-time, no longer fighting the tourists for space on the ships that act as our lifeline to the mainland. Yet I was happier when I first moved there, joining the half-asleep army of commuters on the six-ten AM water taxi for my marketing job at a telecommunications firm in downtown Seattle, than I am now, running my own business.

~ ~ ~

I stop for a coffee along the Seattle waterfront—my third this morning—intent on vibrating the mile and a half from the ferry terminal to Belltown. I feel excited, and slightly nervous. Not only do I have no idea who I am looking for, I have no idea what I will say if I find him. I talked myself out of this trip following my discussion with Jake yesterday, but when I woke up in the middle of the night obsessing over the message I had found, I changed my mind again. This morning I changed it back and went about my usual routine until the café was up and running. Then, after the early breakfast rush had crested, I looked up the bus schedule, arranged with Molly to manage without me, and ran out the door just in time to catch a bus to the eight-fifteen boat—the last water taxi of the morning.

I soon find myself looking through a green metal security gate that houses units 168 and 170 at Cascadia Court. The gate seems pointless; a person could easily pass over or under it if they wanted to. The building is a plain six-story structure accented by a tasteful blend of stonework and earth-tone stucco. It is art that brings unit 168 to life. Hand-crafted wind chimes hang in the entryway, a sign on the door reads "Love lives here," and a crudely drawn picture of a smiling family—what appears to be a father, a mother and a son—is posted in the window above the front door.

Looking toward the corner of the building half a block away, I see a doorway with a security keypad. En route to the main door, an archway opens to expose a courtyard in the middle of the building, filled with plants, fountains and a small playground. The simple sight of a lemonade stand underneath the archway floods me with fond memories of toys and treats that I once funded through the sale of over-priced sugar water.

I approach the stand, attended by a boy about seven or eight years old with a round chubby face and adult front teeth that his face has not quite grown into. About a dozen glass jars in a plastic bin labeled "clean" sit beside an empty bin labeled "dirty." Behind him is a small bucket of soapy water, a cloth and a dish towel. On the front of the stand a sign reads in the clear printing of a child:

Organic Lemonade
by donation
All money goes to homeless cats

I order a glass of lemonade and hand the boy ten dollars.

"I have to get change from my mom," he says.

"No," I reply. "I don't need change. That's my donation."

"Wow, thanks!" The boy stares at the bill with wide eyes.

"What gave you the idea to raise money for cats?" I ask, wishing I could find so much joy in ten dollars. In anything, really.

"I like cats."

I take a sip of lemonade. It is the work of a master. Real lemons, just the right amount of sugar, neither too strong nor too watery.

"This is fantastic. Did you make it yourself?"

"Yeah, I make lemonade all the time. My mom taught me how. We buy lemons from the farmers' market, and we buy sugar from the health food store. It's more expensive but it's better. Organic means they didn't use any chemicals to kill bugs or anything."

"So are there bugs in this?" I ask, and the boy smiles nervously until I crack a smile. Quick to catch on to my humor, he laughs.

Holding out my hand I speak in my most formal tone, "I am pleased to meet a young man who makes such a great glass of lemonade. My name is Oliver. And you are …?"

"Charlie," he says, reaching his hand to shake mine. Then he is running toward the playground waving the money and yelling, "Mom! Mom! I got a ten dollar donation!"

My eyes follow Charlie as he reaches a woman in a flowered sundress, standing barefoot by a bright red jungle gym that two toddlers are playing beneath. She is speaking to another woman while holding a baby in the crook of her arm, the child's head resting on her shoulder. She bends down on one knee to meet Charlie at his level and listens to him, then looks at me and mouths out the words, "Thank you." I tip my lemonade in a salute to her son's beverage-making skills.

She hands the baby to the other woman and walks toward me with Charlie at her side. I feel a knot in my stomach. I struggle to think of something intelligent to say. Upon her arrival she smiles, shattering the last of my composure.

"Your son makes a mean lemonade," is all I can get out before I run out of breath. Her beauty is more a matter of complexity than complexion; she wears her imperfections—a slightly crooked nose and a small mole on her chin—with grace, and she smiles with her whole being. I wonder at her ethnic background—brown eyes and high cheekbones accentuate soft olive skin with no sign of make-up. I guess her to be in her late twenties or early thirties.

"Thank you so much," she says. "Charlie hasn't sold much today. This is not really a lemonade stand kind of community, and not a lot of people buy lemonade on a cool spring morning. But he was determined."

"Well, it hit the spot for me." My nerves are calming, and I sense a connection with this woman. We stand in a comfortable silence until I remember why I am here. "Oh. I'm just over from Vashon Island. I'm looking for someone. He, or she, lives in this building. I think."

Charlie starts to wander off toward the playground and his mother calls him back, reminding him that they have to pack up. As she talks to him she lifts her hand and runs it through her hair. I notice her wedding ring, a simple gold band, and I wonder if she has seen mine.

"Hey," I say, almost blurting it out. "Can I help you carry your stuff?"

"Um, sure," she says. "Thank you."

I reach out my hand. "I'm sorry. I haven't even intro-duced myself. I'm Oliver. Oliver Bruce."

She accepts my handshake. "Hi Oliver. I'm Annie. You mentioned that you're looking for someone who lives here?"

"Yes. You wouldn't happen to know someone named Porter from unit 168, would you?"

The color seems to drain from Annie's cheeks. Her eyes narrow into a questioning stare. "Why do you ask?"

"I found a letter with that return address—not the whole letter—I mean, it was in the garbage, the recycling ... I was intrigued, so I—"

"I'm sorry," she says, her voice brittle. "I don't even know who you are—or who you are with."

Charlie breaks in—"Mom, I have to go to the bathroom."

Annie looks at her son. "Okay, hon. We'll go right away." Then she turns back to me.

"I'm sorry," I continue, "I know this is strange. I thought it was important somehow, with the reference to Quito ... and from what I can figure out ... something to do with solar energy."

Annie's face has tightened. I wait for her to speak, but she abruptly starts packing up the lemonade stand. I make an awkward attempt to join her. "I'm not with anyone," I say as I reach for the table that Annie has cleared, just as she reaches for it as well. I am closer to her than I intended, so I back up slightly. Then our eyes lock and I add, "I just run a small restaurant, and I usually mind my own business. I thought maybe it was important and got thrown out by accident. It didn't seem like the sort of thing someone would throw out. I'm sorry if I've upset you." Her face softens a bit as we both straighten up. I reach into my pocket and hand her the message. She takes it but does not look at it, though I can tell she wants to. "I know it sounds crazy, but on Sunday, just after my accident—"

"Accident?"

I hesitate, not sure how much to tell her, realizing how ridiculous this must seem. While I search for the right words, she holds the letter up and reads it. Her eyes well up as she looks at me and says, "Why do you have this?"

"It's ... I—"

"What on earth do you want from me?" Her tone catches me by surprise. I feel like an intruder. Which is exactly what I am. I should have followed Jake's advice and left this alone.

I look down at Charlie, who is starting to squeeze his legs together. "I don't want to hold you up. Charlie needs the bathroom."

Annie continues to gather Charlie's stuff. She is flustered, and I wonder if I should leave. But I see that there is too much for them to carry in one load, so I use this as an opportunity to extend my stay.

We pack up and then walk in silence until we stop in front of unit 168. Annie hands Charlie a key and sends him through the green gate that she props open with the table from the lemonade stand. Charlie disappears into the apartment.

Annie turns toward me and holds up the letter. "So you found this at a recycling bin? And why did that lead you here?"

"I don't know. At first it was just curiosity. It seemed odd that—I mean, I could see that it was important—and I thought, what's it doing in the garbage? Your address was on the envelope, so I came here."

Annie looks at the letter again, and then back at me.

"Did you write this?" I ask.

"No," she says. "My husband did."

I want to ask about her husband, but I am afraid to push further. So I stand awkwardly, shifting my weight back and forth between my feet.

Charlie opens the door and says, "Mom, I'm hungry."

"Okay, hon." Annie smiles at her son, who lingers in the doorway.

"I'm sorry to have bothered you today," I say. "I should go and let you tend to your son."

"Thank you for your help." Her gratitude seems authentic, her tone less defensive.

Charlie adds, "Thanks for the donation."

"You're welcome," I say to both of them as Charlie retreats into the house, closing the door behind him. I look at Annie and say, "Again, my apologies for intruding on your life."

"I'm getting used to it," she says, but she does not elaborate.

I start to walk away as Annie moves the lemonade supplies into the gated area in front of her door. *I'm not likely to ever see this woman again.* I stop and turn around. "Your husband—" I can't think of how to finish the question.

Annie's voice is barely audible. "Daniel died almost a year ago."

~ ~ ~

Tyler Thomas is unusually alert this morning thanks to a double-strength espresso on his way to the control center. In a less attentive state, he might have ignored the Level Five indicator on a Category C file set to expire in a few days. But something caught his eye, causing him to click on the "Manual Review" button.

Despite the background noise from the outdoor feed, he hears the words clearly—Quito ... solar energy ... Daniel. The machine rarely misses nowadays, its algorithms finely tuned to learn the subtle intonations of each subject, becoming more accurate every time it gathers input. But the man's voice is new—it doesn't match any of their records.

It's probably nothing, Tyler thinks. Not worthy of escalation—yet—but enough to tag the file for extension.

Six

"Hi." I open the passenger door of the motor home. "Where's Isaac?"

"I dropped him off with Beth." Emily barely looks in my direction as she pulls away from the ferry terminal. When I phoned her after lunch from a payphone in Seattle, she reminded me that I was supposed to hang out with Isaac this afternoon while she attended a meeting about a new pottery collective. Then she grunted that she would see me at the ferry terminal, and hung up.

"Thanks for coming to get me."

"Mm-hmm," she mumbles.

"Sorry about your meeting. How was it?"

"It's still going. I just popped out to get you."

"If we had another vehicle ..." I trail off before finishing my thought.

"Let's not turn this into a debate."

"I don't get—"

"I had to pay the Visa with the MasterCard." Emily's voice is flat. "It's embarrassing."

"Summer's coming. We'll get our heads above water again. We usually do."

"Yeah," she says. "I guess."

"Did you hear back from the insurance company?"

"Yeah. Looks like a fifty percent increase if we get a new vehicle."

"Any injury claims?"

"None yet," she says. "Good thing that wasn't a full bus, or we'd probably have a dozen people claiming whiplash."

The reality of my accident sets in, and I realize how appreciative I am that I did not hurt anyone. Alternative outcomes battle for mindshare—thoughts of the tragedies I might have caused if my daydreaming had not been thwarted by two larger vehicles. I feel an odd sense of grief for what might have been.

Emily changes the subject. "So you just decided to up and go to Seattle this morning?"

"Yeah," I reply.

"Why?"

"I picked up spices." My thin attempt at a peace offering misses its mark.

"Ah. You went to Seattle for spices?"

"I wanted to check out the return address on that letter."

"Seriously?" She turns her head sharply toward me, then turns back to focus on the road.

"I kept waking up last night, thinking about it. I—"

"You could've called before—"

"I ran out the door. It was a last-minute decision."

"You've known about this meeting for weeks. I reminded you yesterday."

"Yeah." I stare straight ahead, watching the windshield wipers push aside the light rain. It seems heavier than it is because Emily is driving faster than usual down the island highway.

"It's not like I'm usually forgetful. And how often do I do something impulsive?"

"More often than you think."

"What do you mean by that?"

Emily shrugs.

"Our conversations used to be civilized."

"This is civilized. I can do stark raving mad if you'd—"

"No, let's not."

"I'm guessing you didn't pack a lunch?"

"Sure, I made myself a Reuben as I was running to catch the bus." The harshness of my voice surprises me.

"I'm not in the mood—"

"That's a big shock."

Silence. I rarely allow myself to broach the subject of intimacy; it feels like an immovable object. Every time I allow something like this to slip out of my mouth, I add mass to the wall that stands between Emily and me—a wall that forms like a glacier, one thin layer at a time.

She pulls up in front of the Arts Co-op. Built in the 1960's, the plain exterior of the building gives no indication of the charm that lives within. I long for my own small studio, now packed in boxes until we can find another place to house it, and my frustration grows—a frustration that used to find an outlet on the canvas, but now escapes my lips in tiny acidic morsels, often at Em's expense.

"I should be about an hour." Emily breaks my trance as she opens her door and climbs out of the RV.

"'Kay," I reply. My voice is cool, but warm shades of anger seep from my pores.

~ ~ ~

I loop around Burton, a small peninsula in the center of Quartermaster Harbor, and turn right at Vashon Highway. I suppress a craving for more caffeine when I pass the Burton Coffee Stand. A short distance up the highway, I turn right onto Quartermaster Drive and head toward Maury Island, across the isthmus—a manmade land bridge that forms the northern tip of the harbor and connects the two islands. After a couple more turns, I stop in front of the parking lot for Point Robinson Park. My anger has subsided and I realize, as usual, that Emily has reason to be upset with me.

I let off the brake and turn on Luana Beach Road, where I begin a winding descent through my favorite place on Maury Island—a colorful mixture of homes and cottages scattered along the island's northeast shore, nestled at the edge of a pristine temporal rainforest. The brakes squeal as I navigate a narrow turn, and a young couple at the edge of the road flash a pair of mocking grins. Even the SUV felt big on this road; the motor home feels totally out of place.

I complete a partial loop of Maury Island. As I approach the coastline of the isthmus, I abruptly pull off and park beside the ocean. The rain has diminished to a sprinkle. I climb out of the motor home and walk over to the motley assortment of stationary bikes that islanders have placed on the beach— derelict models with missing parts; classic bikes that are only beginning to rust; and a recently added cycle that has not yet weathered a winter of wind and salt water. A mostly intact treadmill sits among the bikes like a seagull amidst a murder of crows. I have driven past these contraptions probably a hundred times or more, even slowed to take note of additions or changes, but I have never stopped at them before.

I climb on the new cycle; for a moment I yearn for my SUV. I begin to pedal, and I wonder how long it will take for this shiny new bike to look as weathered as its counterparts. I think of my own aging body—of the growing list of aches and pains that are becoming a part of day-to-day life. A slight breeze mists my face with the last remnants of afternoon rain as I scan the scene around me.

People come here to see the sun rise or set from these bikes; I wonder what it would be like to see both in one sitting—what other activity one might witness through the course of a day. I imagine kayaks, sailboats, ferries and tankers sharing the Salish Sea, while vehicles and bikes pass behind me, along with the occasional pedestrian—few, if any, likely to stop at this sleepy alcove, once home to a general store that now sits vacant across the road.

To the west, I see blue sky emerging over Vashon—the larger of the two islands. I think of Charlie and his lemonade stand. Of his beautiful mother and her dead husband. Of why I could not bring myself to ask how he died. She gave me a glimpse of vulnerability—the hint of an expression that said all I had to do was ask and she would spill the grief that was locked inside of her. But I halted, ever so slightly, and the moment passed. When Charlie reappeared in the doorway, I bid them goodbye and walked toward my wife's favorite spice shop near the Seattle waterfront, where I spent the afternoon drinking coffee and contemplating my lot in life.

Seven

"Hey Chief, two guys here to see you. Look like they came from the dump." Frank is appropriately named, a master of candor if not tact.

I am surprised to find Arlo seated in the back corner of the café. I had offered him a free meal for helping me clean up the recycling, but I did not expect him to take me up on it. Nor that he would bring a friend. Both of them are dressed as if they have just come from the landfill, which they probably have.

"Arlo!" I reach out my hand, less reluctant to shake his than I was a few days ago.

"Oliver." Arlo grips my hand vigorously.

"Nice to see you again." I smile in the direction of Arlo's friend, a slight man with scraggly gray hair and a wiry, unkempt beard. Though I have never met him, he is a familiar figure, one of the island's more eccentric characters. I have seen him driving a 1970's Westfalia or riding a scooter of similar vintage, stopping to pick up bottles or garbage along the way.

"Oliver," Arlo says, "this is my good friend Eddy." I am about to shake the smaller man's hand when Molly interrupts, calling from the kitchen door.

"Oliver, phone's for you."

"Excuse me," I say to Arlo and Eddy. "I'll ask Molly to get your order. I'll be back in a bit."

I pass close by Molly on the way to the kitchen. "Breakfast for those two guys in the corner is on me."

"Oh?" she says.

I nod for her to follow me as I walk into the kitchen. "One of them gave me a hand the other day, so I offered him a free meal."

"That was nice. Anything they want?"

"Sure. Who's on the phone?"

"I don't know. Just some guy who asked for you."

I pick up the phone. "Hello."

"Mr. Bruce?"

"Yes."

"This is John Stevens from the University of Washington Records Office."

"Oh, thanks for calling me back."

"Your message said you're looking for one of our faculty members?"

"Maybe. I don't know. I've made a few similar calls."

"Can you tell me why you need to track down this person?"

"It's a research project," I say, repeating the script I have used a few times over the past two days. "About solar energy. I don't know what university he's from. I had no idea there were so many in Seattle."

"Your message was vague. You're looking for a Dr. Robert someone who might live on Vashon Island? How is it you don't know his name?"

"I found part of a paper, and most of his last name was missing. Look, I know this sounds strange. I'm just hoping—"

He cuts me off. "There is a Professor Emeritus in our Mechanical Engineering department named Robert McKinnon. He specializes in renewable energies."

"Really?" I reach for a pen and paper. "Sounds like my guy. Could you give me his contact info?"

"I'm afraid not. I'm told he allowed his office phone and e-mail to lapse. Emeritus means he's retired. He turned down his option to retain an office here."

"Do you know if he lives on Vashon Island?"

"I know he did. But I only show a post office box."

"Could you provide that to me?"

"I'm afraid not."

"Okay, well, thank you. If you come across anything or hear of his whereabouts, could you contact me?"

"Sure, I'll make a note." I have a feeling this is a brush-off, so I thank him again and hang up the phone.

Helen, who waits tables for a few hours each weekday morning, wears a sassy smile as she carries a load of dirty dishes from the dining room into the kitchen.

"What's so funny?" I ask.

"Molly's getting an earful from one of the hobos."

"About what?"

"About the quality of our menu. Apparently the dumpsters he dines at serve only the finest cuisine." A spry seventy, Helen has not changed much since I took over as her manager when we bought the Sunshine Café. A lifelong islander, Helen is part of the shrinking conservative core on Vashon.

"Which guy is it?"

"The bearded one," she says as she sets the dishes into the sink with a small crash.

"Hmm. I was expecting it to be the other guy. I guess they're both opinionated."

The door swings open and Molly enters the kitchen.

"I hear you got an earful," I say to Molly.

"About what?" she asks.

"About our food quality. From my new friend at the corner table?"

"Oh, a little, I guess. He's gruff, but he's got a point."

"That's a glowing compliment. At least he doesn't have to pay for his breakfast."

"It's a free meal?" Helen chimes in. "Then he should shut his welfare hole and eat what we give him."

"Settle down," I say.

"He actually has some good ideas," Molly says. "Might be worth having a chat with him. He seems to know a lot about food."

I help Frank catch up on a backlog of orders, including the one for Arlo and Eddy, which I deliver myself. Arlo's eyes widen when I place our largest breakfast option in front of him—an impressive helping of meat and vegetables served over a three-egg omelet, all resting on a bed of hash-browned potatoes. Eddy opted for granola, yogurt and fresh fruit.

"Thank you, Oliver," Arlo says with a smile. "This looks like a feast."

"Thank you," Eddy adds.

"I understand you have some suggestions about our menu?" I say.

"I think there is room for improvement," Eddy replies. "Do you have any idea where your food comes from?" His voice is surprisingly deep with a hint of a southern drawl.

"From a wholesaler." I know that is not what he meant, but I'm not in the mood for a lecture.

"I mean its origin," he says. "Have you ever grown your own food?"

"My wife and I plant a small garden."

"Well, I don't want to be an ungrateful prick," he replies, a little loud for my liking, "but I think that if you run a restaurant, it would be a good idea to know the origin of the food you serve."

"Fair enough," I say, my tone belying the defensiveness I am feeling.

Arlo has already eaten a quarter of his hash. He spits out a few morsels of food as he says, "Don't mind Eddy. He's a bit cantankerous sometimes."

"No problem," I reply. "I'd like to catch up, but they're quite busy in the kitchen. I'd better get back. Maybe I'll see you at the recycling bins."

"I'll be there," Arlo says before stuffing a large forkful of eggs in his mouth.

Eight

The next few weeks are a blur. In the midst of packing and working we make time to look at a couple of new listings, hoping to find a place we can move into right away. Our search for a new home highlights how far Emily and I have drifted from one another. I am adamant that we will need more space as the children grow, while Emily wants a smaller place that is less expensive and easier to maintain.

On the last day of May we lock the doors to our house, hand over the keys to our realtor, climb into our motor home and drive to Cedars RV Resort, the only campground on the island with electricity, water and laundry.

While Isabella and Isaac are occupied playing cards in the motor home, Emily and I walk to the park's lone building to fold a heap of laundry that we did not have time to finish during our move.

"So," I say, diving into a pile of towels, "we are now living in a trailer park."

"It's an RV resort," Emily says with a hint of sarcasm.

"Shouldn't a resort have more amenities than a laundry room? Like, maybe a hot tub?"

"You might think." We fold in silence before Emily speaks again. "Thanks for doing this."

"No problem. Laundry's as close as we come to a date."

"I mean moving here ... until we find the right place to land."

"Oh, that."

"It's nice to see the bank account in the black again."

"Yeah. I hope we don't burn through our down payment."

"I don't think we will. Life just got a whole lot cheaper."

"True," I say. "I guess an RV is a pretty cheap house."

"Yeah. I've been wanting to get rid of it ever since we got it. Now it's gone from an expensive luxury to a modest home."

I flash a coy smile. "I told you we'd use it."

"But not for a holiday."

"Just pretend we're in Florida."

"Sure," she laughs. "Actually, it's not so bad."

I hope Emily is right, but I fear my light mood tonight is a product of novelty. After the chaos of cramming a houseful of stuff into two large storage containers, the simplicity of this moment feels almost like a vacation.

"We should do laundry more often," I say. "This resembles a conversation."

"It does," Emily agrees. "Hey, did you ever learn anything about that doctor you were trying to track down? It's been so busy ... but I know that was eating at you."

"Oh yeah. I found out his name a while ago. Robert McKinnon. Used to work at U of W in Seattle, but he's retired."

"That's something," Emily says. "Does he live on Vashon?"

"Most likely. The guy said he used to, but he only has a P.O. Box and he couldn't give it to me."

"You could write to him at the university. Maybe they'd forward it to him."

"Good point." I am inspired by Emily's suggestion—and embarrassed that I did not think of it. The truth is that my interest in the message has faded. But my interest in seeing

Annie again has not, and I feel a sense of renewed hope that I might find an excuse for that to happen.

Emily and I chat about an assortment of things as we finish up in the laundry room, then we go back to the motor home and join our kids in a rare family game of Uno. Both Isabella and Isaac are unusually cooperative at bed time, their jack-and-jill bunks in the back corner of the RV—Isaac sleeping directly above his sister—providing a nice change after spending the past few nights on air mattresses in an almost empty house.

Once the kids are in bed, I use the narrow stretch of hallway between the kitchen and bathroom for the nightly stretches that keep my back from seizing up. By the time I climb into the bunk above the cab, Emily appears to be asleep on her side, facing the front of the RV. Encouraged by the warmth of our discussion this evening, I reach around and caress her stomach, moving my hand up toward her breasts. She puts her hand firmly on mine and holds it in place, stopping its progress. After a few moments she loosens her grip. Stifled, I pull my hand away and lie on my back, listening to a light rain land on the roof. My frustration wells briefly, then dissolves as I force my mind elsewhere. In my head I begin to draft a letter to Dr. Robert McKinnon.

~ ~ ~

On our second evening at the RV Park, I run into Arlo during a visit to the on-site recycling bins.

"Arlo!" I approach the bins with a small bag of recycling. "Doing your rounds?"

"Oliver," he replies in a gruff but animated tone. "Welcome to my humble abode. What are you doin' here?"

"We're staying here while we search for a new house. We sold ours a couple of days ago."

"Ah," he replies. "Downsizin'?"

"Only for now. How about you? You live here?"

Arlo points to a well-worn travel trailer two rows away. "In the old Nash. That's my twenty-eight feet o' paradise. Keeps me warm and cozy. What are you livin' in these days?"

I point toward our newer model Class C motor home, across the path from the bins.

"Nice rig," he says. "Not a lot of house for a family though. You got kids, right?"

"Yup, two of them. Seven and twelve, going on thirty and sixteen. How about you? Are you on your own?"

"Yeah, I had a dog, but she died in January. Haven't been ready to look for another one yet."

"I'm sorry," I say. "But hey, I'm glad we'll be neighbors for a while. I enjoyed our talk when you helped me that day."

"You mean my soliloquy?" Arlo asks with a sense of self-mockery.

"Whatever you call it, you got me thinking. About freedom and fear."

"Freedom and fear, huh?" laughs Arlo. "Two of my three favorite topics."

"Three?" I realize too late that I have invited Arlo to step back onto his soapbox.

"Anarchy, my friend. Anarchy. But you don't have time for that now."

I grin, not wanting to admit that I do have time tonight. "Hey, sorry we didn't have a chance to talk more when you came into the café."

"Who could get a word in with the doc critiquin' your food?"

"The doc?"

"Yeah, Eddy. My analytical, hyper-critical friend. He's crazy smart, but he could use a few lessons in etiquette."

I try not to laugh at the irony of Arlo's suggestion. "Why do you call him the doc?"

"'Cause he's a doctor. Not a medical one. A PhD."

"A PhD? In what?"

"Engineerin'."

"Hmm. Wouldn't have guessed that."

"That's how he affords that fancy Airstream." Arlo points toward a shiny aluminum trailer.

"Really?" I look toward the trailer, and my mind churns. "Does he work at a university?"

"He did work at U of W. He's retired now."

"Really?" I ask. "I'd like to talk to him. He might be able to help me find someone."

"I'd suggest we drop by his tin can, but the doc's an early bird. Maybe tomorrow."

I bid Arlo goodnight and walk back to my RV, noting the diversity that populates this place. Luxurious motor homes with multiple slide-outs and automatic levelers—mini-mansions on wheels—parked next to semi-permanent, older model trailers covered in dirt, moss and algae. I smile at the unlikely friendship of a dumpster diver and his highly educated friend, and wonder if I might yet make sense of the mysterious letter I found.

Nine

"Your friends are here again." I am sitting at the computer in the makeshift office and do not acknowledge Molly until she adds, "The hobos, as Helen affectionately calls them."

Arlo and Eddy are seated at the same booth they occupied during their first visit to the café. Eddy's beard is more unkempt than I remember, which is saying something. I approach their table with a smile.

"Hi, Arlo. This is a nice surprise. And hi Doc—I mean, Eddy."

Eddy throws me a menacing glance. "Bad enough Arlo calls me that."

"Doc's the real McCoy," Arlo persists. "He was *this* close to a Nobel Prize. Right, Doc?"

"Yeah, right."

"If it wasn't for the accident," Arlo adds.

Eddy looks like he might snap. "Are we here to eat, or to waste our Goddamned time gossiping?"

But my mind is just gearing up. "What accident?"

Arlo is eager to continue the discussion. "Bus crash. Eddy's colleague got killed in Ecuador. A young physics whiz. On the verge of a breakthrough in solar energy—"

"Enough already!" Eddy barks.

"Ecuador?" My head is spinning. I am connecting dots, but the picture is not clear. "Are you … does this have anything to do with Doctor Robert McKinnon?"

Arlo rumbles with laughter. "How's that for serendipity? Mr. Sunshine Café—" he sweeps his arm in a grand gesture "—I would like to introduce you to your neighbor, the one and only Doctor Robert Edward—Eddy—McKinnon."

"Well I'll be damned." I stare at Eddy, dumbfounded. I feel for him—there is something beyond his seething crust that tells me Arlo has pierced him to the core. I proceed cautiously. "I'm sorry, Eddy. Was your colleague—the one who died in Ecuador—was that Daniel Porter?"

"What of it?" he snarls. "What business is it of yours?"

"I found a letter at the recycling bin … from Daniel. It was addressed to you."

"How careless of me." Eddy maintains a stoic expression, his arms crossed in a rigid posture. Though he is small of stature, he is an intimidating presence. His blue eyes burrow right into mine, forcing me to look down.

"What happened to him, exactly? I mean, the accident."

"So"—Eddy's voice is flat—"you intercepted a personal message that I discarded, and now you want me to tell you what I know about a friend of mine who died tragically?"

"I—" I begin.

"Well," Eddy cuts me off, "I would like to point out that I did not invite you to stick your nose into something that was clearly not intended for you."

"I understand. I got a similar reaction when I saw Annie—"

"Annie?!"

"Yes, Daniel's wife. I went to Seattle to find the person who wrote the letter."

"You are too nosy for your own good, young man."

"Maybe," I say. "But ... I didn't go looking for the letter. It kind of found me."

"Ah, yes," Eddy says. "I can see it sitting in the recycling bin calling, 'Pick me up! Please come and meddle in matters that don't concern you.'"

The table goes quiet. I suppress a blend of anger and embarrassment and ask, "Can I offer either of you anything from the menu? It's on me."

"Is your coffee shade grown and fair trade?" Eddy asks.

"I don't know."

"Then I'll have a glass of water, thank you."

"I'm not as choosy as him," Arlo adds. "I'll start with a cup of coffee, please. And another one o' those breakfast hashes, if you'd be so kind."

"Sure thing." I glance over at Eddy and say, "Look, I'm sorry I've offended you."

Eddy's face softens. He stares out the window, and then speaks with a composed drawl. "Daniel was a dear friend. Perhaps you have dredged up some feelings I would prefer to leave dormant."

Ten

The view from Vashon Heights ferry terminal reminds me of the Great Smoky Mountains with a Cascadian twist. Majestic peaks stand in the distance, layered against an orange morning sky—silhouettes barely visible through a haze that has fallen over the Pacific Northwest.

My thoughts drift to a childhood trip to Tennessee when I was ten years old, the only time my father took enough time off work to go further afield than his parents' corn farm near Olivia, Minnesota. Dad was going to see the world when he retired from his middle management position at a short-haul trucking company. Lung cancer took him shortly after my twelfth birthday and made sure he never had the chance.

"Oliver!" Jake calls from the cab of his cargo van. "Boat's about to load."

I walk around the van and climb into the passenger seat. "Sorry, I was daydreaming."

"And sleepwalking, I'll bet. These are bakers' hours. But hey, I'm glad you finally joined me for one of these."

"It's about time you invited me," I jibe. "I was beginning to think you didn't care."

"I was only being polite because I thought you'd say no again. All those invitations to Maui—I was kidding about those too."

"I think you're safe there," I say. "At least until they build a trans-Pacific bridge."

~ ~ ~

The auction is chaotic, but oddly enjoyable. When the best of the cappuccino makers comes up on the block, Jake elbows me repeatedly, prompting me to hold my card in the air. When my last bid goes uncontested, he smiles and elbows me again.

"Good boy," Jake says. "It's time to put a little café into that café of yours. Now we just have to do something about your coffee."

"Are you inferring that our coffee sucks?"

"Yes."

"You've hurt my feelings again."

"What are friends for?"

"You know you're going to have to teach us how to use this machine you made me buy."

"What?" he says. "And give away our trade secrets? Next thing I know you'll be asking me for bread recipes."

~ ~ ~

As we approach downtown Seattle heading south on the I-5, I turn to Jake. "Any chance you could drop me off in Belltown? I could swing by to pick up the machine tomorrow, if that's alright?"

"Belltown?" Jake says, lifting his eyebrows as he turns to look at me. "Isn't that where—"

"Where Annie Porter lives? Yes."

"And you're going to—"

"Yes," I say. "I'm going to see if she'll talk to me about her husband."

"I thought you were letting that go."

"I was, until I met the recipient of the letter yesterday."

Jake raises his eyebrows again, but says nothing.

"Actually, I'd already met him. But now I know who he is. It's a long story."

"You say that a lot."

"What?"

"That it's a long story."

"I'll fill you in sometime over a decaf mocha Americano thingy at the café."

Jake laughs. "I think we'll start your training with coffee lingo 101."

~ ~ ~

"Hello?"

I lean toward the microphone. "Hi Annie. It's Oliver Bruce. We met a few weeks ago. I bought lemonade and ... brought a letter."

Silence.

"How can I help you?" she says at last.

"I'd like to talk, if we could. I mean, not over a loud-speaker."

Another pause, and then, "Okay. Come on around. Do you remember the unit?"

"Yes," I reply. *Like I remember the mole on your chin and the flowers on your sundress.*

Annie is partially concealed behind the front door of her apartment when I approach the green gate.

"Hi Oliver," she says flatly, but with a hint of warmth.

"Hi Annie."

We look at each other through the bars.

"I wondered if ..." Though I've rehearsed this meeting many times, the script is lodged in my throat. Finally I spit it out. "I met the person your husband's letter was addressed to. Dr. McKinnon. Turns out he's my neighbor."

"Oh?" Annie's tone softens, along with her stance. "How is Eddy?"

"Gruff."

She almost smiles. "Sounds like Eddy."

"I came into the city for an auction. I thought, maybe ... last time I was here, I wanted to ask more, but I couldn't ..." I trail off, and then add, "Is Charlie at school?"

"Charlie is homeschooled. He's with my mom today."

I look into Annie's eyes and sense the same vulnerability that I saw when she told me Daniel had died. This time, I will not walk away. "Would you join me for a coffee?"

"Okay," she says without hesitation.

I wait while Annie gets ready. The sun has burned off the morning haze, but a light breeze gives the otherwise warm air an occasional bite. Annie emerges from her apartment wearing an elegant black pantsuit and a bright violet shawl. She opens the gate and smiles cautiously before turning to walk down the street. "Your timing was good. I was ready for a break."

"From what?" I walk quickly to match her pace.

"I do bookkeeping for a few friends. It helps pay the bills without having to get a full-time job."

"That's one skill that'll never go out of fashion. It's not my forte, but I appreciate it."

"You own a restaurant, right?" I am pleased that Annie remembers something of our first conversation. Then she asks, "I guess you don't do your own books?"

"Emily does," I say, then reluctantly add, "my wife."

When we reach the coffee shop I hold the door open for Annie. She accepts my chivalry and makes her way through a crowd toward an empty table in the back corner.

"What can I get you?" I ask as she removes the hand-woven shawl from bare shoulders and places it on the back of her chair. I wonder if the shawl is from Ecuador, but I decide not to ask.

"A house blend would be great. Black."

I order two coffees, add two heaps of sugar and a large dose of cream to mine, and return to the table. I am happy that our location, combined with the background noise of other discussions, provides a shroud of privacy to the table Annie chose.

"Thank you," Annie says. "So what brought you back here?"

You, I think, but I lean on my pre-fabricated excuse. "I kind of forgot about the letter. Then I met Eddy. Actually …

I met him just after I met you, but I only made the connection yesterday."

"Really? That's quite a coincidence."

"Yeah, it is. I'd seen him around, but I would never have guessed that he was a Professor of Engineering."

"He doesn't look the part, does he?"

"No."

Another long silence.

"I'm really sorry about Daniel."

"Thanks." Annie takes a sip of coffee, holding her mug in both hands.

"I didn't want to pry. I—"

"It's okay. I've looked at that letter a few times, and ..."

"And what?" I ask.

"I wonder if my husband's research was too important ..."

I nod, urging her to continue. When she doesn't, I ask, "Did he tell you much about his work?"

"Not a lot. I couldn't speak his language."

"Can you tell me—"

"Why? Why do you want to know about Daniel?"

"I'm not sure." I search for a more intelligent answer, but I cannot locate one.

Annie looks down at her mug. I wait while she stares into the pool of black liquid, wondering how I would feel if our roles were reversed. After a while she speaks in a hushed tone. "Daniel set out to change the world. Said he was going to harness the sun like nobody had ever done before."

"Did he?"

"I don't know." She looks me in the eyes and shakes her head, causing strands of dark hair to fall loosely over her shoulder. "I don't know if there's a person alive who does. If there is, I'd guess it would be Eddy."

"Why did you say yes to coffee today?" My question surprises me. So does my being here. Not that I have any intention to stray from my marriage, but the occasional tingle across the whole of my skin reminds me of my own motive for coming today.

Annie's reply is casual, almost cheerful. "I was happy for the company."

"I'm sure this can't be easy to talk about."

"No." She looks down and speaks to her coffee again. "It never gets easy. You just find a way to live with it."

Silence is my only appropriate reply. I learned a long time ago that every grief is inimitable, each loss unique. So we sit, wordless. I begin to hear the murmur of others in the coffee shop, and I realize how immersed I have become in every aspect of Annie's presence. Then I look into her face, and I see a distant smile form. Her eyes glaze over, and she begins to speak.

"I miss him. I miss his passion. His quirky sense of humor. His smell. I even miss his pig-headedness. Once Daniel got an idea, there was no stopping him. I knew the first time he called from Ecuador that we'd lost him—that even if he came home, he would never really leave there." A tear streaks down Annie's cheek, and I reach over to hand her a napkin.

"What about Charlie?" I ask. "How is he—"

"Total denial," she says. "It's like he expects Daniel to walk in the door any day. Of course he knows that won't happen, but the truth just sits there, and I let him believe whatever he needs to." She pauses, and then continues. "Kids are resilient. I'm not as worried about Charlie as I used to be. His mother's a wreck, but he'll know I did my best. And his father ... he was always a bit of a myth."

I don't know what to make of any of this. I just want Annie to keep talking.

"What was Daniel's idea? How was he going to change the world?"

"He wanted to put an end to our dependence on fossil fuels. He was onto something big. But he was conflicted too."

"In what way?"

"I'm not sure. The very last time we spoke, he mentioned something about Frankenstein. It was a phone call, and the connection was bad, and Charlie was hungry. I was in mom mode—in no mood for Daniel's philosophy. He could be rather esoteric—he would wrap his feelings into abstract thoughts and deliver them in code for me to figure out on my own time. But I remember his tone that day ... he was concerned ... about his work."

"What did he say about Frankenstein?"

"I don't remember," she says. "I hadn't read it yet. I did recently. Have you?"

I think of Mary Shelley's most famous work—about Victor Frankenstein and the complex, lonely creature he created. A pang of empathy courses through me for a monster that never existed—or perhaps lives within us all. Then I think of Frankenstein telling Captain Walton to turn back from his ambitious journey. I look at Annie and nod. "It's one of my favorite books."

We sit frozen, studying each other as if reading the book through one another's eyes. "What did you take away from it?" I ask her.

"I don't know," Annie says, pausing to consider my question. "There were so many layers. What I wouldn't give to have that conversation again—to really listen to Daniel that last time we spoke. The thing is, I'm not sure which character he was relating to."

~ ~ ~

"What do you make of that?"

"She sounds hot." Tyler leans back in his chair and returns the headphones to his associate, pondering the recorded phone call that he listened to three times.

"Which one? Mom or grandma?"

"Take your pick," Tyler quips. "The apple never falls far from the tree."

Tyler Testosterone, the young man thinks.

"Looks like this dude is making the rounds," Tyler says, thinking of the conversation he listened to earlier—between the guy with the heavy drawl and his friend who speaks at volume eleven. Two conversations, both mentioning the same name. Oliver Bruce.

"What should we do with it?" the young man asks.

"Bump them up to Category B," Tyler says. "And submit a request for information on the new guy."

Eleven

After three hours of Jake's training and a few dozen attempts at making a variety of warm beverages, Molly and I are buzzed on caffeine. We received our first order of locally roasted coffee this morning, a product that I confess tastes better than the canned grounds we have been brewing for years.

I leave work a bit early and ride the bus back to the RV park, where I notice Arlo poking through the recycling bins.

"Arlo!" I holler, walking toward him. "How are you?"

Arlo looks up. "Sparkling," he says, enunciating the full word. I can't help smiling at his answer.

"Hey, do you know if Eddy's around today?"

"He's layin' low, fightin' a bug."

"Well, next time you see him ... could you tell him that I now have fair trade, organic, shade grown coffee and a shiny new cappuccino maker? Not that I'm trying to bait him—okay, maybe a little bit. I'd like to ask him a few questions."

"I'll let him know," Arlo says. "Of course, there might be a delivery fee."

"Of course. Your choice of beverage is on me."

~ ~ ~

Arlo and Eddy arrive at the Sunshine Café the next afternoon.

"I hear you finally have some real coffee here," Eddy says as he moves toward their now familiar table.

"I like to think we've evolved. What can I get for you this afternoon?"

"I don't need any of that fancy stuff. Just a good, strong cup of coffee, black."

"How about you, Arlo? Can I interest you in something more adventurous?"

"I'll try whatever you bring me." Arlo's reply is a charming contrast to his friend's brusque manner.

I prepare Arlo's café latte, swirling the frothed milk into a pattern that vaguely resembles a leaf. Then I pour a fresh dark roast for Eddy and return to their table.

While Arlo admires the artwork on his latte, Eddy smells his coffee, tips the mug, takes a small sip and swirls it around in his mouth.

"Not bad," Eddy says.

Arlo takes a swig of his latte and sets the cup down, looking up to me with a steamed milk moustache. "Could use some sugar, but all in all it's rather tasty."

As I reach for the container of white sugar packets, Eddy gives me another judging look. "You go to all the fuss of making a decent cup of coffee …"

I smile at Eddy's audacity. "By the way," he says, "you mentioned you'd seen Annie. How is she?"

"Yes, and I've seen her again recently. She's okay. Still grieving, of course, but she seems like a strong woman." I pull a chair up to the end of their table. Eddy shifts in his seat, putting space between us. The restaurant is almost empty now, as it tends to be most afternoons, so I venture into the taboo subject. "Can you tell me anything more about Daniel's invention?"

Eddy takes another sip of his coffee and glances down at the table before looking me straight in the eye.

"You seem like a decent chap," Eddy says. "But a bit naive. What makes you think you have any business in Daniel's world?"

"I don't know."

Eddy stares at me and I look away. "What is it you're hoping to learn?"

I look back at his chin, unable to match his gaze. "His invention—Annie said it was very important." He doesn't respond, so I continue. "If it was so important, why hasn't anyone else carried on his work? Or have they? She said that if anyone would know, it would be you."

"Daniel was a bit of a lone wolf. We had a lot in common that way." After another sip of coffee, Eddy adds, "Fair trade and shade grown, you say?"

"Yes," I smile. "So, did he succeed?"

"I never saw it, if that's what you're asking."

"What was your role in the project?"

"I offered him support; consultation on some of the more pedestrian aspects of his work."

"My friend is a tad humble," Arlo interjects.

"I know my strengths," Eddy says. "I'm a damn good mechanical engineer, but I'm no physicist. Daniel was one of the best."

"But you must understand the essence of Daniel's invention," I suggest.

"The essence, yes," Eddy replies.

"Could you share any of your knowledge with me?"

Eddy bristles. "I already have."

"I mean about the invention."

"You wouldn't comprehend it."

"Probably not, but you could try me."

Eddy's face lights up. "If I were you, I would build on this cup of coffee. It really is quite good."

"Right," I sigh. "I'm glad you approve."

Twelve

When I see Eddy's Westfalia pull into the RV Park, I slip on my sandals and open the screen door, deeply appreciative of the July sun after a long, wet spring. My mood has improved dramatically along with the weather, a gradual if not entirely linear progression that began on the day I almost died.

"Where are you going?" Emily asks.

"Over to Eddy's."

"You've been spending a lot of time with those guys lately."

"I know. It's like a free university course."

"Don't forget that I have to go to the kiln this afternoon," Emily says.

"I won't be long." I imagine Emily rolling her eyes while I jog down the gravel lane toward Eddy's trailer.

When I reach Eddy's site, he is wrestling a five-gallon container out of his vehicle. I reach in to get a second container.

"What's in these?" I ask. "Looks like oil."

"It is." Eddy sets down his jug. "Vegetable oil. I get it from Chong's."

"Why?"

"It's my fuel."

"For your Westy?"

"No, for my spaceship."

Arlo walks into the site and points to the top of Eddy's trailer. "Has he shown you his solar panels? He only has to plug in this beast durin' the winter."

"Hi Arlo." I look at the crowded array of technology on Eddy's roof. "An engineer's trailer, huh?"

We all sit down by the empty fire pit in Eddy's site.

"Any news on the home front?" Arlo asks.

"No," I say. "We've reached a stalemate, and Em's too busy to think about it. She's working like mad to get some pottery ready for the Strawberry Festival. Do you guys go to that?"

"Sometimes," Arlo replies. "I go for the freebies."

"I don't bother," Eddy says. "Too many people and not enough strawberries. Thanks to FDR."

"Huh?" I say.

"Executive Order 9066. Signed by Franklin Delano Roosevelt on February 19, 1942."

Arlo groans, "Eddy and his dates."

"The internment. In the land of the free—" Eddy continues, and Arlo finishes his sentence "—except when our government thinks you might be a threat."

We all sit in silence, reflecting on this black mark of American history—the internment camps that robbed people of Japanese descent of their land, and Vashon Island of its strawberry farms—until I change the subject. "Hey, I have a question about Daniel's invention."

"I thought—" Eddy says, glaring at me.

"I know," I interrupt. "But with all our talk about the importance of renewable energy, how can we let Daniel's invention fade off into oblivion?"

"Look, Oliver," Eddy drawls. "You've grown on me a bit, kind of like a fungus. But I've said it before and I'll say—"

"Eddy," I say firmly, "I may seem like a simpleton, but I do have a brain in my head."

"I never said you didn't. In fact, I think you are quite an intelligent specimen."

"Specimen?" I am both humored and offended by Eddy's choice of words.

Arlo lets out a hearty laugh. "Don't mind the doc. He's called me names I had to look up in the dictionary—it's his way of showin' affection."

"Bah," Eddy growls, but I see the hint of a smirk crease his cheeks.

"Eddy," I continue. "I *dare* you to explain Daniel's invention to me."

Eddy bristles, and I can see that I've struck a chord. He stares at me until I begin to squirm, his smirk more obvious now. Making people uncomfortable is a favorite pastime for Eddy. After weeks of these discussions, I no longer take it personally.

"Oliver," he says, "how much do you know about computers?"

"I play a mean game of Tetris."

Eddy ignores my attempt at humor. "Have you ever heard of Moore's Law?"

"No."

"Well here's a little background. The speed of a computer has to do with how closely you can pack the transistors on an integrated circuit chip. Moore's Law states, in so many words, that we should be able to double the number of transistors on an integrated circuit every two years, which, in turn, will double the speed of a computer. Moore's prediction has turned out to be quite accurate, in part because scientists use it as a guideline."

"Okay, so—" I begin, but Eddy has no intention of letting me ask questions.

"Daniel came up with a paradigm shift for absorbing solar energy, using intense magnification and a new material—a sponge of sorts. He believed that the scope of power created, through iterative improvement of the magnification process, could be doubled frequently—like Moore's Law. Now as you can imagine, the implications of such an advancement would be quite revolutionary."

"Catch all that?" Arlo asks.

"I think so," I reply. "Daniel created a process that magnifies energy from the sun and stores it using some sort of new material. Kind of like a solar battery, except that the power it generates will increase exponentially over time."

Eddy leans in and looks me up and down. "Not quite, but close enough. My hunch was right. You are smarter than the average turkey."

"Comin' from the doc," Arlo says, "I'd take that as a compliment."

"So are you telling me that Daniel's invention was kind of like the computer of solar energy?"

Eddy begins to laugh, which turns into a cough. He clears his throat and says, "Imagine a solar pod the size of a football that can power a house. Now imagine that kind of energy on an industrial scale."

"And imagine," Arlo chimes in, "what some people might do to get their hands on that kind of power."

"Are you …" I begin. "Do you think—"

"I think they call it power for a reason," Arlo says.

I look at him and feel the synapses firing in my brain. "So if people knew what Daniel was working on …"

"My friend here is a conspiracy theorist," Eddy says as he waves his arms, "with a very active imagination."

"How did Daniel die?" I ask. "I mean, I know it was a bus crash, but … what happened?"

"Landslide," Eddy says. "Up in the Andes, near where he worked. Took the whole bus, along with a good chunk of the road."

"So they say," Arlo adds. "So they say …"

Thirteen

The air is unusually moist this evening, still warm from a rare scorcher on the island, as we sit around a fire that is not required for its heat. The laughter of four kids pours through the screen door from the table inside the RV. Though they range in age from seven to seventeen, our children have always found ways to enjoy each other's company while we savor a bit of adult conversation. Jake and Beth's oldest son, Jackson, sometimes joins the adults, but to the delight of Isabella and Isaac he has chosen to be a child tonight.

"So how does it feel to be forty?" Jake asks. "It didn't hit me very hard, but fifty is coming on faster than I'd like."

"It's odd," I reply. "I guess I'm in denial. If you guys had let me, I would've been happy to ignore it."

"We had to do something," Beth says. "It's a big milestone."

"I guess," I mumble. I appreciate the attention at home this evening, but I was a little disappointed that nobody at the café acknowledged my birthday. In fairness, it was one of our busiest days on record. "We've been off the charts at work," I say to Jake. "How about you?"

"Probably our best summer yet."

"Timing couldn't be better," Emily adds. "This is the first time in years that our bank account has actually grown. July was really good, and the first half of August has been even better."

"Any headway on the house?" Beth asks.

Emily and I look at each other, and then she answers for us, "No. Every time we try to talk about it we end up arguing about whether to go bigger or smaller. So we haven't talked about it much lately."

Beth looks confused. "I thought you guys were trying to find a bigger place so you could both do your art."

"We were," I say, indignant, "until Em started reading about tiny homes. Our plan—or lack thereof—changed midstream."

"It was your idea to sell the house," Emily says flatly.

"Yeah," I reply, "but not with the idea of going smaller."

Emily turns toward Beth and says, "I used to want my own pottery setup, but then we started the Arts Co-op this spring."

"How's that going?" Beth asks.

"Great," Emily says. "I go down there a couple times a week, and there's plenty for the kids to do. It's a magical place—so many talented people, all feeding off one another. I feel giddy when I'm there, like I'm frolicking in some sort of artists' playground."

I listen to Emily speak with passion about her artistic community while I stew, untended. Part of me is glad to see her thriving, but I miss my own art—and my wife. The flicker of romance that sometimes found enough oxygen to burn when we lived in a house has been snuffed out completely by the cramped space of our motor home.

"What about that trip?" Jake asks during a break in the conversation. "Are you guys going or not?"

Emily's happiness turns to frustration as she points to me. "Ask him."

With all eyes upon me, I shrug. "I don't know. Ask me after the summer."

Jake turns toward Emily, pointing his thumb at me. "I keep telling this guy that these things are called *mobile* homes for a reason." Then he looks at me. "If I was you, I'd get somewhere warmer and drier before monsoon season hits."

Emily smacks me on the thigh and beams at Jake. "I like the way you think, Jake Turcott. Now if you can just keep working on this husband of mine ..."

~ ~ ~

They trickle in slowly enough that it takes me a while to catch on. Jake and his family enter first. Then Arlo and Eddy show up—their second visit today. When my family appears, I realize I've been had. All of our regular staff—Molly, Frank, Sal and Helen—appear in unison from the kitchen, carrying a cake that looks sure to set off the fire alarm.

I wait for the entire group to sing Happy Birthday, unable to contain my smile. "Okay, you got me," I say.

"It wasn't easy to play dumb yesterday," Helen says, "especially with all the fishing you were doing."

"I wasn't fishing." I mock a sneer.

"Yeah, right," Helen says. "That's why you said you were feeling older than usual?"

"Okay," I agree. "Maybe just a little."

I turn to face my family, and they are radiant. The kids' wide grins reveal pride for their roles in pulling off a surprise on old Dad. Emily looks more beautiful than I remember seeing her in a long time. I smile at her and she smiles back, reminding me of our earliest days together.

For a brief moment, the Sunshine Café brings me authentic joy as a gathering place for the disparate group of friends and family that has become my community. After cake is served—a wonderful home-baked creation from Helen—Molly hands me a gift wrapped in newsprint.

"The Complete US Road Atlas," I say, looking around at everyone. "You guys are really tired of looking at my ugly mug, aren't you?"

Molly looks at Jake, who hands me an envelope. I open it and pull out a card, pushing aside a large wad of bills to read various greetings from everyone at the party, plus a few people who could not attend.

Handling the wad of cash, I look around the room and stammer, "Wow, thank you. I didn't ... you didn't—"

"It's gas money," Jake says. "We tried to collect enough to get you to Tennessee and back, but in that house on wheels you'll be lucky to make it to Idaho. It's a start, any-way."

"Wow," I say again, before looking at Emily. "Were you in on this?"

She nods. "A little. But it was Jake's idea. I only mentioned the destination. I know how much you've wanted to show the Great Smoky Mountains to Izzy and Isaac."

"And to you," I smile. "It's about the only place I've been that you haven't."

After gifts, the party winds down quickly. I grab a broom to help Molly and Sal clean up, but Emily comes close and whispers, "Why don't you let them finish cleaning? This is your party."

"I'm just—" I begin.

Emily places a finger to my lips. "In case you hadn't noticed, Izzy and Isaac left with the Turcotts."

"What?"

"They're doing a movie marathon sleepover. It's been planned for a while now. It's just you and me tonight, Oliver."

"Well, in that case …" I set the broom back where I found it. A spark lights in my core, a primal feeling that has been buried beneath layers of discontent. For one night, I will allow myself to be spoiled.

Fourteen

"How are you making out?" Emily calls from the doorway of the motor home.

I pull my head out of the storage compartment where I am packing the last of our outside gear—chairs, sports equipment and a small barbeque. "Almost ready. You?"

"I just need to sweep the floors. The kids are already belted in. They're a little excited, especially since their friends are back in school."

"Yeah," I say, closing the compartment. "I hope they can catch up when we get home."

"They'll learn more on the road than they could in any classroom."

"If you say so. Speaking of classrooms, I'm gonna pop over and say goodbye to my teachers."

"Say bye for me too." Emily shuts the screen door and disappears.

When I approach Eddy's campsite, he and Arlo are sitting beside the empty fire pit arguing like an old married couple.

"What's up?" I ask.

"There's the travelin' man," Arlo says. "I'm just chastisin' Eddy for his new habit o' skippin' breakfast."

"When do you set sail?" Eddy snips, ignoring Arlo's comment.

"We're almost ready to go. I just came over to say goodbye."

"Good riddance to you too," Eddy says.

"Happy trails," Arlo says. "I'll miss your coffee art."

"I'll miss our chats," I say. "But I hope to bring more to the conversation when I get back."

"Enjoy the Smokies," Eddy says, his voice softer than usual. "They're something special."

"You've been?" I ask.

"Once. Many Octobers ago." A nostalgic smile fills Eddy's face, and his eyes become moist. It hasn't been easy to get past Eddy's crust, and this seems like a rare invitation.

"Who were you there with?" I ask.

After a long pause he looks up and says, "Always let the people you love know that you love them, Oliver."

~ ~ ~

"Thanks for embracing this," Emily says, looking over at me with a warm smile.

"Thanks for not giving me a choice."

The kids sit face-to-face at bench seats that double as our dining room while we cruise east along the I-90. Izzy reads and Isaac plays with a tablet computer while Emily and I enjoy the landscape. I marvel at this natural setting so close to Seattle, a passing scene that I scarcely recall from my journey from Minneapolis over fifteen years ago.

After a peaceful two hours, Isaac says that he has to use the bathroom.

"I'll pull over when I can," I yell over my shoulder.

"Why don't we stop for dinner?" Emily suggests. "It's less than five minutes to Ellensburg."

We soon pull into a stall on Pine Street, on a block full of historic buildings mostly made of brick and stone. Isaac bolts to the bathroom the second we stop. Emily sets to making a simple dinner of sandwiches, and I reach to the console and pick up our cell phone to check for messages.

"That's interesting," I say nonchalantly. "I got an e-mail from Annie Porter."

"What does it say?" I know Emily wasn't pleased when I returned to Belltown on the day of the auction, but she let it go. I pretended to do the same after Annie and I parted ways in front of her apartment, exchanging e-mail addresses with promises to keep in touch. Annie often crosses my mind, but I have not reached out to her.

"She just said, 'Oliver, please call when you have a moment.' And a phone number."

"Hmm," Emily says.

My chest tightens at the prospect of speaking to Annie again. I step out of the RV and dial her number. Annie answers on the second ring.

"Annie," I say. "It's Oliver. I got your message."

The warmth in Annie's voice seems that of an old friend. "Oliver," she says. "Thanks for calling. How are you?"

"I'm good. It's nice to hear from you. How are you? How's your summer been?"

"I am well. I was wondering if you could put me in touch with Eddy. I couldn't find his contact info."

"Sure," I say. "I just saw him this morning. Your best bet is to call Cedars RV Resort on Vashon and talk to the manager, Jane. Eddy doesn't have a phone. For an engineer, he's not much for using technology."

"Neither was Daniel," she laughs. "I guess they made quite a pair."

"So, what's— "

"I found a letter that Daniel had written, which I felt Eddy should receive."

"Oh?" I hope my tone urges Annie to continue.

"It was tucked in a book that was sent to me from the village where he was living in Ecuador. I stacked most of Daniel's things in a closet when they arrived here ... and I'm finally going through them."

Closets full of memories take me back to the home where I grew up—the home I cleaned out on my own almost two decades ago. In some way I feel that I am there with Annie, uncovering her grief one layer at a time. "How is Charlie?" I ask.

"He's good, thanks. He still talks about the man with the ten dollar donation … while he tries to sell lemonade at nine o'clock in the morning. You've set quite an unrealistic expectation."

"Sorry," I laugh. "Guess I'll have to come and buy another lemonade when I get back."

"Back?" she says. "From where?"

"I'm on my way to Tennessee. A long overdue family vacation."

"That sounds great. Sorry for interrupting your holiday."

"No, not at all. It's good to hear from you. Let me know if you can't reach Eddy. I can get a message to him through my restaurant."

"Will do," Annie says. A long silence follows before she adds, "Thanks."

There is so much I want to say, but I keep it all in. This trip is an investment in my family. In my marriage. So I say goodbye to Annie and make my way back into the RV. I wonder why she did not ask such a simple question in her e-mail message, and I'm sure Emily will wonder the same thing.

~ ~ ~

Hues of red, orange, and yellow rest upon jagged peaks, layered like sand in a glass, surrounding our campground in Badlands National Park. Three days into our journey, this stop along the longer southern route that included a brief side trip to Mount Rushmore National Memorial is a welcome change from the monotonous rhythm of asphalt rolling under our tires.

"Stunning, isn't it?" Emily wraps her arms around me in a show of affection that I am sure the sunset deserves credit for.

"Yes," I reply. We watch as Isaac gleefully runs from his sister at the playground across from our campsite, engaged in a game of three-dimensional tag on a sparse array of equipment.

Emily's voice is calm, relaxed. "What say we take our time tomorrow, maybe spend some time at the visitor center and do a short hike?"

"Yeah, maybe," I reply. "But I'd like to keep moving."

"We have two days to get to Olivia," she says. "It's less than eight hours from here."

"Yeah, I guess." I have been more comfortable on the road than at any of our stops thus far—unable to fully appreciate any of the places we have seen, or to convince my mind to slow down. I think of work—of Molly's ability to manage the café for more than a few days, and of the bleak financial picture the restaurant paints through the fall and winter months. I think of Arlo and Eddy. I think of Annie and Charlie. And Daniel. Standing in awe of a most brilliant sky, I wonder if Annie has been able to locate Eddy.

"Do we have coverage?" I ask without thinking, realizing too late that I have interrupted a romantic moment.

"I don't know," Emily sighs, and her arms drop away from my waist. "Who were you going to call?"

"I want to find out if Annie reached Eddy."

"Right," she says coldly.

Emily and I return to our separate lives. She walks toward the playground to let the kids know it is almost time to come in, and I go to the motor home to grab the cell phone. One bar tells me a text message is a better bet than a phone call.

I type in the phone number Annie sent me a few days ago, which has already lodged itself into my memory, then tap out a message. *"Hi Annie. Did you reach Eddy?"*

I set down the phone and begin to put away dishes that have dried in a rack beside the sink. The phone rings, and I see it is Annie's number.

"Hi Annie."

"Hi Oliver. Where are you now?"

"The Badlands, in South Dakota. Have you ever been here?"

"No," she says.

"I'm glad we have a decent connection. I wasn't sure we would, hence the text message. Did you reach Eddy?"

"Yes," Annie says. "I sent him the letter." Something in her voice tells me she has more to say, so I wait. After a moment she speaks again. "I read it. It felt inappropriate to read someone else's mail."

"He was your husband," I say in an attempt at support.

"I guess." Her voice is faint.

"I don't suppose you'd want to be even more inappropriate and share the contents of the letter with me?"

She pauses before responding. "I would like to talk about it, but it's probably best if you ask Eddy. I'm sure he'll make more sense of it than I could."

"Understood," I reply.

Another long silence.

"Oliver?"

"Yes?"

"I'm glad you found us."

"Me too."

"I don't know why that letter was unsent."

"You said you found it in a book?"

"Yes, a Physics tome. I flipped through it page by page, like I have felt every piece of Daniel's clothing ... rubbed my hands over every one of his belongings. It seems like I'm trying to hold my husband tightly one last time before letting him go."

I stop breathing as I wait for Annie to continue.

"Oliver," she says, "I think you might want to talk to Eddy about the letter. It's possible ... Daniel implied—"

~ ~ ~

"Sir," Tyler says, *trying to sound confident in the presence of a senior official,* "we've picked up something on a Category B file— Daniel Porter."

"Porter?" *Harold McIntyre replies, trying to place the name.*

"He was a physicist—" *Tyler adds* "—in Ecuador."

"Of course," *Harold says. Daniel Porter. He was one of her favorites.* "What about him?"

"I think the file might be worthy of escalation."

"Why is that?"

"There's a strong indication that Mr. Porter's invention still exists."

Fifteen

"Oliver." My aunt greets us on the porch, opening her arms wide to receive me. "It's been far too long. Danny's wedding, maybe?"

"Lily." I lean in to hug her, trying to remember when her son, my best friend for the first twelve years of my life, was married. "Yes, I think that was the last time."

I rarely saw any of my dad's family after he died. When my paternal grandparents both followed within two years, my mother was unwilling—or unable—to maintain our family ties. Granny and Pops had been like parents to my mother, who had little interest in communicating with her own dysfunctional family in Iowa. Losing the three people she depended on most left a deep void in her heart—a void that she filled with alcohol and antidepressants. Only the practicality of daily life and her determination to see me through to adulthood delayed my mother's descent into the abyss that eventually absorbed her.

"Oliver"—Lily has released me from her embrace—"are you okay?"

"Oh," I say, "Yeah, I'm—is Danny going to make it out today?"

"He'll be here for dinner," Lily says. "Just wait 'til you see his boys—well, I'm not sure I can call them boys anymore."

"Where's Uncle Herb?"

"He's been working out past the creek. He knows you're coming. He'll be in soon."

"I guess we picked a busy time for a visit, huh?"

"Sure," Lily says, "but we're managing. Still remember how to drive a combine?"

I laugh. "I never really did. I just sat on my dad's lap. I am definitely not farmer material."

"Bah!" Lily waves off my reply. "We're all farmer material. Most people have just forgotten how."

We head inside for tea, the kids following reluctantly. When Lily serves them hot chocolate with marshmallows, their boredom turns to a sudden liking for their great Aunt Lily.

"Oliver!" Uncle Herb's booming voice surprises me as he walks into the kitchen. "So good to see you, lad. And this good-looking bunch must be your family."

"Uncle Herb." I stand up to greet him with a handshake. He ignores my offer and wraps me in a bear hug. Then he grabs my shoulders and stands at arm's length, eyeing me up and down.

"You sure look like a Bruce," he says. "All grown up and complete with your own offspring."

I smile at his comment, and I realize that in this instant I feel anything but grown up. In my mind, I am the same age as my daughter.

~ ~ ~

This half section of cropland outside of Olivia, Minnesota—the self-declared Corn Capital of the World—looks much as it did when I was a child. I watch Isabella push Isaac on the tire swing that was installed when the farmhouse was raised—with a great deal of food, drink and song—during the summer when I turned seven. The house has been added to and updated, and a rectangular workshop has been built into the side of the Quonset. The garden is larger than I remember, and a few less animals roam the nearby pasture. But this is very much the same place that I have only ever known as *The Farm*.

"Oliver," Emily calls from the porch. "Danny called. He'll be here in an hour or so. We'll hold off serving dinner until then."

"Okay, thanks." I turn to my kids. "You want to see something cool?"

"Yeah," Izzy replies, and Isaac nods in agreement.

We walk into the Quonset and turn on three sets of lights. The huge bulbs set in large steel bowls illuminate an assortment of farm equipment, including a newish green and yellow John Deere tractor, a rusty old combine that I used to ride with my dad, and the rake trailer that I pulled on my own—with a great deal of pride—during the one summer trip I made to the farm as a teenager. Beyond them, in the back corner, she stares at me like a long lost puppy. I feel her headlights follow me as I walk toward her, and then around to the driver's side. A small patch of rust mars the bright red fender above the front wheel well, but she is still a thing of beauty. Her canvas looks almost new as it stretches from the trunk to the top of her windshield.

"Wow!" Isaac says, "That looks old."

"1964. Older than me. They call her a '64-and-a-half Mustang Convertible. Sally, we called her. Mustang Sally."

"Pretty stylin'," Izzy says.

"Yeah." I run my hand along the door, then lift the handle and open it to look inside. "She was my dad's."

"Why's she out here?" Izzy asks, peering into the open door.

"Good question." Herb is standing inside the door of the Quonset. "I uncovered her just for you. You know, Oliver, all you have to do is ask for the keys. I'm only her babysitter. Have been all these years."

I smile at my uncle, a man who was once a huge part of my life. "Thanks, Uncle Herb. Maybe one day ... I'm not sure." Sally represents everything I left behind, intentionally and otherwise. I can't tell if this stopover at the family farm is a first step toward reconnecting with my family, or a final farewell to a place I used to call home.

~ ~ ~

Bowing my head to say the Lord's Prayer that I must have recited ten thousand times as a child, I glance at my bewildered children. Isabella manages to feign compliance, but Isaac looks around the room with curiosity. God left me the day my father died, and He has not returned. I do not call myself an atheist; I am too indifferent for such a strong label. But once I started questioning the Father, the Son and the Holy Ghost, I couldn't stop. I have come to accept myself as merely one of several billion humans, surrounded by countless other organisms on a rock that is barely a grain of sand in an almost infinite universe.

"It's so great to see you, cousin." Danny breaks me out of my introspection.

"You too," I reply. "Sorry it's been so long."

"I haven't made it out west either." He places a large helping of ham on his plate. "When I get a chance to go away, we usually head to Mexico or Florida, or sometimes a Caribbean cruise."

I begin to serve myself while Emily helps Isaac navigate the hearty feast. "I don't blame you. I wouldn't recommend Seattle in the winter."

"I'd like to see your restaurant," says Paula, Danny's wife and mother of three strapping young men, ranging in age from fourteen to nineteen and all at least three inches taller than my five-foot-ten frame.

"It's not much to look at," I say, "but it almost pays the bills. I can't remember what you're doing these days, Danny. You're not farming, are you?"

"I help with the harvest when I can," Danny says between bites, "but no, my day job is in sales for Talgenic. I'm in the city a couple days a week, and I spend a lot of time on the road."

"I think I've heard of them," I say. "What does Talgenic do?"

"It's a seed company," he replies.

"It's a chemical company," adds Josh, Danny's oldest boy. Josh is taking a weekend break from attending my alma mater in the Twin Cities, and is here to help his grandparents with the harvest.

"Josh"—Danny stares down his eldest son—"let's not, okay? I haven't seen my cousin since before you were born."

Danny nods toward Isaac and Isabella, then turns to me. "I'm telling you, cuz, before you know it they'll be challenging your every move."

"It's nice to meet your boys," I say. "So, Josh, I hear you're at U of M?"

"Yeah," Josh replies.

"What are you taking?"

"Environmental Studies. I want to work in the Amazon."

"The Amazon?"

"Yeah. I'm saving up for a semester in Ecuador next year."

"Ecuador," Emily says. "Go figure."

Josh looks confused, but he continues. "I'm going to Yasuni National Park. They say it's the most bio-diverse place on Earth, and it's sitting on a few billion dollars' worth of oil."

"Hmm," I say. "Sounds like a recipe for disaster."

~ ~ ~

"It was nice to finally meet some of your family." Emily's voice is almost too soft to hear over the buzz of crickets and katydids—a unique blend of sounds that triggers an abundance of memories. A sense of home.

"Yeah," I reply, staring up at the clearest night sky that I have seen in years.

"You don't sound thrilled."

"No, it's good."

"It's been a long time. Is it—are they—what you expected?"

"I guess. I mean, they're twenty years older. Danny's put on a lot of weight. But once they started talking … yeah, they're the same people."

"How about you?"

"I don't know. Danny and I spent so much time here, talking about what we wanted to be when we grew up— pilots, astronauts, football players, rock stars."

"Farmers?" Emily asks.

"No," I laugh. "Anything but. That was way too much work for a city kid, and Danny couldn't wait to get off the farm."

"Sounds like you had a good discussion with Josh?"

"Yeah. He's a nice kid. He's pretty stoked about visiting the Amazon. Is it just me, or are kids these days smarter than we were?"

"Maybe," Em says. "But they get to build on the wisdom of an extra generation." She looks up at the sky and asks, "Why haven't we been here before?"

"I don't know. Hasn't been a priority, I guess."

"I think it's more than that."

"I guess."

"This is hard for you, isn't it?"

"In a way."

"Well, it's nice to see a new part of you. It's good for the kids too."

"Yeah."

"Want to stick around here for a few extra days? Maybe even go into Minneapolis? We're not in a rush."

"No," I respond. "Let's get back on the road."

Sixteen

My life plays in rewind as we chart a path from Minnesota to Tennessee. Our departure from the farm was difficult—complete with hugs, hollow promises to keep in touch and vague talk of a family reunion. Danny gave me the biggest embrace of all, and in that moment I relived the whole of my youth. Watching my cousin say goodbye to Lily and Herb made me long for my own parents, for a time when I could not imagine the loneliness that would find me.

During a brief stop in Des Moines, Iowa, I find my mother's childhood home, looking much as it did in the pictures she showed me when I was young. A modest bungalow, recently updated to include a new roof and vinyl siding—no sign of the basement that housed ten children—looks small and old-fashioned compared to the newer homes that overshadow it. The house, like the community surrounding it, is nicer than I imagined it would be. The pictures—a few snapshots of relatively happy times—were all I knew of my mother's childhood when I was young. The darker stories came during my teen years. They seeped out of my mother like poison—sharp words about my grandfather's belt or my grandmother's denigrations—memories triggered by events that escaped my perception, recalled in sound bites too small to provide my mother with lasting relief.

Heading south, we stay at campgrounds just outside of St. Louis and Nashville, scheduling our days to avoid urban travel during rush hour. I am on a mission to reach our destination and return home as soon as possible. I have never been away from the café for this long, and anxiety—about payroll and bills and the slower winter months that lie ahead—eats at me despite daily reports from Molly that everything is fine. I question my importance and whether the Sunshine Café has become too big a piece of my identity. And I wonder why I am so eager to keep moving.

About halfway along the two-hour drive from Nashville to Chattanooga, Emily loses patience with my pace. "I think we might have seen more of the landscape if we'd taken a plane," she says with more than a hint of sarcasm.

"Sorry." I keep my eyes on the freeway to avoid meeting hers.

"Can we set up shop in Chattanooga for a few days? It looks like there's a lot to do there."

Memories of Chattanooga fill my head—of sitting on a bridge over the Tennessee River, watching dozens of rowers pass underneath; of squeezing my way between massive stone formations at Rock City, daring my parents to follow me; of standing in awe of Ruby Falls, watching a constant flow of water fall more than a hundred feet into an underground cavern. I think of my parents' lives, and of dreams unfulfilled—both theirs and mine. I am about to say something when Isaac yells from the back seat, "Are we going to stop soon?"

"Okay, buddy," I holler back. Then I look at Emily and nod. "Okay, let's do that."

~ ~ ~

The news hits me harder than it has a right to. Arlo's words flow from the phone into my ear, reaching down to my chest, unlocking a lifetime of sorrow.

I walk back to the motor home and lean against it, dropping my head to stare at the ground, fixating for a moment on the bubbling and crackling of our still warm engine. Forty hours of driving to reach Tennessee, and I arrive to this.

I straighten up and climb into the motor home. I lean against the counter, a knot forming in my throat. Emily cuts carrots at the table.

"Hey, Em."

"Oliver?" She stops cutting and looks up at me. "What's wrong?"

"It's Eddy. He's dying. Esophageal cancer."

"Seriously? How long—"

"They don't know. Not long. A month, maybe less."

"I'm sorry."

"Me too."

"Where is he now?"

"At home. He's refusing treatment. It's too late to do anything but control the pain."

"How did they find out?"

"I guess he could hardly eat. Arlo convinced him to visit the clinic yesterday, and they whisked him into Seattle for tests. They just found out this morning." Molly's text message a few minutes ago—*Can you call here? Arlo needs to talk to you*—told me that something was wrong. I think I knew before I dialed that it had to do with Eddy. As the summer wore on he had been coughing more and eating less, and I could see that he was losing weight. But I ignored the symptoms as I enjoyed getting to know the complex man who was becoming a mentor—perhaps even a friend.

Emily stares down at the carrots and slumps her shoulders. "Oh, Oliver. That's so sad."

"Yeah. I think I'll go for a walk around the campground."

"Okay. Dinner will be ready soon."

I walk the perimeter of the campground. When Emily challenged me to stop here, I started to look forward to exploring this hidden gem of a city with my children. But I feel like the child here, waiting for his father to lead the way. The news about Eddy is a kick to the head.

On my second loop around the campground I am joined by Glenn Miller and his orchestra, with my mother singing the lead. Her melodic voice—the sweet, soothing contralto that filled my home as a child—sings to me from another lifetime.

When you hear the whistle blowin' eight to the bar
Then you know that Tennessee is not very far
Shovel all the coal in
Gotta keep it rollin'
Woo, woo, Chattanooga there you are.

Seventeen

A morning tour of the caverns near our campground sets the tone for a busy afternoon downtown. My funk loosens its grip as we emerge from the Walnut Street pedestrian bridge, delivering us across the Tennessee River. Coolidge Park, with its classic carousel of hand-carved wooden horses and a play fountain that invites all of us to escape the southern September sun, displaces my gloom with a flash of unbridled joy. *So this is what a vacation feels like.*

Heading back to our motor home, I hear the alert for a text message buried within the knapsack I am carrying. I stop at a bench and dig through the pack until I find the phone.

"Who is it?" Emily asks.

"Molly," I reply. "She says Arlo wants me to call him at the RV park. It has something to do with Eddy." My throat catches on what cannot be said. I look up the number for Cedars RV Resort and dial it into the phone. I speak to Jane briefly, and then wait for her to get Arlo.

"Ollie," he says at last, "it's Eddy. He's askin' for you."

"For me? Why?"

"It has to do with the project in Ecuador. He got a letter the other day—"

"From Annie," I interrupt.

"You know about it?"

"Just a little. Is he there? Can I talk to him?"

"You know Eddy. He won't take a call at the best o' times. And these certainly aren't the best o' times. He'd bite my arm off if I tried to drag him to the office."

"What about a cell phone?" I ask. "I'm sure you could borrow one."

"No, Ollie, you need to come here."

"When? I won't be back for at least a couple of weeks— longer if Em has her way."

"There's not much left of him, Ollie." The sadness in Arlo's voice knocks the wind out of me. I picture him standing in the small office, and I realize that he is about to lose his best friend.

"I'd like to see him, Arlo. I really would."

"He wants you to go to Ecuador."

"*Me*?" I stammer. "Go to *Ecuador*?

"Yes."

"Why me?"

"Because the universe picked you, my friend. At least that's how I see it."

I pause to consider Arlo's words. "No, I don't think so. Terrified of flying, only speaks English... I'm halfway across the country—with a wife and kids. No, Arlo, I don't think the universe got the right guy."

"It always gets the right guy," he says. "The question is whether the right guy is up to the challenge."

"No," I reply. "I don't think I am. Are you sure you can't get Eddy on the phone?"

"You have to come see him, Oliver. He's even willin' to pay for your flight."

~ ~ ~

"What are you searching for?" Emily asks. She rests a hand on my shoulder and peers past my head to study the laptop screen. Isaac is already asleep, and Isabella is in bed reading about Tennessee's role in the Civil War.

"Train schedules. I thought maybe the Chattanooga Choo Choo could take me home, but there isn't even a route from here anymore."

"What do you think Eddy needs you to do?"

"Whatever it is, I can't imagine doing it. But I'm thinking—if I could talk to Eddy, see him before he dies—I know I'd be glad I went. Did I ever tell you about my aunt Eleanor?"

"What about her?"

"That I didn't go to see her when she was dying. I claimed I was too busy at school, but I found time to go out drinking every weekend. I couldn't handle being around any more illness or death, so I tried to believe it wasn't happening. I didn't even go to her funeral."

"She was your grandma's twin, right?"

"Yeah. For a while she was the glue that held my mom together. She came into the city quite a bit during my school years, but I lost contact when I started university. When she got sick."

Emily wraps her arms around me while I stare blankly at the screen. She leans forward and points at the Amtrak map. "There are stations in Memphis and Atlanta. Maybe you could bus it to one of those?"

"Yeah, I checked. It'd take me three days to get home in either case."

"Ouch."

"I'm thinking of flying," I say matter-of-factly.

"You must be serious." A soft expression forms on Emily's face, close to mine. "Whatever you need to do, go ahead. I'll manage with the kids."

"Thanks." I give her a half-hearted smile, and for a moment I remember why Emily and I have stayed together for almost fifteen years.

I leave the computer running and get ready for bed. Emily is snoring lightly when I emerge from the bathroom ten minutes later. I step over to the kids' bunks and rearrange Isaac's blankets. Izzy has fallen asleep with the book in her hands. I place a bookmark, kiss her on the forehead and shut off her light.

I go back to the table and pull up the airline reservation page. After a moment of contemplation, I click *Book Now*. I type in my credit card details, and then I hesitate. I have made it this far before, most recently at Christmas a few years ago when I almost booked a family vacation to Maui, but opted instead for a weekend getaway to the Olympic Peninsula.

My nerves tug at me as I click *Confirm*, and tighten their grip with a final prompt—*Are you sure you want to confirm this flight?* I click *Yes*. Seconds later, an e-mail confirmation tells me that in two days I am supposed to board a plane destined for Atlanta. And then do it all over again to fly from Atlanta to Seattle. I smile at my courage. Then I shut down the computer and climb into bed beside my sleeping wife.

Eighteen

On the surface, the approach into SeaTac Airport is calm. Under cover of a tranquil façade, anxiety wraps itself around my lungs and works its way to my windpipe, suffocating me. A few moments before touchdown my hands grip the ends of the armrests and I will myself to breathe. My heartbeat reaches a crescendo as the tires of the Boeing 767 bounce once, twice, three times, before settling on the runway. My grip loosens as we pull into the gate. This was a marked improvement over the abject terror I felt during my first ever landing in Atlanta, less than eight hours ago.

The damp autumn air shocks my system when I exit the airport toward the taxi area. Standing in the short queue, I turn on the pay-as-you-go phone that I bought at Chattanooga Airport, happy to see a reply to the message I sent before boarding my plane.

"Hi Oliver," Annie's message reads. *"It would be nice to see you. Call anytime. So sorry to hear about Eddy."*

"Just landed," I type. *"Heading to my hotel now."*

Her reply is immediate— *"Have u eaten?"*

My fingers spring to life. *"I suffered through supper on the plane."*

"Do you drink wine?"

"Only on days that end in 'y'."

It takes a while for the next message to arrive. When it does, it causes me to smile. *"TodaY qualifies. When shall I expect u?"*

I check the time and then type, *"8:30? Need me to pick up a bottle?"*

"I have lots. See you soon."

~ ~ ~

Annie offers me a friendly hug before waving me into her apartment. I hand her a plastic bag containing bagel chips, chutney and goat cheese that I bought on the short walk from my Belltown hotel to her apartment.

"Thank you," Annie says, looking into the bag. "Yum." She walks into the kitchen and takes the food out of the bag, setting it on the counter. "You can hang your coat over a chair. How is your trip going?"

"I can't complain." I remove my shoes and follow Annie into the kitchen.

"Where are you heading again?" she asks. "Tennessee?"

"Yeah, we're going to the Great Smoky Mountains. I went there as a kid and fell in love with the place." On the counter I see two empty wine goblets in front of a row of glass jars filled with lentils, rice, sugar and dried fruit. A stack of cloth napkins in various bright colors rests on the table. *Strawberry Fields* is playing from a speaker in the living room. "Great song," I say. "Living is easy with eyes closed—"

Annie finishes the line, "—misunderstanding all you see."

"Reminds me of a conversation I had with Eddy a while back. Did you know that Vashon Island was known for its strawberry fields until World War II? Until the Japanese farmers were interned."

"I didn't know about the strawberries, but I know about the internment camps." Annie reaches toward a wine rack above the counter. "Is red okay?"

"Sure. What do you know about the camps?"

"My grandfather—my dad's dad—was Japanese American. He spent time in a camp while his father served in World War II. What's your preference—shiraz, cabernet, merlot?"

"I don't mind. I'm not a connoisseur. So that's where your exotic beauty comes from?"

Annie blushes. "I'm no expert either. But my friends must think I'm a wino with all the bottles they give me."

"So your grandfather was in the war?"

"My great-grandfather." She organizes the food I brought onto a plate. "He died in France."

"How?"

"Stepped on a mine during a routine patrol."

Annie pours the wine, picks up the plate and the bottle, and motions for me to join her. I grab the goblets and follow her into the living room. Charlie's art adorns pale yellow walls under the warmth of a few track lights. The dark hardwood floor is furnished with a small leather couch, a matching chair and one large beanbag seat, all centered around a wooden coffee table covered in books. As we sit down—Annie on the couch and me on the chair—I notice a family photograph standing in a frame amidst the books.

"Is that Daniel?" I ask, looking more closely at the picture.

"Yes," she replies, offering nothing more.

I search for the lost thread of our previous conversation, wanting to bring back the casual feeling we shared a moment ago. "Is your grandfather still alive?"

"No. I lost my father when I was twelve, and both of his parents within a year of that. I still have my mom and my sister, thank God. And Charlie, of course."

"Where is Charlie?"

"He fell asleep. He got up early this morning. He was exhausted, so I didn't tell him you were coming."

"That's too bad. I was hoping to see him." In fact, I am appreciative of this opportunity to be alone with Annie.

"He would have liked that too."

The wine is already sanding the rough edge from my nerves. "So you dealt with a lot of loss when you were young?"

"Yes," she says. "Seventh grade was a tough year."

"I can relate to that. Almost exactly. It sounds like we've lived parallel lives." Then I add, "Though I'm guessing I turned twelve a long time before you did."

Over a full bottle of shiraz, our discussion meanders from childhood grief to the challenges of parenthood to anecdotes of teenage stupidity. While I am telling her about tin foil bombs that I used to make with Danny when he came to visit me in the suburbs of Minneapolis, her expression turns serious.

"Are you okay?" I ask.

"Yes. You just reminded me of something."

"Of what?"

"Daniel also used to blow things up as a child. He said that destruction is the genesis of invention."

"Oh, I'm sorry for bringing it up."

She waves off my apology, and for the first time I notice that she is not wearing her wedding ring. "Not at all. It just got me thinking about Daniel. And Eddy. And why you're here."

My heart sinks at the reminder of my real reason for this visit. "Yeah," I sigh. "I kind of forgot about Eddy for a minute."

Annie sets down her wine goblet and looks at me. "It was nice of you to leave your vacation to see him. It seems you've become friends."

"Yeah," I reply, and I realize it's true. "But it's more than that. Eddy wants me to go to Ecuador. This is an all-expenses paid trip so he can pitch me on going there."

Annie tilts her head and narrows her eyes. "Really? What does he want?"

"I don't know. I'm hoping to find out tomorrow. I assume it has something to do with the letter you sent him."

She takes her time to reply. "Yes, it probably does."

"I haven't wanted to pry. But I am rather curious."

"It's okay. I just … when I read it, I felt like Daniel was here."

I wait a bit before asking, "So can you tell me anything about the letter?"

Annie shakes her head. "Like I said, Eddy will make more sense of it than I can." Then she changes course. "Do you think he'll choose to die at home?"

"I don't know. Arlo wants to check him into a hospice in Seattle. But Eddy is a Vashonite if I've ever seen one, so I don't imagine it'll be easy to get him out of his trailer."

"Stubborn." Annie shakes her head. "Just like Daniel."

A prolonged silence tells me that the tone of our discussion has shifted irreversibly. "I should probably go, and let you get some sleep."

"I've enjoyed your company," she replies. "But yes, six o'clock is going to come early."

Walking into the kitchen I try to think of anything I could say to prolong this night. Nothing comes to mind. Annie follows me with the empty wine bottle, which she sets on the counter while I reach for my jacket.

"Oliver," Annie says as I approach the door, "thank you. For the visit, the food, and one of the best discussions I've had in a while."

"My pleasure. I haven't enjoyed a woman's company this much in a very long time."

Annie frowns. "What about your wife?"

"Ah, we're an old married couple now, you know. We mostly talk about work or the kids. I guess we've heard each other's stories too many times."

"You must be creating some new stories on your vacation."

"Yeah, I guess." I put on my jacket and unlock the door.

She smiles warmly. "Let me know how it goes tomorrow, will you?"

"I will. Would you … I'll be back in the city tomorrow night. Would you like to get together again?"

Annie's face drops. "I would, but … I already have plans."

"Oh." I feign a casual tone, but I am sure my disappointment shows. "No problem. I'll send you a message once I've seen Eddy."

"Thanks," Annie says. There is an almost indistinguishable change in the way she looks at me.

"A date?" I ask, more blunt than I intended.

Annie half nods, half shrugs. "Yeah. It feels strange to call it that."

"Is it your first? I mean, since—"

"Sort of," she says. "I've known Martin for a long time. He's an old friend, and a client. It's just … I'm bringing Charlie tomorrow. They know each other, but this is different."

I force a brave face to the surface. "I'm glad you've found someone. I'm sure that if you like him, Charlie will too."

"Thank you," Annie says.

I open the door a crack, and then turn to offer Annie a hug. She steps into me and wraps her arms around my back, resting her head on my shoulder. I close my eyes and take in the subtle scent of oil from her skin and hair, mixed with a hint of wine—and I hold on tight until she releases her arms, backs away and smiles. Some part of me is relieved that Annie is not available. I know that I am not either. But a visceral hollowness spreads through me, and there is nothing I can do to stop it. Against the flow, I return her smile. "Goodnight, Annie. Say hi to Charlie for me." Then I turn and head for the green gate before the wine has a chance to speak.

"Goodnight, Oliver," she says, softly closing her door.

Nineteen

"How were the Smokies?" Eddy is propped up on a stack of pillows on the couch. It is not much larger than a loveseat and is nestled smartly into the living room of Eddy's Airstream, butting against a dinette that is covered in neat stacks of books and paperwork. A small coffee table flanks the couch, and a swivel chair has been placed—by Arlo, I am sure—near the head of Eddy's makeshift bed.

I sit on the chair and shake my head. "Haven't been there yet. Had to interrupt my trip to visit a friend."

"Thanks for coming." Though he is quickly fading, Eddy still speaks with authority.

"Helluva way to get my attention." When I learned of Eddy's condition, I looked up esophageal cancer on the Internet. I remember hearing once that the human body regenerates itself every seven years; in fact, life is more complicated than that. Some cells last a lifetime while others turn over within days. The lining of the esophagus is particularly adept at regeneration, which allows it to heal quickly from minor irritations; or conversely, when infested with cancer, to deteriorate at an alarming rate.

I cut to the chase. "Arlo said you want me to go to Ecuador. This has to do with the letter Annie sent you, right?"

"She told you about it?"

"Yeah. But not what it said."

He begins to cough and reaches for a glass of water. I get the glass from the coffee table and hand it to him. He takes a sip and hands it back to me. Like an infant, this once strong man is now dependent on others—mostly Arlo, who checks on Eddy many times a day.

"Are you planning to stay here?" I ask.

"I don't know. Arlo wants to take me to a hospice."

"I know. He's a good friend."

"Yes," he agrees. "There's more to that man than meets the eye."

"Yup, there is. So what do you want me to do in Ecuador?"

"Deliver a message."

"To who?"

"To someone in the village where Daniel worked."

"Why me?"

Eddy shrugs. "Because I trust you."

"Thanks," I say. "What's the message?"

Eddy points toward the kitchen across from the couch. "There's a screwdriver in the top drawer beside the sink. Take that and remove the microwave."

"Okay." I get the screwdriver and remove four screws from around the microwave, which I pull out of its cabinet and set on the floor. I reach up and retrieve a small zipped pouch, setting it down on the counter along with the screwdriver. Then I lean down to pick up the microwave again.

"Don't bother," Eddy growls. "Damn thing never should have been invented in the first place. Turns perfectly good food into inedible pulp."

I stifle a smile as I pick up the pouch and try to hand it to him.

"It's yours now. You'll need it in Ecuador."

"Who says I'm going?"

"I'll pay your way."

"That's very generous, Eddy, but—"

Eddy tries to clear his throat, so I hand him water again. After a few sips, he seems revitalized.

"Open it," he says, pointing at the pouch.

I unzip the pouch and pull out a single quarter.

I open my mouth to speak, but Eddy places a finger to his lips and looks around the trailer suspiciously. Then he reaches under the cushion below him, pulls out an envelope, and hands it to me. "Read this. To yourself."

I drop the quarter back in the pouch, open the envelope, unfold a single page of paper, and read the letter:

Dear Eddy,

For the first time today I saw the future in action. Your thermo-electric generator is a thing of beauty. It worked, as I knew it would. There are some remaining challenges in the magnification process, but all of the major roadblocks are behind us.

We are on the verge of a paradigm shift that could lead to monumental changes in the economic and political landscape of our planet. People in positions of power are taking notice of this tiny village. I grow ever more concerned about finding an appropriate way to introduce what we have created. If left in the hands of a profit-based economy (or government?) I fear what our creation may become.

Therefore, I have banked everything I know into one secure repository, just in case. Should anything happen to me, you must bring the sponge and our key and seek out the Pachamama for further instruction.

I look forward to discussing all of this in more detail when I see you in Seattle this summer. We will formulate a more cohesive plan then.

Your friend,
Daniel

I stare at the letter for a while, re-reading it and trying to absorb the implications of Daniel's words. I can tell that Eddy is looking at me, gauging my reaction; but I do not know how to react, or what to say.

"Bring me that pen and paper, by those books," he says. "On the table there."

"Why?"

"Because I don't trust them."

"Trust who?"

"I don't know. You read the damn letter."

I retrieve the pen and pad of paper, and Eddy begins to write. After a few moments, he hands the paper to me and tosses the pen, which hits the coffee table and rolls off. His handwriting is neater than I expected.

The key is Einsteinium. You are holding the sponge. You must take this to the Pachamama. She is the grand matron of Pueblo del Sol. And yes, it is safe to touch.

I look at Eddy, who has overcome his weakness to appear almost excited. He nods toward the pouch, so I reach into it and take out the coin again.

"This?" I ask.

"Take a closer look at the words." A wry smile creases his cheeks.

I look at the quote to the right of George Washington. IN DOG WE TRUST. I chortle and Eddy laughs too, which quickly turns to an uncontrollable cough. I hand him the water and he takes a sip.

"So how do you want me to deliver this message?"

"Sign up as a volunteer."

"At the village?"

"Yes."

"Doing what?"

"General labor. They're always looking for people."

"Have you been there?"

"No," he says. "I did my work in the hallowed halls of the university."

I chew on my thumbnail and shake my head, "I don't know, Eddy. This is huge."

Eddy nods. "I can't decide for you. I've never allowed anyone to tell me what to do—probably why I never married. Let's make this real easy. There's a checkbook in the second drawer. Bring that to me, will you?"

"What for?"

"What do you think? What did it cost you to come out here?"

"About five hundred dollars."

"I'll write two checks. Cash the first one now, and the second when you go to Ecuador. If you don't go, rip up the second check. Or cash it anyway. Or frame it if you want to. It's not going to do me any good."

"But I—"

"Just get me the damn checkbook," Eddy growls. "It's up to you whether or not you cash it."

I walk over to the drawer and bring the checkbook back to Eddy.

"Pen!" he barks.

I pick up the pen and hand it to him. He writes out two checks and gives them to me. "You'll need to fill in your last name. I only know you as Oliver."

"It's Bruce," I say, then look down at the checks. "*Five thousand dollars?*"

"The volunteer program is a minimum of three weeks. That should be plenty to get you there and pay for your volunteer stint. And enough to put your family up in a nice place while you're away."

"Three weeks? I thought you only wanted me to deliver a message."

"If I knew Daniel as well as I think I did, you'll have to follow some breadcrumbs."

"But … I don't understand. As you've told me a few times, I'm no scientist."

"That's just me being an arrogant prick. You're a smart guy. You'll do fine."

"I need to think about all of this … and talk it over with Em."

"Of course," he says.

"How long do you—"

"I don't know. Sooner the better, as far as I'm concerned. This is no way to live."

"I can imagine. But if I go … assuming you're up for it … how can I reach you?"

"Through Arlo. You can trust him with whatever you need to say."

"Is there anything else you can tell me?"

"Not that I can think of. You'll figure it out." He looks more relaxed now. "There is one thing. Thank you. I don't say that often enough. It means a lot that you came here. And I couldn't pick a better man to send in my place. So, yes, thank you."

Eddy reaches out his hand, and I cup it with both of mine. We sit in silence, our friendship cemented by the trust he has placed in me. Tranquility seeps into Eddy's face. I see bitterness evaporate, and I feel energy flow through our touch. I hold his hand until he falls asleep, and then I gently release it.

Twenty

Somewhere over the Midwest, my decision becomes as clear as the morning sky. The cropland below reminds me of the discussion I had with Josh on my uncle and aunt's farm, and I marvel at the irony that I might see Ecuador before he does.

~ ~ ~

"Daddy!" Isaac yells, running toward me as I step through the arrivals gate at Chattanooga Airport. "You have to see the aquarium. We saw stingrays and sharks and eels and—"

"Hi Dad," Isabella beams, approaching me with open arms. I could swear that both kids have grown an inch since I saw them only two days ago. I wonder how long it has been since I really looked at them.

I kneel for a group hug with Isaac and Isabella before standing to receive Emily's lukewarm greeting. The kids tell me about their action-packed days as we walk to the parking lot and Emily begins to drive. When we reach the campground, she parks the motor home and says, "Want to help me fold laundry and tell me about your trip? I put two loads in the dryer before we came to get you."

"Sure," I reply.

"Izzy," Emily says. "Dad and I are going to the laundry room. Can you take your brother to the playground?"

"Can't he take himself?" Isabella moans.

Emily turns and glares at her.

"O-kay." Isabella stands up and taps her brother on the back of the head. "Let's go, punk."

Emily and I walk over to the laundry room in silence. She pulls clothes from a dryer and tosses them on a counter.

"Was it a lot of work on your own?" I ask.

"Yeah, but it was kind of nice, too. Sometimes it's easier when I don't have a fourth agenda to manage. So are you glad you went?"

"Definitely."

"How did Eddy seem?"

"Weak, but only physically. His mind was as sharp as ever."

"And you went to Annie's?" Her abrupt change of topic catches me off guard.

"Yeah, I did. It was … she started seeing someone recently."

"Oh?" Emily's mood lightens. "So what's up with Ecuador?"

"I need to go there. Eddy wants me to deliver a message."

Emily stops folding and looks at me. "Can't he pick up a phone?"

"Not for this. Anyway, I'm not convinced he knows how to use one."

"How long does he want you to go for?"

"Three weeks, maybe a bit more."

"That's a long time."

We both return to folding. The cyclical tapping of zippers and buttons in a nearby dryer fills the room until I speak again. "I hatched a bit of a plan."

"What do you mean?"

"I think we could drive down to Orlando—we can get there in a day or two—and I'll set you up at Disney World while I'm away." I sneak a glance at her, but she continues to stare at the clothes she is folding.

"Sounds expensive."

"Eddy gave me five thousand dollars to cover it. Said to put you up in a nice place while I'm gone."

"Five thousand dollars? Seriously?"

"Yup. And he reimbursed me for the trip out there to see him."

She looks at me again. "What about the Smoky Mountains?"

"We can see them on the way home."

"We might miss the fall colors."

"Nah. I'll be back in time."

Emily folds at half speed, as if she is expending much of her energy on thinking. "I take it you're over your fear of flying?"

"No. I almost shit my pants every time I land. But I know I can do it now."

Emily looks up at me, and I can't quite read her expression. "Disney World, huh? Just me and the kids?"

"Yeah. It's not my cup of tea anyway."

"How do you know?"

"I don't, really. Call it an educated guess."

"I don't know what to do with this," Em says. "The Oliver I know wouldn't hop on a flight to South America. Do you even know a word of Spanish?"

"Sure. Abre. It means open. I learned that watching Dora the Explorer."

She lets out a chuckle. "I had no idea you were so worldly."

"I'm sure I have many talents you're not aware of. Actually, no, I think that's the only one. But I'll be a lot more interesting after a trip to Ecuador."

~ ~ ~

Emily and I stare down the freeway, our independent thoughts interrupted only by random acts of small talk. Behind us, Isabella reads and Isaac plays video games—a familiar scene that makes me wonder if my kids are taking in any of the landscape that passes by on their first major road trip.

On the outskirts of Atlanta, Emily breaks the monotony. "What do we need to buy you for your trip?"

"I can't remember everything." I point toward the console between our seats. "I wrote it on the notepad."

Emily picks up the notepad and flips until she finds my list.

"Too bad my backpack is in storage," she says.

"That's okay. I can use a suitcase."

"Suitcases are for tourists," she scoffs. "Travelers need backpacks. Trust me, you'll appreciate having one."

We discuss the recommended list of supplies—insect repellent, sunscreen, flashlight, mosquito net, rubber boots—and then Em asks, "What about vaccinations? I needed Yellow Fever when I went to Peru."

I shake my head. "No, you only need shots if you're visiting the Amazon or parts of the coast. I won't be going to either of those."

"Where exactly *are* you going?"

"It's a cloud forest—basically a jungle in the mountains."

"A jungle?"

"Well, they have monkeys and pumas and pit vipers ... and tarantulas."

"Sounds like a jungle," Emily agrees. "And you're actually going there?"

"Yeah. Hard to believe, huh?"

"Mm-hmm. Are you excited?"

"Yes. And terrified."

~ ~ ~

"What do you have?" Harold asks.

"Mister Bruce is going to Ecuador," Tyler replies. "He booked a flight to Quito."

"When does he leave?"

"Sunday. I called recon, and they have an itinerary. Do you want me to track that for you?"

"No," Harold says. "You've done your part. Thank you. We'll shift this to field ops now."

Disappointment creases Tyler's brow. This is one file that he would like to follow, to explore in greater depth. But he knows his boundaries all too well. Information is power—the seniors know that, and they use it to their own advantage. Minions like Tyler

Thomas are merely instruments—a network of sensors feeding a higher intelligence.

Part 2 - Confiar

Twenty-One

People lie motionless, slumped over seats and resting in the aisle amidst twisted, smoking wreckage. There is no blood—all of the bodies are intact, in contrast to the debris that surrounds them. It is as if everyone is sleeping in the most uncomfortable of positions, but they are frozen in time, breathless. From my window seat I climb over the young man beside me and walk down the aisle, stepping over others as I approach the emergency exit—nothing more than a distorted set of letters over an opening that leads directly onto the tarmac. I pass through the exit and see a man standing in the distance, a lone figure in front of a lifeless terminal where dozens of aircraft sit, motionless. I walk toward the man, who seems to be waiting for me. Daniel is tall and thin, with dark hair and a disheveled beard. I stop and stand before him.

Daniel says something in Spanish, which I do not understand. I am surprised at how serene I feel. I turn and look behind me. Soft bird and insect noises add to the rumble of a flowing river that I cannot see. I survey the crash site. It is no longer a plane, but the flattened remnants of a multi-colored bus—resting in a clearing against the backdrop of a steep cliff. I turn back to Daniel, who is no longer there. In his place stands Eddy, saying with a Spanish accent, "Please ensure your seat backs and table are in their upright and locked positions."

The fleece that I am using as a pillow provides little cushion between my head and the window. I rub my kinked neck. My eyes come into focus and I look out to see what must be Quito in the distance, etched into a rocky landscape. From this height it is neither beautiful nor unpleasant.

My anxiety heightens as the airplane descends, but it does not grip me the way it has on previous flights—the dream infusing my mind with an inexplicable calming effect. As the beauty of the mountainous setting around Quito becomes clear, the airport resting atop a plateau in a sparsely populated region far outside of the city's core, I wonder what Daniel said to me.

~ ~ ~

Modern and orderly, Mariscal Sucre Airport is nothing like the mob scene Emily described from her trip to Peru almost twenty years ago. The customs agent greets me with impeccable English, and my backpack arrives without incident. I am officially a world traveler.

A short, lean man of about forty is waiting for me at the arrivals gate, holding up a sign with my name on it.

"Buenos dias," I say, practicing one of the quotes that I gleaned from my Ecuador travel guide. "I am Oliver."

"Buenos dias," he replies. "¿Habla usted español?"

"Sorry?"

"I am Carlos," he says with a friendly tone. "I speak little English. Welcome to Quito."

Carlos guides me out to the parking lot, where he throws my backpack in the open box of a Ford King Cab and climbs into the driver's seat while I get into the passenger side. He turns on the engine, and his stereo belts out *Hells Bells*. The familiarity of this scene is instantly comforting.

"You like classic rock?" I ask.

"Classic rock," he smiles as he pulls out of the parking stall, giving me a thumbs-up sign. "You like?"

"Yeah." I am unsure whether he would understand a more thorough answer.

The highway that leads west from the airport merges into a maze of smaller roads, ranging from asphalt thruways to narrow cobblestone paths. Carlos names a variety of locations as we pass through them, attempting to tell me a few things in Spanish. Eventually, he says "Quito." A dramatic, sprawling metropolis perched on lofty cliffs that drop hundreds of feet to lush valleys, Quito is like a different planet.

Carlos points toward a peak that towers over the city. "Pichincha." Then he adds, "Volcano."

"Ah. Is it active?"

He nods. "Yo lo llamo El Dragón."

We make a few more feeble attempts at conversation as we weave through the city, passing a chaotic blend of contemporary buildings, shanties and everything in between. Many of the buildings have rebar sticking out of the top with no other sign of construction. I wonder if these are works in progress—temporarily delayed—or perpetual signs of unrealistic optimism.

Carlos parks the truck on the curb in front of the hostel, a Spanish colonial building that is about half as charming as its picture on the Internet.

"You come to get me tomorrow morning?" I point at myself, and then at the front of the hostel.

Carlos says something in Spanish. I look at him blankly until he adds, "Tomorrow. Eight o'clock."

"Yes. Here?"

"Si."

Carlos climbs out of the truck onto a cobblestone road, and I step out of the passenger seat onto a brick sidewalk.

He pulls out my backpack and holds it up for me to slip my arms into.

"Thank you."

"Gracias," he says. "Mucho gusto. That mean nice to meet you."

"Mucho gusto," I smile in return.

As Carlos drives away my comfort evaporates, leaving me with an acute sense of displacement. I wear my backpack on my back and my knapsack on my front, as Emily suggested. Feeling awkward and weighed down, I press the buzzer beside the door of the hostel and wait, taking in the scene around me. Pedestrians—wearing hip outfits and speaking on mobile phones—saunter along narrow sidewalks on either side of a steep street while a variety of cars and trucks rush by, the latter leaving trails of black smoke. Two middle-aged women with dark wrinkled skin sit beside a basket of fruit directly across the street from the hostel. Their colorful dresses, white shirts and round, narrow-brimmed hats suggest that these women belong to a different century.

I hear someone bound down a set of stairs inside. The door opens and a young man grins at me with perfect white teeth tucked behind a thick blond beard, dreadlocks falling wildly about halfway down the back of a blue t-shirt.

"Welcome!" he says in the mellow tone of a surfer dude. "You Oliver?"

"Yes," I reply, instantly calmed by the man's relaxed demeanor.

"Let me take one of your packs," he says.

I try to remove my backpack before realizing my knapsack straps are inhibiting its release. After a brief struggle I manage to shed both packs. Dreadlock surfer dude picks up the larger one, handling it with ease, and I follow him into the hostel.

"Where you from?" he asks as we climb the stairs to the second floor.

"The US, near Seattle. How about you?"

"Portland. There's a few of us Northwesterners here. I think we're colonizing the place." Dreadlock lets out a hearty laugh as he unlocks a door and lets me into a large private room. It is furnished with a queen-sized bed, a wardrobe, and a night table holding a bedside lamp. An expansive window looks at an ugly pinkish building across the street, blocking what I had hoped would be a panoramic view of Quito's Old Town.

He sets my backpack by the bed and offers me a tour of the place. I cling to my knapsack as he shows me around and explains a few things about the hostel—breakfast is included with my room; dinner costs an extra five dollars; there is a lounge downstairs and restrooms with showers on each of the two floors. This is not the enchanting villa I had envisioned—it is old and outdated, with a musty scent and dust bunnies in every corner.

We walk into a common kitchen where half a dozen visitors are seated around a wooden table, each one of them ogling a piece of technology. I feel old compared to this bunch of twenty-somethings.

"Howdy," I say. A few of the guests look up and smile. A cute young woman with a long black braid and round face looks up, smiles and says "Hi" before turning back to her computer. A man of about thirty says "How are you?" then resumes typing on his phone before I have a chance to answer.

I turn to Dreadlock. "I read that you have Internet?"

"Yeah," he replies. "It's slower than a three-toed sloth, but it works." He reaches up to a shelf beside the table and retrieves an ancient laptop computer. I thank him while he sets it down and plugs it in, and then I sit at the table and wait for it to boot up.

I look across the table and catch the woman with the black braid looking at me. She immediately looks down. I wonder what she is thinking—probably questioning what would bring a middle-aged man to stay in a young person's haven.

I click on the browser icon and continue to wait. I look at the woman again. She is more than cute—stunning would be a better description. She looks up and smiles, and then we both go back to our computers.

.I force myself to stare at the screen as my e-mail loads. Then I sift through a short list of junk mail and click on a memo from Annie—a reply to my message that told her I was going to Ecuador:

Oliver,

I'm not sure if you are in Quito yet. I was hoping you could call me. I could use a rational opinion on something.

Best,
Annie

I briefly smile at Annie's invitation, then my face tightens when I see the next item in my inbox. Molly's subject simply reads, *Eddy*. I click on it and hesitate before reading the message:

Hi Oliver,

Arlo was just in to tell us Eddy passed away this morning. He wanted me to send you a message right away, and to let you know that he died peacefully. He dropped by to check on him and said he wasn't responding. It's a sad day here at the café. I hope your trip has been good so far, and I'm sorry to be the bearer of bad news.

Love Molly

~ ~ ~

I lock the door of the restroom and set my clean clothes on the counter. I take off my jeans and drop them on the floor. It is difficult to focus. I open my money belt and check the contents of its main pocket—as if they had anywhere to go. Passport, credit cards, cash ... all there. I reach into a separate pocket and take out a small bundle of plastic wrap, damp with sweat. I unravel the plastic, exposing the sponge. *Why have I brought this to Ecuador, along with a message from a dead man?* My eyes bore holes into the sponge; then I wrap it again and put it back in my money belt. I place the belt on the counter and stare into the mirror. *What the hell am I doing here?*

My abdomen cramps, retaliating for a day full of fast food and avoidance of dirty restrooms. I sit on the toilet for minutes that feel like hours. Finally, my bowels empty.

Standing up to wipe myself, I see a sign beside the toilet. *Please do not flush toilet paper! Deposit used paper in the bin.* Beside the toilet, a bin overflows with scrunched up tissue, some of it noticeably soiled. Attempting to stuff my own paper into the bin, I touch someone else's. I look at my hand and see a small patch of shit smeared on my index finger. I don't know if it's mine. *Fuck!*

I turn on the sink with my clean hand. A fury festers. Every muscle in my core is tense. Emily talked me into staying at a hostel—*it'll be cheaper and more social than a hotel,* she said. She did not tell me that I would have to share a bin of excrement with my fellow travelers. Typical Em.

I wash my hands repeatedly, waiting in vain for hot water. Then I strip down and start the shower. A lukewarm stream is the best I can hope for. I step in and get wet, then hop out of the water and lather from head to toe. Stepping back into the stream I reach up to rinse my underarm and a surge of electricity shoots down my arm, through my rib cage, and into my hip. *Bloody hell!* I look up to see exposed wires leading to the showerhead. Angry tears form in my eyes. My jaw tightens, then my neck. It takes me a moment to realize the water is now cold. A delayed shiver washes over me, running the full length of my body. I stand in the stream, arms down, letting the frigid water run off me. The punch surprises me. "FUCK!" I yell with the full force of my voice—sheer rage, or pain from punching the wall, I'm not sure which.

My body relaxes slightly, goose bumps forming on my skin. I step in and out of the water to rinse off the remaining soap, then lean down and turn off the faucet.

I climb out of the shower onto a well-used bath mat and retrieve my towel from the counter. I pat down my body with quivering hands and wrap the towel around my waist. Then I stand at the counter and gaze into the mirror.

"Damn you, Eddy," I mutter, staring through my reflection.

Twenty-Two

Three people are waiting for the restroom when I enter the hallway. I don't know how long it took to regain my composure, but I imagine I was in there for quite a while.

The woman with the black braid is second in line. Her green eyes meet mine, and I wonder if she heard my outburst in the shower. I purse my lips and nod at her, feeling slightly embarrassed.

I put my towel and dirty clothes in my room, then walk down the stairs and open the front door of the hostel. Disoriented, I stare out into the busy street and wonder why I am standing here. I consider going for a walk, but the doorway feels like an invisible threshold into a magical realm. After some time my fog lifts and I close the door. Unsure what to do or where to go, I walk to the lounge and flop down on an old leather couch. Mindlessly, I pick up a remote control and turn on the television, flipping through a dozen or more channels—a mixture of Spanish and English content—not stopping at any one for long enough to see what is on. When I start to recognize channels that I have already passed over, I turn off the TV and pick up a Quito visitors' guide. I browse through it, staring at the pages, but I cannot focus on the words. I flip the guide onto the coffee table and sit back, rest my head against the couch and stare at the ceiling.

"Hi." Her voice surprises me.

I lift my head and see the woman with the black braid. "Hey."

"Long day?"

"You could say that." I sit up and meet her eyes. Even in the darkness of the lounge, I am taken aback by the bright-ness of her jade green irises.

She sits down on a loveseat adjacent to the couch and opens a Lonely Planet book.

I fidget with my hands for a while before I sit forward and ask, "Do you know where I might find a phone around here?"

She looks up from her book. "There's a cabina just up the road a few blocks. I need to go there for a SIM card before dinner. You're welcome to join me."

"Sure," I say. "I'm Oliver, by the way."

"Jen," she replies.

~ ~ ~

We step out into Quito's colonial district and walk about half a block down the street—south, I believe. I am glad for Jen's company on my first walk in a foreign city. I look around, wary of pickpockets and other hoodlums. With the exception of a few men glancing at Jen, everyone seems to be minding their own business.

"So what are you doing in Ecuador?" I ask, stepping onto the road during a break in traffic.

"I've been teaching English in Quito for the past three months. But I'm finally getting out of here tomorrow. You?"

"I'm volunteering in a cloud forest."

"Where?"

"It's called Pueblo del Sol. It's—"

"Really?" She stops walking. "Small world. Me too."

"Huh," I say, surprised.

"I got a job there with the solar team. I've been waiting a few days for the paperwork to come through, but it's all systems go now."

"Small world indeed." I resume walking, amazed that in this city of three million people I have already met someone who is bound for the same tiny village as me.

"What will you be doing at the village?" Jen asks.

"Grunt labor, mostly. Taking a break from the daily grind at home. How about you? Are you an engineer?"

"Close enough. A software engineer."

"What are you working on?"

"Sorry," she says. "Can't say much about that. I had to sign a non-disclosure agreement."

I struggle to keep up with Jen as we walk up the hill. I admire the impressive architecture that spans the road as it climbs a few dozen blocks up an increasingly steep mountainside. Interconnected buildings—mostly three or four stories high and made of rock and pastel-colored stucco—line both sides of the street. Many have oversized wooden doors, some embedded with rich carvings and patterns.

I pause to catch my breath, raising my hand to let Jen know that I need a break. I hope the cabina is not much farther.

She smiles and puts her hand on my shoulder. "It can take a few days to adjust to the elevation. As for the pollution … you never really get used to that. Anyway, this is the place." She points into a small shop that contains a variety of electronics, two phone booths and a few Internet stations.

Inside the store, Jen gets into a lengthy discussion with the shopkeeper in what I deem to be very fluent Spanish. With the help of my guidebook, I manage to ask a teenager, whom I assume to be the shopkeeper's son, how much it costs to access the Internet.

He answers in English, pointing toward one of the well-used terminals.

I sit down and peck out a few words to Molly—I was too stunned to reply to her message when I first read it at the hostel—and start to draft an update to Emily. I cancel my message and log out, then ask the teenager how to make an international call on one of the payphones.

I reach Emily's voicemail. I debate whether to hang up and try again later, but I don't know when I will have access to a phone again. I leave a brief message, telling Em that I made it here and informing her about Eddy's passing. Then I hang up and dial Annie's number.

"Hello." She answers on the first ring.

"Hi Annie, it's Oliver."

We exchange pleasantries about my flight and the weather, and then I dispense with the small talk. "Have you heard about Eddy?"

"What about him? Is he—"

"He passed away this morning."

"Oh, I'm so sorry to hear that."

"Me too. What's happening there? The tone of your e-mail …"

"It's … it's probably nothing."

"But …?"

"I'm feeling a bit paranoid."

"Why?"

"There's this guy … I saw him a few days ago … and I've seen him a couple of times since."

"Uh-huh." I wait for Annie to gather her thoughts.

"It feels like he's following me."

"Really? Have you—what about Martin?"

"Martin said it wouldn't be the first man who can't take his eyes off of me."

"Well … he does have a point." I compliment Annie with unusual ease, in the tone of an old friend.

"You guys," she sighs. "That's very flattering, but …"

"But what?"

"You're right. It's probably nothing."

"I didn't say that. I just agreed with Martin's assessment. But if you're concerned …"

I notice that Jen is standing near the phone booth looking at cameras, close enough to hear my conversation. I shift in her presence, suddenly self-conscious.

"I—" I want to say more, but not with Jen standing so close. "Look, I'm …"

"Don't worry about me," Annie says.

"Trust your instincts. I just …"

"I'm okay," she says. "I didn't expect you to call all the way from Quito. I thought I might catch you before you left."

I promise Annie I will check in again soon. Then I hang up the phone and look at Jen. "Did you get your SIM card?"

"What?" Jen seems surprised that I am off the phone, but I wonder if it is an act. "Oh, no. They don't have the right type. Nobody seems to. He wanted me to cough up another hundred bucks for a new phone."

Walking down the hill, my conversation with Jen is forced, my intuition about her unclear. When we reach the hostel, I thank her for leading me to the cabina and tell her I will see her at dinner. But I don't make it that far. I lie down on my bed and it grabs hold of me. My body is tired from a long day of travel, and my mind is a muddle of emotions and thoughts—about Eddy and Emily and Annie and Jen, and about my reasons for coming to Ecuador. I sense a widening gap between divergent instincts—one voice telling me to explore every corner of my new reality while another urges me to turn around and go home. Unable to process everything I have taken in today, I drift into an uneasy sleep.

Twenty-Three

My bladder coerces me out of bed shortly after sunrise. The hostel is calm when I stumble down the hall to the restroom. After a quick, careful shower, I head into the breakfast area. Jen is sipping coffee at the dining table where two volunteers are serving breakfast to a few early risers.

"Good morning." I fake a happy tone.

Jen looks up and smiles. "Good morning. How did you sleep?"

"Horribly, thanks. You?"

"Like a baby. Did you go out for dinner last night?"

"No, I crashed when we got back from the phone shop. Seemed like a good idea at the time. Then I woke up at midnight and couldn't get back to sleep."

"Jetlag?" she asks.

"Partly, I guess. The drunks in the hallway didn't help either."

Jen nods knowingly. "It takes a while to get used to this place."

I help myself to a coffee and sit kitty-corner to Jen, who has already finished her breakfast. One of the volunteers—a redheaded woman whose dreadlocks match the man who checked me in yesterday—offers me a plate with two pieces of toast, a dish of marmalade and a small portion of scrambled eggs. She returns a moment later with a glass of juice. I thank her and turn to Jen.

"Is it okay to drink the juice?"

"Hasn't killed me yet."

I drink my juice in two gulps and inhale my eggs. While I spread the marmalade on my toast I look out the window toward a hill in the distance. A statue stands at the top, looming large above the city.

"What is that statue on the hill?" I ask.

"That's the Virgen de Quito. And the hill is called El Panecillo. It represents the Woman of the Apocalypse from the Book of Revelation."

"Sounds cheery. Are you well studied in such matters?"

"Am I religious?" Jen asks. "Not in the least. I just said that to sound impressive. How about you?"

"I'm a recovering Lutheran." The effortlessness of our discussion this morning is reassuring after my misgivings last night. Though I have known Jen for less than a day, she is now the most familiar person in an unfamiliar place. And this hostel—that only yesterday seemed old and dank—

already feels like home compared to the alien world beyond its walls.

Jen looks back toward the statue and says, "I think she looks like some sort of fairy angel." Then she gets up and stretches her arms high in the air. "I guess I'd better get packed up. I assume you're going with Carlos too?"

"Supposedly," I reply.

"What do you mean?"

"I might go home."

"Why would you do that?"

"It's a long story."

"Is something wrong?"

"Yes and no." I can't imagine turning back. But I can't imagine going forward either.

"Well, I hope you come." Jen pauses, and then leaves the room. I finish my toast, take one last swig of tepid coffee and get up to pack my bag.

~ ~ ~

I approach the front door intent on telling Jen that I will not be joining her—that I am going to ask Carlos to take me to the airport, where I will pay whatever it costs to book the next flight back to Orlando. My resolve wavers when I see her smile, and when she places her hand on my arm and says, "I'm glad you're coming," I abandon it altogether.

"What the hell," I say, unable to make sense of my impulsive decision—or of my purpose here now that Eddy is gone.

Carlos pulls up to the curb and helps us into his truck. He drives us about fifteen minutes to the Quito office of the Sostenible de la Fundación Tierra—*the Sustainable Earth Foundation*—where we wait for the foundation's manager, Elsa, to arrive. When she appears, Elsa speaks rapid Spanish into a cell phone held between her shoulder and her ear while she fumbles to get keys from a purse. Unlocking the door to her office, she plants a kiss on Carlos' cheek, shakes hands with Jen and me, and waves us into her office without missing a beat in her telephone conversation. She is animated and irritable when she finally says "Ciao!" and hangs up the phone.

"You must be Oliver and Jennifer," she states with a mild accent, continuing before we can respond. "We have a problem—a landslide in the mountains between here and Tandapi. The road is washed out and won't re-open for a few days. You have to take a different route from the north station to Santo Domingo, where Alejandro will meet you to guide you to the village."

It is a small inconvenience, but it feels like a punch in the gut. Another wrench in the plan, pushing me deeper into a debate about whether to continue on this journey. Something powerful is telling me to go back to the airport, climb on a plane and join my family at Disney World.

"Can we still get there today?" Jen asks.

"Maybe," Elsa says.

I stand in a daze as they continue to speak. My thoughts drift to Daniel ... to a landslide in the Andes a year and a half ago ... to a bus lying in the bottom of a canyon, buried under tons of rock. "Was anyone hurt?" I blurt out, interrupting their discussion.

"No," Elsa says. "Thank God. It was not a big area, but it made a mess of the road."

Elsa buzzes around the office as she explains travel plans that I am not ready to absorb. Then she asks, "Do you have flashlights?"

"Yes," Jen says.

The image of a landslide returns. I cannot get the picture of Daniel's bus out of my mind.

"Oliver," Jen says.

"Yeah?" I half answer.

"Are you okay?"

"Yeah. No. I don't know."

Elsa resumes speaking. I miss most of what she says, but I catch the last part. "You know there is a two kilometer walk uphill to reach the village?"

I nod—the only response I can muster. I look at Jen and see a concerned expression. Elsa is telling us something about the village as she guides us to sit and sets a small stack of papers in front of us.

"We need you to sign waivers."

"Didn't I already—" I begin.

"No," Elsa interrupts. "Not this one. You must read it carefully and sign it."

For the first time since we arrived in her office, Elsa attempts to be patient. I force myself to focus on the letter in front of me. This is no small waiver, mentioning many dangers associated with the village—wildlife; sharp drop-offs; lack of medical assistance; acts of God—and including a section about non-disclosure of confidential information. I read it for a second time, but I do not sign it.

"You must go," Elsa says, her impatience returning. "If you are to make the bus. Please, sign the form."

I look at Jen, who has already signed her waiver. Then I look back down at mine and stare at it, as if waiting for it to tell me what to do. Although I feel Elsa's glare, I continue to stare at the page. "I don't know."

"You're not going to make me go alone, are you?" I look up and see Jen's eyes, dazzling in the midst of a forlorn expression. Then I look back down at the page. *Who is this woman, and why does she care if I join her?*

"You really must go now," Elsa urges, "or you will miss the bus."

I pick up the pen and feel a thin film of sweat on my fingertips. Despite Elsa's hovering presence, I sit frozen, my hand suspended above the page. I think of my car accident, and of the letter I found. I think of Eddy and his dying wish to deliver a message on his behalf. The pen feels slippery in my hand, fuelled by a vague sense of unease. Then I recall the dream sequence that brought me peace on my arrival into Quito and I press my doubts aside, dropping my hand to the page to sign the form.

Twenty-Four

Carlos stops in front of a *No Parking* sign at Terminal Carcelén, helps us with our bags and accepts ten dollars, then climbs back into his truck and darts into traffic with a wave.

Jen buys tickets to Santo Domingo, and we are immediately ushered onto the bus—a modern beast with over forty seats. Within minutes we are passing through a lengthy series of suburbs with buildings that range from upscale to dilapidated.

Driving through a particularly run-down slum, Jen speaks to the window. "How would you define progress, Oliver?"

I am paralyzed by the question.

"I know"—she interrupts my thoughts—"it's hard to define."

I have never seen a place like this, even from the comfort of a bus. I have seen poverty before, on the streets of Seattle or Minneapolis, but this feels different, if only because it is less familiar.

"I'm a big fan of invention," Jen continues. "I mean, we can't turn back the clock. I'm as much of an environmentalist as the next person, but I think we need to focus on innovation."

"Like solar?" I ask.

"Yeah," she says.

"Which is why you're heading to Pueblo del Sol?"

"Yeah."

"So what exactly are you doing up there?"

"I signed an NDA, remember?"

"So did I," I reply, undeterred.

"You mean the waiver? They made me sign something a lot more onerous."

"More onerous than accepting the risk of being eaten by a puma?"

"A different kind of onerous."

"Ah, okay." I don't press her further.

Reaching the outer limits of Quito, urban sprawl yields to increasingly dense vegetation. Jen pushes up the armrest between us, leans against the window and twists to face me, cradling her knees up against her chest. Her sandaled feet press gently against my leg, and I notice that her toenails are painted in a variety of vibrant colors. I sense a dissonance within Jen—an old soul and a girl sharing the same body.

"How about you?" Jen asks. "What brought you to Ecuador?"

I shift slightly to face her. "A friend sent me here. He thought I'd like the village."

"Was he a volunteer there?"

"No. He just knew about it."

"Why were you thinking of going home?"

"I … I found out he died yesterday."

"Oh my God." Jen's eyes narrow and her face drops as she briefly places her hand on my thigh and then pulls it away. "I'm sorry. How?"

I smile softly. "He was very sick. Cancer. I was just surprised how quickly he went." It feels good to talk about Eddy, and for a moment I think of saying more. But I stop myself, unwilling to admit that the man who sent me here was behind Jen's work at Pueblo del Sol.

~ ~ ~

Jen has dozed off. I watch her from time to time, studying features made more youthful by the innocence of sleep. Complex emotions wrestle within me as I recognize my own youth slipping away. One moment we are young, vibrant, free … and then, suddenly, we are middle-aged, teetering on the verge of old. I have not come to terms with that yet. In my heart I am still twenty-something, but my aging self— the wrinkles on my face, the thinning of my hair, the random aches and pains that are now a part of daily life— mocks me, informing me in little ways that I am past my best-before date.

Before I can avert my eyes, Jen opens hers. I offer a gentle, "Morning, Sunshine."

"Morning?" she whispers hoarsely. "I hope not. Where are we, Lima?"

"No, you've only been sleeping for an hour or so."

"How long have you been looking at me? Was I drooling?"

"Only a little," I chuckle. "Watching you, I mean. So far no drool. I was envying your ability to sleep on a roller coaster."

"Have I missed anything?"

"Yes. Some amazing views and a badly dubbed comedy that I can't understand."

Jen looks up at the TV. "I saw that back home. I think you picked the better program."

"Do you mean you or the landscape?" I tease.

"Me, of course," she replies with a tone of false vanity.

"So tell me," I say—watching the brightness return to Jen's eyes following her slumber—"what brought you to South America three months ago?"

"Do you want the long story or the short one?"

"The long one."

"A broken heart and a sense of adventure."

"That would be a short story."

"Yeah," she says. "I guess I'm not ready for the long one."

~ ~ ~

Alejandro is short, solid, intense. He speaks almost no English, so I daydream as Jen communicates with him in Spanish. I am distracted by my surroundings—the bus terminal is chaotic and run-down, and the dim light of the late afternoon sun, blocked almost entirely by thick, low cloud cover, paints Santo Domingo as even more foreign than Quito. I try to reassure myself that this small city is surely a safer place than Ecuador's capital, but I cannot quell my apprehension.

As Alejandro leads us to a cab that is parked in front of the bus terminal, Jen quickly updates me on the basics—we will stay at a motel in Santo Domingo tonight and travel to the village in the morning. Inside the cab I feel temporarily at ease, in part because I know that we will not be traveling into the night.

In less than five minutes we are inside the motel office, where Jen explains the situation to me while Alejandro speaks to the clerk behind the counter. "They only have one room," she says. "With twin beds. It will cost twenty-five dollars in total. Are you okay with that?"

"Sure," I reply. "Beats walking up that hill to the village in the dark."

Jen communicates our approval to Alejandro and to the clerk, who picks up the key to show us to our room. Alejandro bids us goodnight with one of the few Spanish phrases that I now recognize. "Buenas noches!"

"Where is he going?" I ask.

"Home," Jen replies. "His family lives here."

We pick up our bags and follow the clerk outside, walking through a light rain to our room. He opens the door and waves us in with a proud smile.

I see one double bed. "What do you make of that?"

Jen asks the clerk something in Spanish, to which he offers a lengthy reply. She turns back to me and says, "Looks like it's going to be a cozy night. This is the only room they have left. There's a political rally in town."

"I guess they have a different idea of twin beds than I do."

"Yup," Jen agrees. "Either that or my Spanish still has a few holes."

Our evening alone in the motel room is awkward but pleasant. Jen changes into a t-shirt and shorts, and I do the same, forgoing my custom of wearing only boxer shorts to bed. We devour an odd mix of snacks that I brought from Orlando—beef jerky, almonds, apple chips and raisins—while Jen flips through channels until she concludes there is nothing worth watching. Then she sits very close to me at the foot of the bed—our bare legs pressed together, the sweetness of her breath almost palpable—and teaches me

Spanish phrases from her Lonely Planet guide. We both laugh at my lack of linguistic skills, but Jen is a patient teacher.

"I guess we should call it a night," she says when it is clear that I have reached my capacity for taking in new information.

"Yeah," I reluctantly agree. I have been enjoying my private lesson, appreciating such closeness with another human being, brought further into focus against the backdrop of a foreign setting. I am also apprehensive about climbing into the same bed with Jen. It feels surreal, unreal ... like those visions I have had—that we have all had some version of, I am sure—of finding myself on a deserted island in the sole company of a beautiful woman.

We take turns brushing our teeth, Jen going first. By the time I am done, she is already under the covers. I gingerly enter the bed from the other side and wish her a good sleep. She turns off the bedside lamp and rolls on her side to say goodnight, the light of a streetlamp illuminating her face in narrow lateral strips caused by a half-open blind. Then she turns onto her other side and falls asleep. I spend the rest of the night teetering on my edge of the bed, equally worried that I might fall off or grope Jen in my sleep. The image of Jen's face in the shadows, like a sultry dame from a film noir detective flick, taunts me. At one point during the night, I wake up sweating. The details of my dream dissipate quickly, but my erection reminds me of its theme.

Twenty-Five

Morning arrives too soon. Jen and I scurry through our own routines, small talk replacing the intimacy of yesterday's discussion, as we prepare for a six AM departure. Despite a comfortable shower—this one lacking the excitement of loose electrical wires—I am barely awake when Alejandro knocks on our door. He leads us out to the street under a red morning sky that illuminates the already bustling city of Santo Domingo. There are few pedestrians at this hour, but vehicles dart through traffic circles in a convoluted pattern of organized chaos.

Though he says very little, Alejandro's presence soothes me as we climb onto an almost full bus. I hesitate slightly when he asks for my backpack, but when Jen yields hers without question I shed mine as well. He points us toward two individual seats—the last two available—and then disappears to store our packs in the vehicle's underbelly before re-entering the bus and standing beside the driver. I hug my knapsack as I sit beside a man in a business suit. Looking around, I see a variety of people not altogether different than what I experienced during my brief period as a bus rider on Vashon Island. People from all walks of life, rich and poor, young and old, sharing a common mode of transportation en route to very different lives.

I am transfixed by the landscape that passes by as we weave our way through the Andes, its greenery providing only occasional glimpses of the river that carves out the valley below. My eyes feel heavy as the bus sways back and forth, my head bobbing from time to time as I struggle to stay awake. Just when I think I cannot fend off sleep any longer, Alejandro is tapping me on the shoulder and signaling me to follow him. Moments later, Alejandro, Jen and I are standing on the river side of the highway, across from a tiny village comprised of a few houses, one restaurant and a small wooden kiosk that appears to be a convenience store. Traffic is sparse along the narrow road, so we cross easily. Only a few people mill about the village, and nobody is tending the store. I feel like an extra on a movie set—or perhaps we are the stars of the show, and nobody has let me in on the storyline.

Just beyond the kiosk I see a stone archway leading toward a trail that inclines rapidly into the forest. Jen looks at me and we both smile, acknowledging without words what we both recognize to be The Hill.

The Hill does not disappoint. My quadriceps are burning by the time we reach the last of a dozen or so switchbacks separating Pueblo del Sol from the highway below. The path—a primitive assortment of stone, dirt and gravel mixed with recently trimmed grass—cuts its way through a densely forested mountain. Various chirps and squawks fill the canopy above, coupling with the buzz of insects to remind me—with some apprehension—that we are only one of the species in this forest.

The path levels out and the forest thins, exposing the staff accommodation that I will call home for the next few weeks—a three-story building made from a combination of concrete, bamboo and twine mesh, covered by a thatch roof. Alejandro directs us to set our backpacks down at the base of a wide staircase that leads up to bedrooms on the second and third floors.

We continue a few hundred yards down the path toward an assortment of earthy structures and fabric yurts that form a rough circle around a wind turbine and a communication tower. Set in a large clearing, the village sits adjacent to a field containing a four-by-six grid of solar panels. Beyond that lies a large swath of land pasturing a few head of cattle and a handful of sheep.

As we walk toward an open structure providing coverage for a woodstove and sink, a petite brunette woman rushes from a nearby shelter to meet us.

"You must be Oliver and Jen?" she says with a French accent. "Welcome to Pueblo del Sol. Are you hungry for breakfast?"

"Very," Jen says.

"Yes, thank you." I am famished.

"I am Nadine," the woman says, reaching out to shake our hands.

"Mucho gusto," I say, even though English is the village's primary language.

"Mucho gusto," Nadine echoes.

Nadine leads us into a covered open-air dining area where people are seated around three large tables. "Oliver," she says. "Conlan will be your roommate. He will show you to your room after breakfast."

A tall, thin man with short reddish-brown hair and smiling blue eyes stands up, leans across a table and shakes my hand. With the hint of an accent he says, "Nice to have you on board, Oliver. Apologies in advance for everything I've strewn about the room. Guess I'll have to get used to a roommate again."

"Nice to meet you," I reply.

"Jen," Nadine continues, "you will be paired with Katherine." A gorgeous young woman with straight shoulder-length brown hair looks up, smiles, raises her hand in a half wave and says hello. Her accent is strong—Australian, perhaps.

Nadine fills us in on village life—meal times, chores, accommodations and rules. Then she adds, "We have plenty of electricity, but only one Internet connection—which is broken right now. We hope to have it fixed soon."

"We're the village of Luddite nerds," Conlan adds. "A technology think tank with cold showers and sporadic Internet. And right now, we don't even have water."

"Ah, yes," Nadine says. "We have plenty of drinking water stored, but you will have to rely on rainwater for bathing and washing clothes until the system is fixed."

I move to an open seat at one of the tables. Jen slides into a seat across from me.

"Help yourself"—Conlan points to containers of bread, oatmeal, coffee, milk, juice and bananas—"before us vultures finish it off. Breakfast is serious business around here."

"Thank you," I say while reaching for the coffee.

A large, stocky man with a few days' growth on his gray beard—I guess him to be around fifty—tips his head toward Jen. "Sae Oliver, it could'nae been too tough on ye spending a day in the company ah this lovely lassie?" His Scottish accent is thick.

"No, I could've been stuck with worse."

"Thanks for the compliment," Jen says.

"Let me rephrase that—I was very fortunate to travel in the company of this brilliant and beautiful young lady."

Jen tosses back her head and rolls her eyes.

"Andrew will enjoy having a new audience for his tall tales," Conlan says, pointing toward the large Scot.

"Yer jes' jealous," Andrew says, "'cause ye daen't have as much wisdom as ah do."

"That's because you're older than dirt," Conlan sneers.

Andrew turns to me and says, "Daen't mind him. He's harmless enough. Ye jes' need to feed him three times a day and rub behind his ears every sae often."

"I take it you two have worked together for a while?" I ask.

"About six months," Andrew says. "Whit's about six months too long."

"Yeah, right," Conlan quips. "If I wasn't here, who would laugh at your horrendous jokes?"

Andrew looks at me again and tips his head toward Conlan. "Ah hafta dumb down meh jokes fer his ears. He's got Irish in the blood, y'know? Gotta stick to monosyllabic words or he gits confused."

"Don't be fooled by the old brute," Conlan says. "He runs around quoting Robbie Burns like he was a close personal friend. Mind you, he probably was. We only keep him around because he's not half bad on a football pitch. For an old guy, anyway."

Andrew sits up and opens his arms, speaking with the authority of a stage actor. "O, wad some power the giftie gie us / To see oursels as others see us! / It wad frae monie a blunder free us / An' foolish notion."

"Welcome to the jungle," Katherine says. "As you can see, we keep a few of our own wild animals."

~ ~ ~

"We're good to go." Eldon Hewitt speaks into the cell phone from his table in the corner of an upscale restaurant in Quito's Old Town. "We dusted off the old system."

"Who's we?" Harold asks.

"Nathan went in … with one of our partners from Crescoil."

Harold clenches his jaw. "Why did you involve Crescoil?"

"It was an easy in—he tagged along on one of their routine visits."

"Was he undercover?"

"Practically invisible."

"Let's keep it that way," Harold says, lamenting the lack of resources at his disposal. He contemplates involving one of the other agencies—someone with real resources—but this wouldn't even register on their radar. Best to keep it in the family for now. It's most likely a non-starter anyway—just another one of her pet projects.

Twenty-Six

After breakfast, Alejandro doles out the chores to our group of volunteers and full-time laborers, eight people in total, while a slightly larger group—including Jen and Katherine—head off toward the science center to work under the guidance of Professor Jordan Wilson from UCLA.

I walk with Conlan from the breakfast area to our accommodation. "So you're Irish?"

"No," Conlan replies. "I'm from St. John's, Newfoundland. I'm a fifth generation Canadian."

"Do you two joke like that all the time?"

"Pretty much," he says. "If he ever stops giving me a hard time, I'll worry about the old man."

"So what are you doing here?"

"I came for a three-month volunteer stint … two years ago."

"Two years? What do you do here?"

"Everything. We're all here in one way or another to support the renewable energies team, but we spend most of our time doing grunt work. I chip in with a bit of everything and try to learn as much as I can."

"I'm only here for three weeks. I hope I can find some way to contribute."

Conlan smiles as we approach the bunkhouse. "Every log you move or tree you plant is something that wouldn't have gotten done if you weren't here. Just try not to expect too much of yourself. Things move at a pretty slow pace. It can be frustrating at first, but you get used to it."

I pick up my backpack and follow Conlan up the stairs. "Where will I find the Pachamama?"

"Carmen? She's gone to visit her family on the coast."

"Oh. When will she be back?"

Conlan opens the door to our room and waves me in. "I think she's gone for at least a month, maybe longer."

"A month?" I stop in my tracks. "Doesn't she run the place?"

"She owns it, but Alejandro and Nadine run it."

Conlan goes into the room while I consider what he has told me. Eventually I follow him in and set my bags down against the wall. Conlan takes two packs of Oreos off a shelf and throws one to me. "Second breakfast?"

"Thanks." I catch the pack and twirl it in my hands, thinking about the Pachamama, frustrated at myself for not confirming that she would be here. "How far is the coast from here?"

Conlan already has an Oreo in his mouth, so it takes him a while to reply. "Their farm is near Puerto Lopez. That's probably an eight hour bus ride from here."

"Damn."

"Why?" he asks as he begins to clear out his stuff from my half of the room. True to his word, Conlan has spread out with a variety of clothes, books, posters and packaged foods.

"A friend wanted me to pass on a message to her."

"Huh," he says. "Talk to Nadine. If our frickin' communication tower ever gets fixed, I'm sure she can reach Carmen's family."

"I will ... but I kind of need to see her in person. By the way, why is she called the Pachamama?"

"It's the Quechua word for Mother Earth. If you meet her, you'll understand."

"What's Quechua?"

"The main Indigenous language of Ecuador. It's also the name of the people who speak it." Conlan points to a large pile of brown pellets in the corner of the floor near the foot of my bed. "Sorry about the bat shit."

I follow his eyes up to the highest corner of the ceiling, where I can barely make out a bunch of small, dark shapes.

"At least they keep the mosquitoes at bay," Conlan adds. "We'll have to shake out your mosquito net too. It probably hasn't been touched since Daniel ..." He pauses and looks down at the bed.

"Daniel Porter?" I ask before I can stop myself.

"Yeah," he says, looking at me curiously. "Did you know him?"

I shake my head. "No. But I know *of* him. Sounds like he was quite the scientist."

"Yeah," Conlan says, relaxing again as he goes back to picking up his stuff. "He was a good guy."

"So this was his bed?" I ask.

"Yup."

I attempt to reconcile Daniel's presence in the room as I wrestle with the mosquito net that hangs from the ceiling and drapes over the four posts of the single bed. Conlan grabs one end of the net and flips it over the end posts, and I follow his lead at the head of the bed. He detaches the net from a carabiner to release it from the ceiling, and we walk outside to shake it over the edge of a covered porch.

"Hey," Conlan says as we re-enter our room, "I'm overdue for some beach time. What say we get a few people together for a trip to Canoa this weekend? Maybe have a few drinks and tear up a dance floor or two?" He waits while I absorb his question, then adds, "It should be a pretty easy bus ride from there to Carmen's farm."

~ ~ ~

I spend my first morning at Pueblo del Sol working with Andrew in the vegetable garden. I am glad I wore rubber boots, long pants and work gloves, but I regret choosing a short-sleeved t-shirt. The black flies launch intermittent attacks on my elbows, undaunted by my insect repellant. Swatting away a particularly determined fly, I grumble, "Nasty little buggers, huh?"

"Yep," Andrew says. "They dinnae give a shit about Deet neither. Try thes." He reaches into his pocket, pulls out a small glass bottle and hands it to me. "Smells awful, but it does the job and it's good fer yer skin. Especially here." He points to his bald spot, causing me to chuckle.

I rub the oil over my arms, neck, face and hair, my fingers making note of the receding line on my forehead. The oil smells like garlic and it seems to work. The flies land on my skin, but they don't stay long enough to bite.

"Thanks," I say. "This stuff is magical."

"Keep it. Ah hae lots of it. Ah learned about Neem in the Amazon."

Andrew reminds me of Arlo—an observation that is reinforced when he launches into a rant about the US election while hoeing a large raised bed.

"Fools they are, every one ah them. Call themsel's leaders, but they're all bloody followers, catering tae polls and lobbyists. Whatever'll get 'em back into power. Democracy's broken, Oliver."

I look up from where I am digging a shallow trench for a row of carrots. "I gave up on politics a long time ago."

"Daen't say I blame yeh," Andrew says. "What's gonna save this world is grassroots action, not fat-cat politicians. We can't jes' buy our way outta this hole wae dug oursel's inta. We're so hung up on the plight ah the day that we're losing the forest fer the trees."

"Hmm," I say, trying to think of a suitable response.

"So what really brings ye here, Ollie?"

I stop digging and look up at Andrew. "What do you mean?"

"Ah mean, we're all here for some reason. Ah left a good woman and a stable job. Jes' had to see what was beyond the island I was raised on. We ain't no spring chickens, you and me ... gotta be some sorta mid-life crisis brings us here."

"Yeah," I agree. "There's some truth to that."

"Yer not connected with that young lassie from Crescoil, are ye?"

"Who do you mean?"

"Jennifer Morris. I hear she has a black spot on her resume. As in, an oil patch."

"Jen? She works for Crescoil?"

"So ahm told," Andrew says. "They've sent in a few spies—ah mean, business development managers—to check on the progress of our science team. But what dae ah know? Ahm like a mushroom around here … left in the dark and covered in ye-know-what."

~ ~ ~

Discussion at lunch is sparse. Hoping the positive reviews I have read about food safety at the village are true, I stuff myself with my entire ration of salad, rice and beans.

After lunch, Jen and I take our first turn doing dishes.

"How was your morning?" I ask.

"Mind opening. It's a steep learning curve. How about you?"

"Good. It was nice to do something outdoors for a change."

"Conlan mentioned something about a weekend on the coast?"

I am surprised that news has already made it to Jen. "Uh, yeah. Are you thinking of coming?"

"I'm not sure. I guess we're off Friday, and Katherine sounds keen. Would you care for some female company, or would you prefer a boys' weekend?"

"Ahm sure we'd enjoy havin' some lovely lassies in tow, so long as yeh wear yer bikinis to the beach." My lame imitation of Andrew's accent lands me a whip of Jen's dish-towel, catching me in the abdomen with a wicked snap.

"Oh, I'm sorry," she says, her tone genuinely apologetic. "I didn't mean to make contact."

"I didn't realize you were so mischievous. You seem so sweet and innocent."

"I am," Jen smiles, and I see more than one side of her—another hint of the complex woman I glimpsed last night.

"You're complicated, aren't you?"

"Aren't we all?" She continues to grin. "Hey, Katherine told me there's a swimming hole about ten minutes from here, down that trail over there." She points to a trail leading out of the clearing behind one of the yurts. "They use it sometimes when the showers are down. We're meeting at the trailhead around four o-clock, if you want to join us."

I hesitate for a moment, feeling every one of my forty years. "Who's going?"

"I'm not sure," she says. "At least Katherine, Conlan and Andrew, I think."

"Sure," I reply, glad to hear Andrew's name—glad that I will not be the oldest man in the pool.

Twenty-Seven

At home I have allowed the exotic to become ordinary. Although this cloud forest is no more spectacular than my own backyard, the unfamiliar shades, scents and sounds grab hold of my senses. I look up into the trees above, listening to a variety of chirps, cheeps and ker-caws, trying to ignore the flies that seek out patches of uncovered skin.

"Boo!"

"Bloody hell!" I screech.

"Sorry," Jen laughs.

"You scared the crap out of me!"

"You looked so intense. What were you searching for?"

I hold up my hand while I catch my breath. "Birds. I was trying to match sounds to birds."

"Your heart okay?"

"I'll let you know when I find it. Where are the others?"

Jen starts to walk down the path. "Katherine's still working, but she'll join us in a bit. I don't know about the others."

"Did you learn how to save the world this afternoon?" I ask.

"Hardly," she says, "But I will say there is a ton of potential in this little village."

We walk in a silence that is both comfortable and tense. I want to ask Jen a million questions—about her work here and her experience with a global oil giant; about Crescoil's interest in a solar project taking place in the middle of an Andean cloud forest; about what she already knows regarding Daniel's research; about the long version of what brought her to Ecuador. I want to know everything about my enigmatic travel mate—this woman who toggles between mischievous and innocent, between girl next door and sultry dame. But I keep my questions tucked away in my overactive mind.

We emerge from the forest into a circular clearing about fifty yards in diameter, most of which is covered by a murky pond. A small wooden dock extends almost halfway into the pond, and the trail skirts the water in a semi-circle for about twenty yards before turning back into the forest. The clouds have parted following a brief but heavy rain that ended my afternoon gardening session, and the late afternoon sun is beating directly down on the clearing.

"Are you going to join me?" Jen asks.

"I was, but ..." I had pictured a clear pond. The dark water I see is anything but inviting.

Jen walks to the end of the dock, pulls her shirt over her head and drops it by her side. Then she unclips her bra and sets it on her shirt. It takes me a moment to avert my stare from her athletic frame. I look into the forest and hear a splash as she jumps into the center of the pond.

"You should really join me," she says. "It's very nice in here."

I shake my head. "I'm putting my faith in Alejandro and Conlan to get the showers working."

"Don't you like swimming?"

"Sure, in a small, clean pool with water that's, oh, about a hundred and four."

"It's warm in here."

"Not hot tub warm." I don't want to admit the real reason for my trepidation, but Jen seems to detect it.

"If you're worried about getting eaten, I'd be more concerned about the flies out there."

"You're probably right, but I have a long list of irrational fears. Swimming in a murky pond in the jungle is one of them. Actually, when I say it that way, it sounds perfectly rational."

The vulnerability of Jen's nude body makes me uncomfortable. My own clothing feels thicker, heavier, as I attempt to make small talk with the naked woman treading water under my watch. Her smile tells me that she is enjoying my discomfort—but my fear stands like a wall between us. So I begin to undress, starting with my boots and socks and then removing my shirt. "What the hell. I'm scared of flying too, and that didn't stop me from coming to Ecuador."

Jen turns away while I take off my pants and remove my money belt. I slide the wedding ring off my finger and place it in my belt—not stopping to analyze my reason for doing so—and stuff the belt inside of my pants. After a brief pause I peel off my boxers, run to the end of the dock and jump into the pond. Exhilarated, I come up for air, treading water about ten feet from Jen.

"Would you believe that I've never skinny-dipped before?".

"Yes," she says.

Our eyes lock, and my entire body shivers. It takes me a moment to realize that I am not cold; I am aroused. Every nerve springs to life simultaneously, begging to be touched, caressed—feelings all but forgotten in the practical reality of family life. I tread closer to Jen. The tingling intensifies, concentrating in my pelvis. She does not move away when I approach, her smile spreading to occupy her eyes, imploring me to come closer.

I stop a few feet away. An image of James Bond enters my mind, and a droll smile forms on my face.

"What are you smiling at?" Jen asks.

"James Bond."

She laughs, a girlish giggle.

"You know who he is, right?"

"Yeah, I know. Are you feeling like Daniel Craig?"

"I'm thinking Sean Connery."

"And who am I?"

"That's what I'm trying to figure out."

"I'm just a girl," Jen says innocently.

I hear a faint whistle—a familiar song that I cannot place—and instinctively I move away from Jen. Before anyone else arrives I ask, "Are you coming to the coast?"

"I think so," she says.

"Good."

I question what I have got myself into. Whatever it is, at this moment I am in no hurry to get out of it.

~ ~ ~

Conlan and I lie on our backs under mosquito nets, listening to frogs and insects living beyond our mesh walls—and probably within them—as we share stories of who we are and where we are from. I talk about the challenges of marriage and parenthood, and I begin to open up about my mother's rapid decay during my college years. This topic hits close to home for Conlan—his parents being no strangers to the bottle either. I am relieved when Conlan hijacks the discussion about a topic I rarely make space for. The temporary desire to explore my own youth subsides as I listen to him vent about his screwed-up childhood.

Conlan left home at seventeen and spent ten years bouncing between jobs and girlfriends in a variety of Maritime communities before he stuffed everything that mattered to him into a backpack and bought a plane ticket to South America. When he ran out of money, he agreed to work for room and board at the village—a gig that eventually turned into a low-paying job. He tells me a few stories about life in the village, expanding my view of the people I met today. The way he speaks of *Kath* gives me the sense that an Australian brunette may be why Conlan has turned a three-month stay at Pueblo del Sol into two years and counting. I certainly don't believe it is the manual labor that keeps him here.

"This reminds me of talking to Daniel," Conlan says. "We'd lie awake chatting deep into the night sometimes. He was a quiet guy most of the time, but once you got him talking he had a lot to say."

"Were you two good friends?"

"Yeah. The jungle has a way of binding people. You get to feel like family pretty quickly."

"I can see that already. It sounds like you're close to everyone."

"Sometimes too close. Like any family, we have our challenges."

"Like what?"

Conlan delays for a moment before responding. "You might be better surfing than diving."

"Meaning ... don't ask?"

"It's fine. It's just ..."

I change course. "What is Crescoil's role at the village? I hear they've taken quite an interest in the research."

"You're a quick study. Their role here is rather divisive."

"Why's that?"

"Some people trust their motives—they claim they're investing heavily in renewable energy—but others think they're trying to squash anything that might compete with almighty crude."

"What do you think?"

"I don't know. I try to keep my nose out of it. I like to think that even the biggest companies can change. I guess I'm an optimist that way. Besides, I'm not sure they'll find much up here now that Daniel's gone."

"It must have been rough when he died, huh?"

"Yeah, it was a kick in the nuts, for sure. I didn't really believe it at first. In some ways I'm not sure I do now."

"What do you mean?"

Conlan is silent. Maybe I have asked too much for my first night here. But I did not come all this way to keep my questions bottled up. I feel Conlan is trustworthy—something I haven't yet decided about Jen—so I will follow my gut and see what he can tell me.

When Conlan finally speaks, his voice is serious. "Daniel had a bit of Walden in him. He was really taken by Thoreau. He'd talk of fading into the jungle for a while. He often went away for a few days on his own, and when I'd ask him where he'd been, he'd sing a song I introduced him to, a Canadian ditty that he really liked." Conlan sings the lines—*"Where am I going? Wouldn't you like to know? But if I told you then everyone would wanna go."*

"Really?" I say. "He never told you?"

"No. Daniel was funny that way. He could be the most engaging guy one minute, and totally distant the next. Sometimes I got the feeling the rest of the team got in his way. He talked about an engineering prof from your neck of the woods though. Seemed to be one of the only people he truly respected."

"Eddy," I say. "Dr. Robert Edward McKinnon."

"Yeah, that's his name. You know him?"

"I did. He died while I was flying down here. Cancer."

"No shit," Conlan says. "Life's a bitch, huh? So is that why you're here? Does he have anything to do with you looking for Carmen?"

"Yeah," I reply, offering no further explanation.

Twenty-Eight

Alejandro informed me this morning that I would join him and Conlan on horseback to help with trail maintenance and plumbing repair—their second attempt to fix the village's water source. I did not confess that I am inept at horseback riding, despite my prairie upbringing. To my relief, Whiskey is a dependable steed. We chit-chat along the way as Alejandro points out various species of flora and fauna. It takes us at least two hours to reach the place where they found the leak yesterday.

The source of the leak is obvious. Alejandro dismounts and unpacks a variety of supplies, then walks toward a modest stream where water sprays from a heavy black garden hose. He holds up a large piece of rubber tubing, then says something and emits a triumphant cackle. I laugh as well, though I have no clue what he said.

Conlan says, "Yesterday we used tape, which clearly didn't work. Today he has a new piece of hose, and doesn't plan to fail twice."

It takes Alejandro only a few minutes to patch the leak. I am amazed to learn that a single hose combines with gravity to provide sufficient water for the whole village, provided it is used sparingly.

On our way back down the mountain, we make a few stops to clear out dense brush with machetes, uncovering rarely used trails that apparently bear some importance that I am unaware of. Turning a corner maybe halfway back to the village, the ground to our left slopes down toward a small valley. Alejandro points to a stream of gray smoke that billows above the tree line. "Walter. Walter es el hogar."

Conlan turns to translate for me. "That's where Alejandro's brother lives. Walter."

"What's he doing way up here?"

"He helps manage the upper part of the estate. One of his jobs is to make sure the water is running, but he's been away in Quito this week. He must have come home this morning. He probably caught a ride in the Land Cruiser with one of the other workers."

Whiskey comes to a stop, and Alejandro ties all three horses to a tree as Conlan and I dismount. My arms are tired from trail clearing, and from holding onto the reins with far too much intensity. The insides of my knees ache, and my buttocks feel bruised from the saddle.

"That's hard on the ass," I say.

"It's a horse," Conlan quips, flashing a wry grin.

I follow Alejandro as he guides us down a well-worn path through the forest. The trail is mostly dry, but an occasional mud puddle threatens to steal one of my boots. I fend off a mild bout of claustrophobia as the density of vegetation increases, but the trail is wide enough to keep my anxiety at bay.

After a few hundred yards we reach a small clearing, where the trail continues through low-cut grass to a set of stairs leading up to Walter's cabin—a simple but elegant timber structure with a covered porch containing two chairs. I am surprised to see a newly shingled roof with six solar panels mounted beside a smoking metal chimney.

Alejandro walks to the front door of the cottage and pounds on the door, yelling "Walter! Abra la puerta!" The door opens and a taller, thinner version of Alejandro greets us. An attractive woman with dark brown eyes appears behind him with a baby in her arms. Their appearance is more modern than I would expect for people who live in the woods, their clothing and hairstyles similar to those I saw in Quito.

"Oliver," Conlan says, "meet Walter, Maria and their son, Luca." Then he turns to our hosts and says, "Este es mi nuevo amigo, Oliver."

Maria smiles widely. Luca, a spritely boy with his dad's hair and his mother's eyes, stares at us with wonder from the crook of Maria's arm.

We enter the cabin, a dimly lit space of about five hundred square feet, including a small bedroom and bathroom that I can't quite see. The lighting is mostly natural from two small windows. A pot sits on the woodstove, steam billowing past a metal lid. My eyes wander to a refrigerator, and then to a laptop computer sitting on a small desk.

"I wouldn't have expected to find a fridge and a computer all the way up here," I say.

Walter cups his hand over his heart and, looking up to the ceiling, says, "Gracias a Daniel y el sol."

Conlan adds, "Daniel provided the solar panels."

Walter, Alejandro and Maria speak in Spanish while Conlan shares a bit of background about these people. I learn that Walter is a journalist by trade. An avid reader and prolific writer, Walter has just finished writing his first novel.

"What's the novel about?" I ask Conlan.

"Oil and greed." Walter surprises me with his English. "In Amazonia."

"You speak English?" I ask Walter.

"Only a little. I learn in Quito, but I am not good."

"So, what is the premise of the story? Can you tell me what happens?"

Walter begins to speak, but he seems frustrated trying to convey complex messages in simple language. He turns to Conlan and speaks in rapid Spanish. Conlan nods a few times, and then translates.

"It's a story of an Indigenous tribe in the Western Amazon Basin that fights to keep oil and gas exploration off its land. A bit of background … in 2006 Ecuador began to squeeze out global oil companies, and shortly after that they granted rights—similar to those of humans—to the land itself. It all looked promising, but a lot of environmentalists question whether those changes have really made a difference. Oil exports remain the main driver for Ecuador's economy, and exploitation of the Amazon Basin is increasing."

I voice a question as it strikes me. "What would happen if they stopped drilling for oil? Wouldn't that kill their economy?"

Conlan paraphrases another round of translations. "Yes, that's a huge issue. But it scares Walter that Ecuador is so dependent on its oil, especially because most of that oil is sitting underneath the Amazon Basin."

"Okay," I say. "But if one tribe wins their battle, won't that just push the oil companies to another location in the Amazon?"

"Not if they were frightened," Walter says. "If …" he begins, then turns toward Conlan and continues in Spanish.

"He says that sometimes we must fight fire with fire," Conlan tells me.

Walter looks at me curiously, scrutinizing my face for a reaction. I do not know how to respond.

"But this is fiction, right?"

"Fiction," Walter says after an awkward pause. "An idea." His body language—or perhaps his choice of words—makes me uneasy.

"It sounds like a game of hot potato," I say. "I mean, we're going to need more energy in the future, not less."

"Sure," Conlan agrees. "But the Amazon Basin is like the lungs of our planet. Surely we can bring ourselves to leave it alone and go drill somewhere else."

"Or find an alternative," I add.

"Yes," Walter says, smiling.

Alejandro tells Conlan and me that it is time to head back to the village. I say goodbye to the family and tell Walter that I would like to learn more about his book.

Walter smiles and says, "You must read. Conlan translate to English."

We walk off the porch toward the trail. Alejandro changes course abruptly, pointing for Conlan and me to follow him to a path at the opposite side of the clearing from where we entered.

"Oh," Conlan says, "Alejandro must like you."

"Why's that?"

"You'll see. He's only brought me here a couple of times."

Alejandro walks a few hundred yards before turning on-to a side trail that leads about the same distance down a steep slope, until we come to the top of a small set of rapids set in a crystal clear stream. He removes his boots, pants and shirt, setting them beside the creek along with his machete. With a hoot and a wave of his hand, he jumps into the rapids feet first. Laughing all the while, he slides down a twisting chute that stretches forty or fifty feet to a natural pool below.

Conlan follows Alejandro closely, and I challenge myself to follow them both. The water is refreshing, and the ride exhilarating. The rock has been shaped by water over many millennia to form an almost perfect slide, and the pool at the bottom—a gentle whirlpool that holds the water coming from the slide momentarily before sending it further down the creek bed—is an ideal landing spot. At the edge of the pool is another trailhead.

"Where does that lead?" I ask, pointing at the trail. Alejandro, who is already climbing up the rocks beside the slide, shoots me a questioning glance, shakes his head and says, "En ninguna parte."

"He said nowhere," Conlan shrugs.

Twenty-Nine

We skip out of work after lunch on Thursday to embark on the long journey to Canoa—an eight-hour bus ride full of epic views, interspersed with hectic urban stops in Santo

Domingo and Pedernales. I am glad to be traveling in a group, but my dependency on new friends is humbling.

It is past dark when the six of us—Conlan, Andrew, Jen, Nadine, Katherine and I—trudge up a dirt road that runs parallel to the ocean, about two blocks from the beach. The street is packed with stores, most of which are closed for the night, along with a few restaurants and bars containing a handful of patrons. A smattering of streetlights casts a dim glow over the town, which could be mistaken for the set of an old western film if not for the thatch-roof architecture. Our walk terminates at the north end of town, where a modern structure reads "Hostal Vista al Mar." A large middle-aged man with a sleeveless white undershirt unlocks the front door and lets us in.

We pay for our stay and carry our packs to the third floor. I stop to look over a row of shorter buildings, where the light of a half moon illuminates whitecaps lapping up on shore. Strings of colored lights adorn a series of grass huts, each consuming a portion of the beach to house a handful of tables and a dance floor.

I follow Andrew and Conlan into a dorm room containing three sets of bunk beds. Mosquito nets patched with black tape hang from each bed, while equally imperfect screens cover two large window frames.

"Sae I hear yer headin' to Puerto Lopez tomorrow," Andrew says to me. "But you'll join us fer a drink or six tonight?"

"I don't know if my body can handle that."

"Ah, yer bum's oot the windae," Andrew says.

I turn to Conlan. "Translation, please?"

"I don't speak thug," Conlan says. "But knowing Andrew, I'd guess he's challenging you to a Scotch-drinking contest."

I walk down to the lobby to check e-mail on a computer that I noticed on my way into the hostel. I sift through four days of junk mail before I see a message from Annie.

Oliver,

I saw my "friend" again. Nothing else to report, just a bit thrown. I'd love to hear from you to know that all is well there.

Best,
Annie

I get up and ask the hostel manager if there is a public phone. There is not, and every cabina in town is closed for the night, so I return to the computer and peck out a quick message to Annie voicing concern about her safety. Moments later, a reply appears in my inbox.

Oliver,

I'm glad to hear from you. I don't mean to scare you. I'm sure everything is okay, but in any case Martin is going to stay with us for a while. Keep in touch, and I'll do the same.

Best,
Annie

Something shifts inside of me as I think of Annie, her new beau, and the man who may be following her. Our friendship cemented by circumstance and any hint of romance put to rest, her presence no longer makes me nervous—at least not from a few thousand miles away. But something about Annie—her situation, her past, her connection to my being here—unsettles me as I stare at the screen, searching for some way to communicate my mixed emotions. Unable to find the words I am looking for, I close my e-mail and shut down the computer, then head back upstairs to rejoin my friends.

~ ~ ~

"What do you think of village life?" Katherine yells across our beachside table, loud enough for me to hear over the pop tune radiating from a massive speaker about ten feet from my head. The bar is sparsely populated, making the volume seem ridiculous and unnecessary. "Any highlights so far?" she adds.

I yell in response, "I would have to say the tree planting I did this morning."

"They let ye out of the garden?" Andrew leans in to join the conversation.

"Yes," I reply, my throat raw from the yelling and the consumption of two large bottles of beer. "They even let me use a machete again."

"Did that make you feel macho?" Katherine reaches out to grab my bicep.

I recoil from her playful inquiry. "Yeah. You can call me Rambo." Katherine nods vacantly and I cringe at my dated reference to pop culture.

A quieter song—a catchy Latin number dominated by gentle, busy percussion—allows a reprieve from our shouting match. Nadine leans in to ask the whole group, "Who are going to be couples this weekend?"

"Oliver and Jen are attached at the hip," Conlan says. Before I have time to feel embarrassed, he continues. "Kath and I can put on a good act, so I guess that leaves you with Andrew."

"Act?" Katherine licks her lips as she raises her eyebrows at Conlan. "Speak for yourself, handsome."

Conlan groans. "Save it for later, Kath. It won't be easy to act like you're attracted to my starch white ass when I'm face down in a pool of my own vomit."

"Ew," Nadine says, scrunching her face. "That is repugnant."

I look at Jen and she shrugs. "So what's the deal?" I ask.

Conlan explains. "There's a gaggle of guys here who run around the beach all day playing soccer and showing off their physiques—and a few older guys that lurk around the bars at night. We refer to them as—"

"Canoa Creepers," Katherine interrupts.

"They come out in full force on the weekend," Conlan adds. "Most of them are resting up for tomorrow, but you may see a few of them tonight. They're harmless for the most part, but they're relentless. So for the next few days, you and Jen are an item."

"Lucky me," I say, raising my eyebrows to look at Jen again. She smirks and rolls her eyes.

We each have a few drinks, and then we start to dance as a mob. For the next couple of hours, I alternate between beer and water as we move to and from the dance floor. My bladder finally says enough, and Nadine points me in the direction of a bar across the street where there is a restroom. I peel off from the crowd. I notice a middle-aged guy with short brown hair, a collared shirt and khaki trousers sitting on his own at the bar. When he sees me looking at him, he casually looks down at his drink. I wonder if he is one of the so-called Canoa Creepers.

When I come back from the bar with a fresh beer and a glass of water, the man is gone. I shrug off my misgivings about him and return to the table where Jen is sitting alone while the others dance. Andrew and Nadine are be-bopping like a father and daughter would dance, while Katherine and Conlan dance close and intimate, like a pair of Latin lovers.

I lean over to Jen and ask, "What do you make of Conlan and Kath?"

"They seem close," Jen replies. "But I think she's spoken for already."

"Oh? What do you mean?"

"Let's just say that my roommate's bed has been empty since I arrived."

"Really? Who?"

"Dr. Wilson. Though I understand he's married."

"Sounds like I've missed out on some juicy village gossip."

"You want juicy?" Jen says. "Try this. Katherine was apparently Daniel Porter's lover as well—have you heard of him?"

"Yeah," I reply. The song ends abruptly and our group returns to the table. Dumbfounded, I watch Katherine. She is wrapped around Conlan, who is thoroughly enjoying the attention.

Upon Nadine's suggestion we move to the beach, where we all listen to the Pacific Ocean lap upon the shore, melding with the soothing tones of Reggaeton music.

"Sae what are ye hopin' to learn from the Pachamama?" Andrew asks.

"I need to deliver a message from a friend," I reply.

"This is about Daniel Porter, isn't it?"

Taken aback by his bluntness, I pause before responding, "Indirectly. It's a message from Dr. McKinnon."

"Ah half expected ye to say it was a message from Daniel himself," Andrew says. "That boy is like a modern day Elvis."

"That's not funny!" Katherine snaps.

Andrew winces. "Keep the heid, Kath! What'd ah say?"

We are all silent until Katherine looks at me and says, "One of the former volunteers swore she saw Daniel with a woman at Guayaquil Airport about two weeks after the bus crash. By the time she made her way through the crowd, he was gone."

Andrew leans toward me, more serious now. "There's a persistent rumor that Daniel staged his own death. Ye dinnae know anythin' about that, dae ye Oliver?"

"Why would I?" I ask.

"Ye seem tae know a lot for someone whose jes volunteerin'."

"Don't interrogate the poor guy," Conlan says to Andrew. Then he adds to me, "There's been a lot of speculation about Daniel's disappearance. The only thing everyone agrees on is that we wouldn't put anything past him."

~ ~ ~

The six of us stumble up the stairs of the hostel, collectively singing, "Tú eres mi luz en la oscuridad." *You are my light in the dark.* When we reach the third story, Jen attempts a fancy Salsa move, our legs tangle and we fall in a heap on the floor. We lie on our backs, laughing, while I try to assess if I have hurt anything.

"You two okay?" Conlan asks.

"No," I laugh. "I'm drunk."

Jen tries to say something, but her laugh turns into a guffaw and she cannot get the words out.

I force myself to get up, walk into my room, and return with a bottle of water. Jen is no longer sitting against the wall.

"Over here," she calls from a bench that overlooks the street below.

I sit down and Jen sidles up against me, wrapping her arm around my waist. We take turns drinking water from my bottle.

"Can I come with you tomorrow?" she asks.

"What?" I am surprised by her request—and confused.

"Can I help you find your Pachamama?" Jen asks.

"That makes me feel like a lost kitten."

She laughs. It takes a moment for either of us to speak again.

"I don't know," I say. "It's something I have to do."

"It's okay. If you need to go on your own …"

My brain tells me to turn her down, but the rest of me resists. Finally I say, "No, it would be nice to have you there. We might have to upgrade rooms though. Nadine arranged my travel, and I assume she only booked one bed."

Jen shrugs. "It's not like we haven't shared one before."

Thirty

Warm moist air carries fruity perfume, sweat and diesel fuel, along with the occasional whiff of fish canneries that provide the economic backbone for this region. Latin music blares overhead, its upbeat percussion and robust horn section matching the colorful interior of the bus—a charming if outdated mix of patterned orange and blue seats with bright orange curtains that hang from tattered ropes. Outside, tall broad trees stand guard like giant broccoli stalks above a dense array of vegetation that melds together as a single organism, blanketing the fertile earth below in countless shades of green.

Jen is asleep on my shoulder, still nursing a hangover from last night's excess. "I never have more than a drink or two," she told us as she pushed the eggs around on her plate at breakfast, just before she ran to the restroom to throw up.

"Are we there yet?" Jen mumbles as she begins to stir.

"Just a little farther," I reply.

"Really?"

"No. But we passed Manta quite a while ago, so we're over halfway."

Jen sits up and chugs the last of her water, looking more awake—and more sober—than she has all morning.

"Thanks for coming along," I say.

"Wouldn't have missed it. I need to find out what you're up to."

"What if I'm not up to anything?"

"Then why would you come all the way down here to see the Pachamama?"

"I told you. I have to deliver a message."

"Your trip here is about more than you're letting on, isn't it?" She looks at me seriously. "Can you tell me about the message you're delivering?"

"Not really."

"Why not?"

"Maybe I signed an NDA," I say with a smirk.

"Touché. Did you?"

"Not exactly. It was more of a promise."

"Don't turn out to be a spy, okay?"

"You neither."

A statue of a corncob—at least ten feet high—appears in the window, reminding me of my recent trip to Minnesota. I point toward the cob, which hosts a sign that reads, "Jipija-pa Mi Tierra." According to my guidebook, the bus will turn west from Jipijapa toward a twenty-mile length of coastline that stretches from Puerto Cayo to Puerto Lopez, between which lies Machalilla National Park. It is on the edge of this park, at a small organic farm called Naturaleza Jardín, where I hope to meet Carmen—the Pachamama.

We stop at a large cement parking lot in front of a nondescript building. There are a few buses parked in seemingly random locations, and maybe fifty people milling about the area. Our driver gets off the bus, and the attendant who took our money says something in Spanish.

"We have fifteen minutes," Jen says. "Any chance you'd buy me some water? My head's still pounding." She pulls a dollar coin from her pocket and hands it to me.

"Sure. I have to use the restroom anyway." I stand and pick up my knapsack.

"You can leave that here. I'm not going anywhere."

I hesitate for a moment as I envision Jen looking through my stuff. I shake off my doubt, willing myself to believe that Jen is only here because she enjoys my company. In any case, the only valuables I am carrying are in my money belt. So I nod and set the pack down on my seat.

I get off the bus and walk to the terminal entrance, where a woman stands at a small kiosk selling snacks, beverages and magazines. I use my improving Spanish skills—and the coin Jen gave me—to buy two bottles of water and ask where the bathroom is. The woman points at a wall in the back of the station and my feet follow her direction. I am about to enter the restroom when an elderly woman reaches out her arm and blocks my entry.

"Diez centavos," she says, holding out her hand.

"Pardon?"

"Diez centavos."

"Ten cents?"

"Si," she nods.

I dig around in my pocket, but any change I have is in my knapsack. I reach into my money belt and pull out a five-dollar bill, handing it to the woman. She turns and gives it to a girl of about ten, saying something in Spanish while she blocks my entry with her arm. The girl runs out of the station and out of sight.

"Change?" I say. "Is she going to get change?"

"Si."

"I need to go to the baño now. Can I get my change after that?"

The woman tilts her head and stares at me.

"I. Need. To. Go." I squeeze my legs together and point at my crotch. Then I point into the restroom.

"Si," she says, dropping her arm to her side.

The only stall in the restroom is occupied. I wait impatiently for a few minutes, my bowels rumbling in anticipation. Finally, a familiar man comes out of the stall and I rush in to take his place. *Where have I seen him?* I set the water bottles on the floor and wipe off the seat, dumping my paper in the toilet before I remember the obligatory shit bin that I am supposed to use. I line the seat with paper and sit down.

I release an explosive combination of beer, rice, beans and eggs. When I am finished, I look at the overflowing trash bin and, remembering my messy experience at the hostel in Quito, I drop my soiled paper into the toilet—fully conscious that I am breaking the rules. I flush the toilet and begin to pull up my pants. The bowl fills too quickly, a messy concoction of water, excrement and tissue rising toward its brim. I reach down to rescue the water bottles and step back just as the bowl overflows. The surging mess retracts gradually, but the damage is already done. Karma. The toes of both my shoes are splattered with my own feces.

Pulling a large wad of toilet paper off the roll, I feel a pang of guilt for the person who will have to clean up after me. I exit the stall and walk to the sink, thankful there is no lineup for the toilet I just flooded. I dampen the paper to wipe down my shoes, then scrub my hands with a bar of soap that teeters on the edge of the sink.

Another man enters the restroom and heads toward the vacant stall. I look down and make a hasty exit. The old woman grabs my shirt gently and points at the young girl, who has returned. "Cambio," the woman says.

I pause while the girl reaches into her pocket and sifts through an assortment of lint, pebbles, coins and plastic charms. I'm running out of time before the bus leaves—and embarrassed about the mess I have left behind. One coin at a time, the girl counts out four dollars and ninety cents in Spanish. I see a bit of Isaac in her—a pride in her thoroughness—and I relax a little, trying to show appreciation for her effort.

"Gracias," I say when the girl hands me the last of the coins with a huge smile. Then it hits me. *The guy I saw when I entered the restroom—he's the same guy I saw at the bar last night.* I'm quite certain I hear a bus start, and I feel a surge of panic—the time ... the man from the bar ... Jen asking me to buy her water ... offering to watch my knapsack—the details are merging together, and I don't like what they imply. I pocket the change, run to the door of the terminal, and burst out into the parking lot. A huge sigh escapes me when I see the bus, sitting where I left it with its side door still open. My run slows and I settle into a fast walk, taking in every detail of the bus—the multi-colored exterior and the Latin music that pours out of it along with a potpourri of familiar scents. The green curtains scrunched at the edges of each window. *Green* curtains. Our bus has *orange* curtains. A numbness falls over me. My arms fall to my side. I scan the parking lot for Jen, then turn back toward the bus. I manage to focus, this time on the sign beside the door. It reads *Manta*. The bus with green curtains is going to Manta—the largest city in this region—the city we drove through about an hour ago.

Thirty-One

"Shit! Fuck … Fuck!" I look around and see dozens of people staring at me. I am standing in the middle of the parking lot at the Jipijapa terminal, swearing loudly at a bus, waving two water bottles like machetes.

I could not have been in the terminal for more than fifteen minutes. *Where is the fucking bus?* Questions flood my head. *Is Jen still on it? How could she allow it to leave without me? Is the man I saw in Canoa with Jen?* I want to believe that I am being irrational, but no matter how I look at my situation my mind is awash with suspicion.

I look around the parking lot again, and then walk briskly through the terminal. I see no sign of Jen or the mystery man. Trying to abort my mind from connecting dots, I walk up to the terminal's lone ticket counter and ask the agent, in the calmest voice I can manage, if she can reach the bus driver. Her English is almost non-existent, every word accompanied by a vigorous head shake. My face tingles as sweat pokes at my skin from the inside, trying to escape the turbulence within. My eyes survey the terminal for someone—anyone—who might speak the only language I know. I am clinging to the faint glimmer of hope that somebody in this Goddamned terminal can help me find the bus that is carrying my knapsack—and Jen.

I walk up to a young man and ask him if he speaks English. He looks at me blankly. I ask the same question of an elderly woman, a middle-aged man and a teenage girl—all of whom respond with grunts or shrugs. Finally, I yell out to nobody in particular, "Does anyone here speak English?"

A young woman on her way out of the terminal stops and turns to face me. "I speak a little."

"I was on a bus to Puerto Lopez," I say, relieved. "It left while I was using the toilet."

"Another bus will go to Puerto Lopez today," she says.

"But the one I was on … I need to reach the driver. Can you help me do that?"

"No," she says. "Is it gone already?"

"Yes. It's gone. Could you help me talk to the woman at the ticket counter?"

The young woman pleads my case to the ticket agent. Following their brief discussion, the young woman says, "She does not know how to reach the driver. Many buses stop here, and many drivers. I am sorry."

"Thank you," I say, my shoulders slumping. "Do you know … is there a phone or an Internet café nearby?"

"The nearest Internet is quite far. A thirty minute walk." She points toward the terminal door and adds, "There is a payphone outside."

The woman helps me buy a ticket for the next bus to Puerto Lopez—three hours from now—and then asks if she can do anything else.

"No," I say. "You have done plenty. Thank you."

She smiles and says, "You are welcome." Then she walks out of the door, and I stand in the middle of the crowded terminal. A cloud of inter-mingled conversations—all in Spanish—floods my ears, and I notice that the terminal smells musty, oily, humid. Alien.

Sensing that if I continue to stand here I will slowly go mad, I retrieve ten dollars from my money belt and clumsily buy a phone card from a kiosk in the terminal. I walk out to the phone and attempt to call Emily.

After three rings I reach Emily's voice mail. I put on a cheerful voice and wish her well, saying that I will call again when I have a chance. I do not mention my plight.

I dial Annie next, reaching her voice mail as well. I leave a rambling message and ask her to send me an e-mail to confirm that she is doing okay.

Desperate to talk to someone familiar, I dial a third number and let it ring until my friend's voice answers, "The Jakery."

I let out a breath of relief. "Jake, it's me, Oliver."

"Oliver? Where the hell are you?"

"Jipijapa. It's near the coast in Ecuador."

"Hippy what? What are you doing on the coast? I thought you were in the mountains."

"That's the million dollar question. I'm supposed to be on my way to Puerto Lopez."

"I have no idea where Yappy Hippy or Porto Lopez are, but it's good to hear from you. Why the surprise call?"

"I need you to find a hotel for me."

"Seems like an odd way to find a hotel in Ecuador. What's going on?"

"Um … "

"Let me guess"—Jake answers his own question—"it's a long story. Are you alright?"

"In general, yes. Right now, not so much. I missed a bus and lost a girl."

"Lost a girl? Now I'm really curious."

I explain my predicament—sticking to the facts, saying nothing of my misgivings about Jen and the mystery man—and I ask Jake to read out a list of hotels in Puerto Lopez, hoping that one of them will trigger a memory of the name that Nadine wrote down in my journal. To my dismay, none of the names sound familiar.

"Do you need me to call some of these for you?" Jake asks.

"It seems a bit ridiculous."

"Your whole trip seems a bit ridiculous. Look, I'll just call a few of these places and see if I can find your reservation. If I find it, do you want me to pass on a message to this friend of yours ... Jen?"

It strikes me that I do not have the slightest clue what I would say to Jen right now. "You know," I say, "I think I need to sit on this for a bit. Will you be there for a while?"

"At least a couple of hours," Jake replies. "And you can reach me on my cell after that."

"Thanks. I'll see if I can make sense of this. If I'm still stuck, I might call you back in a while."

"You sure?"

"Yeah."

"Okay, but ... what are you trying to make sense of?"

"I'm not sure."

"Sounds like we have a lot to catch up on when you get back."

"Yeah."

"You okay?" Jake asks.

"Yeah," I reply, unwilling to admit that I am not.

I say goodbye to Jake and hang up the phone. Instantly, I feel the madness begin to creep back into the void that stillness creates. I enter the doors near the phone and wander aimlessly around the terminal. The shock of my abandonment gives way to a deeper, more concerning emotion. Fear. It has ridden with me for much of this journey, in the backseat of my mind. Now, alone and adrift, it is impossible to ignore the feeling that coming to Ecuador might have been a grave mistake.

Long minutes turn to three long hours, an agonizing wait as I hover around the terminal, unable to walk beyond the invisible perimeter of its parking lot. Doubts nag at me—both personal and practical—but I know there is no turning back. Something is driving me to continue—a newfound strength that I cannot quite identify. A strength fed by discomfort and uncertainty, and by the memory of my dad voicing his favorite cliché: "What doesn't kill you makes you stronger."

By the time the next bus to Puerto Lopez arrives, I am oddly at ease. None of my questions have been answered. I have simply, for reasons unclear, submitted to the invisible force that pushes me forward.

~ ~ ~

"You lost him?" Harold asks, not even trying to mask his frustration.

"Yeah."

"How?"

Nathan Jacques breathes heavily, looking out across the Pacific Ocean. There are worse places to be stuck, he thinks—at least the dick isn't here in person to chastise me. "He didn't make the bus," he says.

"And you let it go without him?" Harold snaps.

"I lost track of him for a moment. I assumed he was back."

"Nice work, Sherlock."

Nathan fumes in silence.

"How about Ms. Morris?" Harold asks, the edge fading from his voice.

"She's here."

"How's your cover?"

"I can't tell. Maybe …"

"Maybe what?"

Nathan recalls the looks he shared with Oliver Bruce, both in Canoa and in the Jipijapa bus terminal. "He might have seen me. I'm not sure."

"Great," Harold sighs into the phone.

"What should I do?" Nathan asks.

"Pull back," Harold says. "It's still early."

"Where to?" Nathan says.

"Get back to Quito. We'll monitor the situation from there."

Thirty-Two

Settling into the only vacant seat on a bus similar to the one that deserted me three hours ago, I am hit with a wave of nausea triggered by a sweet and sour odor—a tangy brew of dirt, sweat and vinegar that wafts from the window seat beside me. Turning to the source of this unbearable smell, I am met by the mostly toothless grin of a middle-aged Indigenous mother, traditionally dressed in a round hat, dark skirt and multi-colored shawl—garments that I imagine to be held together by grime. She openly nurses an infant who is maybe one year old.

As we make our way out of Jipijapa, I attempt to look beyond the woman and child toward the lush forest that passes by, but I find myself watching her shower the infant with affection—a display of love that reduces her scent from intolerable to inconvenient. The road carves a winding path toward the ocean, and people disembark at various towns along the way. At every stop I consider moving to one of the vacated seats. Each time I choose to stay put.

South of Puerto Cayo, the bus lurches left and right, up and down, through a series of hills that occasionally overlook the ocean. At times it seems the driver is pressing simultaneously on the brake and the accelerator. I chew at my nails while we pass through Machalilla National Park, which ends a few miles north of Puerto Lopez. I am thinking of Jen—of her intelligent eyes and her quick wit, of her lithe body and the scent of her breath. An image laced with jealousy and paranoia cuts through my mind—of Jen and the mystery man spending the night together in Puerto Lopez, pulling the strings of a marionette named Oliver Bruce.

The bus pulls to a stop on the dirt shoulder at the north edge of Puerto Lopez. It is late afternoon—leaving me little time to find my hotel before dark. I stand up and prepare for a mad scramble through town. The hotel that Nadine booked for me is somewhere on the ocean—I know that much. Surely it can't be too hard to find.

~ ~ ~

"You're here," I say, stepping onto the shoulder of the highway. My voice quavers with a combination of anger and relief—relief that is both fleeting and incomplete. I need answers. A credible story for why I spent the afternoon alone in Jipijapa while Jen carried on along the path to Puerto Lopez.

"I am *so* sorry." Jen scrunches her face apologetically.

"So ... what the hell?"

"I fell asleep. Passed out would be a more accurate description."

"Huh," I grunt.

"I woke up when we were driving into Puerto Cayo. I almost got off there."

"How did you—" I take in a deep breath while I form my words and suppress what I really want to say—*how the hell did you fall asleep in the few minutes I was gone, after you promised to watch my seat and my stuff?* "How did you know I'd be on this bus?" I ask in the calmest voice I can muster.

Jen's face brightens as she returns to her usual bubbly tone, a little too quickly for my liking. "I decided to go ahead, rather than miss you on the flip-flop. I checked in at the hotel and then looked up numbers for the bus station in Jipijapa. Eventually, I tracked down the woman who sold you a ticket."

I stare at Jen, still tense. "Where's my knapsack?"

"I took it to the hotel. It made a good pillow on the bus—thanks." Jen turns to walk west toward the ocean and tips her head for me to follow. I stand for a moment, then fall into line beside her, my shoes kicking up dust from the dirt road. Puerto Lopez reminds me of Canoa—plain and dusty, yet charming in a way that only a plain, dusty seaside town could be.

About halfway down the road, I speak again. "I saw a guy in Jipijapa. I also saw him at the bar in Canoa last night." I glance at Jen to gauge her reaction.

"And?"

"I wondered if you knew him."

"Why would I know him?" She seems genuinely perplexed.

"I don't know. Did you see anyone today that you recognized?"

"No."

"My spidey senses were tingling when I saw him last night, and then I saw him in the terminal today. Then, poof, you were both gone, along with the bus ... and my pack ..."

Jen stops and glares at me. "And you think—"

"I don't know what to think. But I was sure glad to see you on the side of the road back there."

We commence walking, and I sense that Jen is brooding over my implication of mistrust. After a block or so, I try to lighten the mood. "How did your hangover do on those hills?"

A look of disgust crosses Jen's face. I am not sure if it is directed at me or the bus ride. "I felt every turn," she says. "But the ocean air is doing wonders."

"How's the hotel?"

"Horrible. We're in an ugly little hut in the garden, and the restaurant has a hideous veranda that overlooks the beach."

"Sounds awful. How many beds does it have?"

"One."

I look at Jen curiously. Her mouth widens into a smirk, but her eyes are still angry. "Just kidding. It has two twins. You won't have to worry about me spooning you in my sleep."

"I was more concerned about me spooning you," I tease, "and you calling the Ecuadorian police to arrest me. If you spooned me and I called the cops, they'd call me lucky and tell me to go back to bed. It's a complete double standard."

Jen smiles again, but I can see that she is still perturbed.

"Look, I didn't mean to imply anything back there. I'm just—"

"It's okay. I guess … I thought we were more comfortable with each other." We reach the edge of the beach—similarly spectacular to the one in Canoa—and turn toward a series of small buildings that face the ocean.

"I'm not really comfortable with anything down here. Especially you."

"What do you mean?" Her voice stiffens.

I stop and face Jen. Her soft skin radiates against a post-card-worthy backdrop—whitecaps reflecting the falling sun through a grove of palm trees at the edge of the beach. "Here's the picture," I say. "A run-of-the-mill, middle-aged guy travels to a tiny village in Ecuador to deliver a message. Along the way he meets a gorgeous woman who's going to the same place ..." Jen waits while I search for words. "They hang out like old friends, dancing, swimming—skinny-dipping, for Christ's sake. Then he sees this mystery man—twice—and he finds himself deserted in Jipijapa ... no sign of the man or the woman ... and he remembers hearing that she works for an oil company with ties to the village—"

"Is that what this is about? My work term with Crescoil?"

"You tell me. I hear they've been poking around in the village and that you—"

"I worked there for one summer. I was a peon. What do you think? That I'm part of Crescoil's global reconnaissance team?" Jen turns and enters a hotel property, bypassing the main lodge and walking briskly toward a thatch-roof hut, separated from neighboring units by dense, meticulously pruned vegetation. She doesn't hold the door, allowing it to slam closed behind her. I open it and peer inside. Other than the separation of twin beds, the hut is a honeymooner's dream—with lush duvets, a glass table, a vase holding fresh-cut flowers, and housecoats with matching slippers.

"This place really is awful," I say, trying to lighten the mood.

Jen sits down on one of the beds and scowls at me.

"Look, I'm not trying to be an asshole, okay? It's just ... I have no idea what I'm doing here, and I'm a little bit para-noid. More than a little after what happened today. And, if you want the truth ... if you weren't so Goddamned beauti-ful, I wouldn't find it so hard to believe that you want to hang out with me."

Jen refuses to acknowledge my compliment.

"Is your stomach up for dinner?" I ask. "My treat. Consider it an apology for accusing you of espionage."

Jen glares at me for a long while, but I see the hint of a smile form at the edges of her mouth. "Okay," she says at last. "Only because you're paying. Asshole."

~ ~ ~

The sun drops below the horizon, casting bands of orange and yellow across the sky above the gentle surf of the Pacific. Jen and I sit alone drinking coffee served with crystallized sugar and frothed milk. Her mood has improved throughout our meal, our casual discussion gradually rebuilding the rapport that we were developing prior to Jipijapa.

"You seem lost in thought," Jen says.

"Yeah," I nod.

"What are you thinking about?"

"Eddy—Dr. McKinnon. He's the friend who sent me here—the one who died. He would have liked this coffee."

"How did you know him?"

I look out at the sea, and then turn to face Jen. I want to open up to her, to trust her with everything. My mind tells me I have no grounds for such confidence, but the look in her eyes or the idyllic setting—probably a bit of both—spurs me to let down my guard. "Eddy was my neighbor. I found a letter addressed to him from Daniel Porter." Jen shifts in her seat at the mention of Daniel, and I continue. "I found it by accident—in a bunch of recycling. It was talking about some invention that could change the world. So naturally I was curious. It took me a while to figure out that it was addressed to Eddy. Anyway, I went on this grand vacation with my family, and in the middle of my holiday—in Chattanooga, Tennessee—I learned that Eddy was dying of cancer. So I flew back home to see him."

Jen leans forward and puts her chin on her hand.

"His dying wish ... was for me to come here and deliver a message to the Pachamama."

"Why?" Jen asks. "What's so important about this message?"

"I don't know for sure, but ... it's possible that Carmen knows something about Daniel's invention."

"Wow." Jen sits back in her chair and stares at me. "So you really are on some kind of secret mission."

"Yeah, of sorts."

"Can you tell me what the message is?"

I shake my head. "I swore to secrecy on that. I don't know what it means anyway." I wonder if I have said too much. "So how about you? Why are you here? I want to hear the *long* story." I tread carefully. "And tell me, what was it like working for Crescoil? What's a day in the life of a summer student at an oil company?"

Jen tells me that she worked at Crescoil for four months last year—with a vague reference to a boyfriend whose dad is a senior executive there. That was where she first heard of Pueblo del Sol. "Actually," she says, "I'm a little embarrassed about that part of my resume."

"Why's that?"

"I guess it depends on whose company I'm in. It was a primo job at the university, but down here amongst all these idealists and hippies ... it doesn't feel like something to be proud of."

"What about your boyfriend?"

"*Ex*-boyfriend," Jen says.

"Okay, who is this *ex*-boyfriend whose dad works for Crescoil?"

Jen takes a moment to reply. "His name is Austin McAlister. The Third—which should've been my first clue that he was high on himself. He was the valedictorian of our high school, one of those guys who oozes charisma." Jen looks out to the ocean and continues. "When he's with you, he makes you feel like you're the most important person in the world."

"Sounds like a good trait."

"I guess. But it's a thin veneer." Jen looks at me again. "He's brilliant—top of his class at Harvard Law School—but he's really shallow at the same time. He comes from money. I'm sure he'll make a killing ... but I think he's losing himself along the way."

"So what happened between you two?"

"The guy's a walking penis," Jen says. "I'm pretty sure he screwed half the women at Harvard. Fortunately for me, his roommate—Cal, who's been my friend since first grade—came home one night and found Austin's bare ass on their couch, screwing the brains out of one of their professors."

"Ouch," I cringe. "So Cal told you?"

Jen takes a sip of coffee and chews on her reply. "Yes ... sort of. I called Austin the next day. He was out at the time, and Cal suggested that maybe I didn't really want to know where he was. So I cornered Austin the next time he came to see me, and he admitted that he was falling for his prof. Said he was just waiting to tell me in person. I got the rest of the story from Cal, along with Austin's nickname in their dorm—Thumper. It had to do with his headboard banging against the wall ... which wouldn't be so incriminating if I had ever visited Harvard. Guess I know why he always came to see me."

I wince at Jen. "I'm sorry to hear that."

"I'm just glad I found out before he proposed to me. Cal said he was planning to."

"Would you have married him?"

Jen nods. "In a heartbeat."

"So that's why you came to Ecuador?"

"Yeah. I figured maybe I could run away from my pain."

"Has it worked?"

"Somewhat." When she looks at me, the suspicion I felt this afternoon melts away.

"I'm sorry about earlier."

"Me too."

I look out at the last vestiges of daylight resting on the surface of the sea. "I've had my doubts about this whole crazy adventure, but right now I have to admit that I'm really glad I came."

"Me too," Jen says again. Then we fall into a contented silence but for the recurring whoosh of the ocean upon the shore. Finally she speaks again. "You said earlier that Daniel's letter was in some recycling. How did you accidentally find it?"

It is a simple question, but I feel a long answer forming. I am not sure I want to share intimate details with Jen or how deep I want to go—but I begin to speak anyway.

"When I was younger I wanted to be a travel journalist. The next thing I knew, I was approaching forty … married with two kids, running a restaurant, just trying to pay the bills. This past winter—in January—it had been raining for two weeks straight, and I was being a miserable bastard to my whole family. My wife and I had a fight one night, and she told me that I was sucking the joy out of everyone around me. So I sat up late and wrote a letter, then rewrote it a couple of times. By the time I was done, I realized that I desperately wanted to get away, to see the world, to find some sort of purpose that was more rewarding than running a café. So my free-writing exercise had turned into a kind of manifesto. I put it away for a while. Then one day in May I pulled it out and figured there was no way I was going to act on it. I thought of destroying it, but I couldn't because it was the most honest piece of writing I'd ever done. So I dropped it in the recycling bin—sort of like a message in a bottle. And then driving home I was daydreaming—and bang—I wind up sandwiched between a bus and a dump truck."

"Oh my God! Seriously?"

"Yeah. I totaled an SUV and walked away without a scratch. In fact, right after the accident I walked back to the recycling bin to get my manifesto. That's when I found the letter." I laugh out loud as my mind replays the picture of meeting Arlo, and how I wondered which one of us was crazier.

Jen is laughing too. "Wow," she says. "You throw away your dream of adventure … and dumping it leads you here to Puerto Lopez. That's quite the irony."

"Yeah, I guess it is."

After dinner we walk to the other end of town and back, past a number of bars and food kiosks, all lined with patio lights, each playing its own music. We park ourselves on the sand in front of the hotel and sit close, looking at the stars as we continue to talk. After an hour or more, we return to our room and take turns getting ready for bed.

I shut off the bedside lamp and drop the mosquito net around my bed, looking over at Jen, barely discernible in the dim glow of a distant light.

"That was a really great evening," I say. "One of the best I've had."

"I concur," Jen says. "Thank you."

"Well, buenas noches, I guess."

"Buenas noches."

"Still think I'm an asshole?" I ask.

"No," she says. "Still mad at me for deserting you in Jipi-japa?"

"No," I reply, smiling to myself in the darkness.

I lie awake, and I can tell that Jen does too. We say nothing, but the energy in the room is undeniable. I am both comforted and tortured by the three feet and two mosquito nets that lie between us. I try to suppress the tension that radiates between my heart and my groin, but focusing on it only increases my yearning.

After a painfully long time—half an hour, an hour … I'm not really sure—Jen's breathing drifts into the gentle rhythm of sleep. My mind has shifted from mistrust to faith—in Jen's character and in my being here. I liken this instant to the moments before I fell asleep on my flight to Quito—allowing myself to trust for reasons that I cannot comprehend.

Thirty-Three

Our taxi is some sort of motorized three-wheel rickshaw, a bright yellow contraption with a partially enclosed cart for us and a shielded seating area for the driver. Over the high-pitched buzz of the motor, Jen and I marvel at the wide range of plants, birds and farm animals that adorn the hilly terrain as we are carried inland, skirting along the south edge of Machalilla National Park. We pass through a few tiny villages during the half hour ride to Rio Blanco, from where we will need to walk another half hour or so to our destination, Naturaleza Jardín.

Riding past a handful of houses along one stretch of the road, I notice that the architecture of each house is unique from the others. One appears to be made of bamboo and straw, while the one beside it is made of wood, sitting on stilts about ten feet off the ground. A third house, made of brick, makes me chuckle.

"What's so funny?" Jen asks.

"I'm expecting the big bad wolf to come along." I point to the three consecutive structures.

Jen laughs. "You're right. It's like we're heading into some fairytale wonderland."

"I hope we're not Hansel and Gretel," I add. "If Carmen's house is made of candy, I'm running like hell."

A few minutes later we pull to a stop in Rio Blanco—a dozen or so buildings surrounded by patches of farmland at the edge of a hill. Jen gets out to discuss a plan with the driver, then relays it to me. "He'll be back at eleven thirty. That should give us at least two hours up there, and have us back in Canoa by suppertime."

I pay the driver and we walk toward a wide pathway that cuts through a mixture of shrubs and shorter trees. Just outside the village, we encounter a young Indigenous man wearing a bright yellow soccer jersey, jeans and rubber boots. He is holding the reins of a donkey pulling a large log; behind them walks a baby donkey.

"That is so adorable," Jen says, and then she turns to speak to the man in Spanish. After a brief conversation she tells me, "We're on the right track. He works for the farm, and he says Carmen is there."

"That's a relief," I reply.

Civilization greets us next in the form of three huge mutts, light brown beasts with flat faces and stocky bodies, barking ferociously as they run down the path toward us. Jen grabs hold of my arm, and we brace as one against our assailants. The dogs calm down as they approach us, their short tails wagging as they compete for our affection. We follow the dogs up the path and find ourselves on the edge of an expansive pasture, separated by a barbed-wire fence from half a dozen cattle, two horses and a llama.

About fifty yards down the path sits a two-story farmhouse beside a semi-enclosed barn. I see about ten people scattered throughout a series of crops and gardens, interspersed with banana trees, in an area that stretches a few hundred yards past the buildings.

As we approach the farmhouse, a tall, lean black man emerges from a group of people who are weeding a garden. He walks toward us with a wide smile.

"Hola. Bienvenidos. Yo soy Domingo."

I reach out my hand to shake Domingo's. "Hola. Mucho gusto. Yo soy Oliver, and ..." I try to recall the word for friend, but I cannot.

Jen steps forward and adds, "Yo soy Jen. Mucho Gusto."

"Nice to meet you too," Domingo says, clearly enunciating every syllable. He greets Jen with a kiss on her cheek. "What bring you to Naturaleza Jardin?"

"We're looking for the Pachamama," I reply. "Carmen."

Domingo smiles. "I let Mother Carmen know you are here." He disappears into the cob building—a classic mix of natural off-white paint and dark wood moldings—and returns a short while later. He leads Jen and me through a small entrance hall into a sitting room decorated with a variety of paintings, complementing a rustic set of bamboo furniture. An elderly woman rises from one of two loveseats to receive us.

"Carmen," says Domingo, turning to face us. "This is Jen and Oliver. English is their language."

"Pleased to meet you," I say, leaning forward to accept her hand and one light kiss on the cheek. Her wrinkled skin and thin gray hair are juxtaposed against the fluidity of her gestures. She has the grace of an aging dancer, further emphasized by a deep blue dress that flows with her movements.

"Hello," Jen says, receiving a similar greeting from Carmen.

"To what do I owe the pleasure of this visit?" Carmen's eyes are clear, her voice lucid.

"We're working at Pueblo del Sol," I say. "I was sent here with a message for you. I'd like to speak in private, if you don't mind."

Carmen looks toward Domingo, who nods his head and leaves the room. Then she turns to Jen, who is staring at me, looking a little hurt.

"I might be able to help." Jen's voice is assertive. Conflicted feelings dance a slow waltz in my mind. *This is my mission—alone.* I know I should excuse Jen and speak with Carmen on my own, but after the closeness we shared last night I feel inclined to let Jen in, to pull her closer and invite her deeper into my world.

After an uncomfortably long pause, I nod at Jen before speaking to Carmen. "I'm here to deliver a message ... from Dr. Robert McKinnon. It was a request from Daniel Porter."

Carmen sits back down on her loveseat and gestures for Jen and me to take seats.

"I was expecting Dr. McKinnon over a year ago," she says. "I had come to believe that message was lost."

"It was ... until recently. Eddy—Dr. McKinnon—only received it a few weeks ago, when he was dying of cancer. He asked me to come here, and then he died while I was on my way to Ecuador."

"I'm sorry to hear that," Carmen says. "The project that began with such hope has also brought great sadness."

"Yes, it has."

"Do you have the key?" Carmen asks.

I look at Jen, and then back to Carmen. Both of them sit patiently, waiting for me to speak. The key is only one piece of the puzzle. I wonder if Carmen knows about the sponge. The mental image of the magical object in my money belt gives me comfort. Finally I say the word. "Einsteinium."

Carmen smiles. "Very well. I shall tell you what I know. It is your choice whether I tell it to you alone, or share it with your friend."

I don't hesitate this time. "She's a part of it now. Please tell both of us what you know."

"Very well," Carmen says again. "I know a little, but not much. You have to trust that your story will unfold as it is meant to."

I grow impatient with the slow pace of Carmen's words, but I try not to let it show.

"What I can give you," Carmen says, "is another key in exchange for the one you have provided."

"What is it?" I ask, my heartbeat accelerating.

She smiles again, causing my anticipation to swell. Then she says, "Enola Gay."

"Enola Gay," I say.

"As in the OMD song?" Jen asks.

"Yes," Carmen replies, "I read there was a song by that name. Do you know why it was written?"

"It was an anti-war tune. Orchestral Movements in the Dark. About the nuclear bomb they dropped on Hiroshima. One of my classmates wrote an essay about it. Enola Gay was the name of the plane used to drop the bomb."

"That is correct," Carmen says.

"So what is the relevance here?" I ask.

"I don't know."

"I was hoping you would tell me something more concrete. Do you know … what else can you tell me?"

"That you must reach Daniel's brother," Carmen says. "Liam holds the next answer."

"Daniel has a brother?" I ask, surprised.

"Yes," Carmen says. "You need to contact Liam Porter and tell him that I have given you the key. He will tell you what to do with it."

"This rabbit hole keeps getting deeper," I mutter. "I feel like a pawn in somebody else's chess match."

"And what is wrong with a pawn?" Carmen asks. "Pawns are underestimated, often ignored. And yet they may become queens. Oliver, I cannot make you do anything … but surely you have not come all this way for nothing."

I look at Jen and see that she is waiting for me to say something. I think of Eddy—he told me, in so many words, that there was more to this journey than delivering a message. *Breadcrumbs*, he had said. "I guess I was hoping," I begin, "that if I gave you the key, that you'd unlock everything and tell me why I came here."

Carmen shakes her head. "I am only a messenger, and an old one at that. But you, Oliver, you are much more than that."

I consider her words for a long moment. "Where do I find Liam?" I ask.

"He works for the Amazon Liberation Organization. If you contact their head office in New York, they will know how to reach him."

"What does the organization do?"

"That depends on your perspective," Carmen replies. "ALO is a controversial group. You may form your own opinion of their work."

Thirty-Four

Jen is waiting for me in the hallway of our hostel. We walk downstairs and onto the street, where the diminishing light of the afternoon sun accompanies us to a nearby Internet café. Upon our arrival back in Canoa this afternoon, we made plans to meet the rest of the group at a bar on the beach, where we will spend our last night on the coast before heading back to the village tomorrow.

"Thanks for trusting me," Jen says.

"You're all in now," I reply. "I sure hope you're not one of those Bond girls."

"Whatever you say, James."

"I'm just using you for your language skills—and your knowledge of eighties music. I've always been more into the classics."

"*Enola Gay* is a classic."

"If you're twenty-three," I say. "I'm thinking more like the British Invasion."

Jen laughs. "Wow, you *are* old."

We find two computers in the corner of the café. I scan my e-email for anything worth reading, while hoping that Annie has replied to my latest voice mail.

Finding nothing of substance, I switch to a browser and search for *Enola Gay*. I read the Wikipedia page just loud enough for Jen to hear. "On August 6, 1945, the Enola Gay became the first aircraft to drop an atomic bomb as a weapon of war. The bomb, code-named Little Boy, was targeted at the city of Hiroshima, Japan, and caused unprecedented destruction."

Jen sings quietly, "Enola Gay, is mother proud of Little Boy today? Aha the kiss you give, it's never going to fade away."

"That's creepy."

"Yup. So is this." Jen makes room for me to roll my chair over and read her screen. I learn that the pilot who dropped the bomb on Hiroshima, Paul Tibbets, named the plane after his mother, Enola Gay Tibbets. The inspiration for her name was apparently the book *Enola; or Her Fatal Mistake*, written in 1886 by Mary Young Ridenbaugh. The book starts with the poem:

Oh, fatal day – oh, day of sorrow,
It was no trouble she could borrow;
But in the future she could see
The clouds of infelicity.

I lean in to read the rest of the passage on Jen's screen, seeing how eerily relevant the contents of a book, written about a nineteenth-century cyclone, were to the naming of a warplane over half a century later. We continue to read together, making notes in our journals as we communicate in sound bites, engrossed in a topic that is both fascinating and depressing.

Jen sits back and says, "I wonder what any of this has to do with the key."

"Beats me." I move back to my computer and type *Liam Porter Amazon Liberation Organization* into the search window of my browser. I choose the ALO website from the search results, where I read about the organization's mandate to protect the Amazon through research and direct action. Unable to find direct contact info for Liam, I note the e-mail and phone number for their head office in New York. Then I go back to the search results and click on a news report from May which references Liam Porter. I skim the page for a moment before stopping cold—"Oh my God. Look at this."

Jen scans my screen and lets out an audible gasp. I read the passage again.

Charges have been dropped against American environmental activist Liam Porter for his purported role in a plot to bomb the Brazilian headquarters of Crescoil Energy Corporation. An official statement from the Brazilian Federal Police indicates that charges against three other suspects, including a member of the Amazon Liberation Organization which employs Porter, have been upheld, and further charges may be forthcoming.

Thirty-Five

It strikes me that gardening, like parenting, is about embracing dirt. I began my work this afternoon by delicately spreading the soft earth and planting peanuts one-by-one in a chasm I had neatly created, trying not to get too messy in the process. After Andrew flung a handful of mud at me, determined to loosen up my pedantic style, I began to immerse myself more fully in the task at hand. Now thoroughly coated in mud, I place my last row of peanuts without regard for hygiene or vanity.

"Ye still plannin' to huff down The Hill after thes?" Andrew asks.

"Unless you've fixed the communication tower today."

"Ahm not much use to ye there. Ah daen't think I can patch that lightning rod with a strap ah duct tape."

It's been three days since I received the new key from Carmen. Three days attempting to track down Liam Porter's phone number through a convoluted series of calls to the Amazon Liberation Organization. Yesterday I walked down The Hill twice, where I paid a king's ransom to use the only cell phone in the vicinity with a worthwhile connection—to no avail. This morning I finally reached Liam's voice mail, but my latest attempt to call Annie led to a *mailbox full* message. Trudging back up The Hill, I struggled to keep my mind from exploring outlandish possibilities.

After my gardening session with Andrew, I return to the bunkhouse and climb into a frigid shower, dancing in and out of the icy stream, peeling off layers of mud. Almost clean, I wrap myself in a towel and step outside. Jen emerges from a restroom stall and joins me on the wide stairway leading to our rooms.

"Hi," she says, placing her hand on my arm as we walk up the stairs. "Nice goose bumps."

"I'm blaming Andrew for those."

"Oh? Was he in the shower with you?"

"Worse. The garden."

At the top of the stairs, Jen speaks softly. "Will you come to my room after supper? I have a movie you might want to see."

"A movie?"

"Yeah. It's a documentary. Nadine found it with some of Daniel's stuff when she was cleaning out a closet this morning. Oh, and I learned something else today. I'll explain later."

My skin tingles. I am excited about the prospect of a new lead, and about sharing space with Jen in the privacy of her room. We have hardly been alone since our night in Puerto Lopez, and I am aching for her company.

~ ~ ~

Jen is bursting to tell me something, so she quickly closes the door behind me. "Daniel was a nuclear physicist before he got into solar power. I asked Kath about the video. She said he worked at a power plant in Brazil before he came here."

"Really?" I pick up a DVD that it is still wrapped in cellophane. *Splitting Atoms for Power and Profit*. "So this just magically appeared today?"

"Nadine found it with a pile of Daniel's stuff. I saw it on the table when I was grabbing a cup of tea, so I claimed first dibs on watching it."

"I thought everything was sent to his wife. Did you see what else she found?"

"There was a coffee mug that said *World's Best Dad*. That made me sad. Other than that, just a Tom Clancy novel and a pair of sunglasses."

We arrange ourselves side-by-side across Jen's bed, our backs against the wall, and play the movie on her laptop computer, which rests on a pile of books between our feet. The film presents a history of nuclear energy in Latin America, its tone shifting from hope to consternation as it documents an industry that currently provides a small percentage of energy to South and Central America. It seems that support for nuclear energy as a panacea for the continent's growing energy requirements has been increasing in recent years, and it is clear that the filmmaker does not share this burgeoning optimism.

The movie begins to drag when the director parades out a chain of researchers, mostly speaking in scientific language that I cannot understand. I am distracted sitting so close to Jen. Distracted by her t-shirt and baby blue shorts, and by the exposed skin that takes me back to my earliest memory of sexual tension—to watching movies with a group of middle school friends in Natalie Shorthouse's basement, frozen in fear of my own desire as I sidled up against my hostess's bare legs. My eyes drift to Jen's thighs, and I fantasize about placing a hand on one of them. My elbow recoils from the thought.

Suddenly he is there, talking directly to us, pulling me into the screen.

"I hold some hope for fusion," Daniel says, "because it presents greater power with minimal risk of a radioactive disaster. If we could unlock a safe way to generate the heat for a fusion reaction, it would be a world-changer. But right now the only way we can do that is through a fission trigger, which, as we know, can have catastrophic consequences."

"When I saw you speak at the Alternative Energies Symposium in Buenos Aires two years ago," the interviewer says, "you stated that the work you were undertaking in solar energy was also dependent on nuclear fission, albeit in its early stages of exploration. What can you tell us about this connection between solar energy and nuclear fission?"

Daniel takes his time to respond. "I believe what I said was that my research into nuclear power paved the way for my transition to solar energy."

"Not exactly," says the interviewer, looking at his notes. "To quote you directly, what you stated was, 'Under exceptional but repeatable conditions, it is possible for nuclear fission to generate a synthetic element which may bond in adequate quantity, and with sufficient stability, to manifest as a tangible component for scientific exploitation.' And you went on to say, 'this metallic element may be capable of absorbing and retaining a level of energy which would far exceed the absorptive qualities of any other known material.'"

"The sponge," I say.

"What?" Jen asks.

"Nothing," I mutter, focusing on the screen.

Daniel looks stunned, but he gathers himself to respond. "That speech was made a long time ago. A great deal has happened since then. Perhaps I was overzealous in communicating my early optimism."

"So is it safe to say that your research did not yield the results you were hoping for?"

"I'm afraid I'm not able to speak further about my work at the reactor." Daniel speaks with an air of formality. "As scientists we investigate a wide range of potential advancements. A few lead to success, but most are false starts."

The interviewer continues to press. "So was this a success, or a false start?"

Daniel's reply is curt. "As I said, I can't speak further about my work at the reactor."

~ ~ ~

Jen closes the lid of her laptop and turns toward me. "What did you say about a sponge?"

"It's just … something Eddy mentioned." I'd hoped she had not heard me, but I must have struck a chord.

"The sponge," Jen says, growing animated while lowering her voice to little more than a whisper. "It's a critical component. It's almost mythical around here. That's the first evidence I've heard that such a thing might actually exist."

"Really?"

"What do you know about it?"

"Not much. I'm a restaurant owner, not a scientist." I hope my deflection sounds plausible.

"This might explain Daniel's first key," Jen says. "I looked into it on the weekend. Einsteinium is a by-product of nuclear fission, but it only lasts for an instant before it mutates into something else."

I shrug, not ready to admit that I have also read everything I could find about Einsteinium.

Jen looks into my eyes and grins. "Daniel discovered a new element—*an energy sponge*—and then he tried to deny it. I'll bet that's what we're looking for."

I smile ingenuously, not sure how to respond.

Jen places a hand on my knee, and her expression shifts ever so slightly—she is suddenly more woman than girl. I am transfixed by the intensity of her eyes and the placement of her hand. I look down at my feet, hoping that she will say something. She slowly removes her hand from my leg, her fingers brushing my thigh as they retreat.

Unable to read the situation—and not wanting to make a fool of myself—I reach my legs over the side of the bed and say, "I'd better go."

"Okay," Jen says, and I start toward the door. She begins to speak, and then stops.

"What was that?" I ask, turning back to her.

She shakes her head. "Nothing. I'll see you tomorrow."

It didn't sound like *nothing*, but I don't press. "Okay," I smile. "Goodnight."

I turn back to the door and pause for a moment before opening it. Then I go out into the hallway and close the door, not daring to look back.

Conlan is already asleep when I enter our room. I tiptoe in to get my toiletries, then head downstairs to the bathroom. Unable to get Jen off my mind, I turn on the overhead light that dimly illuminates two shower stalls, then enter one of the stalls and close the door behind me. I am half inclined to walk back upstairs and knock on Jen's door, but I know that the best outcome I could hope for from such a bold move would be rejection. So I unzip my pants and begin to drop them, intent on relieving my passions. Right then, a spider skitters across the floor in front of my feet—a hairy creature larger than a silver dollar. I jump back a foot or so and gasp. Within seconds, my pants are done up and I am standing in front of the sink, staring back at the shower as if the beast I just saw—a young tarantula, perhaps—is going to come out of the stall with a thousand of its closest friends.

After a few moments my pulse slows and I recognize the irrationality of my fear. Occasional shivers still run across the skin on my chest, up into my shoulders. Unwilling to expose my private parts to whatever else might lurk in the shower stalls at night, I brush my teeth and get back to my room as quickly as possible.

I closely inspect my bed with a flashlight before climbing in and making sure the mosquito net is pulled down on all sides. I try not to think about things that slither or crawl. Jen comes to the rescue; more specifically, the image of Jen's naked form jumping into the swimming hole, invoking me to join her, basking in the sunlit pool—and in the discrepancy between her comfort and mine. Between my vivid thoughts and Conlan's unusually loud snoring, I am quite certain that sleep will not find me soon.

Thirty-Six

"This'll heal what ails ye." Andrew is distributing beer from his own secret stash. Almost everyone who works or volunteers at Pueblo del Sol is gathered in the small open air common room that occupies one corner of the bunkhouse, all huddled inside of an invisible wall that separates us from the afternoon downpour that ended our football match. I missed my first opportunity, or obligation, to join the weekly tradition of *Wednesday Wellieball*—soccer in rubber boots—thanks to a relentless deluge last Wednesday. There was no consideration of skipping this week's game due to a moderate rain, but once it reached monsoon proportions we all headed for drier ground.

After lugging heavy lumber out of the woods for much of the day, running around on a muddy field in loose boots was probably the last thing I needed. Now that I am seated, I am not sure I will ever stand up again. I can already feel my quadriceps starting to burn, and I have blisters on both feet. Andrew's appearance with a beer is nothing short of angelic.

"You weren't half bad out there," Conlan says from the seat beside me.

"I'm not sure what game you were watching," I reply. "I hardly touched the ball."

"Maybe not, but you covered a lot of field."

I look down at the mud caked all over my pants. "I'd say the field did a better job of covering me."

As Conlan dissects the football match—a game that was as humorous as it was competitive—I notice Jen talking to Marco, a resident employee at Pueblo del Sol who was clearly the best player on the pitch today. A strapping young man from a local village, Marco has an infectious smile and an insatiable work ethic. I have only attempted to speak with him once, during a tree-planting session earlier this week, but the language gap between us felt unbridgeable. He and Jen seem to have hit it off, their conversation laced with laughter and frequent touch—arms around shoulders, hands on legs. I try to tell myself this is just the way Latin American people communicate, but I am not sure I believe that's all it is. My attention wanders back and forth between watching Jen's touchy-feely conversation with Marco and acknowledging Conlan's moving lips—providing just enough feedback to keep him talking while I stew about Jen. I have no right to be jealous, but it is a difficult emotion to fend off.

"What do you think?" Conlan asks, and I realize I have no idea what he is asking me about.

"Sorry, I ..." My eyes lock on Conlan as I search for something intelligent to say. "I lost you there for a second."

"I was asking you about Cotipaxi. Do you want to go there this weekend?"

Somehow I missed the shift from soccer to travel. Now I scramble to catch up on the thread. "Where is Cotipaxi?"

"It's south of Quito. We can go into the city on Friday and take an excursion from there."

"And it's ... sorry ... what's there?" I struggle to stay focused on this discussion—to keep my eyes from wandering back to Jen and Marco.

"It's an active volcano," Conlan says. "One of the world's highest. We want to check it out, and look into climbing it."

"Who's we?" I ask.

"Me and Kath ... and I think Jen's going."

"That's it?"

"Yeah, as far as I know."

"Sure," I say. "I'd like that."

~ ~ ~

We wind along the edge of a steep cliff above a vast and picturesque valley, light mist dampening the windshield as the bus to Quito carves its way around corners that seem too narrow for its long chassis. The sun fights its way through distant clouds to cast hazy rays upon the valley floor. A rainbow stretches up from the ground until it is absorbed within the sun's light.

I think of Daniel.

"Hey," I say to Katherine, who is reading beside me while Conlan sits with Jen a few rows back. "Where did Daniel's bus ..."

Katherine looks around to get her bearings, and then speaks, her usually strong accent barely evident. "We just passed it. I didn't realize we'd gone that far already."

"Did any of you visit the site afterwards?"

"Conlan brought me here right after the accident—we borrowed the Land Cruiser. They wouldn't let us get very close. A whole piece of the road had fallen. It took a few weeks to get it open again, and when we came back it was as if nothing had happened. There was a shiny new piece of road where the old one had fallen. We stopped and placed flowers ... but I haven't been back since. I've driven past it, but I never stop."

"I hear you and Daniel were close."

Katherine nods. "Yeah."

"Do you miss him?" It's a stupid question, I know.

"Yeah," she sighs. "I'm not sure why we connected so well. We just did."

"It happens, doesn't it?" I think of Jen and the discomfiting tension between us, and I wonder if she is thinking about me.

~ ~ ~

"Hi Dad!" Isabella's voice reminds me how rarely I have thought of home for the past two weeks, and how quickly I have become engrossed in Ecuadorian life. In an instant, I miss my children dearly.

"Hi Sweetheart. How's Disney World?"

"It's great, but it would be even better if you were here."

"I wish I could be here and there at the same time."

"Do you want to talk to Isaac or Mom?"

"I want to talk to *you*," I say. "I have so much to ask you."

"I'm … in the middle of a movie."

"Okay. Why don't you get me Isaac then?"

"Okay. I miss you."

"I miss you too."

Isaac speaks as if I have gone out to run errands. "Hi Dad. We went swimming today. A girl pooped in the pool, so they had to shut it down."

"Sounds gross."

"Did you notice that pool starts with the word *poo*?"

"Um, no. I hadn't thought of that before."

"Wanna talk to Mom?"

"Sure, buddy, but first … how are—"

"Moooooooooommmmm!"

"—you?" I finish to nobody.

After a long pause I hear Emily's voice. "Hi Oliver. How are you?"

"I'm good. How about you? Sounds like a day in the life there?"

"Yeah."

"I have to say ... if I measured my self-worth by the level of interest my kids show in me, my ego would be the size of a pinhead."

Emily laughs. It is nice to hear her happy. She provides me with a quick overview of their activities, and then I lose her attention as well. "Sorry, but I'd better go before Isaac tears apart the motor home."

"No problem. I'm looking forward to seeing all of you next week."

"Us too. Oh, he's found my chocolate stash ... gotta go."

"Good night, Em."

"Good night. Thanks for calling."

The phone clicks as I begin to say, "I love you."

Half a world away, and my family gives me what? Five minutes? One by one, my emotional dependencies are peeling away as my romantic facades fade into reality. I have lost touch with Annie, leaving me concerned for—and disconnected from—the one person who might understand what drove me to Ecuador. Jen has begun to find her own path at Pueblo del Sol, loosening the bond of shared experience that brought us together during our first week and a half together; I can't tell if she has pushed me away or if I have pushed her, but something changed between us after we watched the movie in her room. And Emily, the one woman who, for a brief period years ago, seemed to accept me for everything that I was, now barely tolerates me. I believe Emily sees me as a convenient obligation—like she has figured out the minimum amount of energy required to keep me around. In fairness, I don't give her much in return.

I can blame it on work or kids or the million little tasks that make up our family life, but I know that Emily's emotions toward me are merely a reflection of the energy that I invest in her.

Reluctant to look deeper into my own shortcomings, I force my mind back to the present. I pick up the phone again and dial Liam Porter's number. I've called it so many times this week, it is probably etched into my brain forever. My imagination wanders as the phone rings.

"Liam Porter." His voice shocks me into reality.

"Um, hi." I pause for a moment to find the words that I rehearsed earlier this week. "This is Oliver Bruce. I've left you a couple of messages."

"Hi Oliver."

"Do you have any idea why I'm calling you?"

"I do now."

"What do you mean?"

"I just got off the phone with Annie. She mentioned you, told me you're walking in my brother's footsteps."

"You spoke to Annie? How is she? I've been trying to reach her." I exhale a breath that I have been holding all week.

"She's fine. She went away for a few days, but she's back home now. Look, I don't know exactly what you're doing in Ecuador—"

"I have the key," I interrupt. "From the Pachamama—Carmen."

Silence.

"I understand you know what I'm to do with it?"

"Annie said that Eddy sent you there."

"Yes," I say.

I hear Liam take in a deep breath and then exhale. "You need to find Daniel's cabin."

"What cabin? Where?"

"In the woods near Pueblo del Sol."

"Do you mean the one Walter and Maria live in?"

"No."

"You know them?"

"Yes, I know Walter well. We've worked together."

"So there's another cabin?"

"Yes."

"Where?"

"I don't know. You'll have to ask Walter—or Alejandro—tell them you've spoken to me. They know where it is. I've never been there. Daniel was going to take me to the cabin when I came to the village last year. I … I didn't get the chance."

I hear myself breathing into the phone. "I'm sorry about your brother."

"Thanks."

"Is there anything else you can tell me?"

"Yes. There's a safe in the floor. The key has something to do with entry to the safe."

"Can you be more specific?"

"No. Daniel said Eddy would understand it. I guess you knew Eddy quite well?"

"I was starting to," I say in little more than a whisper. *So I've been left to unlock the mind of a dead man.* I laugh, though I do not mean to. "I'm sorry. This becomes more ludicrous by the day. I haven't the slightest clue what to do with the key."

Liam's voice indicates that he does not share my sense of humor. "Find the cabin, and maybe it'll make sense."

My voice becomes dead serious, matching Liam's. "Why are you trusting me with this? How do you even know—"

"Annie spoke highly of you."

"Oh. That's—"

"And from what Daniel told me, we could broadcast the location of the safe on CNN. Without the combination, I'd bet the US Military couldn't crack it."

"Your brother sounds like a very bright guy."

It is Liam's turn to laugh. "That's an understatement. It wasn't easy to grow up with Daniel Porter." Then he adds with a thoughtful tone, "But I sure miss living in his shadow."

"I can imagine. Look, I …" A part of me wants to give the key to Liam, to pass the torch and let it go. Another part knows that this is my journey now.

"What is it?" Liam asks.

"It's … nothing. I am wondering one thing though. I read about your organization, and about the charges against you."

"The charges were dropped."

"I know. It's none of my business, but … why were you charged?"

Liam speaks with a reassuring tone. "Don't worry Oliver, I'm a man of peace. Beyond that, I can't say much. My lawyer has asked me to keep my mouth shut until the investigation is complete. I look forward to sharing my side of the story, but for now … I just have to accept the sideways stares and the gossip."

I thank Liam, hang up the phone and turn toward the counter.

He is standing near the exit, about to walk out the door. "Hey!" I yell, but he quickly exits and turns onto the busy sidewalk. I race to the door, open it and step outside. I hear the shop attendant say something about paying for my phone call, but I wave him off. I look up and down the block through a maze of people and cars, hoping to catch a glimpse of the man I saw in Canoa—and again in Jipijapa—but he has vanished once again.

Thirty-Seven

I pay the attendant for my phone calls and step out onto Avenue Juan León Mera. I walk toward the heart of Quito's La Mariscal region, looking all around for the mystery man, half expecting him to creep up on me when I let down my guard. I imagine the cold, hard terror of a gun in my ribs, and my whole upper body tenses. But there is no sign of him. I enter the upscale restaurant where my friends told me to meet them. They are seated beside a window that looks out onto Plaza Foch.

"Manage to reach anyone?" Jen asks as I sit down across from her.

"Yeah." I nod and try to convey with my eyes that I will explain later. "How about you guys? What did you find out about Cotipaxi?"

"That we don't have enough warm clothes," Conlan says, referring to the altitude—over 19,000 feet—of the volcano we were hoping to climb tomorrow. "The forecast is colder than usual."

"And usual isn't exactly tropical," Katherine adds from the seat beside me. "We might try again next weekend."

I look at a menu, forcing myself to focus long enough to order seafood curry. I glance across at Jen; her eyes are serious, questioning. She can tell that something is not right. I smile reassuringly, but this only causes her to raise her eyebrows. Unspoken questions hang in the air between us.

Conlan and Katherine are chatting about what they will do tomorrow now that their plans to scale Cotipaxi have fallen through. I use their conversation as a cover, whispering to Jen, "I reached Liam ... and I saw that guy again."

Her eyes widen. "You'll have to fill me in."

The waiter brings an appetizer of ceviche—raw fish cured in citrus juice and aji peppers—along with a small loaf of warm bread with butter. A silence falls over the table as everyone savors the taste of something more interesting than rice and lentils.

I am the first to speak. "I have to go back to the village tomorrow."

"Oh?" Katherine says. "Why's that?"

"I have to talk to Alejandro or Walter."

"And this is urgent?"

"It's just ... I only have a week left here, and I have some questions."

Conlan takes a sip of water to help him swallow a large mouthful of food. Then he says, "They're both gone."

"Gone?" I ask. "What do you mean? Where to?"

"The coast. Carmen's farm ... they're with a documentary crew, filming in the national park down there."

"Machalilla?" I ask.

"Yeah," Conlan says. "What do you need to ask them?"

"It has to do with the message I delivered to Carmen. When will they be back?"

Conlan shrugs. "I don't know. At least a few days. Alejandro mentioned it in passing this morning."

"Shit," I say.

"What's the big deal?" Katherine asks.

I look down at my food and ponder my options. *Fuck it. I have to find that cabin.* I lift my head and say, "There's another cabin in the woods above the village. Not Walter's place—another one. Have you heard of it?"

"Not me," Conlan says. Katherine looks away and fidgets with her fork.

"Kath?" I prod. "It's Daniel's cabin. It's really important that I find it."

Katherine stops moving and stares down for a while, nobody daring to speak while she processes my question. Then she nods. "I went there. Twice."

"Really?" Conlan says. "Daniel had a cabin?"

"Yeah."

"Can you tell me where it is?" I ask.

She shakes her head. "I don't know. Crazy as that sounds, he never told me exactly where we were. It's in a clearing somewhere up the mountain. Daniel borrowed the Land Cruiser and drove us up an obscure path from the bottom of The Hill."

"How far of a drive is it?"

"I don't know. Twenty minutes, maybe half an hour."

"Could you lead me there?" I ask.

"No," she says. "I tried to find it a few times. The last time I got lost, and scared myself out of trying again."

"What were you looking for?" I ask. "Some sort of closure?"

"No," Katherine says. "Exactly the opposite. I was looking for Daniel."

Silence falls over the table. Fragments of questions trip over my tongue before I ask the simplest question I can think of. "What does the cabin look like?"

"It's small and square. A wooden cottage with a front porch. It has a metal roof and a woodstove." Katherine's words drip with nostalgia. "It's such an incredible place—rustic, but modern. He even added a micro-hydro dam—and solar panels, of course."

"Did you see anything else *around* the cabin?" Jen asks.

"Yes," I echo. "Any landmarks that might help me find it?"

A melancholy film forms over Katherine's eyes. She fights to hold back tears as her smile twists to a frown. We all wait for her to find the words. "There was a pond a little way upstream from his place—with the most amazing water slide."

Conlan sits up straight and stops chewing.

"A water slide?" I say. "Can you describe it?"

"Yes. The water had carved into the rocks and had so flawlessly eroded them that it made a perfect slide, around a bend and into a shallow pool. We spent hours th—"

"The path to nowhere," Conlan blurts.

I look across at Jen, who is surveying all of us, trying to make sense of everything she has just heard. I grin at her and say, "I have to get back to the village tomorrow." I hesitate for a moment, and then—before I can stop myself—I add, "Care to join me for a hike?"

~ ~ ~

"Mission accomplished," Nathan says.

"Good." Coming from Harold McIntyre, that is almost a compliment.

"What's next?"

"Stay put," Harold says. "We'll go in when we need to. For now, we might need you to do some follow-up on the ALO file."

Harold hangs up the phone and considers his next move—and what to tell the boss. His friend and mentor, the strongest person he knows—the woman who now seems too human, too fragile, for the system she walked into. Perhaps it would be best to keep this to himself.

Thirty-Eight

On our own again the next morning, Jen and I fall back into a comfortable dialogue. Our discussion is casual and humorous and philosophical. We skirt around matters of the heart, as if neither of us wishes to dredge up the feelings and wants that accompanied us to Ecuador—or those that have grown since we met. I would like to know everything I don't already know about Jen—about her highest highs, her lowest lows and everything in between—but today, unlike our conversation in Puerto Lopez last weekend, we stick to heady topics. We speak of electric cars and politics and fair trade certification; of mathematics and language and the price of bananas. We speak of everything, it seems, except ourselves.

Before I know it we are walking into the village. I have been so wrapped up in our discussion that I hardly noticed the scenery along the way. Even The Hill barely registered with my conscious mind. My legs simply carried me while Jen's intellect kept me occupied.

Though I am disappointed to confirm what Conlan told me—that Alejandro and Walter left for the coast to work on a documentary about Ecuador's national parks, a trip that could keep them away from the village for a week or more—I am relieved to find that only Nadine and a couple of Pueblo del Sol's female employees stuck around for the weekend. No sign of Marco means no need to share Jen's company.

Our trek up the mountain feels much farther on foot than it did on horseback—its relentless incline gradually deadening the discussion that carried Jen and me for most of the day. Jen's knapsack—containing a few snacks, two large bottles of water and an extra t-shirt for each of us—becomes sweatier as we go, pressing the dampness of my own shirt against my back each time I take my turn carrying it.

It is mid-afternoon when I realize that we have walked some distance beyond the trailhead we are looking for. Backtracking down the hill, it takes two failed attempts before I recognize what feels like a familiar trail. Within a few minutes we emerge into the clearing that hosts Walter and Maria's home. Although Nadine told us that Maria was going to stay with family in Santo Domingo, I knock on the cabin door anyway.

Nobody answers, so Jen and I walk across the clearing and enter the trail toward the water slide. When we reach the top of the slide, Jen tugs at my elbow. "This is amazing!"

"Quite spectacular, isn't it?"

"Last one in is a speckled toad," Jen says. Then she is on the slide. "Whoo!" she yells as she skims down the rock face on her butt. I follow her onto the slide and splash down in the pool, landing next to her. We are both laughing, drenched from head to toe.

"Uh-oh," I say, taking the knapsack off my back. It has been fully submerged and is half full of water. "So much for changing into our *dry* clothes. Sorry."

"Oops," she says, struggling to suppress another chuckle. "But it *was* fun!"

"Indeed."

We climb out of the pond and pick up the trail I asked Alejandro about last time I was here. The water sloshes in our gumboots as we trudge down the path leading away from the pond at the bottom of the slide. After about ten minutes I see a small channel that has been diverted from the stream, leading to a turbine about two feet long and one foot in diameter. A tube emerges from the turbine, leading downward along the bank of the stream.

"Well, I'll be damned," I utter, as much to myself as to Jen. "This must be Daniel's micro-hydro plant."

"Cool," Jen says. "I wish I had one of these at home. That and my own personal stream."

"Let's keep going. We must be close."

We follow the tube downstream. The forest becomes dense around us, but remains passable. Birds serenade us from all corners of the canopy that shelters us from the scorching sun. The cloud forest betrays its name today, and I am thankful for the cool dampness of my clothing.

"This trail seems maintained, doesn't it?" I ask.

"Yeah, it does," Jen agrees. "Around here a trail like this would be overgrown if you left it for a week."

Sunlight increases as we near an opening in the trees. We both pick up our pace, walking as fast as we can while avoiding the roots and vines that complicate our path. All at once we are there, standing on the edge of a circular clearing, beholding a cottage that looks similar to Walter's—a small, wooden structure with a chimney and a metal roof equipped with six solar panels. I see an electrical box that is fed by the tube we followed from the hydro plant.

A twinge of fear enters my mind. *Does anyone else know that we're here?* My breaths shorten into shallow bursts, and my pulse quickens. "What now?" I ask in a hushed tone.

"I don't know," Jen says. I sense that my fear has rubbed off on her.

I look at the lush forest around us and listen to the jungle—to the same sounds that only two weeks ago were completely alien. Now they bring me peace. I turn and smile at Jen, then walk toward the cabin, vigilant but calm. Jen follows, and we walk up two steps to the covered porch. I knock on the door and say, "Hello. Is anyone home?"

I knock again and repeat my query more loudly than the first time. Jen echoes my words in Spanish. Receiving no answer, we walk a full circle around the cabin. Every window is equipped with metal bars, and curtains block us from seeing inside. When we return to the front door—a beast made of hardwood and iron—we find it locked with an industrial-grade deadbolt.

"Well that kind of spoils the party," Jen says.

"Yeah. I—it seems obvious now, that it would be locked. I guess I only thought as far as finding the cabin ... like that would be the hard part."

Jen sits on a small boulder beside the door, and I slump down against the wall beside her. "Maybe Kath can help us when she gets back from Quito," Jen says.

"I hope so," I agree.

~ ~ ~

I now know what it feels like to be a minority, maybe even an outcast. Jen and Nadine occasionally translate something for me, but for the most part I listen to their dialogue with half a dozen of the locals—none of whom speak English—as I might listen to a group of animals. I know they are communicating, but I have no idea what they are saying.

"Jen," I say during a brief break in her conversation with Marco, who returned to the village while she and I were hiking up the mountain.

"What's up?"

"I'm wondering if one of them might know how to get into the cabin."

"Can't hurt to ask," she says.

"Could you find out? Without saying anything, you know … just tell them Carmen suggested we go there."

"Okay," Jen says. Then she gains the attention of everyone and asks a question in Spanish.

I am uncomfortable opening up about Daniel's cabin. I take solace in the recollection of Liam's message that the safe—not the cabin—was Daniel's real secret. I trust that Jen knows better than to mention the safe, which I told her about on our way back from Quito.

After an animated dialogue, Jen turns toward me. "Nobody here is aware of a cabin other than Walter and Maria's. Or at least they won't admit it."

"That seems strange," I say. "You'd think—"

"Yeah," she cuts me off. "But even Conlan didn't know about it."

"Yeah, I guess."

The others resume a loud discussion and Jen turns back to her conversation with Marco. I feel another stab of jealousy when she moves onto the bench beside him. They sit close, touching frequently as they speak.

"I'm heading to bed," I say to the group as I stand up and step away from the fire.

"So soon?" Jen asks, looking up at me.

"Yeah. These old bones need more rest than you young party animals."

Jen's eyes carry their usual warmth as she holds my gaze. I can't decide if she is trying to tell me something, or if I am reading too much into her expression.

"Well, goodnight," Jen says, turning back to Marco again.

I walk back to my room. Sitting on my bed in the dim glow of a candle that I pilfered from Conlan's side of the room, I allow myself to explore my feelings toward Jen. Am I merely the safe older man that eased her journey into a new adventure? Or are there deeper emotions at play for Jen, as there are for me? I recall the friendly embrace that Annie and I shared in Seattle a few weeks ago, after she told me about her new flame, and I wonder if I am living a prolonged re-enactment of that night. My chest tightens at the thought of Jen shutting me down the way Annie did—a gentle but crushing blow. Why am I even pondering possibilities—at best unrealistic and at worst dangerous—that could only lead to heartache?

I briefly think of going downstairs to use the toilet and brush my teeth. Feeling no urgent need to do either, I strip down to my underwear, blow out the candle and lie down on my bed. For the first time since I arrived at the village, an all-too-familiar malaise courses through me.

~ ~ ~

Sunday passes at half speed, a dreary, wet excuse for a day. I spend most of it in my room, reading and thinking and feeling sorry for myself, eating meager bits of packaged food that I accumulated during weekend trips to Canoa and Quito—along with a pack of Conlan's Oreos. I am both relieved to be alone and deeply lonely. On the few occasions when I venture out of the room to fill my water bottle or use the toilet, I see no sign of my colleagues. I try not to think about where Jen might be, or why she has not dropped by.

By the time the sun emerges, it is well on its way to setting over the mountain that looms above the village. I think of Daniel's cabin soaking up the day's only serving of sunshine, and I hope that Conlan or Katherine will be able to help me get into it.

Hungry for a meal, I head to the dining area. Nadine and Jen are already seated across from Marco and two other male employees. I bristle, then recompose and interrupt their friendly banter. "Let me guess ... rice and lentils?"

"Yes," Nadine replies, "but we found some mustard in the fridge, so we are calling this *fancy arroz y lenteja*."

"Where were you today?" Jen asks.

"In my room, reading. How about you?"

"I spent the whole day in the lab. Figured I might as well immerse myself in work on a day like this."

I nod stoically, masking the questions and feelings that lurk beneath the surface, then turn my focus toward my plate of fancy rice and lentils. The dialogue around the table swings comfortably between English and Spanish, but I play no part in it. I feel the dull ache of envy at the realization that I am going home next week, while everyone else at the table will remain in the village.

I am wiping the sauce from my plate with a piece of bread when I hear Conlan's voice. "Hey roomie. Were you successful?" He sits down in the seat beside me.

"Yes and no," I reply. I search for Katherine and direct my attention to her as she sits down across from Conlan. "We found it ... but we couldn't get in. I was hoping you might know, Kath. Do you have a key, or know where I might find one?"

Katherine shakes her head. "No, sorry, I don't."

"Do you remember Daniel using a key to unlock the door?" I ask.

"Yes. He was very diligent about locking it whenever we left, and he kept the key with him."

I look over at Jen and Nadine, who are now listening as well. "We're talking about the cabin," I say to Nadine. "The one Jen mentioned last night. Daniel didn't … do you know if he left any keys behind?"

Nadine thinks for a bit and then says, "No. Whatever the authorities did not take, we sent to Daniel's wife."

"What about with the stuff you found last week?"

"No, mon ami. No keys." Her soft accent lets me down gently.

I speak with a measured tone. "I'm tempted to walk down The Hill to call Annie, but even if she has a key, the chance of getting it here this week is slim."

"This *year*, you mean?" Conlan laughs. "You could probably fly back to the US and pick it up yourself faster than the mail service will get it here."

"Don't give me any ideas," I reply.

"So what are you going to do?" Jen asks.

I stare at the table while I assess my options. "I guess I have to find Alejandro."

Part 3 – Evolución

Thirty-Nine

I toss a spare set of clothes in my knapsack—plus an extra set of underwear and socks for good measure—and tiptoe down the stairs of the volunteer residence under the first rays of daylight. It feels strange to walk down The Hill on my own. My isolation in Jipijapa was good practice for traveling alone, but I long for company. I am more than a bit uneasy about navigating the Ecuadorian bus system, despite a lengthy coaching session from Conlan and a clear list of connections to Puerto Lopez.

During the first leg of my trip, from Tandapi to Santo Domingo, I am wary of anything or anyone that seems out of place. My mind eases slightly when I locate my second bus, and by the time I reach Pedernales, where I have at least an hour until my next connection, I am brave enough to walk almost a block from the bus terminal to order food at a small sit-down restaurant. My server is friendly and courteous, and we attempt to cross a wide language barrier while I down a plate of corn made in every possible way— boiled, fried, mashed and dried. It is not the pork that I thought I had ordered, but it is edible and at times delicious.

I make my last connection without incident. I do not dare to disembark during a brief stop in Jipijapa, but I allow myself to doze off sometime before reaching the coast. When I come to, the bus is passing through Machalilla National Park, just north of my final stop.

Another tinge of loneliness tugs at me when I get off the bus at Puerto Lopez and walk to the hotel. The German lady who owns the resort welcomes me warmly. "Back so soon?" she asks. "Where is your girlfriend?"

"She's just a friend who's a girl," I reply. "She had to work this week."

"Well, you looked good together." While she fills out paperwork for my stay, the woman adds, "She likes you very much."

"You think?" I glance at my bare left hand and recall that my wedding ring is nestled against the sponge in my money belt.

"Own a hotel for fifteen years," she says, "you learn to read people. You like her too."

I blush, embarrassed by her observation.

I drop my pack in the room and go to the same beachside table I shared with Jen last weekend. The sunset is as beautiful as the one we watched together, but my mood is more subdued. I drink a glass of wine and practice a bit of Spanish with another friendly waiter, then walk down to the beach for a few minutes before retreating to my room for the night. The sounds outside of my hut, so peaceful in Jen's company, are more pronounced tonight.

The alarm clock beside my bed rings while it is still dark, echoing the alarm inside my head. Sometime during an erratic sleep, I drew a jagged line between Liam telling me that he and Walter worked together, Liam's alleged connections to a bombing in Brazil, Walter's novel about fighting fire with fire, and Daniel.

I get up and prepare for the day. Within an hour, I am tracing the same route toward Carmen's farm that Jen and I took last week. When the motorized tricycle stops at Rio Blanco, I communicate with its driver in a mixture of English and Spanish until I am almost confident that he will pick me up at noon.

The walk on my own to Naturaleza Jardín is nerve-wracking—every sense on high alert, each unusual sight or sound causing me to freeze momentarily. When the farm's three affectionate mutts run down the path, I greet them with enthusiasm, happy for their company. As the dogs lead me toward the house, I notice that nobody is working in the fields.

"Welcome, my friend." I hear Carmen's voice before I see her standing in the doorway.

"Hello," I say. "I'm glad to find you here."

"And I am glad to see you. Glad and surprised."

"I had no idea I'd be coming back here. I'm looking for Alejandro and Walter."

"I am sorry, Oliver. They left this morning, before dawn. They are on their way to Cuenca to work on a documentary film."

I feel my arms drop to my side in futility. "Cuenca? Where's that?"

"It is southeast of Guayaquil."

"How far is that from here?"

"Guayaquil is about three hours by car. Cuenca is another three hours beyond that."

My lungs deflate, along with my spirit. "Do you know if they have a phone?"

"I do not," Carmen says. "I am not one for using technology." Then she turns and walks into the house, adding, "Come in and join me for breakfast. I will help you as I can."

I join Carmen at a dining table where a woman of about thirty serves me a plate of scrambled eggs and toast, along with a glass of naranjilla juice—a tangy orange-like drink.

"Helen," Carmen says to the woman, "Oliver is working at the village." Then she says to me, "Helen is my granddaughter. She came here to help with the documentary."

"Oh?" I ask, still frustrated about missing Alejandro and Walter. "Do you know how I could reach the film crew?"

Helen sits down across from me. "I know where they are staying in Cuenca. They are with a director named Matt Max. They have finished at Machalilla. Tomorrow they will film at El Cajas near Cuenca, and then they are going to Podocarpus, which is not far from there."

"Why do you need to reach them?" Carmen asks. "Does this have to do with the keys?"

"Yes," I say through a mouthful of toast.

"Did you speak to Liam?"

"Yes." I finish my bite and add, "He told me about a cabin." I look toward Helen, unsure of how much to say in her presence.

"It is okay," Carmen says. "Helen works with Liam and Walter. She is aware of Daniel's cabin, as am I."

"Really? Are you also aware …" I stop, uneasy about sharing what Liam told me.

"Please, feel free to speak openly here," Carmen says. "You are among friends."

I pause for a few seconds and then say, "I'm looking for a key—an actual key for the door—to get into the cabin."

"Then you are looking for the right people," Carmen says.

"You don't—"

"No," she says. "I do not have a key to the cabin. Not many at the village even know about the cabin … perhaps only Alejandro and Walter."

"That's what I guessed." I take a sip of juice, and then I look to Helen and ask, "Did you know Daniel?"

"Yes, I knew him well."

"What did you know about his work?"

"Only that it was very important."

"What can you tell me about him?"

Helen takes a moment to gather her thoughts, and then speaks with authority. "When Daniel first arrived in Ecuador, he was an arrogant scientist. But he died a humble man. Ecuador changed him—the jungle, the people, the way of life here. I think he came here like a missionary, planning to teach us how to live. But he became a student of the Earth." Helen smiles at her grandmother and adds, "And of the Pachamama."

"What about Liam?" I ask. "Were they close?"

"Yes, they were. They led very different lives, but they had a lot in common."

"I read that Liam faced charges."

Helen nods. "Yes, this is a dark time for our organization."

"You also work for—"

"For the ALO, yes."

"Why was Liam charged? And why were the charges dropped?"

Helen takes time to form her words. "Liam found out about a bomb plot which involved people from our organization. He went there to stop them."

"And he did?"

"Yes."

"So he … you don't think he had anything to do with it?"

"No," Helen says without hesitation.

"What about Walter? The novel he's writing has a similar theme …"

"You need not worry about Walter or Liam," Carmen says. "They will be on the right side of history. Now tell me, Oliver … what is it that you are not telling us?"

The compassion in Carmen's voice causes me to open up. I tell her and Helen about the mystery man, about Andrew's suspicion regarding Crescoil and Jen's past connection to the world's largest oil company, and about the rumors of

Daniel perhaps evading death. I tell them about everything, it seems, except the sponge in my money belt.

Carmen waits for me to finish talking, then reaches over and places a hand on my arm. "You say that Daniel was seen two weeks after the accident?"

"That's what—"

"In Guayaquil?"

"Yes. Why?"

It is Helen who replies. "Liam was in Quito to deal with the authorities, after Daniel's accident. Liam and his wife went to the Galapagos to get away from things for a while."

"And so …?"

"All flights to the Galapagos go through Guayaquil," Helen says. "Liam and Daniel—they could have been twins."

Forty

Rolling hills give way to the urban center known as Guayaquil. Slums blend into suburbs, funneling the bus into the heart of a modern port city that is home to nearly four million people. On the surface, Guayaquil seems more contemporary than Quito; it lacks the Colonial Spanish architecture of the capital city, thanks to a devastating fire in 1896.

Kevin, the Peace Corps volunteer from San Francisco who occupies the window seat beside me, is taking a short break from his duties as an environmental educator in

Esmeraldas—a coastal city north of Canoa—to visit the Galapagos Islands.

"Have you seen much of Ecuador?" I ask.

"A fair bit," he replies. "I've been within fifty miles of the Columbian border, hiked Cotopaxi, and I spent a week in the Amazon—in Yasuni."

"Yasuni?" I say. "That's where my cousin's son is going. Sounds like a political hotbed."

"Yeah, it's a lightning rod," he says. "They estimate there's almost a billion barrels of crude oil under the park."

"Josh said something about that. What were you doing there?"

"I wanted to see it before it gets trashed. Now that the ITT Initiative is history—"

"What's that?"

"The ITT? Well, in a nutshell … the Ecuadorian government tried to get other nations to donate billions of dollars to keep the oil in the ground—the UN was going to make sure the funds were put to good use."

"But it failed?"

"Yeah. It was doomed from the start, in my opinion. So now it's business as usual."

"Sounds like extortion."

"Maybe," Kevin says with a hint of aggravation. "Or an innovative global partnership. I mean, we could all spare a cappuccino or two to save the Amazon rainforest."

"Fair enough," I agree. "It's the 'pay us or the rainforest gets it' part that bothers me."

"Gotta fight fire with fire. That's how big oil plays."

"That's the second time I've heard that recently. So I take it you're not a big fan of Crescoil?"

"You don't work for them, do you?"

I laugh. "No, I own a restaurant near Seattle. This is Rainforest 101 for me. Speaking of which—have you ever heard of the Amazon Liberation Organization?"

"The ALO?" Kevin replies. "Yeah—they've been in the news a lot lately."

"What have you heard about them?"

"Just that they're mixed up in some crazy shit. I like what they stand for, but anyone who calls themselves a Liberation Organization scares the crap out of me."

~ ~ ~

During my stopover at the Guayaquil bus station, I phone the hostel in Cuenca and confirm that Matthew Maxwell is staying there, but he has not yet arrived. I book myself a private room and hang up the phone, then dial Annie's number. I finally heard from her via e-mail last night—a simple apology for not being in touch and a request to call her when I have the chance.

"Hello," she answers.

"Annie. I finally reached you."

"Oliver! Where are you?"

"I'm in Guayaquil. It's good to hear your voice."

"I'm sorry for going black on you," she says. "My bad."

"It's alright. I'm glad you're okay. You were away?"

"Yes, Martin took us to his cabin on Mount Baker."

"Is everything okay? You asked me to call. I wondered … have you seen him again? The guy you thought might be … you know, following you?"

"No …" Annie hangs on the word just a little too long.

"But …?"

"I still feel like I'm being watched."

"Huh," I say. "So do I."

"Really? Why?"

"I saw a guy ... three times, in three different places."

"Daniel felt like he was being followed too."

I look around, conscious again of the anxiety that has been riding with me, rearing its head from time to time. Seeing no sign of anyone suspicious, I turn back to the conversation. "Hey, I spoke to Daniel's brother."

"Liam? That's right—he said you were trying to reach him."

"Yes. Thanks for the reference. I think you're the only reason he finally answered my call."

"Why did you need to reach Liam?"

"It's hard to explain," I say. "Eddy sent me on a bit of a goose chase. I didn't even know Daniel had a brother. I seem to learn something new every day."

Annie opens up about Daniel and Liam, and I let her talk. She tells me that the Porter brothers grew up in upstate New York, their mother a lonely housewife and their father a Professor of Philosophy who ultimately chose work—and a curvy young graduate student—over family. Choices that Annie feels shaped the lives of his sons immeasurably. I think of Katherine, and of my knowledge that Daniel walked in his own father's footsteps.

Although her stories bring me no closer to getting into Daniel's cabin, it feels good to hear Annie's voice. I don't want to let go, and I sense that she is not ready to hang up either. But I want to check e-mail before my bus leaves, so I promise to keep in touch and reluctantly place the receiver in its cradle. Then I duck into a tiny shop with two Internet stations, log in and read a brief update from Emily saying that she is taking the kids to Kennedy Space Center.

I am about to close my inbox when a message appears from Molly, entitled *Eddy's trailer*. I open it and read:

Hi Oliver,

Arlo came in this afternoon and told me someone looted Eddy's trailer. He couldn't tell if anything was missing, but they left it in a mess. As far as Arlo knows, Eddy's trailer was the only one hit. Someone probably knows he died recently and saw it as an opportunity, but of course Arlo thinks it's some big conspiracy and he wanted you to know about it. Anyway, everything else is fine here. We are all looking forward to hearing about your trip. AND SEEING PHOTOS!!! Hope the snakes haven't eaten you yet.

Love Molly

Forty-One

The full moon offers a glimpse of tall, fern-like trees and exotic broad-leafed plants jutting through an eerie evening fog. When the clouds part to show that we are perched on a precipice above a deep valley filled with rounded peaks, I feel like I am witnessing my life from above, looking down on the smallness of my existence with a newfound sense of purpose.

My thoughts drift to Eddy's trailer and the way it was trashed. I think of the mystery man I have seen, and of Annie's concern that she is being followed. I do not believe these are unrelated coincidences. I wonder again about Jen, and the trust I have placed in her; I wonder if she misses me, as I do her. I think of my family—of Emily, Izzy and Isaac on their grand Florida adventure—and I feel suddenly incomplete. I look up toward the moon—the same moon that we all share—and I think of the strange interconnected-ness between all of the people who weave in and out of my thoughts. Between everyone I have met and those who have yet to cross my path.

My eyes come back into focus as we cut higher into the mountains, passing rivers and waterfalls before reaching the plateau that hosts Parque Nacional Cajas. Here the moonlight casts a mystical glow over a mostly barren landscape dotted with small lakes and the occasional grove of coniferous forest. I am thankful for the clear sky. Before long we are on the outskirts of tonight's destination, Cuenca. Though any sign of human settlement provides a stark contrast to the natural landscape I have witnessed for the past three hours, this urban center of less than four-hundred thousand people feels tiny compared to Guayaquil.

The Cuenca bus station is still lively at ten PM. I hail a taxi and settle into the backseat. The talkative cab driver tells me in broken English that Cuenca is the most beautiful city in South America. He might be right. A series of streetlamps show off the region's grandeur—quaint Spanish buildings aligned behind neatly tiled sidewalks throughout a grid of well-maintained cobblestone roads. The streets are quiet and most of the shops boarded up, save for a few restaurants and bars hosting a modest bustle of those seeking late-night activity.

I pay the driver, walk to the door of the hostel and press the buzzer. A large, Arabian-looking man with a full black beard appears.

"Oliver?" he asks.

"Yes."

"Goodnight," he says with a smile.

"Hello," I reply.

We walk up a long set of stairs to the front desk. The man hands me a mostly filled-in form and points to where I need to sign, then asks me for my passport and fifteen dollars.

I take a twenty-dollar bill out of my money belt and hand it to the man. "Can you tell me what room Matthew Maxwell is in?"

"Matthew," he smiles. "Matt Max."

"Yes," I say. "What room is he in?"

"You are in room four," he says.

"No, Matthew," I say. "What room is Matthew in?"

"Matthew asleep." The man puts his hands together by his ear and tilts his head in a sleeping symbol.

~ ~ ~

The breakfast area is mostly full when I get there at seven o'clock. I scan the room for signs of Alejandro and Walter, and I try to visualize what a documentary filmmaker might look like. Nobody stands out.

I help myself to toast and coffee, then sit down beside two guys at a large table with two empty chairs. "Buenos diaz. Mind if I join you?"

"Sure," says one of them—a tall, thin man with dark skin and black hair.

"Where are you from?" I ask.

"Canada," replies the other man, a short, stocky fellow with blond hair. He talks with a nervous energy, in contrast to his friend's calm demeanor. "We're near Vancouver. The Sunshine Coast. It's a peninsula, but most people think it's an island, because you can only access it by ferry."

"We have something in common then. I live on an island near Seattle. Hey, I'm looking for a filmmaker who's staying here."

"Matt Max?" the shorter man says. "He's a legend. I met him yesterday. Made my whole trip."

"Ryan here's a filmmaker himself," says the tall guy. "Or a wannabe filmmaker, anyway."

"Oh yeah?" I ask, looking at Ryan.

"Yeah. I'm writing a screenplay about a guy whose body stops aging at twenty-two. His kids pass him, and then his grandkids, and his great-grandkids ... and he winds up dating a bunch of their friends, because everyone he goes out with becomes too old for him."

"It's called *Wishful Thinking*," the taller guy says. "Ryan's dream of staying twenty-two forever."

"Did you pass it by Matt Max?" I ask, slightly amused.

"Yeah," Ryan says. "He didn't seem all that interested."

The tall guy shakes his head and adds, "He's too busy doing unimportant stuff like exposing environmental disasters. For some reason he doesn't have time for narcissistic fiction."

I laugh. "Speaking of Matt Max ... have you seen him this morning?"

"No, they'll be long gone by now," Ryan says. "They were planning to be in El Cajas before sunrise."

"Shit," I say. "Are they coming back here tonight?"

"No. They're moving on to Vilcabamba."

"Where's that?"

"A few hours south of here."

"Oh, man." I bury my face in my hands and shake my head. *Two days of travel and I couldn't bother to get up before sunrise.* Recomposing myself, I look up. "Do you know where they're staying in Vilcabamba?"

"No," tall guy says. "But the whole town is tiny, and it's gringo central. You'll be able to find them there, no problem. Just ask around."

I drop my head and tap my foot against the empty chair beside me. My flight back to Orlando looms large as Daniel's cabin fades into the distance.

After a few minutes of breakfast and small talk with my Canadian hostel mates, I get up and pack my bag. I call Elsa on the hostel phone to let her know my whereabouts and ask her to notify Nadine of my delay—no small ask given the lack of connectivity at the village. As I am about to hang up, it dawns on me to ask, "Hey, do you know how I could reach Alejandro and Walter?"

"No," Elsa says. "They are traveling to the national parks to film a documentary."

"Yeah," I say. "That's why I'm here. Do you know their itinerary?"

"No. Their project has nothing to do with Pueblo del Sol."

"Okay, thanks." I hang up the phone and ask the hostel attendant—a slightly smaller version of the burly man who greeted me last night—to call me a cab to the bus terminal. Less than an hour later, ticket and water bottle in hand, I step up into a motor coach that reads *Loja y Vilcambamba*.

~ ~ ~

"He's tracking just north of the Peruvian border," Nathan says. "Still want me to stay put?"

Harold thinks for a moment, then replies, "Yes. He's not much good to us unless he returns to the village. Just keep me apprised of his whereabouts."

"Will do, sir." Nathan hangs up the phone. He prefers groundwork to this glorified office job. But the boss is the boss, and Nathan knows better than to question authority.

Forty-Two

Vilcabamba rests in a bowl of rounded peaks coated in a velvet layer of grass and shrubs, marbled with the occasional streak of exposed red rock. The hillsides are speckled with adobe-styled buildings that look out over two rivers, the Chamba and the Yambala, which converge in the middle of town to form Rio Vilcabamba.

Perched on the resort's patio, I look out at the valley and sip on a coffee while listening to displaced Americans complain. "You can't buy anything decent here." "Nobody will finance property." "They only accept cash." "You can't even match paint!" "The locals make no attempt to speak English." It strikes me what an entitled culture we have become in the so-called developed world, and I wonder if we are really improving the lives of others by evangelizing our flavor of capitalism throughout the globe. These types of thoughts have visited me with increasing frequency on this journey.

"Are you Oliver?" It takes me a second to find the owner of the voice—a round-faced woman with curly gray hair and rosy cheeks.

"Yes," I reply. "Are you—"

"I'm Martha." She reaches out her hand to shake mine. "My husband and I own the resort. My daughter says you're looking for Matthew Maxwell?"

"Yes," I say. "Is he staying here tonight?"

"Why do you need to know?" she asks. Her manner is kind.

"I'm looking for two of his crew—they work where I'm volunteering. I've been trying to track them down for a few days. Someone at The Village Hostel down the hill said that Matt usually stays here."

"Yes," Martha says. "They're coming here today. We're expecting them before dinner."

Relief washes over me. "You have no idea how happy I am to hear that."

"It must be important," Martha says.

"Maybe," I reply. "I'm not sure yet."

A puzzled look fills Martha's face.

"It's a long story," I say before I can stop myself.

I go back to my room and change into my least filthy clothes, then return to the patio to wait for Matthew. Looking out over the fertile valley below, I realize that I am unlikely to make it back to the village in time to help with the earthly duties that have become my new normal over the course of two weeks. Although my volunteer role was a cover for the real purpose of my trip, I have come to treasure my small contributions—planting trees, hoeing gardens, building trails—toward the important task of maintaining one small piece of cloud forest.

~ ~ ~

Two men climb the stairs to the patio where I sit under the afternoon sun—one carrying a large camera bag and the other a tripod. I waste no time approaching them as they reach the top of the stairs.

"Are either of you Matthew Maxwell?" I ask.

"No," says a very thin guy with a shaved head and a lumberjack beard. He points to the bottom of the long stairway, which another man is just starting to climb. "That's Matt."

"Thanks." I walk down to a landing halfway up the stairs. Matthew is hip and fit, maybe five or ten years younger than me, with a full head of brown hair and a few days' growth on his face.

"Hi," I say, extending my hand and blocking his passage. "My name is Oliver. I work with Alejandro at Pueblo del Sol. I've been trying to reach you guys for a few days."

"We're a long way from Pueblo del Sol," Matthew says, shaking my hand. "Are you a fan or a stalker?"

"I haven't seen your work yet," I reply.

"So, a stalker then," he deadpans. "What can I do for you, Oliver?"

"I need to speak with Alejandro or Walter." I point to a truck parked at the bottom of the stairs. "Are they down there?"

"No. Is everything okay?"

"Yes, it's fine. I just have to get some information from them. Where are they?"

Matt grimaces. "They're with my partner, Brad. We parted ways in Loja a couple of hours ago."

"In Loja?" I ask, recalling the city my bus passed through about an hour north of Vilcabamba. "Are they still there?"

Matthew shakes his head. "Not if their flight's on time. They're flying back to Quito tonight, and to Coca tomorrow morning."

A mixture of frustration and anger festers inside of me. The futility that has been accumulating since I found Daniel's cabin—doors locked and windows barred—burns its way to the surface.

"Of course," I blurt. "Of course they're on their way to Coca. And after that they're probably going to Antarctica, before they head to Mars. You wouldn't happen to have their intergalactic itinerary, would you?" I kick the railing, hard.

Matthew tilts his head and studies my face. "Are you alright, man?"

"No, I'm not alright. I just chased these guys halfway around Ecuador on a bunch of smelly buses, and I finally thought I was going to reach them here. But no, of course that wouldn't happen, because nothing has happened as planned on this whole fucking trip." I realize I am ranting, but the glint in Matthew's eye suggests I can indulge. "I now have three days left to solve some great mystery and save the fucking world. Then I can go back to Orlando and take my family for snow cones at Disney World. If they even have snow cones at Disney World. They'll probably run out of the fucking things just before I get there."

"Tough day?" he says.

"Tough week," I reply, wiping spittle from my mouth with the back of my hand. *Refocus.* "Where's Coca, anyway?"

"At the edge of the Amazon."

"Of course it is. What are they doing there?"

"They're going ahead of us to film in a park there. We're filming in Podocarpus and Cotipaxi, then meeting up with them in Yasuni."

"Yasuni?" I ask, my voice still terse. "All roads point to Yasuni."

"Sadly," Matthew says, "that may soon be true. Do you need me to get a message to Alejandro or Walter?"

I look out at the valley. "Not *to*. I need a message *from* them." Matthew waits patiently as I fret and fume, cursing under my breath. Then I turn to him and say, "Can you reach them?"

"Maybe," he says, "but not easily. They're going into the heart of the jungle tomorrow, and I don't know where they're staying tonight. I can get a message to Brad, but I think your friends are staying with family."

"Do you know where they're going in Yasuni?"

"They're staying at the Pachamama Nature Center, off a tributary of the Napo River."

"Pachamama?" I say. "Of course it's called Pachamama. And how might I get to this Pachamama place? I don't feel like my journey into futility is quite complete."

"Two flights and two canoes," Matthew says matter-of-factly, as if he's suggesting that I catch a cab into town. As if booking two flights and two canoes to a nature center in the Amazon is an everyday occurrence for him. "There's only one travel agent in town," he adds. "She can set you up."

My sneer softens. Pachamama … Yasuni … those names have been calling to me since before I set foot in South America. I feel a blend of dread and exhilaration. I already know that I am going there.

I look at Matthew and allow a smile to form. "Thanks. And sorry for the outburst."

"No problem," he says. "I just wish I'd captured that on film."

~ ~ ~

From the cabina, I stare out at a square of small shops bordering a dirt road. At the center of the square is a park containing two large trees and a handful of benches. I am about to hang up and walk over to one of the benches when I hear Emily's voice on the line.

"Hi Em! I thought I'd missed you again."

"Oliver, how are you? And *where* are you? I'm having a hard time following the bouncing ball."

"Me too. This trip has been … an adventure, to say the least."

"Where are you now?"

"Vilcabamba. It's in the south end of the country. You'd love it here."

"Why are you there?"

"I've been chasing our volunteer coordinator around the country. I'm trying to find a key to get into a cabin. It's way too long of a story to tell you on the phone. Let's just say that this message Eddy sent me with … it's the gift that keeps on giving."

"How are you travelling?"

"By bus, mostly. But I just booked myself a flight—two flights, and two canoes actually—into the Amazon."

"The Amazon?"

"Yeah."

"I can't believe you're going into the Amazon. That's crazy."

"Yeah, it is. Doesn't sound like I'll be roughing it though. They have electricity and running water, and from what I hear their restaurant is first rate. It's called the Pachamama Nature Center—in case I disappear into the jungle."

"Don't even *say* that," Emily exclaims. "You wouldn't keep making me dump these sewer tanks, would you?"

I laugh. "I'm glad to know where my value lies. So how are you guys?"

"We're good. Isaac caught a cold, but it hasn't slowed him down much. I think this trip has been a life-changer for both of them. They miss you tons though."

"I miss them too. Can I talk to them?"

"They're at the playground. Izzy's been a great help, watching Isaac lots so I can get things done. She's grown up a lot these past few weeks."

In the comfort of this conversation, I miss Emily more than I have for a long time. "Give them big hugs for me, will you? And … miss me a little, okay?"

"I will," Emily says. "And … I am … especially in bed."

"Not just at the sewage dump?"

"No."

A passion wells up, carrying with it memories of earlier times with Emily—making love at all hours, in every corner of the apartment we first shared in Seattle. I recall Emily's unsuccessful attempt to get me to skinny dip in a remote corner of Lake Washington, my hesitation the first of many walls that have formed between us over the years. I think of telling Emily about my dip in the pond at Pueblo del Sol, but instead I say, "Em … whatever you're missing … keep thinking about it until I get home, okay?"

We connect in silence—a rare and comfortable stillness for Emily and me, as if the blinds that cut us off from one another have opened, allowing light to flow between us. After a long while I tell Emily that I love her, and for the first time in far too long I feel the truth in those words. She echoes my sentiment and tells me to appreciate every breath of Amazon air—to take it in with all of my senses—before adding, "See you soon, Oliver."

"See you soon," I reply.

I hang up the phone and stand for a moment, allowing my emotions to percolate. There have been times, frequent of late, when I have imagined creating my own separate life. Maybe selling the café and finding a small studio near the Seattle waterfront—a funky spot with a loft where I can host the kids a few days a week, spoiling them with visits to the Experience Music Project, tickets to a Mariners game, or treating them to hot chocolate at Pike Place. Then there are moments like now, when I cannot fathom the appeal of such a lifestyle—that of an urban, middle-aged, part-time father. Moments like now, when I long for my wife and miss my children dearly.

I pay the cabina attendant and step outside. People of all stripes walk, drive and ride along the dirt roads that connect a small web of two- and three-story buildings. A few people—mostly tourists as far as I can tell—congregate around a handful of coffee shops and bars that surround the square. I think of going back to the travel agent to ask her to hail the cab that brought me here, but choose instead to walk the mile or so back to the resort. I feel safe here in the Valley of Longevity, and I enjoy the warmth of the sun on my face and arms.

When I reach the resort, I see Matthew and his crew sitting at a large table with a number of other guests. Still embarrassed about this afternoon, I head for my room.

"Oliver," Matthew hollers, too loudly for me to pretend that I can't hear.

"Hey," I reply, turning as if I am surprised to see them.

"Why don't you join us for dinner?" he asks.

I nod and shake my head at the same time before saying, "Sure. I'll be right back."

I return to my room and wash up, then walk back to the patio and pull a chair up to Matthew's table. I am hardly seated when Martha's daughter places a bottle of beer in front of me.

"Matt said you might need this," she says with a smile.

I am nervous around Matthew—maybe a little star-struck by this celebrity whose work I am not familiar with. A few sips into my beer, the camaraderie and the casual discussion at the table make me feel at home; by the time I finish my salad it seems as if I am in the company of old friends. Jerry, a tall middle-aged man with a thick New York accent, spent the past ten years living in Japan before travelling to Ecuador six months ago for what he thought would be a two-week stay. Phyllis—the feisty chain-smoker whom I guess to be somewhere between fifty and eighty—used the last of her available credit to buy a flight to Quito three years ago, and has yet to notify anyone in the United States of her whereabouts. There are two Johns—one from Toronto and the other from Houston—who have become more than friends during their month-long stay in Vilcabamba. And there is Georgia from Georgia, a plump fifty-something with a constant smile and a girlish giggle, who arrived in Ecuador via Brazil eight months ago after leaving her husband of thirty-one years; she's not sure if he has noticed her missing yet. For all their differences, this cast of loveable expats—some of whom I glowered at earlier today as they complained about Ecuador's inadequacies—all seem to have come here to escape something.

While I savor my main course—a frittata with fresh-cut salsa—Matthew leans over to me and asks, "What led you to Ecuador, Oliver?"

I take another bite of my dinner and ponder his question. I look at the faces around the table, a motley assortment of lonely souls embroiled in a collection of interrelated discussions. "I don't know. I thought I knew, but maybe I didn't. I'm starting to wonder if this whole trip is a snipe hunt."

"What's that?" Matthew asks.

"It's when someone sends you out to hunt for something that doesn't exist."

"Ahh," he says. "Sounds like there's a whole 'nother story there."

"Yeah," I nod. "Maybe I missed the point."

"What point is that?" he asks.

I look around again—at Jerry and Phyllis and John and John and Georgia, at Matt Max and his film crew—and take a large swig of beer before setting the empty bottle firmly on the table. "I don't know," I say. "Maybe just being here. I feel like I've lived more on this trip than I have in the past nineteen years put together."

"Huh. So what happened nineteen years ago?" Matt asks.

I hadn't meant to be so specific. The years form a memory of my mother lying on her back, her light blue bedspread and cream-colored sheet folded down neatly on her chest, head tipped sideways, eyes slightly open. Only the dried sputum on her cheek indicated that any struggle had taken place within her body. The empty highball glass and pill bottle told me all I needed to know. Some small relief came from the medical examiner's report—my mother's death was likely quick, due to both her already weakened condition and the quantity of vodka she had consumed.

"It looks like I've struck a nerve," Matt says.

"Yeah," I reply. "You have. It's a long …" I stop myself from completing the sentence, aborting my standard deflection. "Got all night?" I ask.

Matt hollers over his shoulder to Martha's daughter, "I think we need a couple more beer over here."

Forty-Three

"Hello again." The curly-haired man from New Zealand sits across the aisle from me, yielding the window seat to his partner. I met Jack and Sam, along with two other couples, at the airport counter where we checked in for our expedition to Pachamama Nature Center.

"Hello," I say. "So, what brings you two to the Amazon?"

Sam leans forward and says, "I've joined a protest against oil drilling in Yasuni National Park. I figure I'd better know what I'm talking about."

Jack smiles. "And I'm here because of her. I do like the cause, but I like Sam more."

"Got it. Are you two doing anything with the film crew?"

"What film crew?" Sam asks.

"Matt Max," I say.

"Matt Max is here?" Sam's voice is elevated, emphasizing her accent.

"Not yet, but he's on his way in a couple of days. Part of his crew is already in Yasuni."

"That's awesome," Sam says, and then turns to Jack. "He's the guy who made that film called *The Myth of Clean Coal*."

"That's right," I say, feeling an odd sense of pride at the heartfelt conversation I shared with Matthew in Vilcabamba. "I had dinner with him last night. We stayed up half the night talking. He's a great guy."

"Cool," Jack says with an approving nod.

I stand up to make room for another single traveler to step into the window seat beside me. "Are you heading to Pachamama as well?"

"Yes," he replies.

"Hi. I'm Oliver."

"Richard."

As we prepare for takeoff, I grasp my armrests and distract myself with thoughts of last night. My dialogue with Matt had led to a group therapy session—skeletons emerging like popcorn, knowing nods urging each of us to open up about our darkest moments. By the time I went to my room for what would be a very short night of sleep, I was sad to leave another micro-community—an odd assortment of people brought together by place and circumstance.

When we parted ways, I briefly believed we might make use of the contact information that we all exchanged in a drunken fog. This morning, I recognized last night's discussion for what it was—a fleeting glimpse of humanity in its rawest form, enabled by the anonymity we shared.

Once in the air I turn to Richard. "What brings you here, Richard?"

"Work," he says—another one-word reply—then he picks up a briefcase and pulls out a bunch of papers, turning away as he flips through them.

I run through my itinerary, attempting to create a work-back schedule for the remainder of my trip. It is already Thursday—only three-and-a-half days before I am scheduled to fly back to Orlando. When I reached Elsa from Quito this morning, she sounded doubtful that I could make it back to the village tomorrow—even if I find Alejandro and Walter today, which would be a small miracle in itself.

Unable to formulate a workable plan, I sit back with the booklet I was given at check-in, which describes the history and mandate of the Pachamama Nature Center. Before I am finished reading, we are descending into Coca.

Two men speaking fluent English meet our group of eight at the tiny Coca airport, and usher us onto a bus. The humid air and tropical vegetation remind me of the Ecuadorian coastline, but the city carries a different vibe than its coastal cousins. From what I have gleaned from television and movies, it feels like Coca belongs in the Caribbean.

After a short drive, we are led to a motorized canoe that must be forty feet long. One of the guides, Javier, hands each person a life jacket and a bag lunch as we board. The boat has twelve rows of seats with backs, one on each side of a wide aisle. Fourteen people in total—eight guests and six others, whom I assume to be members of the Quechua tribe that runs the resort—settle into seats and begin to eat lunch as the captain, seated in the front, navigates us onto the Napo River.

"The Napo is the thirteenth largest tributary of the Amazon River," Javier yells over the sound of the motor, referring to the vast body of water that feels more like a long lake than a river. "It will take about two hours to get to our base, where we will transfer into smaller canoes, which we will paddle up to the Pachamama Center. I will provide much more information then. For now, enjoy your ride."

Our ride is not particularly interesting. We pass a few small settlements and a number of other motorized vehicles. Discussion is difficult given our seating arrangement and the motor's noise, so I allow myself to drift off for a while. I awaken to the sound of Javier's voice speaking loudly to Sam, who is seated behind me.

"Yes," he says, "that is one of the drilling sites." I look across the river to see a large yellow flame burning on top of a tower. "It is a big problem," Javier continues, "because bugs flock to the light at night, attracting birds and bats to the area and disrupting the interactions between species."

Moments later I see a flatbed ship carrying a combination of trucks and industrial equipment. "What is that?" I ask, pointing to the ship.

"That is the Napo highway," Javier says. "Carrying equipment to and from the oilfields."

"Aren't there roads leading into the oilfields?" I ask.

"Many of the fields have only localized road systems," he says, "but the number of roads leading into the Amazon is growing quickly. And where there is a road, there is loss of life. There are many reasons for roads out here—oil is only part of the problem."

"What else is there?" I ask.

Javier leans in closer to Sam and me so he doesn't have to yell. "Palm trees, bananas, logging, pastures. People cut down rainforest for many things, and it is irreplaceable."

"Sounds short-sighted," I say.

"It is the human condition," Javier replies. "Even though we know it is not good for us, we do not know how to change."

~ ~ ~

"There are over one hundred thousand species of insects in Yasuni." Javier speaks just above a whisper, interrupting the buzz that accompanies us down a narrow stream. A variety of other sounds—croaks, chirrups, bleats—add to the mystique of this otherwise peaceful voyage. The blue sky that escorted us on the Napo River now plays hide-and-seek through a dense canopy. Bubbles rise to the surface of the murky water, from which I am protected by less than one inch of fiberglass. A chill courses through me as I contemplate the myriad creatures that could be the source of the bubbles.

I am somewhat comforted by the scent of Neem oil that covers all of the exposed flesh on my face and body. It is my only defense against the possibility of contracting Malaria, Yellow Fever or Dengue Fever. I am in no way prepared for this trip; if I'd had time to prepare, there is little chance I would have followed through.

Javier points out a number of animals along the way, including two different types of monkeys—a few white-tailed capuchins and a large, active family of squirrel monkeys—a three-toed sloth, and a family of otters. As the stream widens into a small lake, he directs the two Quechua men paddling our canoe to skirt along the shoreline. Across the water I see a large dock and about a dozen circular, thatch-roof huts resting on the gently sloped, heavily forested banks of the lake. In the back row of this tiny settlement stands a larger building, from which an observation tower rises fifty feet or more.

"There is a Black Cayman." Javier points to a dark lump moving along the surface of the water less than ten feet from our canoe. Focusing on the shape, I see two large eyes set in leathery skin. "Part of the alligator family," he adds.

"How big would he be?" Richard asks.

"Probably four meters long," Javier replies. "He travels like an iceberg."

"Yikes," Jack says. "I don't think I'll go for a dip tonight."

Within a few minutes we reach the dock. Javier helps us out of the canoe while the two Quechua men get our luggage.

A tall man with khaki pants and a collared shirt is standing by a table containing a piece of paper and eight wine glasses, each filled with some sort of dark beverage. "Welcome," he says. "I am Ivan. I manage the Pachamama Nature Center. Please enjoy a glass of blackberry juice, and check the list for your room numbers. You can get comfortable in your rooms, and then join us for dinner at six o-clock."

Ivan sweeps his hand toward the table, inviting each guest to take a glass. While I do so, I make note of my room number.

Ivan looks over my shoulder at the list. "Your name is?"

"Oliver Bruce."

"Your room is over there." He points to a hut on the lakeside, a short distance from the dock.

"Thank you," I say. "Also, I'm looking for two people who are supposed to be here with a film crew—Alejandro and Walter."

"Yes," Ivan says. "They are out filming now, but they will be back for supper."

I am relieved to hear that I have almost located Alejandro and his brother, but I will not believe it until I see them. I down my juice, pick up my pack and head up the path toward my hut.

"Oliver!" Richard calls, catching up with me. "I'd like to have a word with you, if I could. Would you mind meeting me in the bar once you've had a chance to settle in?"

"Sure," I reply. "What's up?"

"I'll fill you in when we meet."

The room I have been assigned reminds me of the one Jen and I shared in Puerto Lopez. Thick, white duvets cover two twin beds, each contained in a bed frame holding a mosquito net bunched like drapes. A chest of drawers, nightstand and wardrobe, all made of bamboo, fill only a small part of the large room. The bathroom is as modern as any I would find back home, complete with shower, sink and flush toilet, as well as a fresh jug of drinking water.

I would like to rest, but I am curious about Richard's request to meet with me. His pleasant invitation was a surprise given his aloof manner on the plane. I brush my teeth with the drinking water and apply a fresh coat of deodorant before heading out.

Thousands of ants line the path to the dining area. About half of them walk toward the lake carrying pieces of leaves, while the other half travel counter-flow, presumably to collect their next load. "Leaf-cutter ants," Richard says, coming up behind me. "They're one of my favorite creatures in the Amazon."

"They're busy," I say. "Where are they taking the leaves?"

"See those mounds of red dirt?" Richard points to a series of hills not far from my hut—some almost as tall as me.

"Those are their anthills. They would be creepy if they weren't so impressive."

"I'll say. So what is it you want to talk to me about?"

Richard scans the area around us, and then he speaks quietly. "I am aware that you are volunteering at Pueblo del Sol, and—"

"How?" I interject. "How could you possibly know that?"

"My company has been tracking the work of Daniel Porter, and it has come to our attention that you may have information about the invention he was working on at the time of his death. Let's continue to the bar, and discuss this over a drink."

Richard resumes walking and I fall into step beside him like an obedient puppy. We walk in silence until we reach the open-air bar at the edge of the dining area.

"What's your poison?" Richard asks.

I hesitate before responding. "A beer, I guess."

Richard orders two bottles of beer, and then invites me to a table in the back corner of the bar.

"I'm confused," I say, "about how you could know anything about my reasons for being in Ecuador, or even the fact that I'm here. Who do you work for?"

"I'm with Crescoil."

"Of course."

"What do you mean?"

"You guys have your fingers all over the village." I think of Jen again, and of the mystery man. "Is that your goon that's been following me, too?"

"Sorry?" Richard tips his head, seeming confused.

"I've seen the same guy three times. In Canoa, Jipijapa and Quito."

Richard shakes his head. "I have no idea. I found out about your itinerary from Elsa Morales in Quito. I spoke to her this morning, and she had just gotten off the phone with you. I scrambled to join your group, because I realized I wouldn't have time to talk to you at the airport. I almost missed the plane to Coca." He chuckles, but I do not share his amusement.

"What does an oil company want with me?"

"We're an energy company," Richard replies, matching my serious tone. "I'm with the renewable energies group."

"This must be important for you to come all this way for a conversation."

"You tell me," he says. "I know you're scheduled to leave Ecuador this weekend, so time is of the essence."

I nod, but I don't say anything. My mind spins in a thousand directions, trying to make sense of my newfound importance. It is both cathartic and disquieting to confirm that people are paying attention to my presence here.

Richard takes a swig of beer and says, "Crescoil Energy is working aggressively to diversify our portfolio of clean energy solutions. We understand that oil is not the only game in town, and we are determined to play a role in every major source of power. Let's face it—people need energy, and we're going to need more of it in the future."

I nod again.

"Look," Richard continues, "we're not the big bad oil company we're made out to be. There are a lot of people who would like to believe we can go back to hunter-gatherer status, but let's face it ... there's no stopping progress. It's grow or die. We need your help, Oliver."

"How can I help?" I ask. "I'm a restaurant owner, not a scientist."

"A restaurant owner who has been entrusted with the wish of a dying man."

I feel myself go cold in the face of this intrusion into my private life—and hot at the vague feeling of betrayal.

"How do you know—"

"I was briefed on your background. Like you, I have been assigned a task. Mine is to find out what you know about Daniel Porter's last invention."

The warmth of his smile, intended to be disarming, begins to sicken me.

"There is no reasonable way that you could—"

"Oliver—" Richard leans close to me "—I know this must be confusing to you. I'm not here to scare you. I'm here to improve your life ... and change the world for the better."

"And how exactly do you intend to do that?"

"We are prepared to compensate you for any assistance you can provide regarding the location of Daniel's design."

"I'm afraid I can't be of much help. I don't know the location of Daniel's design."

Richard reaches into his pocket and pulls out a business card. "If that changes, I would appreciate if you would contact me. And I would like to reiterate what I said about compensation."

"What kind of compensation are you talking about?"

"If you could lead us to the full invention, we're talking seven figures."

"That's not pocket change," I say, taking a moment to realize what seven figures means. *That could buy a lot of house. And a really nice SUV.*

Forty-Four

"Who do you work for, Richard?" Sam leans over her glass of wine, speaking across the table that she, Jack, Richard and I have been assigned for dinner.

"Crescoil," Richard replies with confidence.

"Ah." Sam's retort is snappy, sarcastic. "So you're here to see the rainforest before your company burns it down?"

"I'm with the Clean Energy Division," Richard says, stiffening. "And in any case, Crescoil is not drilling in this part of the Amazon. The Chinese have a lock on most of the oil here."

"So what is *clean* energy to you?" Sam asks.

"Solar, wind, hydro …" Richard says, "and nuclear."

"Nuclear?" Sam snorts. "What could be dirtier than nuclear waste?"

"Every source of energy has its downside." Richard holds a forkful of pork above his plate as he speaks. "To me, clean energy refers to any source of power that does not pollute our atmosphere."

"Oh, I get it," Sam says. "So it's okay if I grow three eyes, as long as I have fresh air."

Richard sets the fork down on his plate as if preparing for a long debate. "That's a gross exaggeration," he says. "With few exceptions, the nuclear power industry has operated with a very high level of efficiency, and has done a fantastic job of containing the impact of its operations."

Sam makes intentional eye contact with Richard and says, "But those exceptions are the definition of environmental catastrophe. Nuclear power plants are time bombs waiting to blow. And when they do, the entire globe is affected."

"That's nonsense," Richard scoffs, picking up his fork again. "Science doesn't support that."

Sam's voice is indignant. "Not the kind of science Crescoil subscribes to."

"For what it's worth," Jack chimes in, "I think you'd be cute with three eyes."

Sam pierces Jack with an expression that says she is not in the mood for humor or adulation.

"Look," Richard says, "I know we're not the most popular company in the world these days, and we have hard choices to make. But when you look at the planet realistically, it's clear that there are no easy answers. Crescoil, like any company, is a vehicle for managing money and resources. It's a publicly traded corporation, meaning anyone can buy a share of it. Millions of people around the world do."

"I've seen the graphs about the one percent," Sam says, her tone subdued. "That's who the market serves."

"The great thing about the countries we live in," Richard says, "is that we're each allowed to have our opinion."

"I'll give you that much," Sam says. "I just wish people would wake up and realize that we need a wholesale change in how we do things."

Richard dabs his mouth with his napkin, and then smiles. "People are waking up, and the world is adapting fast. We're on the same side of this issue, Sam." He gestures toward me. "As Oliver and I discussed this afternoon, one breakthrough in solar energy could put all of this discussion to rest in a heartbeat."

I shift in my seat, uncomfortable with Richard's implication that we are somehow connected. I look at the lake, where the last traces of sunlight fall upon the water. To my surprise, Alejandro and Walter are walking up a trail that leads from the dock to a hut behind the dining room.

"I'll be right back," I say, rising from the table without further explanation.

I walk briskly around the building, looking back to make sure Richard has not followed me. I catch up with the brothers as they are entering their hut.

"Oliver?" Alejandro says, his mouth opening in disbelief.

"Why are you here?" Walter asks.

"I'll explain inside … if that's okay?"

They welcome me into their hut, where Walter asks again, "Why are you not at Pueblo del Sol?"

I look at Alejandro, then turn back to Walter. "I need to find out how to get into Daniel's cabin. I learned about it from Daniel's brother, Liam. I have Carmen's blessing."

"Blessing?" Walter says, confused.

"Carmen told me to find you. I am looking for the key to Daniel's cabin."

Walter turns to Alejandro, who is seated on one of the room's two beds, and translates what I have said. Alejandro's eyes bulge. He speaks rapidly to Walter, who turns back to me and asks, "Why do you need to get into the cabin?"

"Because that is the reason I came to Ecuador. I was sent by Daniel's friend—Dr. McKinnon."

Walter listens intently, then turns to speak with Alejandro again. They both look at me with icy stares, as if assessing my motives. Walter says, "*Why* do you need to get into the cabin? What is it you look for?"

I choose my words carefully. "I am looking for information that Daniel left behind. Dr. McKinnon was supposed to come and get it, but he died. I am here in his place."

Walter describes this to Alejandro, who pauses in thought before responding.

"We will take you there," Walter says, "when we finish here."

"That won't work," I reply, trying to keep my frustration from showing. "I am leaving Ecuador on Sunday, to go back to the United States. I need to go to the cabin before then."

I suddenly see myself through their eyes and realize how difficult it must be for them to trust me. "Please," I say. "Carmen and Liam have given me permission … for Daniel. This is very important." I wait while Alejandro and Walter engage in another discussion. Then Alejandro gets up and paces around the cabin. I can't tell if he is angry or confused or some combination of the two. Finally, Alejandro stops and looks at me, then shakes his head and smiles. He says something that causes Walter to laugh.

Walter translates, "My brother says you would be crazy to come all this way to make up such a story."

"I can accept crazy. So … can you tell me where the key is?"

Alejandro speaks again. Walter turns to me and says, "The key is under a rock, beside the door."

"Under a rock?" I ask, motioning with my hands as if I was picking up a big stone.

"Si," Alejandro replies without waiting for a translation.

"By the door? Of the cabin?"

"Si." Alejandro smiles, and then both brothers begin to laugh.

"You mean …" I think of Jen sitting on a boulder beside the door during our visit to Daniel's cabin. I feel a brief twinge of frustration at the realization that I wasted almost an entire week to find a key that was inches from the cabin door. Then I think of my travels around Ecuador—the places I have seen and the characters I have met along the way—

and I submit myself to the humor of it all. I join Alejandro and Walter in a symphony of laughter, tears of mirth forming in my eyes.

Forty-Five

The crackling fire provides a thin veil for the nocturnal commotion of the jungle as a handful of guests at the Pachamama Nature Center end the night with a quiet fireside discussion. Alien sounds—different from the noises of the cloud forest—force all of my senses to life.

Tuning into the buzz that fills my ears, I close my eyes and yawn wide, inhaling a swampy concoction of smoke, sweat and Neem oil. I taste the wild, moist air on my tongue. I imagine eyes looking out from the dark of the trees, causing my own eyes to open and my lips to snap shut. Suddenly vulnerable, I long for the relative security of my hut.

"I think I'm done," I say, sitting up straight and stretching out my arms.

"Me too," Jack says, and then looks toward Sam. "You ready?"

"Sure," Sam says, and the three of us bid the others goodnight as we start to walk up the path away from the fire.

"Jesus Christ," Jack says as we approach their hut. "Look at that!"

Jack's flashlight illuminates a short post at the edge of the path, where a tarantula the size of my hand straddles two sides of the post.

"Wow," Sam says. "He's beautiful."

Jack says, "Not the word I would have chosen. I guess I know why she's attracted to me."

"Wow indeed." My whole body tenses. "Good luck getting to sleep now."

"You and me both, bro," Jack says. "These huts aren't exactly bug proof. If we're lucky they'll keep the snakes out."

We admire the tarantula for a while, then say goodnight as they enter their hut. I walk to mine and gingerly open the door, shining my flashlight on the light switch. When I turn on the light, a cockroach skitters under the wardrobe.

I get ready for bed in the fully lit hut. I check my bed for bugs, and, relieved to find none, I tuck the mosquito net tightly into each side of the bed, leaving only a small opening to get in. I shut off the light and use my flashlight to get into bed, then tuck in the final section of my net from inside. I do one more scan of the bed before turning off the flashlight.

I think of my conversation with Richard—of his offer to compensate me for information about Daniel's invention. I want to know how Crescoil found out about my connection to Eddy, but I am doubtful that Richard will divulge that information—if he even knows.

I hear a quiet scraping noise above my head. I fumble for the flashlight and turn it on, illuminating the mosquito net above me. A cockroach sits directly above me. I stand up on my bed and flick the net with my finger, sending the roach flying onto the floor of the hut.

Guided by my flashlight, I get out of bed and tiptoe to the door, where I turn on the light again. Though completely exhausted, I am not ready to sleep. My hands tense as I open my knapsack, as if expecting something to jump out at me. I look inside, and then retrieve a large plastic re-sealable freezer bag that contains my guidebook and journal, along with an envelope and a pen. I bring it back to the bed, surround myself with protective netting, and reach in to get my journal. Instead, I pull out the envelope and open it, taking out the foolscap page it contains. I sit cross-legged and begin to read.

If life is a mosaic of experiences and relationships, then mine is tiled in pale shades of brown and gray. I yearn for a more diverse palette, though I am not sure I would know what to do with the colors. My life is the embodiment of ordinary. We all begin with a dream to achieve greatness, but I chose long ago to set my sights on more modest, achievable goals. If I continue on the path I have chosen, my legacy will be written in dust.

I have much to be thankful for, but appreciation does not come easily. I know that Isabella and Isaac are gifts to treasure, yet I rarely show them how much I love them—the small amount of time that I have with my children consumed by the minutiae of everyday life. And Emily, the sheen long since worn from our once bright relationship, has grown tired of my dreary moods. I cannot recall a single moment that pushed us apart—just a gradual drift exacerbated by the pressures of parenthood and business and the financial stress that comes with both. I recall a time when I only had eyes for Emily—eyes that now wander more than I care to admit. I spend more time resenting my family for weighing me down than appreciating them for all that they are. How can I expect them to feel better about me?

When I ask myself what it is that I want out of life, a flood of selfish desires springs to mind. I want to spread my wings as I have never done, to overcome my fears and travel the world—to faraway lands like India, Africa or Indonesia. To escape the responsibility that drags me like a stone, pulling me to the ground as I flap in vain. To live without worrying about anybody else. To be single again, if only for a while. Perhaps what I really want is to regain the part of my childhood that was lost when my father left me, and all but forgotten when my mother gave up her will to live.

So what do I want? I want to write more, to paint more, to play more. I want to smile more, to laugh more, to kiss more. I want a more balanced, more fulfilling life. I want to open my heart and release the fears and faults that shackle me. I want, quite simply, to reach some semblance of my full potential.

When I think of the chasm that lies between the life I am living and the life I imagine, I realize that only a proactive approach to personal growth—to change—can bridge that gap. I am tired of words ... hollow words filled with platitudes and unrealistic goals. What I need is action—some sort of real-life experience to snap me out of an existence that falls somewhere between discontent and depression. I hope that these words, unlike so many that I have uttered in my mind, contain some form of substance. That this might be my own personal manifesto, by its very definition a declaration to act on that which I put into words.

Let this be a promise to myself—that I shall begin to take care of my own needs, to look beyond the confines of the life I have created toward a more rewarding existence; that I shall become strong enough to break free of the malaise that grips me; that I shall find a greater purpose than serving bacon and eggs to people who don't need another helping of bacon and eggs; that I shall seek a richer palette of experiences and relationships with which to reconstruct the mosaic of my life.

"Huh," I say to myself. Then I fold the manifesto, place it in the envelope, and seal it in the plastic bag.

Forty-Six

Another morning brings another round of goodbyes. Following an early breakfast and a heartfelt farewell to Jack and Sam, I walk down to the perfectly still lake to be paddled back to civilization by one of the local guides and his crew. Despite my short sleep, I am wide awake as I look across the mirror-like surface to see the reflection of the jungle under the sun's first light.

Richard joins me as the only other passenger in the canoe, which is powered by the strong paddling of four men. There is little chitchat in the boat this morning—the primary purpose of this voyage is to pick up another boatload of tourists, most of whom will stay at the Pachamama Nature Center for three to seven nights of spoilage. Aside from the cockroaches, my one night in the Amazon was more akin to a five-star luxury resort than a camping trip. The scenery this morning is every bit as stunning as it was on the ride in, and the animals are more active than they were during the afternoon. I take in every sight and scent that I can absorb, more appreciative of my opportunity to see this small patch of rainforest than I was yesterday. Though I am far from confident that I am going to find the key to Daniel's cabin where Alejandro and Walter told me it would be—nothing on this adventure has gone as planned thus far—finding the two brothers was in itself a monumental achievement, and brought with it a sense of fulfillment.

We reach the Napo River in maybe half the time that it took to navigate the smaller tributary yesterday. We are quickly ushered from the human-powered canoe into a larger motorized canoe, where I succumb to the whine of the motor, hunkering down in my seat to nap. Sleep eludes me as a thousand thoughts fight for airtime, none of them lasting long enough to hold my attention. I am not sure what I am trying to figure out, but my game of intellectual whack-a-mole fills the time, and before I know it we are back in Coca.

~ ~ ~

Richard reaches out to shake my hand at the arrivals gate of Mariscal Sucre airport. "Call me if you have anything to share."

I accept his handshake and look into his eyes. "I will."

"The offer ... even partial information could be valuable. It's negotiable."

"Understood," I reply. During our flight from Coca, Richard explained Crescoil's impressive plans—and hopes—for renewable energy. And in a quiet voice as we were about to descend into Quito, he put a firm number on Crescoil's offer for complete access to Daniel's plans. Three million dollars. Since my conversations with Richard yesterday, I have been thinking about what kind of positive changes a big player could make in the development of alternative power. It has been an on-going internal dialogue, the counter-argument to Richard's positive perspective colored by my growing distaste for the tactics employed by corporate America.

We part ways, and then I turn back suddenly and call Richard's name. He stops and walks toward me.

"I might know more in a day or two," I say.

"I hope so." He tips his head and turns away.

I head for the information desk, then pause in front of a pay phone and consider calling my lawyer—or Jake. I decide against making a call, and continue to the desk. The attendant suggests that I take a shuttle bus to the old airport, which has been converted to a park, and then catch a city bus to Terminal Quitumbe on the south side of Quito.

My journey back to Pueblo del Sol starts with a comfortable hour-and-a-half coach ride into the city. Then my limited Spanish skills cause me concern. I climb onto a densely populated bus and engage in a brief flurry of Spanglish with its driver. The price is right—twenty-five cents—but I sense the direction may not be. I ask if anyone around me speaks English but nobody answers my query. I push my way through the crowd, continuing to seek someone who can help me. Finally, a tiny woman says, "Where are you trying to go?"

"Terminal Quitumbe," I reply.

She winces, clearly a bad sign. "This is going to Terminal Carcelan."

"The north terminal?" I say.

"Yes."

"Thanks." I curse to myself, no longer surprised by detours.

The woman advises me to continue to the north terminal and then catch another bus south. I am not sure if it is the fastest way, or merely the only route she knows. I watch many buses pass by, and I question whether I should get off and cross the street. But I follow the woman's directions, watching the day fade along with my hope of reaching Pueblo del Sol today.

I get off at Terminal Carcelan and catch a bus that will take me the full length of Quito to the other bus terminal. It is mid-afternoon when I recognize the popular La Mariscal region. A quick calculation tells me there is no way I will reach the bottom of The Hill before dark. Without thinking further, I jump off the bus at the next stop and make my way to the hostel where we stayed last weekend.

~ ~ ~

"Oliver!" Conlan looks up from his beer at the Irish pub adjacent to Plaza Foch. "What are you doing here?"

"The guy at the hostel told me where to find you. I made an educated guess that you'd be staying there." I nod to Katherine and Andrew, then add, "Where's Jen?"

"Ahm using her ticket," Andrew says. "Thanks to yer tardiness."

"She stayed at the village?"

"Yeah," Katherine says. "She didn't want to miss you. Not that we did, but ..."

"But Cotipaxi awaits," Andrew says.

"So I hear you went into the Amazon," Conlan says. "Did you find Alejandro and Walter?"

"Yeah, at last. How did you know?"

"Elsa sent a message to Nadine—by e-mail, if you can believe that."

"The connection's back up?"

"Yeah. Apparently hell has frozen over."

"So what did you find?" Conlan asks loudly. The empty bottles on the table suggest they are on at least their third round.

Katherine leans forward in her seat. "Do you know how to get into the cabin?"

I look around, wary of my friends' volume. Nobody seems to be paying any attention to us, so I lean in and say, "Yes. I'm going to try again tomorrow."

"What cabin?" Andrew says. "Here ah am again, the mushroom. Please, someone remove this shit from mah eyes sae I can see what the hell yer all talkin' about."

"It's … just a cabin," I say, brushing off Andrew's question. "So what's been going on at the village?"

"Dirt," Andrew replies. "Lots and lots of dirt."

"Crescoil's been around again," Conlan says, looking to Katherine for an explanation.

"Yeah," she adds. "One of their executives was up there soaking up details about Daniel's project."

"Was his name Richard?" I ask.

"Yeah, Richard Brentwick. You know him?"

I nod. "He paid me a visit as well. What was he asking about?"

"He just asked me some technical questions."

"Did my name come up?"

"Not to me," she says. "He talked to everyone though— we didn't compare notes."

"Strange," I say. "I wonder why he didn't tell me he'd been to the village." Then I add to the whole group, "Can we keep this conversation between ourselves? I don't know what I'll find at the cabin, but it's obvious that there are a lot of people interested in it."

"Sure," Conlan says.

Katherine nods in agreement.

Andrew laughs heartily and says, "Daen't worry, mah friend. Ah won't admit that I daen't know anything, no matter who asks."

~ ~ ~

Eldon Hewitt feels silly in the Panama hat that he bought at a tourist market a few blocks from the plaza. It makes him feel conspicuous—precisely the opposite of its intended purpose. But its narrow brim covers enough of his face to bolster his sense of anonymity as he sits alone in a corner booth of the small, lively pub. More importantly, it covers the ear that contains a small amplification device, honed in on a single conversation—filtering out all but the four voices it has been tuned to receive. A techie at heart, Eldon enjoys this part of his job—getting to use gadgets that are a generation ahead of what is available to the rest of the population.

Eldon picks up his phone and punches in his passcode, then taps on the shortcut to Harold McIntyre's number. He adds Nathan Jacques to the recipient list and then types, "OB returning to Pueblo tomorrow. FYI Brentwick's been fishing."

A few seconds later, Harold's reply appears on the small screen. "EH: go to the village ASAP." Then another message follows: "NJ: hold back and await further instruction."

Forty-Seven

I stand up and walk to the front door of the bus, dizzy from the ride—and from last night's pub crawl. I am glad I am not trying to summit a volcano with my friends.

I step off the bus and look across the highway. Jen is there, talking to the woman who runs the convenience stand that provides Pueblo del Sol with Oreos and beer. When Jen sees me, she breaks off her conversation and smiles broadly.

I make my way across the road, where Jen opens her arms to hug me. I pause for a moment before leaning in to accept her greeting. Then I step back and say, "I wasn't expecting a welcoming committee. I guess Nadine got my e-mail?"

"Yes," Jen says. "I've been waiting down here for an hour."

"Thanks. I'll appreciate the company while we trudge up The Hill."

"Actually," she says, "I didn't walk down just to greet you. I came to intercept you."

"What do you mean?"

"Someone showed up at the village first thing this morning. He's here to see you."

"Is it Richard?"

"Who?" she asks.

"Richard Brentwick ... from Crescoil."

"No. But how do you know about Richard?"

"Kath told me he'd been here. He also came to see me in the Amazon."

"I'm confused," Jen says. "But no, it's not him. It's someone with the US Government."

"And he wants to see me?"

"Yup."

"Huh. I seem to be very popular all of a sudden."

"I want to hear all about it. And by the way ... I learned about a detour ... around the village. That is, if you don't feel like talking to the government dude right now."

"I'm not sure," I say.

"What did you ..." Jen starts to form a question, then pauses. "Nadine said you tracked down Alejandro and Walter. Did they have a key to the cabin?"

"No," I reply. "But they told me where to find one. You wouldn't believe how close we were. It's right by the door."

Jen flashes me a bright smile. "Well, let's go! I packed a few snacks for the trail." She taps the top of her knapsack. Her sincerity is unmistakable, her presence comforting.

Jen starts up The Hill, practically jogging. Her energy is contagious, and my hangover abates as I match Jen's pace. When we approach the first switchback, a question comes to mind. "What can you tell me about Crescoil's Clean Energy Division? I'd be interested in another perspective—other than Richard's."

Jen responds without hesitation. "I think it's a façade, for the most part. But I'm sure if they saw a real opportunity … I mean, money is the bottom line, right?"

"Yeah," I agree.

"The one area where they seem to be serious is nuclear. They've been buying up nuclear companies ever since the Fukushima disaster—at bargain basement prices."

"Really?" I think again about the sponge in my money belt. I stop to catch my breath while debating whether to tell Jen about the strange coin that I am carrying. Then something catches my eye on the highway below. A truck stops and a man gets out of the passenger seat. The truck pulls away, and the man crosses the highway. When I see him clearly, my heart stops cold.

"Jen," I say, pointing. "Down there, crossing the road … that's the guy I saw. The one—"

"Your mystery man?"

"Yeah. Where's that detour?"

"It's at the first waterfall."

Without another word, we both begin to jog, pushing ourselves up the steep incline. When we reach the next switchback, I briefly stop and look back down the trail. The man appears around the corner, probably a hundred yards below us.

"Faster," I say.

We run to the next turn before I dare to look back again. The man is nowhere to be seen, so I slow for a moment. Then he appears around the last bend, running as well.

"Mr. Bruce!" His voice carries faintly up the path. I freeze for a second, then turn the corner and run, Jen on my heels. One foot in front of the other, I press myself to continue. My heart pounds and my calves begin to ache; I worry that they might cramp. By the time we reach the next corner, I am gasping for air.

"Just up here," Jen says, passing me, pointing toward the waterfall. It is less than halfway up the next switchback, maybe forty yards ahead, but it seems farther than that.

A wall of water trickles gently down a broad rock face more than twice my height, into a ditch at the edge of the trail. Jen reaches it and climbs up one edge of the rock face, scrambling frantically to scale the wall against the modest flow of water. I am right behind her, matching her intensity.

Jen's foot slips, but she manages to hold on. She regains her footing and changes course. I clamber to follow her lead, reaching … dirt falls away … I can't find anything to hold onto. Finally, a root. My fingers grip the root and I pull with all my strength, trying to find a place to put my foot. Pain rips through my hand and down my wrist as Jen's boot crushes down, using my hand as a foothold. I suppress a shriek. The pressure of her foot increases as she pushes away from my hand, releasing it. I scramble, grabbing for anything … dirt and water falling onto my face. Another root … panic fuelling my climb … and suddenly, I am at the top, pulling myself into the stream that feeds the waterfall. I crawl for a few feet to drier ground, then collapse beside Jen, our pulses racing.

Forty-Eight

Jen and I lie there—a tangled, dripping web of limbs, knapsacks, roots and vines—listening to the babble of the stream. Long seconds pass. Nothing. Seconds more ... still nothing. It dawns on me that I am lying on the floor of a dense forest full of nasty creatures. My fear shifts from the man on the path to the nature around me. I turn around and peer over the edge of the rock face. There is no sign of our pursuer. I get up quickly and sweep off my clothing and hair.

"Let's go," I whisper to Jen. "You lead the way."

Jen rises, shaking off dirt, leaves and moss, and then walks in front of me up a narrow trail beside the stream. We do not dare to speak, and we stop every time we hear a plant rustle or a branch crack. Each sound is a false alarm. With every step our unease diminishes. "So where are we?" I ask at last.

"This used to be the main trail, before they built the road. Conlan showed it to me the other day. We came down to get some stuff from the store, and he brought me this way so he could clear the trail."

"Where does it go from here?"

"It skirts around the village ... up to the swimming pond."

We walk for a while before I speak again. "What did the guy at the village tell you? Why is he here?"

"He asked Nadine and I what we know about Daniel's pod. I told him I don't know much, and that I'm under an NDA. He didn't press me … just said he might have more questions later. He came to talk to you."

"What's his name?" I ask.

"Eldon," she replies. "Eldon Hewitt."

I shake my head—the name means nothing to me. "What about the guy we ditched back there? Who do you think he is?"

"I have no idea," Jen says.

We stop speaking as we near the village. The path offers peekaboo glimpses of the buildings and pasture, but we don't stop to sightsee—walking briskly until we arrive at the pond. From there we follow another trail that intercepts the main path up the mountain. We continue to walk in silence until we reach a bluff above the village. Charcoal clouds converge to squeeze out blue sky, and I feel the first drops of moisture. Fearing detection, Jen and I squat down as we approach the edge of the cliff. We kneel and crawl to the edge, looking a few hundred feet down to the village below. Nothing seems out of the ordinary. A few animals stand in the pasture. Nobody appears to be working today.

Jen tips her head for me to follow as she crouches along the bluff and back into the forest. Once we are both there, we stand to full height and continue walking. We march up the trail under an ever-darkening sky.

"I feel like …" I begin, but I am not able to unscramble my thoughts.

"Like what?" Jen asks.

"Like someone's going to appear."

"They might. How do you think they tracked you here? And why?"

"I don't know. They could have access to my e-mail, phone calls, credit cards—who knows? Maybe they're monitoring my bowel movements too. Jesus, I'm starting to sound like my friend, Arlo." I think of Eddy's paranoia during my last visit to his trailer, and I wonder why it was ransacked—and who might have done it. Then, abruptly, I stop and take off my pack.

"What are you doing?" Jen says as I root around in my knapsack.

"I don't know ... following a hunch ... something about the man ... when I saw him in Quito."

"What are you talking about?"

"He was leaving the store when I spotted him. And he had a look ... like he'd just achieved something. I'd been immersed in phone calls. I think I put my knapsack down. I can't remember keeping my eye on it."

Jen looks at me with a combination of intensity and amusement. I continue to investigate every inch of the knapsack, guided entirely by instinct. I am about to give up, but the image of Eddy's trailer being plundered causes me to continue my search.

On the bottom of my bag, I find something unfamiliar—a small black disc about the size of a nickel but slightly thicker, with the density of a magnet. I try to pry it off but I can see that it has been epoxied to my bag.

"What is that?" Jen asks.

"Beats me. A tracking beacon maybe, or some sort of bug?" I reach into the smallest pocket of my pack and pull out a Swiss Army Knife that Emily packed for me—wondering for a moment how a knife made it to and from the Amazon without being confiscated by airport security. The disc reminds me of a retail security device; maybe it's been there since I bought the pack. In any case, I do not plan to keep it.

I set my pack on a boulder and wedge the largest blade of the knife into a small crack between the disc and my bag.

With a thump of my palm on the dull edge of the knife, the disc pops off and lands in the dirt, taking the epoxy with it.

I look at the disc closely, and then hold it up for Jen to see. I look at it one more time, then toss it into the woods.

We walk up the path a bit before we venture to speak again.

"What just happened?" Jen asks.

"I don't know." I recall the visitor who spoke to Jen at the village this morning. "We'd better check yours too."

We search Jen's bag thoroughly. Finding nothing resembling the disc that adorned my pack, we resume our walk up the trail. The rain starts to fall, lightly at first, and then heavily. I tell Jen about my trip to find Alejandro and Walter; about my discussion with Carmen and her granddaughter; about my journey to the Amazon, via Cuenca and Vilcabamba; and about my meeting with Richard Brentwick. I tell her about everything—except Richard's offer of compensation. I am not ready to share that.

~ ~ ~

This afternoon's downpour behind us, the sun shines in full force when Jen and I reach the top of the water chute. With a giggle, Jen approaches the slide with the same uninhibited joy that she showed during our previous visit here.

"We're already soaked," she says, jumping onto the chute feet first, holding her knapsack in front of her. I shake my head and follow her, sliding down to the pool below.

Standing in the pool next to Jen, I seek her eyes. We look at each other for a long moment—reminding me of the look we shared in her room last week, when it took every ounce of restraint for me to walk out and retreat to my own quarters. I blink to break the spell, then tip my head toward the shore. We climb out of the pool and walk in an excited silence, down the path along the stream, past the micro-hydro dam. I tense as we reach the clearing. We look around for signs of anyone—or anything—that seems out of place. Everything appears as it was the last time we were here. I venture into the clearing and walk cautiously toward the cabin. Jen follows close behind.

We reach the cabin porch. I kneel down and grasp the boulder—about the size of a large watermelon—and tip it at a forty-five degree angle. Jen glances at me, raising her eyebrows, before reaching down to retrieve a key. She studies it for a moment, then hands it to me with a smirk.

I insert the key into the deadbolt and turn it. My heart skips a beat when I hear the bolt slide open.

Forty-Nine

"Is this material?" she asks, looking at the transcript on her desk.

Harold McIntyre shrugs one shoulder and says, "Enough that I thought you should see it."

"How did you learn about this?"

"Routine monitoring," Harold replies.

"Hmm," she says, unconvinced. "So what are you proposing?"

"I think I should go. With no disrespect to our field ops, I don't trust their judgment ... or their negotiating skills."

"That's a big commitment, given the timing."

Harold thinks for a moment before replying, "It's worth a shot, in my opinion. I can be there tonight, back by tomorrow after-noon."

She looks at the transcript again, the letters blurring as she re-treats into her mind. Her grip on power is tenuous—she can feel it slipping away. So many dreams, goals, visions ... all on the verge of blowing like ash into the wind, her only substantial legacy being her gender. It was never good enough just to show up—she came here with a purpose, thus far unfulfilled. And now this ... this smells like an opportunity.

She looks up at Harold. "Yes," she says, "let's find this thing."

"Yes ma'am," Harold says, a rare formality between two old friends.

As he turns away, she speaks again. "Harold ... I want to be there."

Fifty

I flip the switch on the wall beside the door, bringing half a dozen LED bulbs to life to complement the sunlight that pours in through the open doorway.

"It's so—" Jen begins.

"Modern?" I ask.

"Clean," she says. "It seems very well kept, like the trail. Do you think Daniel—"

"Daniel is dead," I say, surprised by my bluntness. "Alejandro and Walter take care of it."

Jen does not reply.

The cabin is well finished with a bamboo floor, hardwood countertops and walls made of vertical wood slats. The main room is an open plan with a kitchen to our right, a loveseat to the left, and a woodstove against the back wall.

In the center of the room is a wooden table with two chairs on top of a tightly woven, multi-colored rug.

"The rug," I say, looking to Jen.

"Do you think ...?"

I am anxious to look for the safe, but a cautious voice from within causes me to slow down. I remove my wet hiking boots and socks and set them by the door with my knapsack. I close and bolt the door, and then point toward a small hallway between the woodstove and kitchen. "Let's check out the cabin first."

We walk together into the hallway, where a desk sits under a large window. Jen looks in the bathroom while I check out the bedroom. We return to the main room and move the chairs and table. Without a word, we pull the carpet aside, exposing a two-by-three foot trapdoor. There is a circular metal ring near one end, with a finger-sized groove allowing access to the ring.

We share an impatient glance. I reach down, lift the ring and pull up the door, flipping its precise hinges one hundred and eighty degrees toward the kitchen, setting it gently on the floor. Under the trapdoor lies a steel door, also containing a metal ring. Next to the ring, a panel of LCD lights—alternating between the words ENTER and CODE—flashes at us in digital red. Beneath the LCD panel is an alphanumeric keypad.

"Holy shit!" I stare at the panel in disbelief.

"I hope it's a safe," Jen quips, "and not a bomb."

"Looks like a bank vault." My heart is pounding against the inside of my ribcage. "Now what?

"I can't believe this."

"I'm just ... this is surreal."

"It's alphanumeric," Jen says. "Eight characters."

I stare at the panel, my mind working overtime. Then I look up at Jen and grin. "Enola Gay."

"Enola Gay," she echoes.

My fingers are methodical as they type the letters. E-N-O-L-A-G-A-Y. I pause and look at Jen again.

"Go on," she says.

I press the ENTER key and wait.

It takes a moment for the message on the display to register. When it does, my heart sinks. "Fail," I say out loud. After about five seconds, the display switches back to alternating between ENTER and CODE.

"Well, that's disappointing," Jen says.

"It seemed so perfect." I stare at the panel for a while. Then I walk over to my knapsack, open it and extract my journal from the freezer bag that saved it from the rain and the waterslide. I flip through my journal until I find what I am looking for.

"Little Boy is nine letters," I say. "Tibbets is seven. Hiroshima … nine."

"Nagasaki is eight!" Jen says, rising to join me.

"Yeah," I reply, scanning my notes again. "But the Enola Gay didn't drop the bomb on Nagasaki."

"Good point." Jen looks over my shoulder at my notes.

While Jen sits on the floor, I walk around the room looking for hints. A small framed photo on the wall beside the loveseat catches my eye. I recognize it instantly from my Internet research in Canoa two weeks ago. A young man with thick, dark eyebrows and a ball cap waves as he sticks his head out the window of a cockpit. Below the window, in crudely painted black letters, is the name of the plane.

"Bingo!" I reach out and tap the words—ENOLA GAY.

Jen scrambles to her feet. As she approaches, I recite a quote that is typed in small print below the photo. "'The release of atomic power has changed everything except our way of thinking … the solution to this problem lies in the heart of mankind. If only I had known, I should have become a watchmaker.' Albert Einstein. 1945."

"Wow." Jen steps close to me, looking over my shoulder at the picture on the wall.

We stand, dumbfounded, analyzing the photo and the quote. Then, in little more than a whisper, Jen says, "Einstein."

"Yeah," I reply, still staring at the quote. "Takes us right back to the first clue ... do you think ...?"

"It's worth a try," she says.

It takes me a moment to pull away from the picture—long enough to tell me I am not at all confident that we have solved the riddle. It seems too simple. Then I think of the key under the rock, and I feel a surge of hope. Perhaps simplicity *is* the key. *Einsteinium* was too long a word, but *Einstein* is just right.

"Yes," I say at last. "It is worth a try."

Jen and I walk back to the vault in unison. I reach down and type E-I-N-S-T-E-I-N into the keypad, and then press ENTER.

My disappointment intensifies when FAIL lights up the screen again.

"Damn," I mutter. "What else could it be?"

"I'm ... I don't ..." Jen trails off as she walks back to the picture.

I am still crouched by the vault when Jen says, "What about trying Tibbets? It's only seven letters, but maybe it doesn't need to be eight."

"Maybe," I say, "but if we open that can of worms, I'm sure there are a bunch of words that could fit."

"True," she says, "but Tibbets was the last name of both the pilot and his mother—Enola Gay Tibbets. It feels like that's the word that ties everything together."

I think about Jen's logic, and it begins to make sense. Almost lackadaisically, I type T-I-B-B-E-T-S into the keypad and press ENTER.

The vault emits a long, low tone that reminds me of an alarm clock. My breathing stops while I wait for the display to light up. When it does, it reads TIMEOUT.

Fifty-One

"Shit!" I say as Jen walks over to the vault. "I guess you only get three tries."

She looks down at the display and says, almost cheerfully, "At least it only says *Timeout*. That implies that it'll let us try again."

"Well, that's looking at the bright side. If only we had a fucking clue what the password is, I might see that as reason for optimism."

I get up and pace around the cabin. Frustration compels me to open the front door and walk outside. I stare out into the forest, and then sit down on the top step. Jen comes out and sits beside me. I feel a strong urge to put my arm around her—more from a sense of camaraderie than attraction, like we are partners in a failed mission. I resist the temptation out of fear that Jen might misinterpret my intentions. Instead, I get up and walk back into the cabin. The display on the vault still reads TIMEOUT.

Practicality takes over. I pull out the wet clothes that are still in my pack and set them along the railing of the porch. I strip down to my boxer shorts, adding my shirt and pants to the impromptu drying rack. Jen removes her pants as well, then reaches under her t-shirt and undoes her bra, leaving on only her panties and shirt. I go to my knapsack and pull out my bottle of Neem oil, liberally applying it to my bare skin before handing it to Jen. I watch her apply the foul-smelling liquid on her skin; despite my continued frustration, the visual arouses me, overriding the scent that accompanies it.

We sit on the porch again, allowing our minds to spin. I finish the last of my drinking water, and Jen offers me snacks that she packed—a few recognizable goodies from the convenience stand at the base of The Hill. "Think we could last the night on granola bars and apples?" I ask.

Jen looks toward the afternoon sky. "I've existed on less."

"We should probably head back," I say, my voice coated in futility.

She looks at me with a warm smile and says, "No, let's stay. We'll figure this out." The confidence in Jen's voice tells me that maybe she is right. After all, we found our way into this cabin—even located the vault within it—based on a series of obscure clues. Perhaps we are on the verge of discovering what I came to Ecuador to find. But I can't help thinking that we missed something—that we came to the cabin before we had all the clues.

Futility gives way to resignation as I consider the options—going back to the village would eliminate any hope of finding whatever is stored within the vault, and staying here feels like a fitting way to spend my last night in Ecuador. So Jen and I get up and scrounge around the cabin. We are surprised to find the cupboards stocked with canned foods—soup, vegetables, three tins of Washington State salmon—and some glass jars filled with dry goods. Under the sink, I find a bunch of sealed one-gallon jugs of drinking water. Jen locates three larger jugs under the desk in the hallway, hidden beneath a tablecloth. Beside them is a bamboo crate with a dozen compartments, most of which contain bottles of red wine.

Jen lifts a bottle into the air. "Our search is complete!"

We agree on a meal of salmon and cold green beans. We check the vault again—to no avail—and go back to the porch, enjoying our dinner while the sun falls below the tree line. A sense of tranquility sets in, and for a moment I forget about the reason we came to the cabin.

"I don't feel like I should be this relaxed," I say.

"I know what you mean," Jen replies.

A thought crosses my mind, and I try to voice it. "You and Marco ... you seem close. Is there ... are you—"

"Marco?" Jen says. "You think ... really?"

"I don't know. It's just ... something in the way you communicate with him. You're both very ... touchy-feely."

"Marco?" she says again. "No ... I mean, he's nice, but ... just, no. He's not my type." Jen looks up at me, and I can see that she is trying to suppress a smile. "Are you jealous?"

After a moment of hesitation—my pause an answer in itself—I shake my head. "Just curious."

Jen allows her smile to form, and I respond with a sheepish grin of my own.

Darkness falls quickly, the sun hidden beyond the trees. A light breeze brushes my bare legs, the crisp mountain air colder than the village below. I look at the woodpile beside the cabin. "Let's light the woodstove. We can use it to dry our stuff ... and keep warm."

"Do you think—what about the smoke? I mean, in case they're looking for us ..."

"We're pretty far up the mountain," I say. "And it's getting dark."

"True," Jen agrees.

We take our dishes into the kitchen, then go outside again to bring in a few loads of wood before night consumes the forest.

"Not much for kindling," I say, picking out the smallest bits from the pile we stacked beside the woodstove. "Should do though. Have you seen any paper?"

"No," Jen says, shaking her head.

"I can use a few pages from my journal. How about a match?"

"I saw a lighter in the drawer." Jen goes to get the lighter while I walk over to the table to retrieve my journal.

I notice the plastic bag still containing my guidebook and manifesto. I pull out the envelope. "Even better," I say.

"What's that?" Jen asks.

"My manifesto."

"The one you told me about?"

"Yeah." I take the page out of its envelope and crumple it up.

"What are you doing? I thought … isn't that important to you?"

"I thought it was. I read it again when I was in the Amazon." I scrunch the envelope and put it in the woodstove along with the manifesto. "It didn't resonate with me any more."

"Why not?"

"I don't know. It just didn't." I assemble the kindling around the crumpled paper. Jen hands me the lighter, and I ignite it with a flick of my thumb.

"Whatever you wrote," Jen says, "you must have felt it at the time. The pen rarely lies."

"I guess." I reach my hand into the woodstove and light the edge of my manifesto, which turns to ash and rises into the chimney. I wait for the kindling to catch fire, and then watch the last of the paper burn while the wood snaps and pops. "I guess it *was* important," I say, "but I think it's served its purpose already."

~ ~ ~

Eldon Hewitt leaves the dining area to receive the call from his superior. He punches in his security code and answers, "Sir, where are you now?"

"Over southern Colombia. We'll be there within the hour. Have you secured landing?"

"Yes," Eldon replies. "in Tandapi—near the highway. It's less likely to attract attention down there."

"Makes sense," Harold says. "I'll text you when we're approaching. Get Nathan and make a graceful exit. Just fade out of there if you can."

Fifty-Two

"I hope Nadine isn't too worried," Jen says. "I only told her I was going to give you a heads-up about our guest."

I go to the woodstove to flip my socks and underwear. "We did leave some clues—for better or worse, I talked up the cabin with a few people. I'm guessing they'll figure it out."

"Yeah," Jen agrees. "How long do you think we have until they find us?"

"Beats me." I pick up Jen's clothes and try not to think about the body they belong to. "Your pants are already dry. Bra's still damp though. Want me to turn it?"

"Yes, please."

I flip Jen's bra and set her pants on a chair. Then I walk over to the vault and look at the display.

"Any change?" Jen asks.

"Nope. Might as well read FUCKOFF. I think this is Daniel's idea of a cruel joke."

"Have you thought of any other password ideas?"

"No. You?"

"No," she says.

Seeing the dirty cans from our dinner on the counter, I walk over to the sink and turn on the tap. The faucet spits for a while, and then settles into a constant flow. "We have running water," I announce.

"How cold is it?" Jen asks.

"Even colder than the village."

"Don't tell me that," she groans. "I'd like to rinse off the pond water."

"I dare you."

Jen flashes me a smile, accepting my dare. "Here goes."

She goes into the bathroom, and I hear the water run. Then I hear a yelp, and I grin at the image of Jen standing naked, trying to wash herself in a stream of icy cold water. I am instantly aroused, unbearably so. I busy myself washing dishes, and then I check the vault again before sitting on the loveseat.

I hear the shower turn off. Jen emerges from the bathroom wrapped in a towel and says, "That is the coldest fucking water I have ever felt. Your turn."

"You do make it sound inviting." I get up and pick up an almost dry set of clothes from a chair beside the woodstove. On my way to the bathroom, I remember the wine rack and I reach down for a bottle. "Want to warm up from the inside out?"

"Yes, please," Jen says. "Unless you can find me some hot cocoa."

I set my clothes in the bathroom and return to the kitchen with the bottle of wine. I root through the drawers until I find a corkscrew.

"Voila," I say, holding up my treasure. I find two mason jars in a cupboard and pour some wine in each, setting one in front of Jen. She is seated on the loveseat, running her fingers through damp hair that falls over a bare shoulder, ending below the towel line at the top of her breasts. A warmth rises from my pelvis to my chest. I allow myself a glance at Jen's athletic legs, the towel reaching only halfway down her thighs. Then I force my eyes back to her face.

"Were you looking at my legs?" she asks.

"Yes," I confess, taking a swig of wine. "That outfit … it's … distracting."

She smiles shyly.

"I'm only stating a fact. You are a *very* beautiful woman, Jen."

"Thank you," she says, reaching for her wine.

I set down my glass. "I think I'd better take my turn with the cold shower."

"Have fun."

I walk into the bathroom and close the door, exposing an on-demand water heater on the wall. I press the *On* button, which causes a single click before a *Pilot Out* indicator lights up. I walk back into the front room, grab a flashlight and slip on my still wet boots.

"Where are you going?" Jen asks.

"To see if there's a propane tank around back."

"Why?"

"So I can turn on the hot water heater."

~ ~ ~

When I get out of the shower, Jen is still wrapped in a towel on the loveseat. I go to the vault.

"Still timed out?" she asks.

"Yup," I reply.

Resigned to waiting, we polish off the bottle of wine in less than an hour. There is little conversation between us. I have the feeling we are both pretending to be content with sitting in silence. In fact, the wait is excruciating. We share space on the loveseat and occasionally exchange glances, each one lingering a little longer. The wine that has dulled the anxiety over our harrowing journey to the cabin now replaces it with a sexual tension that I am sure is mutual.

I turn and face Jen again. This time I don't look away. I study every inch of her face, and then allow my eyes to wander down. I stop briefly at her bare shoulders before scanning the length of her towel. Nervously, I follow my eyes' lead and rest my hand lightly on her thigh. *What have I started?* I feel foolish and frightened, but I keep my hand in place, fighting a strong instinct to retract it and apologize. When Jen rests her hand on mine, all of the tension that has been building dissipates from my body and I shift my face toward hers. She leans in to receive my kiss. My hand reaches around and rubs her back, then wanders up her neck to the base of her head. Passion flows freely between our mouths as I pull at the folds of her towel, allowing it to open. Jen slips her hand up the back of my shirt, and I pull the towel to her waist.

I unlock from Jen's kiss and take in her bare chest. I peck at her chin and neck, moving my lips up to her ear while one hand caresses her back and the other her breasts.

A trace of shame scrabbles at my mind. I press my lips harder against Jen's neck, trying to fend off the emotion that threatens to consume me. I cup Jen's breast hard as I lift my head and smother her mouth with mine. A jumble of thoughts and unwelcome images claw their way through my brain. I push each thought aside, pressing my mouth harder against hers. Jen matches my intensity, scratching at my back, equaling the force of my kiss.

Abruptly, I sit back, searching for an invitation ... begging her to beg me, looking for validation of my desire to take her fully. What I see in the dampness of her bright green eyes is the reflection of my own defenseless heart.

"What?" she says.

I have no answer.

"I didn't ask you to stop." Jen shakes her head, breathing hard, her lips clenched.

"I know. It's just ..."

Her breathing gradually softens. I feel empty, hollow. Slowly, she wraps the towel around her torso and asks, "What is it?"

I stand up and stare at the woodstove. I am afraid to open my mouth, afraid of what will emerge. But it comes out anyway. "You're amazing, Jen. And insanely beautiful. Being here with you ... it's like some crazy dream. This whole trip is like a dream—like I'm this hero who traveled to Ecuador to solve some great mystery ... and he gets the girl too. Only the hero has no wife, no kids, no business. But me? I've got all of those ... and this ... dream."

Jen looks at me patiently, so I continue. "You're incredible. You're kind, intelligent ... we connect on so many levels. But you're closer to my daughter's age than mine. My God, while I was kissing you all I could hear was my son's little voice asking me a million questions ... about space ... and dinosaurs ... and math, for crying out loud. I'm making out with Miss Universe and my son's reciting forty-seven digits of pi in my head."

Jen's face relaxes into a broad smile.

"What?" I ask.

"Forty-seven digits of pi?" she says.

"Yeah. The little bugger knows forty-seven digits of pi. Probably more by now."

Jen starts to laugh.

"Listen," I continue. "A while back I was bitching to my friend, Jake, about how hard it is to be married with kids. He used this brotherly tone that he calls on whenever I'm feeling sorry for myself. He told me to savor every minute of it, because these years will be over far too soon. And he's right. Next thing you know, my babies will be moved out, living in far away places, and I'll be singing Harry Chapin."

Jen looks at me with puzzled eyes.

"You know, *Cat's in the Cradle*?"

She shakes her head.

"You know *Enola Gay* and you haven't heard of Harry Chapin?" I begin to sing, "When you comin' home son? I don't know when ... but we'll get together then, Dad ... you know we'll have a good time then."

Jen waits for me to continue, but I have nothing more to say. My eyes fill with tears, and I wipe at them to keep them from running down my cheeks. She gets up and embraces me in a long hug. "If it makes you feel any better ... that only makes me want you more."

I let out a loud snort—half laughing, half crying. "Oh God, don't tell me that. My monogamous Lutheran morals are hanging by a thread here."

Jen laughs again. "You're a good man, Oliver."

A resigned smile possesses my face. "Would it change your opinion of me if I asked you to pick up where we left off, you know, before my conscience kicked in?"

"Don't tempt me. Look, I'm ... I'm sorry ... that was selfish of me."

"Selfish of *you*? I'm the one with the wife and kids."

"I know," she says. "But I knew that too. I didn't really think … I never expected to be stuck in a cabin with you … and a woodstove, and a bottle of wine." Jen looks me straight in the eye and her face turns deadly serious. "Look, Oliver, I know you aren't happy in your marriage, and I can't entirely relate to that—I'm not even sure that you know why you're unhappy. But I'm on the rebound too. It's a dangerous mix … we're both vulnerable, and you're right … this has gone too far."

I look at the loveseat and see the potential for a second bed. "Can I at least borrow a pillow?"

Jen smiles. "I think that can be arranged."

An incongruous mix of electricity and contentment fills the cabin as we prepare for bed. While Jen is in the bathroom, I refuel the woodstove and turn off all but the bedroom light. Then I tuck myself into a blanket on top of the loveseat cushions on the living room floor. I lie on my back and bask in the glow of an inflated ego. Desire knocks again, but I send it away, turning my thoughts to the family who will greet me in Orlando in less than forty-eight hours.

Jen emerges from the bathroom. "Any change?"

"You mean me or the vault?"

"I meant the vault, but … how are you?"

"I'm fine," I say, though I'm not sure that I am. "As for the vault … no change. How are you doing?"

"Good," Jen says. "I'm kind of sad happy, if you know what I mean."

I nod. "Yeah, I think I do."

"Well, let me know if anything changes—with the vault, I mean."

"I will."

Jen stops outside the bedroom door and says, "Have a good sleep, Oliver."

"You too," I reply.

She hovers for a moment and then adds, "Thanks for blinking first."

"Mm-hmm," I say before she disappears into the bedroom.

I stare at the doorway where Jen was standing, until I am quite certain that she will not reappear. Then I roll over on my side and mutter to myself, "Goodnight, Sunshine."

~ ~ ~

"Showtime?" she asks.

"Not quite," Harold replies. "We're waiting for first light."

"I'll be ready," she says. Then she looks around her office and scans the photos of all those who came before her. Allowing a smile to form, she adds, "Harold, let's change the world tomorrow."

"Yes Muriel," he replies. "That is what we came to do, isn't it?"

Fifty-Three

I awaken for the umpteenth time, uncomfortable and restless. The wine has worn off, and a dull fear has taken its place. In Jen's company, it was easy to forget that we are miles from anyone. Lying alone on the floor of an unfamiliar cabin, it is hard to ignore. Someone is looking for me, and I cannot fully comprehend why. I am certain the source of my recent notoriety rests less than ten feet from my head. If only I knew how to reach it.

Feeling a chill, I get out of bed and add another log to the woodstove. On my way back to bed, I look over at the vault.

Something has changed since the last time I checked. I take two steps toward it and lean down. The word ENTER shows briefly on the vault's display, followed by CODE.

"Welcome back," I say to myself. Reinvigorated, I turn on a lamp and get my journal, then flip through it until I find my notes about the Enola Gay. I pore over the information looking for any clues about the password. Nothing seems to fit.

I consider waking up Jen, but we already went through every option we could think of together, to no avail. So I walk around the room, looking for any new source of inspiration. By the loveseat I take another long look at the framed picture on the wall.

Paul Tibbets stares out above my head, waving and smiling. Each time I see this photo it feels slightly creepier, the reality of its context becoming more evident as I allow myself to search deeper into the image. What would go through a pilot's mind as he prepared to take off in an airplane named after his mother, knowing that he was about to drop an atomic bomb in the middle of an urban area? I recall reading, during my research in Canoa, that the purpose of Tibbets' wave was to get reporters to move away from the airplane's propellers. That doesn't explain his smile.

I pull myself back from 1945, focusing again on the details of the picture. This must be it … this must be my next clue. *What am I missing?* I look at every part of the photo, and then read Einstein's quote again, mumbling to myself, *"I should have become a watchmaker."*

I analyze every aspect of the picture—the photo, the matting, the frame. Then I reach up and take it off the wall. *Why didn't I think of this before?* Excitedly, I look at the back of the frame. Nothing. Disappointment creeps in again as I stare at the wall, and at the back of the frame. Still nothing.

I sit down on my makeshift bed and twist four metal clips that hold the photo in place, then remove the cardboard backing and study it closely. Finding no markings, I look at the back of the photo itself. It too is blank. I scrutinize the matting, and look at everything again. Then I walk back to the wall to see if I have missed something, but all I see is a blank wall with a single nail. I sit down on the bed again, an odd mix of exhaustion, futility and fear coursing through me.

I pick up the photo, now free of its frame, and hold it at arm's length. I see nothing new. Then there—I am not sure if my eyes trigger a memory, or if it is the other way around—but there, in the bottom-left corner of the photo, I see a date, handwritten in light gray ink. *1945-08-06*. August 6, 1945—the day the Enola Gay dropped Little Boy on Hiroshima, killing hundreds of thousands of people and changing the political landscape of the planet. As I shake my head at this new find—*how did I not see this before?*—Arlo's voice fills my mind, a vivid memory of a discussion at Eddy's campsite this summer. *Eddy and his dates*, he had said—something to do with the Japanese internment. *A watchmaker*, I think. *And a date*. It's a weak link ... but this entire puzzle was intended for Eddy to solve, not me. Maybe, just maybe, this would have been obvious to him.

I stare at the date for a long time. Given everything that has happened since I found Daniel's letter in May, it seems impossible that I could be looking at the key to a vault containing a world-changing invention. And yet, it feels entirely plausible. Carrying the picture, I crawl over and kneel beside the vault. Staring at the display, I think again of waking Jen. *No, not yet. Just one try ... either it works or it doesn't.*

I move my fingers to the keypad and slowly enter the digits 1-9-4-5-0-8-0-6. I pull my hand away and force myself to take one full breath, and then another. My pulse quickens despite my efforts to subdue it. Gingerly, I reach down again and press the ENTER key.

Nothing happens.

Seconds later, the vault emits a short beep followed by a click. The LCD panel shows the word CLEAR followed by TO LOCK.

My heart races. I reach down and insert my finger under the metal ring, lift it perpendicular to the vault, and pull. The heavy steel door moves slightly. Then I wrench the door upward, swinging it in an arc above its hinged edge, and set it against the wooden trapdoor that already rests on the kitchen floor. I reach into the vault and retrieve a letter, the pages bound by a paperclip. I recognize Daniel's handwriting.

Fifty-Four

Dear Eddy,

I trust that you will find this message only if you are meant to. Trust does not come easily to me, but my faith in you is steadfast. There is nobody else that I could imagine carrying on my life's work.

For what it's worth, the vault itself is virtually impenetrable. Sometimes I wonder if it will be found thousands of years from now, still unopened, its contents destroyed by some overzealous archaeologist. I laugh at the irony that one scientist's work might be undone by another. Or perhaps it is not ironic at all. Isn't that what we, as scientists, strive to do every single day?

I have never been one for drama, but I own a heightened sense of mortality and a dark sense of humor. The fact that you are reading this cannot be a good sign for what has become of me. Don't cry for me. I've lived a richer life than most, and I've wanted for nothing. If you must acknowledge my passing, consider this my epitaph.

If all goes as planned, this message will be delivered in person. Each time I read it, I think of how impossible this all sounds, and then I re-write it again and burn the previous version. I wonder how different this is from the first letter I placed in this vault, more than a year ago. At that time the pod was only a dream. Now it is a reality.

Yes, my friend, it works. The question is: what do we do with it?

I am beginning to understand what you have known all along: that the scope of the solutions we invent must equal the scope of the problems we face. I used to think you were only referring to magnitude, but now I understand that you were also speaking of complexity. The layers we have placed upon ourselves cannot simply be undone in one broad stroke. There is no panacea for all that ails us. It is essential for people around the world to redefine them-selves, to build sustainable communities at the local level, and to network those communities in a global web of resilience—a world of inter-related yet largely independent villages that live within their means and work together to take care of the planet we share. Technology has its place in a sustainable future, but it also fuels the problems we face.

I know that you understand the relevance of the keys I provided to get here. Our discussions about nuclear power have caused me to face the reality that this invention, no matter how well intended, holds the potential to be used or misused in ways that we cannot yet fathom. I am too immersed in this project to see it objectively. I hope that you are able to see it with a clearer perspective.

There are three fundamental challenges that I see for commercializing this technology:

1. Magnitude of Power: I have been able to power this cottage using a pod smaller than a football. I cannot comprehend the energy that could be generated, stored and deployed by an industrial version of the same device. I rejoice at its potential, and recoil at its destructive power. Perhaps these risks can be mitigated through legislation, but I know that our governments are not always benevolent watchdogs over such matters.

2. Inertia: If we plug a new battery source into the existing machine, is that simply treating the symptom rather than addressing the root cause? How would that serve to curb the myth of perpetual growth and our culture of consumerism? The collective sense of entitlement that grips our western world is already spreading to less developed nations who look to our form of "civilization" and ask how they can be more like us. My time in Ecuador has made me acutely aware of this. It is essential that we bring this invention into being in a way that truly changes the way people think and act, rather than fueling the existing paradigm.

3. Dependency on Fission: The sponge is a man-made substance, the equal of which I have not yet found. Environmental concerns aside (and those are anything but trivial in their own right), I question the energy efficiency of the process. Unless we can find another material to act as a sponge, I do not see how we can call our invention a truly sustainable energy source.

Which leads me to what you will find in this vault, aside from this letter: one thick folder which contains everything you will need to create a solar pod; one memory card containing electronic copies of the folder's contents; and a letter for my dear Annie, which I would ask you to please deliver to her.

I have gone to great lengths to dismantle my prototype, and to ensure that no other copies of this information exist. The sponges are stored in a location equally secure to this one. However, in the documentation provided within, I have included a scientific explanation of how the sponges were created. Even my colleagues at the nuclear plant are unaware of this process. It is, without a doubt, the most controversial aspect of my life's work.

I still feel the optimism that fuelled this journey: the vision of a world no longer dependent on fossil fuels. I have, however, shed the arrogance that drove me when I first met you. Perhaps you can reconcile science with nature—and optimism with fear—in a way that I have not been able to do. I wrote to you before that the future is in our hands. I am sorry if I have left you to carry that load on your own.

Your friend,
Daniel

~ ~ ~

My eyes drift from Daniel's letter back to the vault. An envelope and a memory card sit atop a large folder. I reach down and take out the card, and then retrieve the envelope. It is sealed shut with a crimson disc of wax about the size of a nickel, containing an image of two roses, stems intertwined, surrounded by a double circle. Flipping over the envelope, I see two words in Daniel's distinctive script. *For Annie.*

Fifty-Five

"How much of this do you understand?" Jen asks, setting down Daniel's letter. She leafs through the rest of the vault's documents, which I left strewn about the kitchen table.

"Bits and pieces. Not enough to make sense of it, but enough to realize …"

"To realize what?"

"It's—this is exactly what I came to Ecuador to find. I just can't believe we found it."

Jen flips through the documents while I re-read Daniel's letter. "This must be worth a fortune," she says.

"Yup." *Three million dollars.*

"You look worried," Jen says.

"I'm … confused."

"About what?"

"About what to do with it. It's … you read the letter. Even Daniel was confused. What do you think?" I pass the letter back to her.

Jen scans Daniel's words again. "I think the right thing to do is take it back to the village and share it with the solar team."

"What about government dude? And mystery man?"

"Yeah. I don't know. We could leave it here for now. Then what do we do … lie to them?"

"We could try the truth," I say. "We have a lot of leverage. As far as I know, we're the only two people on the planet who know how to get into the vault."

"Good point."

Jen and I spend the next couple of hours sifting through the documents, only stopping to add wood to the stove. My mind keeps returning to Crescoil's offer.

I stand up to get a glass of water. "Most of that stuff is Greek to me. It must make a lot more sense to you."

Jen sits back in her chair and crosses her arms. "Not really. I do software—this is a very different type of science. One thing's for sure though … the sponge that Daniel mentions … it's a critical piece that we've been missing. The team's going to be stoked about that."

The first light of day is seeping through cracks in the window coverings. I push a curtain aside and look across the clearing to the edge of the woods. "The letter Daniel wrote, it kind of sums up everything I've been hearing these past few weeks. I keep trying to look for simple answers, but life is complicated. Let's leave the documents here for now, like you suggested—lock them up in the vault while we figure out what to do with them. We could talk more on the way to the village."

"You think we should head back?"

"Yeah. I guess. It's hard to believe, but I'm supposed to be at the airport by ten o'clock tonight."

Jen ponders my suggestion for a few minutes, and then gets up. "Mind if I grab a shower first? Warm water is too good to pass up."

"Sure. I might have one too."

Jen disappears into the bathroom and starts the shower. I look at the papers spread across the table and wonder what Eddy would do with them. My thoughts are interrupted by a faint sound—faint but unmistakable. It is the sound of helicopter blades, barely within earshot. I freeze and listen intently to make sure I am not imagining things. I'm not. Already the volume has increased. I hurry to the bathroom door and knock loudly.

"Jen!" I shout. "There's a helicopter!"

The chopper is approaching with remarkable speed. I reach down to my money belt and take out the plastic wrap containing the sponge Eddy gave me. I unwrap the coin-shaped disc and drop it into a small pocket in my knapsack that I use to store change. Through the window I see trees moving in the wind from the helicopter. I quickly gather the documents, stuffing them back in the folder.

For the first time I understand what people mean when they describe their life playing out before their eyes. The journey that led me to this moment replays itself in my mind, pointing me to this cabin in the heart of the Andes—a vivid detailed tapestry of faces, voices, sights and sounds. Then more images, violent, disturbing, as real as the flash-backs. Enormous trees crashing to the earth, undergrowth flattened, rainforest being cut clear by monstrous machines; animals scrambling in all directions—monkeys, birds, snakes, insects—then an explosion and a mushroom cloud. Quechua villagers—men, women and children—run from the wreckage. The image dissolves in a wave of conflicting emotions—hope mixed with futility, love with pain, kind-ness with inhumanity. I feel nauseous ... then suddenly, strangely calm. I know what to do.

~ ~ ~

"What's happening?" Jen is panicked as she runs from the bathroom, wet hair dripping down her shirt and across the floor.

"It's okay," I say. "It'll be okay." I am surprised at the composure of my voice. The helicopter is in the clearing, its blades slowing gradually. I go to the front door and unlock the deadbolt.

"Where are you going?" Her voice is still quavering.

"To greet our guests." I walk onto the front porch. The helicopter seems unusually large—I am surprised that it fits in the clearing. Its windows are heavily tinted, and the only marking on its black body is an emblem with an eagle, surrounded by a circle of print that reads *United States of America*.

The helicopter's side door opens downward, hydraulic arms extending in two stages to form a stairway. Through the opening of a dark curtain covering the chopper's entry-way emerges a man with a thick head of silver hair parted neatly to one side, wearing dark dress pants and a light blue collared shirt. He walks confidently down the stairs toward us. Behind him, another man emerges wearing khakis and a white, short-sleeved dress shirt; I recognize him as the man who chased us up The Hill yesterday. A third man walks through the curtain, also dressed in khakis and a white shirt.

"That's him!" Jen says from behind me. "The man from the government … the one who came to the village yesterday."

"Mr. Bruce," yells the man in front as he approaches us, flanked by his two henchmen. "You are not an easy person to track down."

"It wasn't for lack of trying," I respond over the low rumble of the chopper idling.

"I'm sorry if we've frightened you. That was not our intention." He tips his head toward Jen. "Jennifer Morris, I presume?"

Jen nods.

"So what was your intention?" I ask.

He ignores my question. "My name is Harold McIntyre. These are my associates, Nathan Jacques and Eldon Hewitt. We are with the Office of the President of the United States of America."

"As in … the Secret Service?"

"I report directly to President Baldwin. We're a very small unit … but we're part of the same web. We all serve the same nation. Do you know why we're here?"

"No, I don't," I bluff. "Do you want to tell me?"

"I'll be happy to—" Harold turns and motions toward the helicopter "—in my office. There are a couple of other people who would like to speak to you as well."

"As long as Jen comes too."

"As you wish," Harold says. "Please understand that we will need to do a full search of both of you. And we'll need to search the cabin."

"What jurisdiction do you have here?"

Harold smiles at me. "This is not so much about jurisdiction as responsibility. I trust that you can understand the importance of ensuring that certain technologies do not fall into the wrong hands."

"Sure," I reply. "And whose hands would you be referring to?"

~ ~ ~

Jen wears a stoic mask—equal parts humiliation and indignation—as the security guard pats her down at the door of the helicopter. My hands form into a fist, causing my forearms to tense. I remind myself that the man is only doing his job—and that he could probably snap me like a twig.

The guard gives me an equally thorough search. As he sifts through the contents of my money belt, I wonder if the men searching the cabin have found anything unusual about the change in my knapsack. The guard hands back my money belt and waves me through to the lounge where Harold is seated.

"Sorry for that," Harold says. "Standard protocol. This is a very important, and very expensive, piece of machinery."

"I can imagine," I reply. Jen grunts, no doubt still put off by the search.

Harold signals for us to sit in two swiveling chairs. Jen and I comply, and I look around at the helicopter's interior. The furnishings are elegant but simple. Tinted windows on both sides of the room allow a full view of the clearing. There is a solid wall in front of the entrance, containing a door which I assume leads to the cockpit.

Harold presses a button and two television screens descend from the ceiling on one side of the room. When they are fully lowered, both screens come to life. On one is an image of the President; on the other a man in a suit and tie.

"Jennifer Morris, Oliver Bruce. I introduce Muriel Baldwin, President of the United States of America. And John Flanigan, Chairman and CEO of Crescoil Energy."

"Hello," Jen and I say in unison.

"Hello," the President says.

John Flanigan speaks with a drawl. "I'm pleased to meet you both."

Jen glances over at me with incredulous eyes.

"I assume," Harold says, "that you are both aware we are facing a very tight presidential election in less than two weeks. Despite her incredibly busy schedule, Ms. Baldwin insisted on being part of this meeting. I'm sure I don't have to spell out what that implies about the importance of the invention that you have come to find."

"Have you been tracking me this whole trip?" I blurt. "And what about Eddy's trailer?"

When my question goes unanswered, I feel my anger swelling. "Let me guess—you have video cameras in the cabin too?"

"No," Harold says calmly. "We haven't been filming you."

I look at the screen that holds John Flanigan's beaming face. "What about you?" I say. "You sent Richard Brentwick into the Amazon to buy me. How is Crescoil tied into the US Government?"

"Mr. Bruce," Flanigan says, "Crescoil is working hard to diversify our investment in renewable energy sources. I have been briefed on your discussion with Mr. Brentwick, and the offer he presented to you came directly from me. Crescoil Energy is a major supporter of President Baldwin's re-election campaign, and we have been working with her team to develop an energy mandate that will resonate with the American people. I am here today to demonstrate our commitment to a future based on renewable energy—a message that our president has delivered frequently throughout her campaign."

"The problem," Harold interjects, "is that in times of economic stress, our message of sustainability falls mostly on deaf ears. Polls consistently show that the American people are more interested in jobs and tax cuts than they are in long-term issues like the environment."

"Which means," Flanigan continues, "that the only way for renewable energy to capture the attention of the American public is if it can be seen as a way to create jobs and bolster the economy. I'm a businessman, Mr. Bruce, and I'm here to see if there is a deal to be made. But first we need to understand what you have learned in that cabin."

"The work of Daniel Porter was brought to our attention about two years ago," Harold explains. "Following introductory discussions with Mr. Porter, we developed, in conjunction with our partners—including Crescoil Energy—a re-election campaign based on a viable economic platform fuelled by solar and nuclear energy."

"Was Daniel on board with this?" I ask.

"Let's just say we had piqued his curiosity. As you know, Mr. Porter died tragically, and prematurely. At the time of his death, we understood there was a high probability that he had created a solar pod that could revolutionize the entire energy landscape. Unfortunately, we could not find evidence of the invention. Under routine surveillance earlier this year, it came to our attention that you had picked up on a thread that we were unaware of."

I shake my head in disbelief. "How long have you been monitoring me?"

"Monitoring is a strong word," Harold says. "We have taken an interest in your activities since May."

"How exactly were you ... taking an interest?" I ask.

"I am not at liberty to tell you that," Harold says. "I can only assure you that we have taken the utmost care to ensure both your privacy ... and your safety."

"From who?" Jen asks, breaking her silence. "Who are you keeping us safe *from*?"

"Possibly no one," Harold says. "But like any revolutionary advance in technology, we are treating Daniel Porter's invention as a matter of national importance."

The President's voice calls us all to attention. "Mr. Bruce, and Ms. Morris ... we have no interest in treading on personal liberties. We believe that the future of America, and by extension the world, may be altered by what is inside Daniel Porter's cabin. I am here to ask for your help in this regard, and to gauge whether or not I might be able to deliver a message of hope to our fellow Americans before next week's election."

"Which brings us to the question we all have," Harold says. "What have you found in the cabin?"

"Daniel's documents," I reply.

Harold leans forward, glances at Jen, then looks back at me. "Where are those documents now?"

I look out at the cabin and raise my eyebrows toward the chimney. "Out there. In the smoke."

I hear Jen gasp, but I fix my eyes on Harold and hold them while he processes what I have said.

After a long pause, he asks, "What do you mean?"

"I put them in the woodstove," I reply. "I'm quite certain there's nothing left of them by now."

Fifty-Six

"You burned the documents?" Harold says. "Why would you do such a thing?"

Everyone waits for me to answer. Words fail me when I see Jen's confused expression. Even I do not fully under-stand my impulsive decision. As paper burned to ash in the fire and the memory card melted in the intense heat of the coals, I knew there was no way to undo what I had done. I had closed the door of the woodstove with numb hands, unable to reconcile my actions with the hope that had brought me to Ecuador. Then I walked over and closed the empty vault, pressed the CLEAR button, and listened as it locked shut.

When the words come out, it is as if they are not my own. Perhaps they are not. "Daniel's invention was going to create as many problems as it solved. Maybe more. It was too powerful."

"In what way?" Harold asks.

"In more ways than one. I saw it being used as a weapon. I saw accidents … and bloodshed. I realized what our real problem is … I mean, with energy."

"And what is that?" Flanigan asks.

I look at Harold McIntyre, then at Jen, before locking eyes with the image of John Flanigan. "We use too much of it."

Harold speaks with a hint of anger. "I believe you have made a mistake."

"Time will tell," I reply flatly.

After a long pause, the President speaks. "Mr. Bruce, I am highly disappointed. I had hoped that we might have an opportunity to work together on a new energy strategy, to be part of a solution to the problems we face."

I look at the screen, directly into the president's eyes. A million thoughts come to mind, but a simple message forms on my lips. "Maybe we can," I say. "Once we all realize that we're part of the problem."

~ ~ ~

"That's it?" Harold asks Nathan, the mystery man.

"Yes, sir. The pass code checked out. The vault was empty."

"Thank you," Harold says. "I'll take the documents. You can give the packs to Mr. Bruce and Ms. Morris."

Mystery man hands some stuff to Harold before passing our knapsacks to Jen and me. Harold takes my travel guide out of the bag and flips through it. He sets the guide on his desk and picks up my journal, looking at each page carefully. Then he sets down the journal and picks up the last document—the one piece of Daniel's treasure that I chose not to destroy. As Harold inserts his finger in the envelope flap to break the wax seal, I lurch forward. "That's a personal letter from Daniel to his wife. I'd like to deliver it. Do you really need to open it?"

The security guard takes a step toward me. Harold speaks with quiet authority. "Yes, I do. *If* it is appropriate to do so, I will give it back to you to deliver to Ms. Porter."

Harold reads the letter, places it back in its envelope and hands it to me. He then proceeds to interrogate Jen and me about the contents of the vault. Clearly frustrated by the brevity of our answers, Harold raises his voice considerably. "You are telling me that you reviewed Daniel Porter's documents in detail, and you understood none of it?" Then he looks pointedly at Jen and says, "I understand that of Mr. Bruce, but I have a much harder time believing you, Ms. Morris."

"Give her a break," I say, my neck tightening in anger.

Harold speaks more calmly. "I apologize for my tone. Ms. Morris, is there anything else you can tell us about your understanding of the documents, given your work at the village?"

Jen shakes her head and drops her shoulders. Then she speaks with a combination of confidence and indifference. "I'm a software engineer. My role in this project is to write an algorithm for timing the pulsing of gates that convert heat into electrical energy. So far, my work has been completely theoretical—I rely on data that pretends to come from sensors, and I create events that are supposed to trigger someone else's components to do their job. The modules I write don't have to understand the ones other people write, and vice versa."

Harold rubs his hand from his forehead down to the end of his nose. Then he removes his hand from his face, looks at us with a weak smile and says, "Would you be willing to answer a few questions under oath, and … in the presence of a polygraph system?"

"A lie detector?" I ask.

Harold shrugs. "I prefer to call it a truth validator—that is, assuming you have nothing to hide."

Jen looks at me and shakes her head. "I don't," she says.

"Me neither," I echo. Then I think of the sponge. *Just answer his questions*, I tell myself, *and you'll be fine*. "Okay," I say. "If that'll buy back our privacy."

"This is a voluntary action," Harold says. "We're not forcing you to do anything. But yes, a polygraph should help us to build confidence in your story."

Within moments, Jen and I are both connected to a series of wires, and Harold is peppering us with questions as he looks at a small screen attached to the armrest of his seat. He asks simple questions—our names, where we were born, our parents' lineage—mixed with random queries about childhood, religion and politics. I believe he is trying to throw us off and challenge our integrity, but I answer every question honestly and completely.

Harold broaches the subject of Daniel's invention. He delves into how we found the vault and what we gleaned from its contents. I remain surprisingly calm throughout the process, with only a nagging concern about the sponge resting in the back of my mind. Jen becomes increasingly relaxed as the questioning intensifies, as if the experience is therapeutic for her.

I begin to recognize Harold's words as repackaged questions—repeating things he has already asked using slightly different language—and I become mildly agitated. But I continue to provide earnest answers, trusting that the machine I am attached to will recognize my honesty. Just when I think the questioning might go on for hours, Harold sits back in his chair and instructs his security guard to disconnect us from the polygraph machine.

"You're free to go," Harold says as the guard removes the last lead from my chest.

"That's it?" I ask.

"Unless you have something else to tell me."

"No," Jen and I answer together.

"What about your monitoring efforts?" I ask. "Will you continue ..."

"You have my word that we will respect your privacy." Harold reaches into his pocket and pulls out a business card. "I would appreciate you calling me if you think of anything—anything at all—that you might not have shared with us today."

I stand up to leave.

"Are you okay getting back down the mountain?" Harold asks. "We could make a stop at the village."

I look at Jen. "I don't know about you, but I prefer to keep my feet on the ground."

Jen nods and follows me out the door. We head for the cover of the forest. I glance back and see the chopper's stairway retracting into its belly. I search my mind for some semblance of fear—this all feels too simple, too clean an exit from such an intense experience—but I am still calm.

By the time we reach the forest, the helicopter blades are in full motion. Without looking back, we push forward along the path leading upstream. Over the sound of the water I hear the helicopter rise into the air, then fade into the distance.

Fifty-Seven

Jen and I walk through the woods, past Daniel's micro-hydro plant, until we reach the pond at the base of the water slide. We clamber up the rocks, saying nothing to one another as we continue up the path toward Walter and Maria's cabin. Jen's cheerful demeanor is absent, her bright face expressionless.

Neither of us says a word until we reach the main trail heading back to the village. When Jen finally speaks, her voice is distant.

"Did that just happen?" she says.

"I think so," I reply. "Either that or I'm having one hell of a dream."

"Do you think they're still watching us?"

"I don't know. I'm not sure I'll ever feel totally free again."

"I know what you mean."

"Welcome to the twenty-first century. Maybe there's no such thing as privacy anymore."

"Maybe that's not such a bad thing," Jen says apathetically. "Maybe if we all knew we were being watched, we wouldn't do such awful things to one another."

"Maybe if we were truly free," I reply, "people wouldn't feel the need to."

Silence falls upon us again, and walks with us until its presence becomes unbearable.

"I'm sorry," I finally say.

"I know," Jen answers.

"I didn't plan to do that. I just—"

"Why didn't you tell me?"

"I'm not sure. It all happened so fast."

"I wish you'd waited, so we could've made the decision together."

"You would have tried to talk me out of it."

"Yeah, I would have." Jen takes a few more strides and then stops. "Speaking of secrets … what was that offer about? The one from Crescoil?"

"Oh, that. No big deal—they just offered me three million dollars for the location of Daniel's invention."

Jen's eyes widen. "Three million dollars? Why didn't you tell me?"

"Want the truth?" I ask.

"Um, yeah."

"I didn't trust myself. Telling you would have made it more real … it would have been harder to ignore."

"You're telling me that you threw three million dollars into a woodstove?"

"Yup. Crazy, huh? I'm blaming you, in part."

"What do you mean?"

"After you told me what a good man I am, I had to live up to your expectation."

Jen pierces me with her eyes. "I'm not sure if I love you or hate you right now, but either way … I'm going to miss you."

~ ~ ~

The last time I felt this popular was at my fortieth birthday party. Sitting around the table for one last lunch at Pueblo del Sol, I feel like I am in the midst of family.

"Thanks for the send-off," I say. "I was worried I wouldn't see some of you again."

"I'm glad we made it in time," Conlan says. "So tell us, what did the President's office want with you two?"

"I'm sorry," I say with mock sincerity. "That information is classified."

Andrew smacks me hard on the leg. "Classified? But we're family!"

"It feels like a dream," I say. "It's as if I'm Dorothy, and I'm going to wake up in a pool of sweat—"

"Come on, Dorothy," Katherine says. "We're dying to know what happened up there."

"Did you find it?" Conlan asks.

"It?" Andrew says. "Would someone mind fillin' me in here? I daen't even know what *it* is."

Everyone waits for me to speak. I search for some internal guidance about sharing what Jen and I experienced—this seems like one of those moments when you feign ignorance and pretend that nothing happened. *Why weren't we sworn to secrecy? Isn't that what happens when you meet the President of the United States in a clandestine location to discuss matters of global importance?* Yet nobody asked us to remain silent. We were questioned and released, simple as that. No drama, no gunfire, no bodies falling from the sky. Just people being people—a business opportunity, as John Flanigan put it.

I finally open my mouth and allow the words to come out. "We found Daniel's invention."

A stunned silence falls over the table.

"Well?" Conlan says. "What did you do with it? Was that—did they take it?"

I shake my head. All eyes upon me, I freeze, unable to admit that I destroyed the Holy Grail that has been the driving force behind the work at this village. Scanning the faces around me, I see hope, excitement, curiosity. For a moment I regret saying anything, but on a deeper level it feels right to speak openly about the decision I made. I swallow hard and look at Conlan. "No," I say softly. "I destroyed it."

Andrew spews coffee onto his lap. "Ye did *what?*"

"I burned it." I say. "In Daniel's woodstove."

Nobody is smiling anymore.

"You found Daniel's invention," Katherine says, "and you *destroyed* it?"

"Yes."

"*Why?*" she asks, staring daggers at me.

"Because the world wasn't ready for it."

"What the hell?" Conlan says with an edge that I have not seen in him before.

"It all happened in an instant," I say. "I had to make a decision based on everything I'd learned—and based on Daniel's own words. I ... it just came to me, and I acted." Looking around the room, my confidence returning, I add, "It might be hard for all of you to accept, but ... I know I did the right thing."

"Ye cocky son of a bitch!" Andrew slams his cup on the table. He looks like he might take a swing at me. Then he shakes his head and sits back, crossing his arms. I think he might be planning which way to kill me. Then he shakes his head again and says, "I dinnae know ye had it in ye, Oliver."

~ ~ ~

Jen opens the door before my second tap, already wearing her boots.

"Ready to tackle The Hill?" I ask.

"I'm ready to walk down," she says. "I'm not so sure about the up part."

Heading down the path, I breathe in my last view of this paradise. The birds are vocal this afternoon, a symphony that I imagine to be a farewell refrain.

"I guess you'll have a few hours to reflect on everything," Jen says.

"Yeah. Somehow I have to find the energy to meet my family tomorrow morning ... and hear every minute detail about Disney World."

"You must miss them."

"Yeah, I do."

We walk side-by-side, a comfortable silence bridging our thoughts. When the highway comes into view, Jen asks, "Will you tell your wife about me?"

"Yeah."

"Will you tell her it didn't mean anything?"

"No."

"Why?"

"She'd know I was lying."

When we reach the bus shelter, I put down my backpack and Jen sets down the knapsack that she carried for me. I turn and study her face. "Well, I guess that's it ... for now."

"I guess so," she says.

I reach into my pocket and pull out a sheet of paper. "Here's my contact info. Let's keep in touch."

Jen takes the paper and reads it. Then she reaches into her own pocket and hands a slip of paper to me. "And mine." Her eyes begin to well, and she raises her arm to wipe them.

"Don't dry your cry." I open my arms and Jen folds into me, sobbing. I am too numb to cry. I hold onto Jen, tight, until I hear the hum of the approaching bus.

"Now get back to work," is all I can say, my emotions stoically, stupidly suppressed.

"On what?" Jen asks. "You burned our work, remember?"

"Oh yeah. That. They say the phoenix rises out of the ash. I took care of the ash; the phoenix is up to you."

"Very poetic," Jen says.

"I've been waiting all day to say that."

"I'll think about that," she says. "Right now, I'm going to say goodbye and walk back up The Hill. I don't think I can bear to stand here and wave as you ride out of my life."

"Fair enough. Take care of yourself, okay?"

"You too. Goodbye." And true to her word, Jen turns and walks away.

Fifty-Eight

I stare at a menu in the diner adjacent to the sprawling RV Resort where our motor home is parked. The chaos of this Floridian megalopolis makes me pine for the tranquility of Pueblo del Sol. I am not hungry, despite a long day at the Magic Kingdom. Isaac woke me up before sunrise this morning, intent on making the most of our one family day at Disney World.

I order a bowl of soup from the chatty, chubby waitress, and try to listen to the constant flow of stories coming from Isaac's mouth. Emily and I have hardly spoken, or touched, since I landed in Orlando yesterday morning. "Tonight," I said this morning, "I will tell you about my trip. Once the kids are asleep."

An image on the TV screen hanging across from our booth brings me into focus. President Muriel Baldwin is about to address the nation. During a brief read of a newspaper yesterday—a welcome distraction from my emotional turmoil—I learned that the presidential race is as close as any this nation has known, while a Republican Congress is all but certain. I am suddenly interested in politics, and I wonder what our president will say tonight.

"Daddy," Isaac says, "how many bats did you count in the Haunted Mansion?"

"Sorry, buddy. I really want to hear what the president says, okay?"

"I counted twelve," he says, ignoring me. "How many did you see?"

"Just, please, I need to hear this."

"Since when are you interested in politics?" Emily asks, surprised.

"Since about forty-eight hours ago."

Emily twists her head in curiosity while Isaac moves on to playing tic-tac-toe on his paper menu.

I put up my hand to catch the waitress's attention. "Excuse me. Could you please turn up the TV?"

"You wanna hear that bag o' wind?" the waitress grumbles, reminding me of Helen at the Sunshine Café. Then she laughs and adds, "I'm sorry, hon, was that my outside voice? Sure, I'll turn it up."

The president is trying to quiet the gathering of supporters in her home state of New Hampshire, repeatedly saying "Thank you" while motioning her hands like a quarterback hushes the hometown crowd. Following a few last chants of *Pres-i-dent!* the crowd calms enough for her to speak.

"Thank you. Thank you so much." She pauses to scan the crowd, and then she removes her glasses and replaces them with another pair. As the audience quiets to a murmur, the

President looks toward the camera and holds up the glasses that she just removed. "I won't be needing these tonight. And that is going to make a few people very uncomfortable. You see, these glasses are a technological marvel, delivering words to me in case I forget what I'm going to say. My own personal teleprompter. The thing is ..."

President Baldwin sets the glasses down on the podium in front of her and picks up a stack of paper. Then she continues to speak.

"The thing is that while I was supposed to be rehearsing the speech that was prepared for me today—and a wonderful speech it is—I was actually writing my own. So please forgive me if my delivery is not perfect. It has been a long time since I've spoken my own words in front of a crowd."

I recognize Harold McIntyre crossing the stage toward the president. Gracefully, she turns to him and holds her hand up to stop his advance. The president gathers herself and sets the stack of papers upon the podium.

"My fellow Americans," she begins with a bright smile. "Most of us who enter politics begin our careers with the best of intentions. We believe that we are called to serve our country, and we are willing to do almost anything within our power to reach our highest calling. Then, as we climb the ladder of political success, most of us lose our way. We lose our hearts, if not our souls, as we cater to those who usher us toward the pinnacle. We fall victim to the most hollow of objectives: to win more votes than our political opponents. For the select few who manage to garner enough votes to govern this great nation, we owe too much to too few for helping us along the way. We forget that we are all in this together, that we—regardless of our political leanings—are all Americans. We are all people, who share responsibility for the well-being of this planet with hundreds of other nations, and billions of other people; people not unlike ourselves; people who love their children just as much as we do.

"A few days ago, I met a gentleman in the most unusual of circumstances. He said only a few words to me—ordinary words that on any other day might not have reached me. Ordinary words that, at that particular moment, struck me to the core. He said, quite simply, that to find solutions to the challenges we face we must first realize that we are part of the problem.

"I am not here to deliver a sermon. I am here to acknowledge that I have walked the path that I described, and in doing so I have lost my way. Tonight, I am supposed to be delivering a cautiously crafted speech aimed at winning a few additional votes in critical swing states, with the hope that I will narrowly defeat my adversary, Edwin Mann, and be rewarded with another four years as your president. Four years to do what?"

She looks up from her page and sweeps her head slowly to take in the silent audience. Almost everyone in the restaurant is also silent, staring at the television. Only Isaac is oblivious to the president's message, too caught up in his menu games to notice history in the making.

President Baldwin continues to read. "I am tired of playing the game. I just want to lead—from my heart—and make a real difference in this world. If you choose to re-elect me next week, all I can tell you is that I will be a different president—a better president, and a better person—than I have been for the past four years. Those of you who believe that your president must be sure and unwavering, who look to me as a young child sees a parent—as an unquestioned leader who always has the right answer, the perfect solution to any problem—should not vote for me. Those of you who can see me as a human, no more or less so than you, who is trying to make the most of her brief time on Earth … for those of you, I ask for another chance to lead this great nation.

"I can only make this one promise: to provide the kind of authentic leadership that each and every one of you deserves, and to use the authority you entrust in me to enact changes that will move this world toward a more peaceful, sustainable future. I ask this of you, my fellow Americans— that each of you join me in finding your own purpose, a calling to the greater good, and contribute to the best of your ability toward that purpose."

"Hot damn," our waitress stammers as the news anchor re-appears on the television following the speech. "That almost makes me want to give her another chance."

"That *was* a great speech," Emily says.

I smile warmly at my wife. "I really do have to tell you about my trip."

Fifty-Nine

The chill from a January rainstorm is wearing off as I look at Charlie's art on the wall of Annie's living room. After a whirlwind trip to Vashon Island I am eager to return to Florida, where my family is relaxing at a beachside RV park south of Sarasota.

Annie's voice precedes her as she emerges from the stairway. "He's finally asleep. Thanks for waiting."

"My pleasure," I reply. "It was nice to see him. You both seem ... happy."

"We are," Annie says. "How about you?"

"I'm good. I'm seeing life a lot more clearly than last time I was here. Hey, I hope you don't mind that I brought the mug back to Charlie."

"Not at all," she says. "I want him to remember his father."

"What about you? I don't imagine that letter will be easy to read."

"I read it, just now."

"Oh. How was that?"

Annie's face turns solemn. "It was hard. It was very personal ... more emotionally honest than Daniel ever allowed himself to be in person. I learned some things ... and confirmed some things too."

"Did he speak of ..." I begin, then hesitate.

"Katherine?" she asks matter-of-factly.

I nod.

"Yes," she says. "That was one of the confirmations."

"I'm sorry."

"Don't be. I'm in a good place these days. I'd like you to meet Martin sometime."

"I'd like that too." A sense of contentment tells me that I mean it.

"How long are you here for?" Annie asks.

"Just a couple of days. I had to catch up on a few things at the restaurant, but my staff kicked me out before I had a chance to get in their way. I'm on my way back to Florida now."

"Where will you travel to next?"

"We're going to wait until it warms up enough to drive back through Minnesota. We're planning to spend a bit more time with my extended family before returning to the daily grind."

"That sounds nice. Are you still planning to see the Smoky Mountains?"

"We already did," I reply. "We went there for a few days when I got back from Ecuador."

"Was it everything you hoped it would be?"

I think of the Smokies, and I hear Eddy's voice. *Always let the people you love know that you love them, Oliver.* "Yes," I smile at the rich blend of memories that fills my mind. "Yes, it was."

Part 4 – Selección

Sixty

"Hi," I say.

"Hi," Jen replies, her carry-on bag falling to her side.

"You look … amazing. But you always look amazing."

"Thanks. You look good too."

I open my arms and she steps into them. We embrace for a long while before she pulls away.

"So, what do you want for dinner?" I ask.

"Anything but airplane food."

"Sushi?"

"Sounds good. It's probably the last food I'll recognize for a while."

I fall into stride beside Jen, a familiar intimacy resting in the air between us. "It's so good to see you again," I say. "Strange, but good."

"I was a bit nervous when I told you I'd be stopping here."

"I'm glad you did."

We find a seat in a quiet corner of the Japanese restaurant. I try to read my menu, but I keep looking up at Jen. Five years have only added to her radiance. When the waitress asks for my order, I yield briefly to the inconvenience and accept her suggestion of a bento box C.

I don't know what a bento box C is, and I don't care. All I want is to make the most of my time with this woman whom I last saw on the side of a highway in Ecuador.

"So how have you been?" I ask. "I've been following your blog ... but what about the stuff you don't blog to the world?"

"Like what?" Jen's coy expression matches her tone.

"Like your private life."

"I thought we agreed that privacy no longer existed."

"I'm still holding out hope. So how are you?"

"I'm good," Jen says. "I guess you know that I got my PhD in Computer Science, and I've been carrying on with solar research. I'm really excited about what I'll be doing in China."

"Sounds like an ambitious project."

"Yes and no. That's the beauty of distributed energy. It's more like a bunch of small projects that we hope will add up to major change. We're seeing a huge demand for it—especially overseas. Here it still feels like we're pushing a boulder up a hill. But we've recruited a heavy hitter."

"Oh?" I say.

"Yeah. It's not public knowledge yet, but our favorite former president is about to take the reigns of the Renewable Energy Alliance—and she's bringing some powerful friends with her."

"Seriously? That's great. Have you actually met her—in person?"

"Yes, a couple of times, once while she was still in office, and again last week. I told her I'd be seeing you. She asked me to say hello ... and she said she'd like to meet you one day."

"I'd be honored." Already considered one of the most popular presidents in history, Muriel Baldwin fought relentlessly in her second term to challenge the inertia of a growth-based economy blind to long-term environmental effects. The first president in recent history to successfully hand leadership to her vice president, the equally popular

Thomas McCready, she set into motion an unprecedented level of continuity in government programs and international relations.

I sip a bowl of miso soup, part of the tray of compartmentalized food that appeared without me noticing. "So, I know a bit about your work … but how about your personal life. Are you seeing anyone?"

Jen takes a drink of tea, and I sense that she was dreading my question. After a bit of deliberation, she sets down her cup and says, "I've been dating someone for almost two years. Sam Jaworski. He's a physicist, and ten years my senior. Surprised?"

"Not really," I reply, genuinely happy for Jen, even though I feel a pang of envy for a scientist I have never met. "Two years, huh? Sounds serious."

"It is. He wants me to marry him."

"And?"

"I'm waffling."

"Let me guess … you don't want to change your name to Jennifer Jaworski?"

Jen laughs. "Yeah, that's it."

"He must be a good egg to win your heart."

"He is. He reminds me of you."

"You mean dashing, intelligent and witty?"

"I meant old," Jen deadpans. "Just kidding. I mean that he's kind … and intelligent."

"I'll take that as a compliment. But dashing and witty would be good too."

"Yes, he is all of those things. And so are you. So how's your family?"

"Good. My daughter's practically a woman now—she's seventeen—and my son is twelve."

"How about Emily?"

"She's good. We're good. It's not perfect, but we have a good life." After a long pause I say what has been on my mind since the arrivals gate. "Jen, have you ever wondered—"

"Yes." *No hesitation there.* "More often than I'd care to admit."

"I can relate. You messed me up for a long time. Still do sometimes. I envisioned this honeymoon phase where everything would be incredible ... we'd be having sex on the beach and attending cocktail parties with all your young, cool friends. Then I saw the future ... you hit thirty and your biological clock kicks in ... and all of a sudden I'm rocking my kids and my grandkids to sleep at the same time. Then my arthritis flares up and I have to rest my weary joints ... and you're asking yourself what the hell you were thinking when you married this old guy."

Jen laughs. "I guess I romanticized it more than that."

"Me too. I just needed to create a less pleasant outcome to keep myself from going crazy."

"I'm glad you're doing well," she says. "And your family ... it's good that you held things together."

"Yeah," I agree. "It wasn't easy. I almost left Emily ... then she almost left me ... but we worked it out. You don't want to know how many times I thought of climbing on a plane to come and find you. But then I'd return to that moment in the cabin, and it seemed ... almost too perfect. I didn't want to spoil a beautiful memory."

"What did Emily think of you coming here today?"

"She knew I had to."

The waitress appears to refill our teacups. I look at the tray of food in front of me. My appetite has left me, replaced by the nervous energy that accompanied me through much of my time in Ecuador. Five years of pretending that I was over Jen, undone in half an hour.

"And your restaurant?" Jen asks. "How's that going?"

"I sold it to our star employee, but I work there sometimes—as a barista. I write for an outfit in Quito that is working to save the Amazon, one that Carmen's granddaughter started working for a couple of years ago."

"I'll have to get the link," Jen says.

"Sure. It's just a soapbox of sorts. But I do make a few bucks from it."

"So is that what you're doing now … for work?"

"In part. I'm also doing some painting, and Emily does pottery. We're thinking of becoming starving artists when we grow up."

"Doesn't sound like a bad line of work," Jen says. "Except the starving part."

I fixate on Jen's green eyes. "I don't want this dinner to end."

"You haven't even touched yours."

I look down at my bento box. "I'm just trying to make sure you miss your plane."

I force myself to eat some of the food I ordered, and then I pay for the meal and get up from the table. We walk to the departures area together. I think of a thousand things to say, but none of them feel right. Finally, almost unconsciously, I look into Jen's eyes and say, "I love you."

Her face says more than any words could, and her tears force my own to follow. I make no effort to stop them.

"I love you too, Oliver. I always will."

I attempt to smile. "Now go. Change the world. I'll be watching for your next blog post."

"Okay"—Jen wipes her cheeks with her sleeve—"let's not wait another five years, alright?"

I shrug, my face a damp mess. "We'll cross paths when we're meant to."

I watch Jen pass through the security gate and out of view. Then she re-emerges, kisses her hand and blows it to me. I return her gesture. She smiles and disappears again. I stand and stare at the gate for a long time, wishing her to reappear, knowing that she will not. Finally, I wipe my tears with my arm and allow my feet to carry me in the direction of the exit.

As I walk out the doors of the airport, a security guard is hounding a beggar to get up. The beggar is holding a sign that reads: *I went to war when all I wanted was peace. Now I'd be happy with a sandwich.*

I reach into my pocket and pull out the sponge. I look at it and chuckle at the inscription—IN DOG WE TRUST—and then hand it to the beggar. Then I reach back into my pocket and give him a five-dollar bill.

"God bless," he says, slipping the money into his jacket.

Sixty-One

"How was dinner?" Jake asks as I climb into his car.

"Bittersweet. Thanks for the ride."

"Anytime. So how is your young friend?"

"She's good. Really good."

"Still gorgeous?"

"More than ever."

"Where is she heading to? Japan?"

"China. She's working on a really cool solar project. They're trying to decentralize the energy sector."

"Sounds exciting. Why do I sense that you're going to talk me into spending more money?"

"Saving more money, you mean?"

"Oh yeah, right," Jake says.

Our conversation turns to small talk as we approach the heart of the island. A few blocks before the café I ask, "Would you mind driving over to the isthmus? To the stationary bikes?"

"Sure," Jake says. "Why's that?"

"I ride them sometimes, as a sort of therapy. I'm not ready to face a crowd right now."

"You want to skip the meeting?"

"Yeah. It's half over anyway."

Jake drives us to the isthmus and parks beside the ever-changing row of exercise equipment. "Somebody actually rides these things, huh?"

"Once in a while," I say, climbing out of the car. Jake follows me, and we sit down on two relatively new bikes.

"That was tough on you tonight, wasn't it?" Jake asks as we both begin to pedal, looking across the night sky to the lights of South Seattle.

"Yeah. A part of me wanted to get on the plane."

"A part of you probably did."

"Yup," I agree.

I expect a dose of brotherly advice, but Jake says nothing. We look out over the water, listening to the rhythm of our wheels. I don't think Jake and I have ever spent this much time together without talking.

After ten or fifteen minutes, I stop moving my legs and listen to the wheel slow down. When it finally comes to rest, I break the silence. "Guess I'd better go meet my family."

Jake climbs off his bike. "I'm glad you suggested this. I'm surprised these things even work."

I point to a bike without a seat. "Next time you should try that one. The cold metal pole adds a whole new element of excitement."

"I'll bet," Jake laughs. "But I think it has your name on it."

~ ~ ~

"I'm sorry I missed the meeting." I hug Isabella as she greets me near the door of the bustling Sunshine Café.

"It was good," she says. "We're making progress, Dad. Every meeting we seem to attract a few new people." I brim with pride whenever I see her speak with passion about her role in the Vashon Resilience Group—our local chapter of the global Resilience Movement, a growing beacon of hope for environmentalists everywhere.

"That's great," I say.

"Hey Chief!" Frank yells across the café as he walks toward me. "How it feel your kids smarter than you?"

"It feels great, Frank. I guess Henry can say the same thing, huh?"

"Ya, ya," Frank laughs.

"How is he doing, anyway?"

"Not so good. Still got spirit. Bones weak though."

"I might have to drop by and see him tomorrow. Hey, where's Arlo?"

"He at work," Frank says. I shake my head. It is hard to believe that Arlo dons a uniform five days a week, setting his anarchist beliefs aside to work the docks for the Washington State Ferry Service.

Isaac comes up and gives me a hug. At twelve, hugs are no longer guaranteed—especially in public.

"Hi Dad," he says.

"Hi Son. I hear it was a great meeting?"

"Yeah, we're killing it on the co-op."

"Thanks to their assistant web master," I say, referring to my son's new role with the Vashon Island Car Co-operative. Isaac's exuberance and Isabella's smile reinforce the decisions I have made, and remind me why I have invested so much into being a better husband and father.

I make eye contact across the room with Emily, who is already gathering up her coat and walking toward me. She gives me a hug and a deep passionate kiss.

"You came back," she says.

"Was there any doubt?"

"Maybe a little."

~ ~ ~

"We're finally alone," Emily says as she climbs into bed beside me.

I say nothing, but I look into my wife's face and appreciate her ageless beauty. Gray hairs and laugh lines remind me of the years we have spent together and the memories we have made.

"Are you glad you went today?" Emily asks.

"Yeah. Thanks for your support."

"Of course. Do you need to talk about anything?"

"No. I debriefed myself on the ferry tonight. It was a lively conversation."

"The ferry's good for that."

"Yeah. It's funny ... I saw some toddlers on the boat, and they made me think about grandchildren."

"Whoa," she says. "Aren't you getting a little bit ahead of yourself?"

"Yeah. I just meant ... I might be starting to embrace this age thing."

"Not me," she scoffs. "I'm going down fighting."

I laugh, enjoying Emily's renewed sense of humor. We have laughed a lot more lately, and lived more too. Enjoyed one another's company—simple things like coffee on the porch or watching the kids play soccer. And laundry—there is never a shortage of laundry.

Acknowledgements

There are, of course, too many people to thank. If you ever asked me about this book, encouraged me, challenged me, provided me with inspiration, or served me a warm beverage while I hunkered down in the corner of your coffee shop, then please know that you are appreciated for the contribution you made to this project.

My gratitude starts and ends with my beautiful and talented wife. Sheila, you have supported me in so many ways from the moment we dreamt up the idea of making a movie (a goal that I hijacked and morphed into a novel) to the seemingly countless manuscripts that you have read and edited. Thank you for your honest feedback, and for always pushing me to be better.

To my children, Iris and Simon: thank you for inspiring me every day—in ways both large and small. Watching you grow and expand your knowledge as you expand mine has been the most stimulating and motivating experience of my life. I wrote this book in part for you, to demonstrate that if you really want to achieve something, all you have to do is set your mind to it and persevere. Not that you need me to teach you that—you have both figured that out for yourselves already.

As a new author, I have quickly grown to appreciate the value of a great editor—or in my case, two great editors.

Sheila, a skilled copy editor long before I called myself an author, has taught me to think about every word I choose, by asking critical questions about plot, characters and language. Supportive, exacting and detail-oriented, Sheila has helped me to become a better writer ... all the while honoring my voice and style.

Feeling that Sheila was too close to me—to the anecdotes and people who would inevitably shape my story—I looked to Richard Therrien for a fresh perspective on the style and structure of my novel. Richard taught me so much about dialogue and character development and story structure. More than an editor, Richard was a fantastic mentor and coach as I took the leap from everyday writer to novelist. Richard helped me to understand that writing is a team sport.

I owe great thanks to my beta readers—Sarah Parent, Ben Haggeman, Mark Yellowley, Jan Poynter, Bruce Edwards, Jess Robertson, Lisette Cameron, Weegee Sachtjen, and my parents, Carol and Allan Cameron—for providing thoughtful, thorough and candid feedback. Your input has been incredibly helpful, exposing patterns and gaps within my story that needed to be addressed.

To my cover design team—Bruce Edwards, Beth Hawthorn and Mark Benson—thank you for allowing me to tap into your creativity and professionalism to create a cover that so accurately reflects the mood and story I wanted to convey. It is an honor to have my writing associated with artwork of such quality.

To everyone who urged me to focus on writing—Ruth Baxter, Marg Peterson, Art Aylesworth, John Weisberg,

Anne-Marie Pham, Aaron Pazurik, Natalie Valois, John Geoffrion and more—thank you for helping me to overcoming my feelings of inadequacy as a writer, and for building confidence in my ability to weave a tale.

To Ali Bryan … thank you for your guidance, feedback and support as a fellow author and friend-of-a-friend-become-friend. I have appreciated your encouragement and candor throughout this journey.

To my fellow Spirits—Karl Rebner, Stephen McKenzie, Jaret Clay and Chris McDonald—for two decades of shared experiences that would be inconceivable to most mortals (and perhaps even to superheroes).

To the baristas who kept me caffeinated for the past three years—from my first handwritten pages at Rocky Mountain Bakery in Powell River to the last of my countless visits to Wheatberries Bakery in Gibsons—thanks for providing me coffee, conversation and smiles when I needed them most (at all hours of day and night). Off the top of my head—I'm sure this is not a complete list—I recall writing in the coffee shops of: Powell River, Gibsons, Sechelt, Roberts Creek, Calgary, Palm Springs, Palm Desert, Tucson, Portland, Seattle, Vashon Island, Quito, Cuenca, Vilcabamba, Puerto Lopez; and the quaintest location of them all: Napo Wildlife Reserve in the heart of Yasuni National Park.

To the staff and volunteers at La Hesperia Biological Station, the inspiration for the setting of Pueblo del Sol, I cannot say enough about the effect that your community had on the creation of this novel—and on my life. While none of you are directly present in this story, you are all there in one way or another—your collective awesomeness injecting spirit into the characters that formed within my head. Special thanks to Alister Reid for being a great roommate, and for trying in vain to coax out of me the Scottish dialect that would seem to accompany my name. And special shouts out to Alexandra Hoeneisen, Simon Gray Baker and Leah Corr for your ongoing support of my writing efforts.

To David Rueda and his wife, Mary, who provided me a personalized tour of Quito and surrounding areas ... thank you for introducing me to your amazing country. Thanks also to Derek and Ximena Aylesworth for introducing me to David.

To our tribe of homeschooling/unschooling families—especially the Rosnaus, Yellowleys, Parents and Bretts—I owe you gratitude in so many forms ... for inspiring me, supporting me, feeding me, housing me ... and for providing fun, loving (and fun-loving) environments for my children to thrive while Sheila and I toiled on this project.

To my mom and dad, I owe you the ultimate thanks—for nothing short of everything. To Jan, Ben, Mary, Sarah, Jessica, Paul, Lisette, Julia, Alison, Christy and Mark ... and the rest of the Camerons, Baxters, Aylesworths, Watsons and more ... one could not ask for a better family! Your unwavering support is the basis for everything I have ever accomplished.

Thanks to all the great songwriters who inspired music references in the book. And, by the way, the Canadian ditty Conlan referred to in Chapter 27 is *Where Am I Going?* by Matt Mays.

And last but not least … thanks to you for buying this book. I hope you enjoy it!

Mark Cameron
Gibsons, BC
November, 2015

Author Interview

Is Goodnight Sunshine *based upon experiences that you had? Share with us.*

I began with scenarios that I knew well enough to write about, and then allowed my mind to run wild. I tried to extract myself from the story, and in many ways I accomplished that. But the harder I worked to create plot details and characters that were not reflections of my own life, the more I recognized the essence of this book—Oliver's character and his journey toward self-discovery—as my own. Oliver and I are as different as we are similar—but kindred spirits nonetheless.

So, in a nutshell … yes, *Goodnight Sunshine* is very much an extension of experiences I have had. I live in a west coast community that is dependent on ferries. I have a 12-year-old daughter who loves to read and a 10-year-old son who has memorized 100 digits of pi, and my wife is usually a step ahead of me. I lived with my family in a camper van on and off for almost two years and we spent another year in a trailer in our local RV resort. I've been to Ecuador twice. And I am somewhere in the midst of an existential crisis—a chapter of my life that I am in no hurry to escape.

How are you and Oliver the same, or different? What characteristics does he have that you don't, but wish you did?

Beta readers who know me well had a hard time separating me from Oliver—yet our histories and traits are very different. In hindsight I see that choosing a similar family setting—middle-aged couple with a daughter and son, living in an RV on the west coast—makes Oliver and me seem far more similar than I intended. I've heard that such is the nature of first novels—it is hard to avoid incorporating some elements of poorly veiled memoir into a similar set of circumstances.

As for character traits, I came to like Oliver more as the story (and his character) progressed. In some ways his growth is a reflection of my own, but rather than stretching it over decades and countless small increments, Oliver's growth was forced to happen through a series of more profound changes, over the period of only a few months.

What was the initial inspiration for the novel? At what point did you say to yourself, "I have to write about this!"?

I have wanted to write a novel for many years, but there was no one story that was bursting to get out—just a general sense that I had to start writing. The decision to write *Goodnight Sunshine* was made during a discussion with my wife, Sheila, during a long day of driving in 2012. But the seed was planted—literally, in the form of endangered hardwood saplings—during my first trip to Ecuador in 2011.

How did your travels to Ecuador inspire the story and/or setting for **Goodnight Sunshine?**

In 2011, I spent a few weeks volunteering at a nature reserve called La Hesperia Biological Station, with side trips to a few different locations. My lasting impression of the location that inspired Pueblo del Sol was the sense of instant community that I felt while I was in the cloud forest at La Hesperia. I saw the reserve as a great base for a story, because it was a rich and exotic location full of interesting people from around the globe. Then, once I started writing, I found that my imagination could not be confined by my own experience. I started to write about places I hadn't been to, which gave me a great excuse to return to Ecuador and explore other parts of the country.

I recall one particularly vivid memory from my second trip to Ecuador in 2013. Walking alone on a beach in Puerto Lopez, experiencing a spectacular sunset, I imagined what it would be like to be there as Oliver—with Jen at his side. I felt an odd duality between my real experience in that moment and the one I was living in my head; then a third reality joined the fray—a memory of a very fun weekend in Canoa (a seaside town very similar to Puerto Lopez) with a group of volunteers from La Hesperia. A great deal of content—both plot and character development—stemmed from that moment.

The project originally started out as a screenplay. How did it become a novel? Do you have any intention to take it to the big screen?

I was driving with my family to an unschooling conference in Portland, and Sheila and I were debating how to re-shape our careers following a series of major life changes. Having dabbled with music and writing, and fresh off helping a friend create a full-length remake of The Princess Bride, I was keen to do something that involved various forms of media. Somewhere along Interstate 5 between Seattle and Portland, we decided we were going to make a movie. I'd always wanted to write a book, and we thought it might be better to start with a book and then adapt it to a screenplay. Three years and a great deal of learning later, we're content to see *Goodnight Sunshine* in book form for now ... though we see potential for turning it into a movie one day.

They say writers write to explore. What were you seeking to understand?

I started out wanting to convey a number of messages, but those messages evolved throughout the writing process; I came to see my writing as less of a soapbox and more of a tool for self-exploration. Looking back on the journey, I mostly wanted to test myself, to find out if I could see a novel through to completion.

How has writing this novel impacted/changed you or your way of thinking?

I learned a great deal about myself, about writing, about the editing process, about myself (oh, wait, I already said that). I have to admit that I had a different ending in mind when I began the story. During the writing process, I allowed a lot of information to permeate my own consciousness, which led me to surprise myself with the ending I chose. That in itself was a huge learning experience and an opportunity for growth.

*As a Canadian who wrote a novel centered in the US &
South America, what are your thoughts on travel?*

People are people, wherever you go. Traveling gives me a
much greater appreciation of home, and of what it means to
be Canadian, but it also reminds me that there is beauty—in
the landscape, the culture, the people—everywhere I go.
Traveling to a land where you don't speak the native
tongue(s) is also very humbling, an experience that I would
highly recommend to anyone who hasn't tried it.

*There are eco-friendly overtones throughout the book. Is
that how you live your life? What are your thoughts on the
environment?*

I consider myself an environmentalist, and I have a huge
passion for sustainability. I am a conscious consumer who
works hard to reduce, reuse and recycle (in that order). Yet I
always feel like I could be doing more. I'm trying to mini-
mize my own hypocrisy factor and live responsibly, without
carrying a constant sense of guilt about all the things I'm not
doing to save the planet.

*What is the one thing you would like readers to take away
from your book?*

That we all contribute to the problems we face, and we must
all contribute to their solutions. I wanted to humanize characters as much as possible, no matter their role or stance,
because I think people have a tendency to over-simplify the
views of others—and the challenges we face. I'm not a big
fan of the "good vs. evil" cliché that exists in so many stories, because I believe life is much more complex than that.

They say to write the book you want to read. What was it that compelled you to write this book?

I set out to write an up-tempo, plot-driven story that addressed issues relating to progress, technology and the environment. Then, during the writing process, I realized that I was writing a slow-developing, character-driven story about one man's mid-life awakening. Somewhere along the way I began to see the plot as a bit of an inconvenience. I was getting to know a bunch of characters who had spawned within my head, and I wanted to find out what was going to happen to them. Plot be damned, I was far more interested in the humans! What this taught me was that I love reading books with rich, well-developed characters, and I see plot mostly as a vehicle to develop characters, convey information and engage readers.

Who are your favorite writers?

In terms of classics … Steinbeck for his character development and descriptive text; Hemingway for his bold, direct prose; Mary Shelley for conveying the alienation and anger of a lonely soul. As for more modern writers … Sara Gruen's *Water for Elephants* spoke to me, in part because it helped me to imagine my maternal grandfather's days as a circus worker; Richard Wagamese, whose subtle eloquence provides a rich window into native Canadian life; and Alistair MacLeod, whose *No Great Mischief* was perhaps my first great read.

Can you share some advice for aspiring writers?

Just write. It's far too easy to convince yourself that you can't—that you're not good enough, or you don't have the time, or you need to take courses or join a writing club or whatever other "lacks" are standing in your way. Writing is a journey and a learning experience, and each of us who do it will have moments of pride and moments of humility.

Oh, and find a great editor—don't just use Aunt Millie because she loves books and was once a grade 10 English teacher. I believe that all writers can benefit from a qualified editor—someone who will honor your voice while challenging you to be a better writer.

Anything in the hopper? What can we expect from you going forward?

Yes. I am playing with a few ideas, two in particular which are extremely different from one another. One is inspired by my uncle's story of his father's time in Dieppe during World War II, while the other is a light-hearted look at weddings through the eyes of a loveable loser. I don't know exactly where these stories will take me ... I just know that I now have the bug to write novels, so expect to see more from me soon(ish).

If you would like to connect with Mark, please email him at:
markofwords@gmail.com

If you liked this book, please consider contributing a review on
Amazon or Goodreads.